Water

Book One of the Water Series

Emory Gayle

2nd Print Edition

February 2018

Copyright © Emory Gayle 2017

All rights reserved.

Cover design © Lori Follett of www.HellYes.design

For Jon, my biggest cheerleader. Love you, hun.

Prologue

MY LUNGS BURNED. *Don't breathe. Don't breathe. Don't breathe.*

We dove too deep. I knew it. He knew it. The surface laid sparkling far above our heads, and I was already out of air. *Maybe he can hold his breath this long, but I can't.* I flicked my feet and started for the surface and pulled his hand to go. His hand clamped around mine and yanked me down, wrapping his arms around me. Pain shot through my ribs as his grip fastened tight.

My lungs screamed. I thrashed my legs, but his arms were iron and I couldn't move. Panic broke through my calm as I frantically tried to squirm away from him. He held on, wrapped around me and weighing me down. I punched, kicked, and scratched, but nothing made a difference.

He's going to drown me!

Realization slammed into me, punching me in the gut. My heart raged in my chest as I turned to look into the eyes of the man that I had given my trust to. The one I had given my love to.

But he was gone.

Behind the eyes that I thought I knew so well was a stranger. I was alone and I was going to die because I did what I swore I would never do...

I fell in love.

1

Darrien

"YOU'VE GOT TO BE kidding me!"

"It's not a joke, Darrien." Sands sneered. The smile on his face was infuriating.

"What the hell are you talking about?" I snarled.

"You've been reassigned." He beamed, his smirk stretching far enough to turn his eyes to slits. He was loving this. Alastair Sands, the right hand of the king, the hammer, the mighty and the huge pain in my ass.

"Bullshit," I spat. Sands' hands balled at his sides, his knuckles whitening. A bloom of red appeared beneath the brim of his neatly pressed collar and I tried to hide the feeling of satisfaction getting under his skin gave me.

The man stood a good few inches taller than me and he was almost as wide as he was tall. Everything about him was impeccable: his tailored clothes, his raven colored hair, his pearly teeth, even his voice was low and velvety. But, that didn't keep him from being a bully. He was an intimidating and scary man to most, for no reason other than to make a point of showing how much power he had. But there was one person he couldn't intimidate…me. Even though, I only came to his nose, *my* power didn't come from my height, or being a bully…and he knew it.

"I'm warning you, Locke," he threatened, taking a step toward me, his temper ticking higher. "Keep it up and you will be doing security in the kitchen for the rest of the year."

"I'd like to see you try…*sir*," I sneered not backing down. Sands was a bully to everyone. He had a reputation for his temper and his aggression, both things had won him a lot of power in Court, but not with me. *Ambassador* Sands had no authority over me. I'm the King's Guard and the head of his royal security. My orders came from one person only- the big guy. I was the one person that the Ambassador couldn't push around, and that made me a threat.

2

King's Guard. The High Guard. Darrien. Locke. They were just a few titles I was called around Court. I might not have been the easiest person to get along with, but that went along with the job...*mostly*. My work was my world and that didn't leave room for many acquaintances, let alone friends. Other than my brother, Tyde, I was alone.

Sands stiffened and puffed his chest. "You might be his favorite now, Locke, but that won't last forever. You're being *replaced*." My jaw dropped and a Cheshire cat grin spread across his face. "What? You didn't *know*?" he added with a look of innocence that just screamed for me to slap off his face.

My pulse raced, and I balled my hands, but I refused to let him get anymore enjoyment out of me. Instead, I smiled, gave him a special one finger salute, and walked away without being dismissed, knowing how much all of that would piss him off. I could almost hear his blood pressure rise and I fought to keep the smile from my lips. Alright, I didn't fight that hard...or at all actually.

Reassigned, my ass.

There was *no way* that King Zale would reassign me. Not now. There had been two attempts to assassinate him in the last year. Supposedly, it was all the Sirens' doing. But, while they were nothing to mess around with, my gut was telling me there was more going on than just the Sirens.

The Sirens were a race of mutated and extremely violent Mer that had been a problem for a few generations. While they lived in a city far away from Titus Prime, our home, they made trouble for our people frequently. Recently, their attacks had become bigger and more destructive.

The worst Siren attack happened eleven years ago, when I was nine years old. They laid waste to our city, Titus Prime, after breaking through the dome that protects it.

Losing the dome was devastating. As Mer, we live in the very depths of the ocean, but we don't live in the water day to day. We actually walk around our city, just like they do on land. The dome keeps the cold salt water out and, more importantly, protects us from the dangers of the sea, like the Sirens. Our city is much like those on land, it's just located on the bottom of the ocean.

The day of The Attack, many Mer were slaughtered. Including both my parents. Tyde, my younger brother, and I were orphaned that day. My hatred for the Sirens only grew from that day on.

Sirens can't be trusted. They are born with violence and hate in them. They have no conscience. They kill and torture for sport. In my mind, they need to be wiped out. But that was the *one thing* that King Zale and I differed on. For some unknown reason, Zale had sympathy for Sirens, and that had driven a wedge between us for over a year.

3

After our parents died, Zale took Ty and me under his wing. Zale had been a fatherly influence in our lives since we were young. Before my abilities were even discovered, he took an interest in me because of *who* I was, not *what* I was. That meant more to me than I could say.

A few years ago, the weight of everything that had happened to my family and the discovery of my powers caused me to turn to a dark place. It was Tyde and Zale that brought me back. I will never be able to repay them, but I am willing to spend a lifetime trying. Even if we didn't always see eye to eye, Zale had been there for me since I was young. I owed it to him to follow his requests, even if that meant that he didn't want me at his side anymore.

As I made my way back to my chamber, I looked around at the place Tyde and I had called home for the last year. The buildings in Titus were made of similar materials as buildings on land, such as stone. Court was no different than a medieval castle, in that regard. The walls were polished stone on the inside; they shone and reflected light, so that the building looked like it was glowing from within. Titus Prime looked like light bubbles collecting on the ocean floor, with the largest "bubble" near the center.

Court was the centre of Titus Prime, and all of Mer. It was also where Zale lived, and therefore where I did. Tyde lived with me too. One of the conditions of taking the position as King's Guard was that Ty remained with me. I wasn't leaving my brother behind, not after everything we had been through together. We were a packaged deal. Zale never hesitated. Either he was really desperate for my services or he liked having Ty around just as much as I did. Personally, I think it was the latter.

As I sped through the massive stone hallways and the beautiful coral-and-pearl art on the walls caught my eye I could feel anger start to build as I continued going over everything that Sands had said.

There was no doubt that the guy hated me. He wasn't tip-top of my bestie list either, but would he have been able to convince Zale that he didn't need me anymore? Would Zale listen to him? They were childhood friends from rival families. Their relationship always had confounded me. Zale Reed and Alastair Sands. The Reeds and Sands had been battling it out for centuries for the throne. It seemed that the Sands just couldn't get over the fact that Poseidon himself chose the Reeds to rule Mer. The Sands' should have accepted this and moved on, but they weren't known for being passive. Their stubborn streaks were legendary, and Alastair was no exception. His lack of flexibility often lead to arguments between him and Zale.

Zale and I were close; surely, if he was thinking about reassigning me, he would have talked to me about it. He wouldn't have told Sands first. And yet, there was something eating away at me that I couldn't shake. When I reached the door to my chamber, I threw it open in frustration.

4

Standing in the center of my chamber was a figure that I knew all too well. Zale.

This can't be good.

2

Cora

"WHAT ARE YOUR PLANS FOR THE SUMMER, Cora?" My stomach hit the ground, *hard*. I glanced up at Mrs. Sherwin. I was the last person in English class today…well, every day. It was the last day of classes and everyone was excited for summer holidays, but not me. Nope. I was dawdling…as usual.

"Um…I'm not sure yet," I answered with a shrug, tucking my books into my bag for the last time. "I haven't really thought about it." That was a lie. I thought about it all the time. I was dreading the end to the school year, especially seeing how I had graduated. That meant that I would have to spend every day at home, in that depressing house. It was not a promising or exciting prospect, and I wasn't looking forward to it.

"Have you considered getting a job?" my English teacher asked. I perked up. No, I had not considered it. Mrs. Sherwin could see the look in my eyes and smiled.

"The annual summer job fair is just a few days away. I hear that the book store is looking for some summer students," she explained in a warm voice. My heart leapt and I bit my lips from grinning too big. *A whole summer surrounded by books? Yes, please!* I usually spent my summer days in the library, but working at the book store would allow me to do the same thing and get *paid* for it!

"Thank you!" I blurted loudly, and maybe with a touch of a squeal. She had just offered me a refuge from my boring summer prospects. *Hallelujah!* I thanked her again and ran out the door.

A job at the book store would be *perfect*. I could get out of the house. Bree, my little sister, could come with me some days. They knew me well there, too. I had a habit of wandering the store whenever I needed an escape from home, which was quite often. I was perfect for the job! There was no way I wasn't going to get it. It's not often that I found something to be excited about in town, but this could really change that.

Yorkton was a small city, smack-dab in the middle of Canada's Saskatchewan prairie. We had two high schools, one public and one Catholic. Yorkton was a nice place to raise kids. Nothing horrific ever happened here. Nothing exciting ever happened there either. The kids grew up and moved away, just to return again to have their own kids. Most people liked to retire to the coast when that time came, but our town was like a little prairie retirement community. I guess that happened because at one time we were surrounded by family farms. When farmers couldn't work their land anymore, they moved to the closest city. That was Yorkton.

I was too late to catch the school bus home, but I managed to get on the city bus. The ride took a little longer, but I was okay with that. I lived in a neighborhood that was brand new...in the 1980's. The houses in my neighborhood had begun their outdoor refurbishing. New siding and brick work was showing up all over the place, but not on our house. Nope.

The bus dropped me off right in front of the house. I knew the driver. I might have made a habit of missing the school bus.

We lived in a small one-story bungalow, it was a rental. It had wood siding that was faded and peeling. It hadn't been painted since Dad left, around eleven years ago. The peaks in the roof had beautiful old scroll work that didn't match anything in the rest of the neighborhood. I'm sure when they were new, it looked good, but now it just made our home look like a stale gingerbread house.

The shingles needed replacing badly; they were the cause of a leak in the kitchen at the moment. We had asked the landlord to get them fixed months ago. Still nothing. If it weren't for the ridiculous good deal he gave us on rent, we would be out of there.

I couldn't get the outside windows clean no matter how much I scrubbed at them. And I scrubbed at them a lot. The flower beds had seen better days; they still had dried up dead stems from last year, maybe the year before. The front door was a faded pink. It used to be bright red. I remember painting it with Mom and Ana. It was Ana's favorite colour. My heart hitched thinking about her. Ana, my twin sister, drowned in a boating accident when we were seven. I shook my head to rid myself of that memory.

I walked up the driveway, stopping to adjust the torn and faded paper sign taped to the front step post. It read, 'Keep off. Leave mail in bin. Thank you.' I looked down into the plastic bin, which we used to serve as a make shift mail box. As my eyes travelled downward, I caught a glimpse of the long thin scar on my leg. I fell right through the rotted out front steps last summer, slicing open my calf. Bree had screamed bloody murder and nearly fainted.

Mom came rushing out of the house screaming, too. It was the fastest that I had seen her move in a long time. She was usually too exhausted to get out of her bed. For being such a bad cut, it had healed remarkably well. You could only see the hair line scar in certain lights.

I looked up just in time to see Bree trudging towards the front door, her long blonde hair, tied into a thick high pony, swinging wildly behind her. When she saw me, her blue eyes narrowed.

"You missed the bus again, Cora," she complained.

"I know. I was talking to Mrs. Sherwin. I got gr-"

"Do you know what it's like, riding that school bus by myself?" She cut in. My mouth opened, though no sound came out. I often missed the bus. It was one of the few things I was actually good at. Bree flopped down on the ground next to the dilapidated step.

"No one will sit with me. They all just ignore me," she mumbled. *Aww, B.*

"I'm s-"

"Sorry. Yeah, I know," she grumbled. "You are always sorry, but you never do anything about it," she spat back. *Wow.* That actually hurt. I thought that she knew that I meant it. *I really am sorry.*

"I *am* sorry, B. I just…get stuck in my head sometimes and can't find my way out." I watched her expression soften. "I didn't mean to leave you alone. And just think about it, now we'll have to whole summer together." I painted a smile on my face and stuck it in hers.

"But Mom-"

"I'll figure something out, okay?" I grabbed her hand and sat next to her. She was hurting and I hated that I was the reason for it. "I know it's tough around here in the summer. I'll figure out a way to get you out of here. I *promise.*"

At that, her face lit up a little. The ball of guilt in my stomach loosened a bit and I let out a sigh and a smile. I knew she wasn't excited to be spending two months at home, neither was I. Mom was…difficult to live with.

Things weren't always so rough. Mom wasn't always so scared and worried about the world. She used to be this amazing free spirit. Fun and full of life. People used to stare at her, not just because she was crazy beautiful, but because she exuded passion and happiness. She reminded me of a new flower, bright and fresh. She even smelled sweet like one. I couldn't help but feel better around her.

Mom was always fun; she was always up for trying new things and going new places. There was always an adventure to be had, or something new to learn or see. She fostered imagination and creativity into our home. She was the reason I loved to write. Mom was always the one that brought our family together. She was our glue.

That all ended the day Ana died. It was so hard looking at Mom now and not have the wind knocked out of me. She wasn't half of the person she was before. That spunky woman was discarded after we lost Ana.

On one hand, I understood why. She lost a daughter. That had to be hard. But I lost my *twin*.

Ana was like the other half of me. We did everything together. *Everything.* To me, it was normal. It was wonderful. She knew me better than I knew myself.

I lost part of myself when she died. I didn't know who I was without her. I still didn't.

3
Darrien

"DARRIEN, I HAVE SOME NEWS. Please close the door," Zale said, his long delicate hands clasped and serious.

Oh, Crap.

King Zale was tall and slim. His dark brown hair showed its wave even though he kept it short and his deep set green eyes saw more than most thought. Today his five o'clock shadow was longer than usual, a sign that he hasn't slept well, or maybe not at all. He didn't look regal, as kings should, maybe more in tuned with the earth than most would like. To me, that just made him more personable.

But he was no fool.

He was an excellent judge of character and a great ruler. I was fully behind every appointment he made in Court. Every one, except Sands. That one still had me baffled.

I pulled the door closed behind me, then turned and faced him. My heart was pounding. He had never been in my chamber before. Somehow, it looked smaller with him in it.

As far as a guards' room was concerned, I had the biggest and the best. My room was just across the hall from his. There was also a secret passage from my room to his, in case of an emergency. The chamber was stone-walled and the dark stone was polished to a muted shine. I didn't like the room that bright. I slept during the day a lot, and that much light just kept me up.

My chamber was one large room, with a small bathroom off the back. I had a large four-poster bed, a small table and chairs, a dresser, and a chest. I kept the room simple and tidy, a side effect of my training. Other than sleeping, I really wasn't in it. My job was my life. Even on my so-called days off, I was working in one capacity or another.

"What can I do for you, Sir?" I asked, my fingers tapping against my leg.

"Stop calling me *that*, for one," he sighed. "For the millionth time, I hate it. We're around each other all day, every day. The least you could do is call me Zale," he reprimanded.

"Yes, Sir," I answered. He groaned. I bowed. We did this every day.

"Alright, Darrien. I'm guessing, by the look on your face when you walked in, that you had been talking to Sands," he ventured. He really did know me too well. I swallowed back all the questions I had and let him continue, my hand balling and flexing at my side.

Zale cleared his throat, something that he always did before he delivered bad news. That's when it hit me. *Sands was telling the truth.*

Zale cleared his throat again, "I asked him not to say anything to you," he admitted.

Shit.

"I have to reassign you, Darrien," he blurted. My blood stopped running, replaced by an icy fire that was painful. I bit my lips to stop the outburst that was building, but it didn't work.

"Why are you moving me? After everything we've been through, you're just going to toss me?" I shouted. This man was more of a father to me than the one I'd lost as a child, and the betrayal stung.

My hand raked through my hair and I took a deep breath. I forced down my anger and remembered my place. Through tight lips, I asked, "What did I do, Sir?"

"Darrien, you have done nothing wrong." Zale held out his hands palm up, his voice tender and quiet. My shoulders dropped slightly, though I knew he wasn't done. He paced the floor, rubbing his hands over each other.

"I need you to watch over my *daughter*," he admitted.

His daughter? I wasn't sure my eyelids were ready for the stretch they got with that piece of news.

"What?" I uttered.

"My daughter, Cora. I need you to bring her here, to Titus. Home." His eyes searched mine for an answer, but I didn't have one. Not yet.

"But, she's never been here. She has no idea who you really are, or that any of this is here," I reminded him. Zale's family was living on the surface. He had left Mer when he was young, and had a family up there. Years later, he returned without them. He never talked about why, not even to me.

"I know that," he grunted and started pacing again.

"Well, then don't you think that information should come from *you*?" I bit my tongue. That was completely out of line…even though it was true. Zale's head spun to me and I braced for the reprimand, but it didn't come.

"I *can't* leave," Zale cursed, shoulders sagging.

"But you-"

11

"I have my reasons, Darrien, and I want it left at that," he declared with a sweep of his hand.

"Very well," I muttered, not pleased with that answer.

"Look, there are some things that you are just going to have to trust me on, and this is one of those things."

"It's *your* daughter," I grunted. I respected him very much, but this was one of those times I wondered about his sanity. This was not going to end well.

"Sir, I can't leave," I said, trying to convince him to let me stay. "We have to think about your safety. It would be incredibly reckless to send me away right now, when the assassination attempts are getting more frequent," I stated.

"Darrien, there is more than my life at stake here," he argued back. "My lifeline is tied to the city. I can't protect everyone in Titus if I die and have no heir. The dome must have a ruler to tie to. You know that. If something were to happen to me without my daughter here, the people of Titus would be in great danger. You know what happened during the last Siren attack. They only had a small opening to get through that time. Imagine the devastation if the dome was completely gone. We *need* her."

"I-" *Damn it! I can't argue with that.*

"I have selected the best for your replacement. You won't be disappointed," he added with a triumphant smile.

There it was, just as Sands had said...my *replacement*. It hurt. I had worked so hard to get that job, and just like that...I was replaced.

"Why *me*, Sir? Why not someone else that is-"

"Is *what?*" He interrupted. He stood in front of me, pulling himself up to full height. His face looked younger than his years, though that was thanks to our Mer blood. We lived much longer than humans. But, the years on the throne had weighed heavily on him, literally drooping him under their weight. Now that he pulled himself up, he was taller than me. I had never realized that. He captured me in a look and I stood there.

"You know what it's like to lose family," he began. "You know the value and importance of family. No training can give you that understanding. You are the only person I trust for this job. The *only* one."

"Sir-"

"Your king is sending you to protect the future queen, Darrien. Are you really going to say no?" he asked, knowing full well that I wouldn't turn him down.

And, damn it, he was right. I wouldn't say no.

"Fine." I submitted. I could *do* this job, I just didn't *want* to.

12

I'd get the job done quickly, and then get back here to figure out who wanted to kill Zale. The more time I spent away from Titus, the greater the threat from the Sirens became. I needed to be in the city. I was useless on land if there was a problem.

I knew how to protect a king. A stupid teenage girl shouldn't be a problem. I'd bring her back in a day, and this would all be over.

"Perfect. Just one more thing," Zale added, and cleared his throat. *Uh oh, now what?*

"Yes, Sir?" I asked, narrowing my eyes and crossing my arms.

"She doesn't swim," he said nonchalantly.

"What?" I hollered. "Then how…" I threw my hands out. "How am I supposed to do this?" I exclaimed, a little louder than I intended to.

"I honestly don't know," he admitted. "She has no idea who she is, or *what* she is. You are going to have to show her, somehow," he explained. *Is he serious?*

"I have to show her that she's Mer, when she doesn't even swim? How?"

"I don't know. You're smart. You'll figure it out." He said with a flip of his hand.

"Right. Sure. No problem." I nodded and scrubbed my hair with my hand.

"I've set you up on the surface already. You're going to be working at Camp Crystal. It's a human summer camp that is run by someone I know who lives on the surface. She is Mer. She knows what's going on, and is going to make sure that Cora gets a job there this summer. All you have to do is protect Cora and get her into the water," Zale explained. "Bring her home, Darrien."

"Alright. Who runs the camp?" I asked firmly.

"No one you know." He averted his eyes. *Hold up!*

"But *you* know. Who is it?" I demanded. He was hiding something from me. It was all over his face.

"She's a *friend.* I've known her for a long time, and is someone I have a great deal of respect for." He was stalling.

"Who *is it?*" I insisted.

"Pearl Wasche."

"Wasche. How do I kno-" It hit me…hard.

I was young at the time. It was just after my parents were killed, but I remembered. A Mermaid was accused of smuggling out Sirens, after the decimation of Titus, to avoid their trials. The Sirens were never caught, but she was. She was convicted of Siren Smuggling and sentenced to life on the surface. Many called for her death, but it went against Mer culture to kill our own. A lifetime above the water. Banishment.

Zale was sending me to work with the most notorious Siren Smuggler *of all time.*

4

Cora

BREE AND I ENTERED the house through our faded red door. We were late, and Mom was bound to be agitated. The key was to calm her and get her off to bed before she got too upset.

Mom was sitting at the dining room table. She looked stunning. She was always stunning. Without makeup or styled hair, she still looked like she stepped out of a magazine. She did *not* pass on those genes to me. Her long blonde hair cascaded in waves to her waist, like Bree's. She had huge blue eyes with thick long eyelashes, just like Bree's, and she hadn't aged in years.

"Where have you been?" she demanded and smacked the table with her hand, her eyes working between Bree and me.

"It's fine, Mom. We're both here. We're both safe," I said as I hung up my jacket and backpack on the hook near the door. Bree threw her stuff on the couch and flopped down beside it. I gave her the same look I gave her every day. Just *once*, it would be nice if she would put her stuff away, so I didn't have to. She flipped me a knowing smile and turned her eyes away.

Mom had turned her attention away from us and was absentmindedly looking through the mail, which she usually never did. There was often junk mail for Dad, which upset her more. I hated the mail. I busied myself tidying up the house.

Our living room consisted of a brown, scratchy couch and a television with a small stand. There wasn't even room for a coffee table. The walls were a shabby shade of green and the floor was beige shag carpet. The house needed a facelift, badly. Our dining room table was new, though, and stuck out like a sore thumb amongst the other furniture. The one from our old house bit the dust, and we all shed a few tears seeing it go. The scratches and marker stains from a time when things were better were gone, replaced by a shiny new imposter.

15

The inside of the house was as clean as I could get it. I suppose, I was slightly obsessive about it. I guess it was the one thing that I had control over in my life. This thought struck me as I was scrubbing away at an old stain on the sink counter. I threw down the rag I was using with a grumble.

My eye caught movement in the living room, and I looked over at Bree. She was subtly waving a hand and motioning to Mom with her eyes.

Mom sat at the table, staring at a letter. Her head moved from side to side. She was mumbling to herself, "No. No. No." I took a step toward her, but she wasn't aware of my presence until I touched her shoulder. She jerked, startled at my touch.

"Mom? You okay?" I asked, already afraid of the answer. She didn't say anything, just handed the letter over to me and stared at me with her big blue eyes. It was from the University of Regina.

I gasped. I had sent in my application months ago. I was trying to get into their creative writing program. I didn't want to tell Mom until I had heard back. She *never* checked the mail. I didn't even consider that they would send a letter.

I scanned it quickly, my breath still in my chest, until I saw the one word I was looking for: "Accepted." A huge smile slid across my face. *I did it! I got in!*

"What is it, Cora?" Bree's voice travelled from the couch over to me.

"She's leaving us." Mom's voice cut straight through my happy high.

"What? Cora?" Bree's eyes widened with panic as she looked at me. I stared open-mouthed at Mom. How could she say that to Bree? She made it seem like I was abandoning them. I was going to *school*, for goodness sake!

"I'm not leaving you. I got accepted into a Creative Writing program at the U of R. Look." I handed Bree the letter and sat beside her on the couch. I tossed Mom a glare while I was at it.

"That's amazing, Cor! I didn't know you even applied. Why didn't you tell me?" Bree asked, bouncing on the couch and shaking me by the arms.

"I didn't want to say anything unless I got in." I eyed Mom. She was staring at the doorway in silence.

"Mom, aren't you happy for her?" Bree asked. I laid a hand on her knee and shook my head. I didn't want to start a fight between Bree and Mom. Bree's eyes narrowed as she looked at Mom.

"Of course," Mom mumbled, and then turned to me. "I'm proud of you, my dear."

"Thank you, Mom," I said and waited for the shoe to drop. It always did.

"It's just that-"

"What? What is it, *now*?" *Oh no.* The words came out of me before I knew I was even thinking them. I'm sure I looked as shocked as Mom and Bree did. I wasn't prone to talking back to my Mom. I had been known to have choice words for certain kids at school, but not my mom. Never Mom.

"Cora…" Bree's tone warned of a storm brewing.

"No, it's okay, Bree," Mom said. "Cora is entitled to her frustration, but there is nothing I can do about the fact that we don't have the money for this." Mom confided turning in her chair to face us. She wore her "I'm sorry" expression that left me feeling half guilty for wanting anything for myself and half filled with a rage.

"What? You said that there was money set aside for our education. You told me that I would be fine after high school," I exclaimed, frustration eating away at my patience.

"And I didn't lie," Mom pleaded, her eyes fastened to mine.

"But you didn't tell the truth, either," I added.

"I know. I know…."

"You know. *Right*," I responded. I didn't want to be mean, well maybe I did want to be mean. *I don't know*…I was hurt.

"I'm sorry, Cora. Really, I am. I know this is something that you want to do. I'm sorry." I stared at her, unsure of what else I was supposed to do or say. I felt like my lungs were being squeezed and ripped from my chest. Getting into that writing program had been my focus for a year. I worked really hard on my portfolio to get in and now I wasn't allowed to?

Mom stood from her chair and crossed the room to Bree and me. She sighed, looking at the two of us.

"Cora, please understand. There are things that we just can't do."

"Why not? You always say this but you never tell us why. I'm tired of living like this!" It had been burning a hole in my gut for a long time, it didn't feel good coming out though. Instead I felt like I had opened a can of worms.

"It's just the way that things are for us," she shrugged, clearly not wanting to have that conversation and effectively shutting me out again.

"Whatever," I spat and slumped into the bed.

"Mom. How can you just stand there and tell Cor that she can't have this," Bree argued, sitting up taller on the couch. "She must have worked hard to get into that program. She's earned this, in more than one way. She has looked after us for years, it's time we look after her for once." Bree took my hand and smiled at me. My eyes filled with tears and my heart sang. B was so sweet and kind, in a way that I knew I could never be.

It was true, I had done a lot for our family, but I never complained and I never laid blame. I did it because that's what I did, that was my role. I never expected Bree to feel that way about it though and that warmed my heart so much.

17

"I'm not saying no. I'm saying not right now," Mom answered and got up and paced the room.

"What does *that* mean?" I asked.

"Well, I know this isn't the best timing now, but I have a surprise for you two," she shared with a tentative smile.

"Surprise?" Bree and I responded at the same time, and with the same amount of shock in our voices. Mom didn't do surprises. Bree's big eyes darted to me. I shrugged.

"Yes!" she smiled more. "I, uh…got you both jobs. Summer jobs," she blurted.

"What?" I squeaked.

"I had a visit from a friend of mine. She runs Camp Crystal, that summer camp about an hour away from here?" Bree and I didn't say anything. We just stared at her. "Anyway, she was looking for some help this summer, and I thought you two might want to get out of the city for a while." She looked from one of us to the other. Bree and I just sat there, completely speechless.

Mom had been supremely terrified of everything outside the house for years, and now, all of a sudden, she wanted to send us away for the entire summer? I wasn't buying it. Something didn't add up. But when I thought about it, did I really want to argue? This was our chance to get out of the house for the *whole summer.* We'd be able to do what we wanted without worrying about Mom. This was the opportunity that we had been looking for. If I started digging now, I might ruin it.

Bree was the first to break the silence, "You mean it, Mom? Really?"

I didn't know what to say. I just stared at hopeful-looking Bree and terrified-looking Mom. Things weren't fitting.

"Yes. I mean it," Mom nodded, swallowing hard. "You two are set to start work in a week at Camp Crystal," she exclaimed and smiled, but her smile wasn't right.

"Seriously? Just like that? You got us jobs?" I questioned, letting my uncertainty out.

"Yes. It will be a good experience for the both of you. And I trust Pearl. She'll look after you," she nodded.

"Pearl. You trust Pearl. How have we never heard of her before this?" Mom opened her mouth to answer but I kept going, "I don't *care* about this stupid job! What about school in the fall? What about that?" I demanded.

"I-well…okay. Let's strike a deal," she started.

"A deal?"

"Yes, a deal. If you go for the summer to Pearl's camp, and you still want to pursue creative writing at the university at the end…you can go," she conceded.

18

"What? Really? I can go?" I stood up, hands clenched to my chest. Was this really happening? Was I really going to be able to what I loved?

"Yes. If...*only if* you want to still do this after the summer is over," she restated.

"Okay!" I squealed.

There was nothing that was going to change my mind. *Nothing.*

It was just weird and totally out of character for Mom, but if it was going to get me to university, it was worth it. It was all worth it. Bree jumped off the couch and wrapped me in a big hug, cheering as she did. Mom saw her moment to go, and slipped back into her room before I could ask any more questions about the new job she got us.

Bree bounced into our room and shut the door. I stood there for a second. *A summer away.*

It was a good thing. It wasn't the book store, but it was an escape. Maybe, it was a better one. Working at a camp would be nice. I could get some fresh air, paint a building, maybe, mow the grass, tend the flower boxes...all the stuff I already did at home. I would be fine. Just as long as I didn't have to look after any kids. I'm sure that those positions are reserved for people with certain training, or at least who have been to a camp once in their lives.

No, that won't be my job. I'm sure of it.

5
Darrien

"PEARL WASCHE!" I yelled.

"Yes, Darrien." Zale didn't move a muscle; he held firm to his position.

"You seriously expect me to work with a *Siren Smuggler*?" I didn't give him a chance to respond instead I planted myself dangerously close to him and let my temper do the talking.

"After everything that I have been through because of those *monsters*, you want me to work with someone that has saved their lives? Rescued them from their trials? How *could* you?" This wasn't just ridiculous, it was hurtful. He knew how much I hated Sirens, and he still was asking me to do this.

"Pearl was wrongly accused of that crime," Zale argued. "She didn't aid any Sirens that were involved in the attacks," he responded, backing just the slightest bit away.

"Of course, that's what she would *say*. She's a liar and a traitor. I can't work with her. I *won't* and it is unfair of you to ask this of me," I barked and started pacing the room, hands in hair and breathing heavily. I needed to calm down, but it wasn't happening.

"Like it or not, Darrien, you work for *me*. This job is more important than your vendetta with the Sirens. You *will* go to the surface. You *will* meet Pearl, and you *will* work with her to bring my daughter home. Is that understood?" Zale bellowed.

I stared at him. For the first time since I had met him, he threw his king status in my face. I was well aware that I worked for him, but I thought that there was more to our relationship than just employer employee. I thought he was a friend. I took a deep breath, forcing the anger rotting my guts away to calm. It may have stung, but it infuriated me that he was right. We needed Cora back here. That was more important than my issues with the Smuggler.

"Fine," I growled. "I'll bring Cora home. But I can't promise that I will play nice with the Smuggler-"

"Her name is *Pearl*, and she is a *friend*, Darrien. A very good friend."

"How can you afford to keep a friend like that? Don't you care about what the rest of Court thinks of you? They say you are a sympathizer. That you would let Sirens back into Mer! Those Sirens are trying to *kill* you, you know! Don't you care about *that*?" I yelled. I was starting to lose it again. I needed to cool down. I was acting like an idiot. Whether Zale was a friend or not, he *was* still my boss. At times, it was hard for me to remember that.

"You know, I have never really cared for the popular opinion. I have my reasons, and I assure you that they are for the good. You'll understand once you meet Pearl."

"I won't," I blurted. "But I will do this job for you."

"Thank you, Darrien," he sighed and his posture relaxed.

"Yeah, well, don't thank me just yet. What exactly is the plan?"

"Pearl has reached out to Cora's mother. She has agreed to send her to camp, in the guise that she is working there for the summer."

"So her Mom knows about our world then?" I asked. Zale never talks about the woman that he ran away with.

"Yes, she does." Zale sank down on a chair at the table.

"Wow. Okay. I can't imagine how that conversation went with a human, but okay." I was hoping that he would give me more information, but he didn't. His eyes were focused far away as he drew lines on the table. Then, he snapped out of it and stared at me.

"Well, it doesn't matter. Cora will be there. Your job is to get her to swim. You know what it will take for her Mer powers to kick in." I nodded absentmindedly. It hadn't occurred to me until he said it. "She has to sacrifice herself to the water to survive in it," he reminded me, though I knew full well what he was getting at.

"Of course," I said, flipping my hand in the air. "'cause that won't look like murder to all the other humans running around the place. Are you trying to have me imprisoned in a human jail?" I asked. Zale chuckled warmly.

"I'm really hoping that it won't come to holding her down like that. She's been through enough, Darrien. I want this done delicately. She doesn't need to suffer more trauma." His voice and body language were back to the Zale I knew best. The man that I respected.

"Okay. You know this is a tall order right?" I asked, a half smile sneaking out.

"I know." Zale's smile snuck out too.

"Just making sure."

"You are posing as the swim instructor. I thought that would give you an excuse for needing to get her into the water." I nodded. The irony was not lost on me. "You will be living with the other camp leaders. They are Mer, too. They don't know that Cora is my daughter, though. I have asked them to go and observe human youth."

"Oh? That's an interesting undertaking."

Zale nodded, "I told them that I was putting together a Human Youth Ambassador Team, a group of young Mer that will study the humans, and then inform us of ways that we can use their culture to better our own. They all jumped aboard. Don't let on that you are there for any other purpose than that. When the time comes, their skills will be helpful to you."

"Sounds good. I can do this on my own, though," I clarified.

"It never hurts to have help," he added.

"Speaking of help, you mentioned that you found my replacement. Who is it?" *Who's the jackass taking my job?*

"Tyde," he beamed.

"You chose my *brother*?" I exclaimed, my mouth dropping down and my eyes wide.

"I told you that you wouldn't be disappointed in my choice," he declared, crossing his arms and sporting a smug smile.

I wasn't. I was proud. My little brother would be perfect. I had been training him myself. He knew everything about my job. Even though he was sixteen, he was already a King's Guard. He knew what the risks were and what the job included. He wasn't as big or strong as I was, but he was faster. He was a healer, too, which could be useful.

"Did you tell him yet?" I asked.

"No," he said. "I thought that you would like to do it. I know how much it means to you and Tyde. Go and enjoy the news tonight, because you're leave in the morning."

"Yes, Sir," I answered. My excitement for Ty overwhelmed my worry about leaving Zale in someone else's hands. Tyde was going to be ecstatic!

"Good luck," Zale shook my hand.

"Thank you," I said and walked to the door.

"Darrien?" Zale called.

"Yes?"

"Don't do anything stupid," Zale said with a smile. A surge of determination flashed through me.

"I won't, Sir."

6
Cora

AFTER MOM RETREATED to her room, I found Bree in ours, looking through the clothes that she was going to take to camp. I groaned as she tossed shirt on top of shirt, onto the floor. She eyed me as I came in the door, challenging me to scold her messiness. I didn't. I kept it together. I knew I drove her insane with my need to constantly clean and organize.

Our room was tiny. Bree and I had painted it a few years ago, when we bought a can of paint at our neighbor's garage sale. It wasn't exactly the colour that we would have chosen, but it was better than the bright orange that it was before. The minty green color was fresh, and our own choice, which was good enough for us. We made it work. We always made it work.

We had a twin-sized bunk bed that creaked so much, we both had learned to sleep like the dead to prevent waking each other with our tossing and turning. We shared a tiny wardrobe and a closet that couldn't fit more than ten hangers. Clothes and books spilled out of every drawer and nook in our room. Even my cleaning and organizing couldn't do anything about the lack of space. We lived like two teenage hoarders.

Bree was humming as she destroyed the cleaning I just gave the room. I wanted to be more annoyed, but it was so nice to see her happy. There was a huge smile on her face as she pulled out a drawer and dumped its contents on the floor. *You've got to be kidding me!*

"Okay! What are you looking for?" I asked, taking a moment to steady my breathing before I bent down and started folding and stacking her clothes back into the drawer.

"That necklace that Mom gave me for my birthday," she whispered, so that Mom wouldn't hear us through the paper-thin wall.

"You lost it?" I whispered back, now digging though the clothes a little more carefully.

"I thought it was in this drawer!"

23

"Geez, Bree, you have to be more careful with stuff like that."

"I really don't need a lecture right now, Cora. Just help me find it!" she hissed.

We both dove into separate areas of the bedroom, searching for that necklace. I was going through the dirty laundry and an old toy box. Bree was pulling out more drawers from our dresser. I squeaked when she pulled out mine and dumped it. I knew it wasn't in there. I just organized it again yesterday, but I wasn't about to tell her that. She was starting to mumble to herself, which was never a good sign.

Bree tossed a sweater out of her way and knocked the glass of water from the nightstand onto the bed.

"Watch it B!" I yelled and ran to the kitchen for a towel.

"Sorry, Cor!" B yelled back from the bedroom. I returned with a dish rag and started wiping off my bed. The water had soaked through the covers, sheet, and was in the mattress.

Great. My back is going to be damp all night now. I pressed the cloth to the sheet. *Come on water, get out.* Suddenly, the towel felt really wet and heavy in my hand. I ran from the room, as water dripped from it onto the floor, and held it over the sink.

How? I looked back to the bedroom and the trail of droplets that escaped my hands. I rang out the towel and hung it to dry on the rack. I walked slowly back to my room, sat on my bed, and ran a hand over the spill. Dry. Completely dry. *How is that possible?*

"Is anything ruined?" Bree asked, coming over to the bed.

"No, all good," I said absent mindedly, running a hand over the sheet again.

"Good. Now help!" B nudged me, forcing my mind away from the water and to the search for the necklace.

"Do you think it's odd that Mom is sending us away, all of a sudden?" I asked Bree, as she treated my perfectly folded tanks like they were scrambled eggs in their drawer.

"I don't know. Maybe." She tossed the drawer aside and went towards the chest that we had. I instinctively drew a breath in. That was where I kept all of Ana's keepsakes.

"I'll go through that! You come here and finish with the laundry."

"Okay," she nodded. Bree knew that Ana was a tough subject for me, and we avoided talking about her at all costs. The chest was off limits to Bree. Not that I didn't trust her with the things I kept in there...maybe I didn't trust her or maybe I just wanted Ana to myself.

I opened the lid and gazed down at all the treasures I had salvaged from our past life. Anything that was attached to Ana was in that chest: pictures, toys, books, and even scraps of fabric from clothes. As far as I knew, Mom didn't keep anything.

Bree was mumbling to herself, so to keep us both out of our heads, I decided to keep asking the questions that had been bugging me.

"Don't you think that this friend of Mom's is odd? I mean, when has Mom ever had a friend? I've never heard of her. Have you?" I asked, pulling out a bunch of pictures of Ana and me, which had been tied together with one of her hair ties. My heart gave a great thud. I had a scrap of the matching outfits we wore in the picture somewhere, too. I placed the pictures on the floor next to me, away from the chaos of the room.

"No." Bree's answered faded into the sound of the covers on the bed being tossed.

"I just…I just don't know if we should go," I admitted. That stopped her.

"You're kidding, right?" Her eyes turned to ice, and I started second guessing myself immediately.

"Well, I just think-"

"That's the problem right there. You're thinking. You are always over thinking everything, looking for the problem with it, the conspiracy."

"I don't do that!"

"You don't even realize you do it! I get it. Your phobia is going to be an issue, but don't make this about you, *please!*" she pleaded, and tossed her pillow on top of the heap she had made on the floor. The blood drained from my body. I hadn't even thought about that. I would have to be near open water. The thought made my heart pummel the inside of my chest. It had been years since I had seen open water. I didn't even bathe, for fear of bringing on the panic attacks.

After Ana died in the boating accident, Mom had never allowed us near water again. We stopped having baths, only showers. No pool. No swimming lessons. I knew how to swim- I learned when I was young- but I couldn't do it anymore. Bree never learned. She couldn't swim at all, but not because she feared it, like me.

A heavy cloud of doubt hung above me. How was I going to do this job now? Was my ticket to a summer of freedom worth inducing panic attacks? *No.* I looked up at the chaos of the room and my little sister that made it. *But Bree is.*

I wouldn't do it for myself, but I would do anything for her.

After we lost Ana, Dad left. He took the last spark of happiness Mom had with him. Bree and I were shocked, and hurt beyond words. Dad just left. He didn't say goodbye, and he gave no hint of things not being okay. He was just gone.

25

Mom cried for days. We all did. I tried to keep it together for Bree as best as I could, but I was only seven. At night, I would just hold Bree until she fell asleep in my arms, she was only four. That was around the time she started having night terrors. Mom was out cold from exhaustion most nights, so she never heard Bree's cries. I did. I would crawl into her bed and sing Dad's song to her. It always calmed her and helped her sleep.

Bree's grunts and groans were escalating, as I watched her toss my top bunk. Her long blonde hair swept back and forth across her back as she worked over the sheets and bedding.

Looking at us, we didn't look remotely related. We looked nothing alike. Bree was beautiful, blonde, and skinny - she'd have made a killer model. Then there was me: tall, awkward and gangly, with springy brown hair down past my shoulders. Bree had the most beautiful clear, tanned skin. Mine was all freckly and pale. My eyes were the color of algae, like sludge. I hated them. She had the prettiest blue eyes, big and rimmed with the thickest, longest eyelashes I had ever seen. Even *I* marveled at them, and I wasn't prone to jealousy, at least not towards B.

I peeled my eyes away from the carnage of my bed. She may keep my life in messy chaos, but I loved her more than anyone. Phobia or not, I could do this for her.

"Pack your bags. I guess we're going to camp," I said, and pulled her necklace out from behind the chest, flashing it at her with a triumphant smile.

7

Darrien

SAYING GOODBYE TO TYDE didn't feel good, but he was so excited about his new job that it made things easier. He was sixteen, the same age I was when I started working for Zale. Sure he was young, and it was going to piss off a lot of older guards that he got that job, but in the end it didn't matter. He really was the best for the job, and I wouldn't say that unless it was true. I trusted him completely. I knew he was trained to protect Zale at all costs; after all, *I* trained him.

But, just as a safety precaution, I had hired extra guards, and put the ones that I trusted in more shifts than usual outside Zale's chamber. Tyde was responsible for anyone that got right up to the king. My other guards would, hopefully, stop anyone before they got that close.

We spent the night talking about what his new job included. He had to shadow Zale wherever he went; he should be beside or behind him at all times. There would always be one or two guards with him, or close by, but it was Tyde's job to keep away anyone that posed a threat. He was the last line of defense, and the best one.

Ty was anxious to know all he could. I told him everything about his new duties that I could think of, but I couldn't tell him the real reason I was going to the surface, other than the bogus Human Youth Ambassador Team. It hurt not being totally honest with him. I knew he would understand, but it didn't make lying to his face any easier. Zale didn't trust anyone with the location of his family. Most didn't even know that they existed.

After talking with Ty well into the night, exhaustion finally put an end to his questions and he headed to bed. I spent the rest of the night tossing and turning. My mind was working overtime, making sure that I had covered all areas of Zale's protection and prepared Ty the best I could. Morning came just as I finally nodded off into a book. It took Ty shaking me awake to get me going. I got my things ready, prepped my room for Ty to move in, and said goodbye to Zale.

Tyde came to the pod with me to see me off with a huge hug. When Mer have to travel great distances, we travel in pods, or large bubbles. They moved faster and kept out the elements of the ocean, plus they protected us from Sirens and other dangers of the deep. And there were *many*.

I liked travelling in them. It was relaxing and smooth. I closed my eyes and enjoyed the last semblance of peace I would get before meeting a Siren Smuggler and a Princess.

Pearl was convicted of smuggling a Siren and her mate, which was unheard of, out of Titus and to the surface. She never defended herself; she just stood there during her trial and let the Mer rip into her. When they convicted her, she took her sentence with a smile and left Titus. It happened when I was very young, but people still talked about it. The scars the Siren Attack had left on Titus were slow to heal, and Pearl's name was brought up alongside them every time. That made Pearl that much more of a problem for me.

I arrived at the surface precisely on time. It was so bright. My eyes were watering, and I couldn't squint enough to stop the ensuing blindness. I reached into my bag and took out the shades Tyde gave me. *Where did he get these things? They're huge!* But they worked.

I walked up and out of the water, shedding every drop left from the lake as I stepped onto the sand. Mer can control water, drawing it off of the body, even from hair and clothing. I was thankful for that ability now.

I took a look around at Camp Crystal. The lake was small, but the water was clear and fresh. I could smell the sweet scent of the spring-fed water from where I was standing. Even though Titus Prime was an ocean dwelling, there were gateways to it all over the world. No one would expect to find a Mer settlement at the bottom of a fresh-water lake. To most, those things didn't mesh, so it was the best way to disguise our home. Mer loved fresh water; it was like getting a spa treatment to swim in it, and it was great for our skin and lungs. Filtering out the oxygen was easier, here.

Crystal Lake was the best kind of water to swim in for Mer, and it was also warm, which was another bonus. I would really enjoy taking a dip in it when I could.

The camp itself was well groomed and neatly put together. I was on the main beach, from what I could tell. There were four larger buildings, and one huge structure just off the shore. To the east was the biggest; it looked like a banquet hall. If I could guess, that would be where we would be eating our meals. Next to it were three smaller buildings. From east to west, they got smaller. The one next to the huge structure had flags on all four corners of the roof and a loud speaker on the top. It looked like an office, or a station of some kind. Obviously, this was where she ran the camp from. The shed next to it had no windows, and I immediately knew it was storage. That left the last smaller building, which, now that I really looked at it, was a cabin. I guessed that it must be Pearl's.

The exterior of all the buildings were made of logs. They were painted dark chocolate-brown, with bright white trim. Each had flower beds with brightly colored flowers. The grass was even freshly cut. Everything looked like a lot of pride went into it.

I couldn't see anything other than the buildings on the beach. My guess was that the campers' cabins were through the heavy brush running off of each side of the beach. Looking out across the lake, I could just see the outlines of a few buildings. The trees were tall and close together. A person could get lost easily if they wandered in. I wouldn't have to worry about that, though. I could sense the water from the lake and find my way back with no trouble, but the humans that went to camp here had better be careful. Cora, too.

"Darrien Locke?" A sunny voice asked from the cabin. I turned and looked for the source. On the small deck, hardly big enough for a two to sit, a figure stood. Pearl, I assumed, bounded down from the deck. Her shoulder-cropped salt and pepper hair bounced as she went. Her face was rosy cheeked and her eyes like large almonds. When she got closer, I could see that she was shorter than me. But then, most people were, since I push six-foot-three. Her smile was beaming, her face so sunny *it* was now blinding me.

"Yeah, that's me," I replied and reached out my hand, but she swept past it and threw her arms around me. I went stiff.

"Well now, we are going to have to work on that," she said, releasing me. Her smile was not a touch reduced, even after that awkward exchange. "Welcome, Mr. Locke!"

"Darrien is fine," I said flatly.

"Alright, Darrien it is," she replied.

"I'm guessing you are Pearl?" My tone could have been described as icy, but it didn't seem to faze her.

Pearl's smile didn't fade. "Well, let's get you settled in and started on your work." For a Siren Smuggler, she seemed nice enough, but I that didn't mean that I could trust her.

"Now, Zale said you were going to watch over the princess, but I asked that you come up before she arrives. I don't really have much help around here. There's going to be a lot of work, so a strong guy like yourself will be very handy to have around," she stated. I stopped walking and looked at her. Her smile faltered. "Is something wrong?"

29

"I'm here to bring Cora back, that's it."

"Oh, of course. Zale just told me that you would be happy to be of any assistance that you could." Her smile returned and she kept walking.

"Of course he did," I mumbled to myself and trudged along behind Pearl.

We walked in silence down a pathway, through some foliage to the east of the beach. Once the silence got too much Pearl started talking again.

"So, I hope you are comfortable sharing your living quarters with the other Leaders. I don't have a separate cabin for princess guards." Her smile suggested she was joking, but I knew what she was getting at. I would not be getting preferential treatment here. I didn't respond, but just kept walking.

"Anyway, each one of them will be assigned a group of campers to look after. You aren't getting a group, since you are here as our swim instructor. Cora will have a group to look after, though I haven't broken that news to her, yet. Her sister is going to work in the office with me, and take part in the Red Cabin activities at times, not that you are that concerned about Bree."

I shook my head. I was here for Cora, not Bree. The road was narrow, maybe large enough for a single vehicle. The bush was thick on both sides of the path, and I could barely see the water glimmer through it. Pearl walked along as if this wasn't the most uncomfortable situation in the world. I wasn't up for a chat, but she didn't seem to get that.

"Zale-"

"*King* Zale," I corrected.

"He will always be Zale to me." She smiled sweetly and I glared back at her. She continued, "Bree is Cora's younger sister. She was only about four when Ana was killed in the accident."

"How do you know so much about the Reeds?" I asked. Pearl hadn't been in Titus Prime for a long time, and was gone before the accident occurred. How did she know all of this?

"Zale told you, we're friends. We talk. Don't you have any friends?" She teased.

"No," I admitted.

"Oh. I'm sorry," she uttered.

"Don't be. I'm not." And I wasn't…for the most part.

"Oh, boy. You need to loosen up, darling." My lips tightened and my fists balled but I kept it under control. I had a job to do. I needed to focus on that.

The path opened to reveal a large area that held five cabins, and a larger building at its center. Pearl walked straight to the first cabin, closest to the road. She bounded up the stairs and held the door open for me. I walked in, having to duck to make it through the door. At first glance, my living quarters were almost militaristic. It was a small cabin, but I'd have a twin-sized bed, storage for my very limited things, a shower, and a bathroom. It was actually really nice.

The interior of the cabin showcased the logs it was built of, but they were left to their natural color and stained to seal them. The furniture matched the stain on the logs, giving the whole room the feeling that you were living inside a tree. The bedding on each bed was colored in deep blues and greens; nothing really seemed to match, and yet, the lack of matching fabric worked together somehow. It drove me a little crazy. I liked things to match. Maybe it was the soldier in me.

"Well, I'll leave you to unpack and take a look around. Lunch is at noon, sharp. I'll see you in the Hall, that really big building on the main beach. Have fun!" Pearl's voice rang through the cabin. When I didn't respond she gave me a side grin and walked back to the beach.

I threw my bag on the bed closest to the door. I needed a place to sleep where I could sneak out without disturbing anyone. I actually liked the room. I liked the camp, too. That surprised me, since I didn't spend any time on land as a kid. Land-bound vacations were popular amongst Mer, but, given our situation growing up, Ty and I never got the opportunity to travel anywhere. It wasn't until I was in training that I learned so much about the surface and the culture up there. Zale insisted that I had extensive training and knowledge of the land, maybe it was because he already knew I would be doing this job. Maybe.

I was lucky, I supposed, compared to Ty. I had years more experience on land than he did. After our parents died, Tyde and I were put in the care of the city of Titus Prime. Normally, any child that was orphaned was placed with family. Titus Prime is the largest of the Mer settlements, and there were families for every child whose parents died in the attack, except for Tyde and me. No relatives came to claim us.

The other settlements were even contacted, to see if we had family elsewhere. The deepest, darkest parts of the ocean house our beautiful cities, but not one of them answered back with news of family for us. We had no family.

We were a unique case. They had to do something with us, so we were put into school. We were nine and five years old, and though that was very young to be put into military school, that was the only place that had living quarters in it. Our career paths were chosen for us from a very young age.

We weren't treated any different than any of the other students, although we *were* allowed to live together. We shared two adjoining rooms. One room was our bedroom, and then the adjoining room was our spot to do our homework and, if we were lucky, play. The cabin reminded me of the close quarters that Tyde and I shared for so many years.

After I unpacked my things and had a look outside my cabin, I took a walk around the lake to get an idea of the layout. On the opposite side of the lake from the main beach was a boat house. That was my first stop on my walk. From what I could see, peeking in the windows, there were over a dozen canoes and kayaks in there. I had never been on either, and found myself surprisingly excited about trying them out.

I walked slowly, taking in the sweet-smelling air and the soft pattering of the leaves. I knew I had made it to the girls' side of the camp when I encountered a mirror image of my side, the boys' side. The doors to the campers' cabins on my side were all color coded: black, blue, green and purple. The girls' side had different colors: pink, red, orange and yellow. Both sides had five cabins that backed the lake, one for the Leaders and one for each colored team. There was also a massive shower room across from the cabins. There was no access to the lake at the cabins, just rough brush, and maybe a wildlife trail or two.

The smell out there was invigorating. I couldn't get over how fresh it was. Nothing tainted it. It was as if rain had fallen all day long, or maybe the grass was just cut. I couldn't be sure.

It didn't take me long to walk around the lake, and I got back to the hall in time for lunch. When I walked in the door, the most magnificent scent met me. I couldn't see Pearl around, so I headed to where the heavenly smell was coming from.

A stout woman, wearing a white smock and a hair net, was bent over the stove. She was humming wistfully to herself.

"Hello?" I interrupted. She jumped, startled by my entrance, and spilled a ladle of what she was cooking.

"I apologize, Madam," I said, and stooped to help clean up the mess. The woman's eyes spread wide when she looked at me.

"Hello, Gorgeous!" she exclaimed in a low, clear voice. Her eyes wrinkled at the edges, but they were kind and maybe a bit mischievous. Her greying hair was up in the hair net, though I could tell it was cut short.

"Hello, yourself," I said and chuckled. "I'm Darrien Locke," I introduced, and stuck out my hand.

"Anne Norris." She took my hand in hers, and I was surprised to find a firm but gentle shake. "I'm the cook here at Camp Crystal. You would be?"

"The new swim instructor," I said after a split second of hesitation.

"Ah, right. The pain in the ass nephew Pearl has been talking about. Coming to stay for the summer, huh?"

"What?" I exclaimed.

"Ah, Anne! I see you've met Darrien, my *nephew*!" she said, eyeing me. I looked from Pearl to Anne and back, my jaw tightening.

"Pearl, uh, can I talk to you for a moment? Anne, it was lovely to meet you."

"Likewise, Gorgeous!" she called as I dragged Pearl out of the kitchen and into the dining hall.

"What the hell, Pearl? Why did you tell her that I'm your nephew?" I demanded in a hushed voice.

"You have your cover story for being here. I need one too. Anne has worked with me for years. She knows that I don't get anyone to come up this early. I needed an excuse for you being here. I figured that you were a new position, and a relative would be the easiest way." Pearl shrugged as if it was the most natural thing.

"You can't just go around telling people that we are related," I fumed.

"Look, I know that where you come from, you're a big deal. But, up here, with humans, they have no idea who you are, and they don't care. Get used to it. Here, you are nobody."

"I don't want the other *Mer* to think that we are related," I said through clenched teeth.

"Trust me, there are worse things. You're here to do a job, so focus on that." With that, she walked back into the kitchen and ended the conversation. I raked my head with my hands and filled my lungs to the point of pain. *If we were in Titus Prime...*

But we weren't and things did not improve from there. For days, Pearl tried to get me to work, planting flowers and watering grass, cutting grass and cleaning the cabins. I ignored her. Instead, I took that time to familiarize myself with the camp more. There were trails that led into the woods on the girls' side. I did two every day. Anything, so I didn't have to talk to her.

"Darrien!" Pearl called. I was just coming out of the brush from a walk through the woods, testing my ability to find my way out if I got lost.

"What?" I may have hollered...just a little.

"Geez, who spit in your cereal this morning?" she said, appearing by the girls' shower room. "I need you to come with me."

"What now?" I blurted. It was taking every bit of self-control I had not to do something I would later regret.

"We have to make a trip to town," she explained.

"What for?"

"We're going to visit a Leader that is coming to work here this summer."

"Are you kidding me? I've been here for days now, and *Cora* isn't even here! You think I'm going to go visit someone other than her? Forget it!" I could feel a coil of anger ready to spring.

"Wow, you have a lot of anger in you, Darrien, my dear." She teased and smiled that smug smile. "Well, we actually *are* going t-"

33

"I really don't care what you are going to town for. I'm not going anywhere with you," I shouted.

"But-"

"Listen, I don't want to work with you. I don't want to have anything to do with you." She stood there, unmoving and silent. "I am being forced to be here with you for Zale. He gave me a job to do, and I intend on doing it. I don't need your help, and I certainly don't need to help you run this damn camp." With that said I stormed away, leaving her silent and still.

When the hell is Cora getting here?

8

Cora

THE NEXT FEW DAYS flew by, with Bree in full-watt smile. It had been a really long time since I had seen her that happy. But even her good mood couldn't put me at ease. I was a walking ball of nervous energy.

I had just finished cleaning up lunch and was washing dishes when there was a knock at the door. My hair was tied back in a messy bun, and I was wearing my worst clothes; it was a cleaning day. Well, most days were cleaning days for me. The knock startled me so badly that I splashed water all over myself, soaking my shirt.

"Damn it!" I cursed and went to open the door. There stood a woman I had never seen before.

"Cora?" the woman asked.

"Yes?" I questioned, eyeing up the stranger. She had the biggest green eyes I had ever seen. I guessed she was in her mid-forties, but she looked incredible. She was tall and thin, with an athletic build. Small streaks of grey ran through her chocolate-brown hair, which was cut bluntly at her shoulders. She had a kindness and familiarity to her I couldn't place, but that immediately put me at ease. But I'd never seen her before in my entire life, which brought me to the question, *how did she know who I was?*

"Cora *Reed!* Well, it's such a pleasure to finally meet you!" She was beaming at me.

I took a step back. I didn't know this woman, but she knew me. I was sufficiently creeped out now.

"Umm...who-?" I managed to stammer out.

"Oh! How silly of me! I'm Pearl Wasche." She held out her hand. I reached for it.

"Oh. *Oh*! Mom's friend from the camp," I exclaimed, as it dawned on me that I was meeting my boss.

"Yes! Exactly. I thought I would pop by and introduce myself, and maybe say 'hi' to your Mom," Pearl's smile was a beam of light shining into our dreary house, and it was very welcome.

"Um, okay. Come in." I moved back from the door and let Pearl in. She moved with ease, like she had been there before.

"The place looks great!" she said, taking another step in, though not too far without an invitation.

"Mom's just in the shower, I'll tell her you're here," I said and started for Mom's room.

"Oh, don't worry. I don't want to bother her if she's busy, I was just going to be a second anyway. I mostly came to give you this." She handed over a large envelope. It was full and heavy.

"Thank you." I smiled, unsure of what else to say.

"It's just some information about Camp Crystal for you and your sister before you come out. Is Bree here?" she asked, as her eyes took a tour of the room.

"Oh, um, no. She's out at the moment."

"Oh, I see, well I'll meet her soon anyway," she smiled back and shrugged.

I pulled at my wet shirt, the warm water having turned cold and started sticking to my stomach. "Did Mom tell you that I have a phobia of water?" It tumbled out before it checked itself. I had been thinking a lot about it, maybe too much, but I certainly didn't intend on interrogating her.

"She did. I'm not going to force you into the water if you are not comfortable, Cora. I hope that your time at camp will help you start to work through your fears, not make them worse. No one is going to be tossing you in the water," she assured me.

I smiled with relief. *Thank goodness.*

"I would be lying if I said that wasn't a fear of mine," I laughed. "Sorry, for being such a disaster, you caught me on cleaning day." I brushed at the water on my shirt to help it dry faster and realized that my hand was soaking wet. I grabbed a towel and dried my hand and then went to rub it on the wet patch on my shirt again, but it was gone. I grabbed my shirt and held it out, staring.

"You look fine to me!" Pearl complimented. I looked up at her, mouth open and nodded. I ran my hand over my shirt again. *Yup, dry. So weird.*

"Well, I suppose I'd better be off. There is an issue at camp that I need to deal with immediately, before it gets out of hand," she smiled and shrugged. "My darling nephew has come to stay, and he's a handful."

"Oh. Sorry," I grinned and focused on Pearl.

"Oh, it's nothing I can't handle. Thank you, though. You have a wonderful day, Cora. Say 'hi' to your mother and Bree for me. I can't wait to meet her, by the way," again her smile lit up the doorway as she made her way out.

"I will. And thank you for the information. I appreciate it. It helps," I said.

"You are very welcome." She made a move for the door, and then hesitated. "I know this is kind of out of the blue for you. I just want you to know that I'm there for you if you need anything. We just met, but if you need anything, you have only to ask. Your Mom did me a great service once. She-" Pearl stopped herself there, and just grinned. "I'm very happy to have you coming, Cora." She reached a hand out and squeezed mine. It was a kind, gentle gesture, which meant more than I was able to understand. With that, she headed out the door, hopped into the ancient green truck parked in the street, and waved out the window as she drove off.

I looked at the envelope in my hand, wondering what Mom had gotten me into.

9

Darrien

BOREDOM HAD OVERTAKEN ME so badly that I found myself cleaning out the girls shower room and hanging shower curtains. Part of me wanted to laugh at the situation I found myself in, the other wanted to blast the shit out of the camp and just leave a crater in its place. That's the mood that Pearl found me in when she returned from town.

"Darrien?" Her sunny voice didn't help my mood any.

"What now, Pearl? Want me to do your laundry?" I glared at her.

"No, I think we need to talk," her voice, her face…all serious. It would have taken me back if I wouldn't have been in a foul mood already.

"I'm good, actually." I tried leaving the shower room, but she stepped in front of me. My fists balled and my short finger nails dug into my palm.

"Well, I'm not." Her blunt words shot at me. My temper roared as the power inside me came alive. Without intending to, I mapped the water in her blood. It was a knee jerk reaction to the anger spike in my body. I wasn't about to pull her blood from her. At least, I was pretty sure I wasn't about to.

"What, Pearl?" I stared at her. Willing the tension in my gut to loosen.

"You don't like me." My eyes rolled. "But if we are going to work together, we are going to have to get along."

I laughed, "Yeah, I don't see that happening. I don't like *who* you are, or what *you* have done." I shoved past her and climbed down the stairs, heading for my cabin.

"And what do you think I have done?" She asked, catching up to me and placing herself in front of me again. Her eyes never wavering and her expression unchanged.

"Look, everyone knows you smuggled Sirens." I waited for her to deny it. To say she was wrongly accused. But she just watched me, so I continued. "You saved them. They should have been taken care of, but you let them go without punishment for what they had done! You knew what they were capable of and you *let them go*!" My anger was building as the agony of my parents' death bit at the back of my throat.

"Darrien, I know what happened to your parents," she said, "but that had nothing to do with me."

"Bullshit, Pearl! How can you say that?" The lid that I had held precariously in place for weeks came flying off. "You freed Sirens! You helped them escape their punishment! You may as well have killed my parents yourself!"

It had taken me years to control my temper. I had a huge chip on my shoulder as a kid. I was angry at everything and everyone about what happened to my family. Being here, with her, was dredging it all up again. She was tapping on a raw nerve and I was struggling keeping it together.

Instinctively, when I'm that mad, my powers reach for the quickest source of water. I felt the water in the pipes going to the shower room immediately. The more she talked the louder the groaning got from the pipes, expanding under the pressure of the water. It wouldn't take long for them to burst if I stayed where I was.

I ran further from the shower room. I didn't *want* to do that kind of damage, but I could end up doing it anyway. Standing still when I was upset like this was nearly impossible. I needed to get rid of the energy building inside me safely. I could feel enough power to have blown all the damn cabins to pieces. And I would have. But, I didn't think Zale would have been impressed that I destroyed a children's camp. Pearl caught up to me on the ground in the center of the girls' side. One look at her and I knew I needed an outlet, now.

I settled for the giant rain barrel by the shower room. The water bubbled and boiled. Pearl looked to see what was going on. That's when I let go. All of the water shot out of the barrel and headed sky high. I could feel the sweet release. When the water got high enough I put more anger into it. It exploded, like a water firework. It felt good letting go, but it wasn't enough to calm me completely, just keep me steady.

Pearl's eyes were wide as she looked back at me. She watched me carefully. It dawned on me that I had scared her. I was shocked at the twinge of guilt that panged in my gut. She *should* be afraid of me. So why did that make me feel bad?

Her voice didn't change. It was still calm and steady when she said, "I didn't help *them*, not those particular ones. You don't understand *everything* when it comes to the Sirens, Darrien. You're hurt and angry, and you have every right to be, but *not* at me. All I did was help a friend." I saw her face without a smile for the first time; sadness had slipped across it.

"How am I supposed to believe you?" I spat.

"I don't know." Her eyes searched the area around us, as if an answer might crawl out from under a bush. "I have no reason to lie. You already don't trust me, so I'm not losing that. I want things to be better between us though. We have a really important job to do and we need each other." Her voice was calm.

I don't need you. But, she was right about one thing. We had a job to do. I heaved a great sigh. I owed it to Zale to at least *attempt* a cease fire.

"Alright, change my mind then." I sat on the bench outside the Leader's cabin. The air was crisp as late afternoon set in and the birds chirped in the trees. The sounds and smells of the lake were helping me suppress the energy coursing through my veins, and calm my heart enough to listen to her.

"Ok, I can do that," she answered, "But please let me get through everything before you interrupt." She looked at me pointedly and I gave a nod. She sat beside me, stretched her long legs out next to mine and took a deep breath in, as if she needed to calm herself too.

"Well, to start with, I didn't smuggle out any of the Sirens that were responsible for the attack. I saved the innocents," she said.

I opened my mouth to object but she held up her hand. "Yes, there *are* innocents," she continued. "There are two kinds of Sirens, those born *as a Siren* and those born *as a Mer* that grow into a Siren. I smuggled out the Mer-born Sirens." I was well aware of the genealogy of Sirens, I just never differentiated between the two. A Siren was a Siren, no matter where they were born.

"Now, you may think this is horrible, but there's something that you need to understand. Sirens are extremely rare in a Mer family, as rare as twins, and their characteristics don't show up until the child is older." I knew all this. They usually turned by their sixteenth birthday, then they were dealt with. I remained silent, though, and let her continue.

"When a Mer-born turns Siren, it breaks families apart. It's a cruel thing to raise a child, love them, and then have them ripped from you just because their eyes change color. It's like a family member dying right in front of you, and being helpless to stop it. It's horrible," Pearl confided.

Mer-born Sirens had one indicator, they had violet eyes. It was their only marker. Siren borns had the violet yes and different colored skin, some purple, some green. When a Siren is born to a Mer family, she is taken the moment her eyes change. We can't take the chance that she will grow up and become a full-fledged Siren. The young ones are dealt with. I didn't say it was easy. But it had to be done. If there was a Siren in your family, it was best that they were rid of. It doesn't matter who their family is. I wasn't sure where she was going with this, but so far, I wasn't convinced I should change my mind about her.

Pearl was getting frustrated, I could tell. I wasn't exactly oohing and awing over her sob story. *Sorry, not sorry.* She gathered herself up and said the words that changed my tune completely.

"My little sister was one," Pearl whispered. My heart chilled.

10
Cora

THE DAY FOR CAMP CAME so quickly I didn't feel I had prepared myself for it at all; even though I had read through the information that Pearl had dropped off a solid dozen times. I was shocked to see that she had assigned me to lead a group of campers for the summer. Even though she said that she wasn't going to force me into the water, boating lessons and swim lessons were on the list of things that the campers were supposed to learn. From what I had read, that was going to be my job.

Mom decided that Bree and I needed new clothes. Who knows why or where she got the money, but B and I both got a new wardrobe for Camp Crystal. We both desperately needed summer clothes, but I was concerned about where Mom was planning on getting the money to buy herself food with, after spending it all on us.

When she took us to the bus station it felt like we were never coming back. She hugged us tightly and just a moment longer than normal; that moment that breaks your heart. Tears were in our eyes as she placed a hand on each of our cheeks.

"Look after each other. Stay true to who you are," she whispered. Bree and I promised we would, through our own tears, and gave her another hug.

We took our seats on the bus and waved out the window until we couldn't see her anymore. The most paranoid part of my brain worried that I wouldn't see Mom again. She had been acting weird lately and that was usually a red flag. Bree didn't see it, or maybe she refused to see it. And, she wouldn't let me voice my concern about it, leaving me to feel like I carried it all on my own. I supposed I should be used to that.

Now, I found myself in a stinky bus, on a road I'd never been on, to a camp I had never been to. I was supposed to be a Leader. Did that mean I was expected to be one of those "cool" teenagers who guided kids through the forest, teaching them how to swim, hike and all that nice outdoorsy stuff?

I hoped not. I wasn't an outdoorsy person, or a beach lover. I couldn't swim or maneuver any kind of water craft. I didn't like group activities or sing-alongs. I had less artistic talent in my whole being than a two year old with finger paints. In short, *I'm doomed.*

Thank goodness, I wasn't going alone. At that moment, Bree, was sleeping against my shoulder. Her golden blonde hair cascaded down her shoulders in big beautiful curls. She was deep in dreamland and her lips hinted of a smile. Bree was everything to me, all my friends and family rolled into one.

I had to hand it to Mom. She did the right thing getting Bree to come too. I wouldn't have gone without her anyway. It was going to be nice having my sis with me.

Bree adjusted herself against me. I watched her eyelashes scrunch as her dream took hold. She was so pretty. I guess I did envy her a little. Bree was starting to get attention from guys, now that she was fifteen years old. Though our family life made us social pariahs, guys still stared at her…so did the girls. No one really drew too much attention from her, she wasn't really interested in dating yet…thank goodness. I wasn't ready to lose my sister to a guy yet. I still needed her too much. Selfish, I know, but I didn't care.

Me? I was never at any threat from guys. At eighteen, when a person is supposed to be celebrating life and youth, I was wallowing in it. That might have had something to do with raising your sibling and dealing with a depressed, absentee mother. Being totally socially backward didn't help matters either.

"Mmmm. Did you say something Cor?" Bree mumbled into my shoulder.

"No. Go back to sleep," I whispered back. I felt bad. It took Bree's coaxing to get me going that morning. And, I kept her up pacing the room last night, stressing.

"It's okay, I'm awake. Where are we?" Her big blue eyes couldn't hide her excitement. While I was worried about being able to do the job I was hired for, Bree was ecstatic about the getting out of the house and away from the kids at school for a summer. She didn't give a thought to job she was hired for, she didn't even ask me about it. She was ready and willing for anything.

"I think we're about half an hour away from our stop, then Pearl is picking us up and driving us out to camp," I answered, realizing I only had thirty minutes left to calm down and, somehow, convince myself that this was *not* going to be a total disaster.

I reached into my bag and pulled out a chocolate bar. *Time to get out the big guns.* Nothing made me feel better than chocolate melting over my tongue. *Oh sweet goodness!*

43

I concentrated on every bite for as long as the bar lasted. Before I knew it, we were five minutes away from our stop.

Bree was staring out the window with a look I couldn't read, and that was never good.

"You okay?" I asked, not sure I wanted to hear the answer.

"Yeah, just thinking about Mom," she replied.

"How come?" I asked, picking at the fudge bits stuck in my molars.

"Gross, Cora," she scolded. "You know, you really need some manners."

"Shut up!" I shoved her.

"Seriously, how are you going to date anyone when you do stuff like that?"

"I don't want to date anyone, so I don't really care," I stated with a toss of my head.

"Well, you'll want to date someone someday. And then it *will* matter," she pressed. I stuck out my tongue and laughed. Dating was *so* not going to happen. If I scared or grossed out every guy in a ten mile radius, all the better. I wasn't going to end up like Mom. The further guys were away from me, the better for everyone.

Bree shoved me and stuck out her tongue. We glared at each other for a few seconds, and then the corner of her lip started to flicker. I could see her smile about to break, and in turn I bit my lips to keep from smiling before her. Then, simultaneously, we burst into laughter. Our fights never lasted long. We seemed to know instinctively that it was a waste of time being angry with each other.

We spent the last few moments of our trip giggling. The other passengers on the bus started to stare, but we didn't care. Bree and I had a way of blocking out the rest of the world when we were together. We'd often find ourselves in that place where the giggles came nonstop, and we couldn't remember what started it all. Our laughs were the only thing that tied us together as sisters; they were identical. She was the only person I could do that with now, the only person I could ever be my true self with, and I loved her more than she would ever know for that.

Then, at precisely the same time, my face dropped and Bree's brightened. We had made it to our destination.

11
Darrien

A FEW DAYS HAD PASSED since I had talked to Pearl outside the shower room on the girls' side. Today the first worker was coming and Pearl had headed into town. I was finishing up some of the chores around the camp before everyone started showing up. My mind constantly wandered back to that conversation. My whole world was turned upside down after that. In the days after, I was stuck wondering what to do with all the anger I was feeling, not being able to place it on Pearl anymore. Her voice was stuck in my head after she shared her story.

I didn't want to hear it.

I didn't want to understand her better, not if that meant I would have to excuse what she did. Not if that changed the way I thought.

But that's what happened.

I had depended on my hatred of Sirens. It fueled me. It drove me. It was the reason I was the top of my class in the academy and how I got my job. I didn't *want* that to change. I didn't want to have to look at that part of myself.

What if it changed everything completely? I wouldn't feel the same way about anything- including myself- ever again. And I didn't.

"My little sister was the sunshine of my family," Pearl began. "She was kind and caring. She loved with everything in her. My parents doted on her, and you'd think that would've made me jealous, but I doted on her just as much as they did. You'd never meet a kinder, gentler soul than Lily.

"Then, around her eleventh birthday, her eyes changed from blue to violet. We were horrified! How could our sweet, innocent Lily be a Siren? How? My mom cried for days, and so did Lily.

"We all knew what would happen to her. If we revealed her, they would take her away and be done with her. It would be a death sentence for her. We couldn't do it. She wasn't a real Siren. Lily didn't have a mean bone in her body! Why were they afraid of her?"

Tears started to gently glide down Pearl's face, and as much as I didn't want to, I was starting to understand. I would do anything to keep Tyde safe. I never really thought about what it would be like to have girls in the family. You never knew if any of them would turn. It would be years and years of torture, waiting to see if they woke up with violet eyes. I had never thought of it like that before.

Pearl continued, "So, we hid her. She stayed inside all the time. We barely left the house, but someone got suspicious and they reported us. I still remember the day that the Guard showed up and took her. Lily was screaming, a blood-curdling scream that I can still hear. Begging for us. Begging to be left alone. Mom was sobbing, unable to lift herself off the ground. I tried going after her. It took my neighbors, three of them, to hold me back." Pearl paused, trying to get a hold of her emotions enough to continue. "My heart shattered. She was my other half. I didn't know how to live without her.

"In the end, my parents blamed each other. They fought all the time. Eventually there was silence, but it was worse than the yelling. The family I once knew was gone. I felt alone. The light in my life was snuffed out, and the fallout from that was the destruction of everything I cared about. Months went by in a blur of depression. My parents eventually settled into a routine of quiet hatred. I wasn't allowed to mention or even allude to Lily anymore. The pain was too much for any of us to bear.

"Then, one day I received a letter. It was from Lily." My eyes shot wide. Usually Sirens of any age were destroyed. "I was so surprised. I had assumed she was dead all that time, but she wasn't. She was smuggled out of Titus and taken to the Siren City." I had heard of the Siren City and the thought of that many Sirens gathered together made me shiver.

"The Sirens there are mostly Siren-born, but they smuggled out the Mer-born Sirens when they could. Lily was selected to be saved, and I use that word loosely. It turns out that the Siren-born use the Mer-born as slaves. They humiliate them, bully them, and torture them, as a way of practicing for a time when they could use those skills on Mer captives." Pearl's sadness was replaced by a raging hatred I was well acquainted with.

I knew Sirens were horrible creatures. But then again, if it would have been up to me, I would have killed Lily on sight, and that was something that I would no longer be able to stomach doing.

"My Lilly was taken from me to be treated in the most disgusting way you could imagine." My stomach churned. Pearl was wiping the tears from her face. Her eyes wouldn't meet mine. She stared at the floor as she continued the story.

46

"One day, while Lily was being 'practiced' on, a young Siren stepped in. She cut Lily from her bonds and took her home with her. Lily didn't trust this girl, but was in no condition to fight her off. The young Siren's name was Celia. She befriended Lily and protected her.

"Celia hid Lily in her home, away from the other Sirens. She fed and clothed her and was her companion. Lily wrote that she was so grateful, and that she would have died a horrible death if it wasn't for Celia. Soon, I was accustomed to getting monthly letters from Lily, telling me about her secluded life with Celia. She seemed, not happy, but content.

"Then, without warning, the letters stopped. There was no word from Lily for two months. I got scared, almost frantic. After three months of hearing nothing, I got the last letter I would ever get regarding Lily.

"It was from Celia.

"She told me that her mother discovered that she was hiding Lily. To teach Celia a lesson about what it meant to be a true Siren, she tortured and killed Lily right in front of her."

My blood froze. I clenched my fists so tight they went numb. I knew that Sirens were vicious, but that…if that was Tyde…my heart slammed in my chest in anger and my stomach wanted to empty.

"I can't begin to explain the pain. It hurt in every way possible, all over again. Lily was sweet and kind. She didn't deserve that. She wasn't one of them. She wasn't. And to be murdered, just to teach someone a lesson!" Tears were streaming down Pearl's face. As much as I didn't want it to, my heart broke for her.

"Celia wasn't like the others. She was a Siren-born, but she lacked almost all the traits that came with that. Her mother was a Siren, a very powerful one, the *most* powerful one. But Celia was like Lily, sweet and loving. She saved Lilly for as long as she could. She protected her and gave her the best life Lily could have hoped for amongst the Sirens.

"I loved Celia for that.

"I trusted her for that. For a while, Celia and I exchanged letters. We talked about Lily, mostly. She loved Lily too. She thought of Lily as a sister just as much as I did. I didn't feel so alone in my loss anymore.

"You see, I didn't tell my parents about Lily's letters. I let them mourn her and move on. Celia was the only one that knew what happened to Lily. I grew to love Celia like a sister, too. She told me about her life, her mother, and the other Sirens around her. She was horribly treated. Eventually I realized that Lily's death was probably a blessing, not that it made me any less angry at Celia's mother, but if Lily had to go through a fraction of what Celia talked about, I'm glad she was gone.

"Celia was the bravest girl I had ever known and after what she did for Lilly, I would do anything for her."

I agreed. If Ty was in that position, I would do anything for the person that saved him. I was starting to see things from her position more and more and that scared the crap out of me. But Pearl wasn't finished.

"When the time came to repay a fraction of what she had done for my Lily, I was all too happy to help. And that included smuggling Celia and her husband to the surface, to save them and their unborn children's lives.

"After that, I did my part to try to save as many Mer-borns from a fate like Lily's. I had a contact on the surface that was relocating them on land and my smuggling operation began. After the attack, I knew of a couple whose daughter had changed. I broke into the holding cell to get her out before they killed her. I was caught, but the young girl ran. I'm pretty sure she was captured by the Sirens and taken to Stronghold. I was charged and sentenced to the surface."

She sat back against the bench, her eyes drifted away from me.

"I don't regret it, Darrien. I never have. I did it for Lily, in her memory. No child should have to suffer as she did, and I couldn't live with myself if I didn't do something about that. I saved as many as I could, until I was sent here. Since then, the Sirens have been able to get their hands on all of the Mer-born again. I was the only one in their way."

I was speechless.

Pearl was so far from the person I thought she was it was almost laughable, if it wasn't so disturbing. The guilt for the way that I had treated her and spoken to her was like a rolling thunder storm in my gut. A respect for Pearl had snuck up and taken a hold inside me that shocked me to my core.

"I'm sorry, Pearl. I don't…I can't…."

"It's okay, Darrien. I didn't tell you to make you feel bad. I told you so that we understand each other better. I know what people think I did in Titus. I know I can't go back, even though Zale has asked me to. There's no life for me there. Even my family disowned me. Every move I make would be watched so I wouldn't be able to help the Mer-born either. I can't live there knowing what is really going on." A weak smile caught the edges of her lips.

"Zale is one of the only ones that has understood me. Like I said, we go way back. He was kind to me when I needed it most. He set me up here and found a way for me to be useful again. I can't thank him enough for that. He must think extremely high of you to ask you to do this job for him. He doesn't hand out his trust lightly. You should feel good about that."

Her smile returned but it was different this time. I could see the guards down. That was a smile that had been through a lot and was still strong

48

enough to come out. It was beautiful, in the saddest way possible. I knew what it felt like to try to smile after losing my parents, and truth be told, mine wasn't as strong. I scrubbed my face with my hands, getting rid of the tears that I didn't want Pearl to see.

"Well, what's our next job? The Leaders are coming soon, right?" I asked, and jumped off the bench. I didn't want to prolong the sadness that had spread through us both. Pearl smiled and raised up herself.

"Actually, we have one arriving early. She will be here with her sister in a week, a day before the others."

"Okay, well let's get started." I headed for the door.

"Alright!" Her beaming smile filled the room for the first time in what seemed an age. "Thank you, Darrien."

I nodded and smiled. Next to Zale, Pearl had become the most incredible person I had ever met, and she'd done it in a half hour. No wonder she got on with Zale so well. He had done the same thing. I found myself more willing to help and over the next few days Pearl and I had some really great talks. I started to see what Zale saw in her.

Zale. We had always argued about Sirens, and now I knew why. He knew Pearl's story. He knew there was goodness out there, and he needed me to see it too.

Smooth move, Zale. Smooth move.

12

Cora

BREE AND I STARED out the window as the bus pulled into town. A decrepit wooden sign gave a faded salutation to the passengers: "Welcome to Sturgis".

I scoffed. Bree nudged me with her elbow. My eyes instinctively searched around to see who heard me. Bree had always been more in tune with the feelings of others than I was. She must have thought I was being rude. I wasn't born with the capability of hiding what I thought; my feelings were right there on my face for everyone to see. Bree, on the other hand, was very good at keeping her expressions under control. That's probably why people liked her more. Okay, that and several other endearing features she had. She couldn't hide anything from me, though. I could read her like a book.

We travelled past small streets lined with little houses and neatly trimmed lawns which soon intersected with a major street, and I use "major" loosely…really loosely. Lining this road on both sides were more small houses and businesses. Each place was unique both in architecture and design. Some houses were small one-story bungalows, some were two stories high, some had store fronts, and others featured a little sign in the window. It was the most eclectic grouping of buildings I had ever seen. It would be interesting to wander through town on my days off. I'd have to see if I could bring Bree with me.

"Cor! Look!" Bree jumped up and pointed to something, slamming her finger into the bus window. "Ooww!"

I started laughing. Her brief look of shock, then pain, was priceless! Bree joined in, giggling and holding her throbbing finger. Whatever it was that she pointed at was lost in our bubbling giggles, and one snort, which put us right over the top.

We decided that we'd come back together and have a look through the shops. Mom's birthday was next month and we'd both be missing it because we were there. I was sure we'd be able to find something unique and tacky to get her there. *She loves that stuff.*

The bus made a sharp turn left, and then came to a stop. A gush of air released from the back of it like a great sigh of relief, as if the bus wasn't sure we would make it. I sighed right along with it. *This is it. This is the start.* I closed my eyes, took a deep breath in, and waited. The feeling of full lungs always calmed me a little- when there wasn't time for an entire chocolate bar, that is. I opened my eyes and slowly deflated my lungs through pursed lips.

Bree was watching me. She was used to me doing this. I often had to psych myself up for things that I was nervous about, like tests, hospital visits, and school performances. They were all things that made my stomach flop. Getting off of that bus and heading into the unknown was a legitimate call for some concentrated breathing. Bree sat patiently while I did what I needed to do. It helped having her there. Though she said nothing, it wasn't an angry or annoyed silence, but one of quiet support. Quickly, the panic was over and I was ready to go.

Before I had lifted myself off my seat, Bree already had our things from the floor and overhead gathered. Just standing next to her, I could feel the current of excitement flowing off of her. If I were anyone else, I would've been affected by her spark. But I'm me, and I was too nervous about the weeks to come.

We flung our heavy backpacks on and trudged out the bus door. Well, *I* trudged, Bree skipped. A tall slender brunette stood a few feet away smiling at the two of us. *Pearl.* She was wearing blue jeans and a black Camp Crystal t-shirt. Her eyes were twinkling, and her smile was genuine and kind. I slapped on the most honest smile I could muster.

"Hi, Pearl!" I said, trying desperately to fake enthusiasm. "This is my sister, Bree. Bree, this is Pearl." I gestured to each of them as I introduced them. Pearl put her hand out and Bree took it in a generous handshake. Bree's smile inched higher and higher on her face; for a second I thought it might take off with her ears and we'd never see it again.

"What a lovely pair of sisters!" Pearl gushed. "Welcome to Sturgis, ladies! I hope you are as excited as I am to have you here this summer! Let's get you loaded up so we can get into camp. I have a lot to show you before the others get here! Shall we?"

Pearl grabbed our bags and headed toward a beat up 1970-something Ford half-ton truck. The color reminded me of the mints that Dad used to have in his pocket, a light dusty green. I could smell them just thinking about it. Bree's eyes nearly jumped out of her head as we clambered into the truck. It was a rust bucket. Pearl tossed our bags in the back and jumped in beside us.

"Sorry, dears! I've been meaning to get the seat belts replaced in this old thing, but never get around to it. No worries though, this old beast can't go fast enough to do any damage!" Pearl smiled and laughed to herself as she fired up the engine. The "beast" coughed and groaned to a start. We were off.

We traveled down the rest of Main Street. The same odd assortment of houses met us on both sides of town. I spotted a book store, craft shop, and a clothing store among them, perfect for Mom. I leaned over to tell Bree, but she was staring out the window again, lost in thought. I decided to leave her alone with them. I had my own thoughts to keep me company.

Pearl was humming a tune to herself as she drove. There was a peaceful timbre to the way her voice curved around each note, like it was coaxing a melody out of them. I couldn't place any words to the melody, but it called to a memory somewhere deep inside me.

Soon, we were zipping along the highway. Well, maybe "zipping" was an exaggeration, but we were moving.

I know that people think that the prairies are bleak and boring, but I think they are lovely. In the fall, when the flax fields bloom, there is a sea of blue that waves in the wind, and looks like the ocean travelled all the way across the country to visit us. Then right next to it, the canola blooming bright yellow, like a field of sun. The sky is a blue dome overhead that you can see forever and a day and watch the clouds roam from horizon to horizon. In the winter the northern lights danced across the sky in brilliant pastels to a song they only know. It's so open and fresh, you can really breathe when you're out in the middle of it. It might not be the majesty of mountains or the scent of the sea, but the prairies have a magic all their own. There is a quiet, understated beauty to the prairie, just the way I like it.

One thing that was not magical, however, was the truck we were driving in. I noticed a few more oddities I didn't see before as I plucked up my courage and looked around the cabin. Not only was the truck missing essential safety equipment, like seat belts, it was missing parts of the floor too. If I looked down, I could see the road below us through a quarter sized hole in the floor.

Pearl must have been watching me take in her truck. "Quite the view, isn't it! You let me know if you see a white line any time. That means I'm drifting too close to the ditch!" Pearl stole a glance at me and burst out laughing. I knew that I must have looked horrified...and ridiculous. Bree was giggling and enjoying Pearl's joke at my expense, too.

"Ha ha. Very funny," I retorted, making sure every syllable dripped with sarcasm.

52

Pearl wasn't fazed a bit. She smiled generously at me and winked at Bree. Bree nudged me to let me know that she was sorry for laughing. I grinned back. *I'm so glad she's here.* I was much better at being half-normal when she was around.

It was going to be tough when she had all her new friends and couldn't protect her big sister from herself, though. Bree wouldn't have trouble making friends. She had one of those personalities that people just gravitated to. Unfortunately, the kids at school never gave her a chance. I will admit, I was a little jealous of Bree at times. But, she was too much a part of who I was to let those feelings override my affection for her. She didn't even realize she had any of the qualities I loved about her.

"Welcome to Camp Crystal, ladies!" Pearl announced, as we travelled under a camp crest and welcome sign. We were home for the summer.

13

Cora

IN THE MIDDLE OF THE PRAIRIE, immersed in farm land and crops, sprang a tall collection of trees. We could see them a long distance off, but even so, their height was astounding as we got closer.

We turned into the grove of trees and onto a gravel lane, which lead to a gate. It was a giant wrought iron monstrosity, with the initials "CC" wound in and around each other, appearing on both doors of the gate. It could have been mistaken for the entrance to a mansion, or maybe Jurassic Park, instead of a kids' summer camp. Even though years of rust that had accumulated on it, somehow the gate was still beautiful and intricately detailed.

"You think they keep dinosaurs in there too?" Bree asked. I smiled at her and chuckled to myself. Sometimes she was more like me than she probably wanted to know.

The road was narrow, not paved but rutted dirt. It looked like a wagon trail to me. If we met another vehicle, we'd end up in the bushes for sure, but by the looks of the road I guessed there wasn't a lot of traffic. We were walled in by tall trees on both sides, which created a beautiful flickering canopy of foliage and sunlight above us. The brush underneath was thick, and full of berry bushes and small shrubs.

Soon, the road widened and opened into a large green expanse. My first scan of the open area showed three buildings and one huge hall. Pearl gestured to each building and explained to Bree and me their purpose, going from left to right: there was Pearl's cabin, a storage shed, the Main Office and finally the hall, which served as the cafeteria and meeting room. All of the buildings were built with logs, save for the Hall, but they were all painted the same dark brown with white trim. The Main Office, however, had flair. Flags hung from every corner of the roof, and flowerbeds were meticulously tended and held a brilliant array of colors. It certainly drew attention. There was also a loud speaker attached to the roof, most likely for announcements,

I figured. Pearl's cabin and the storage shed, on the other side of the Main Office, were the same shape, but much less fanfare was given to them. The only difference between the two was that Pearl's cabin had a laundry line outside, while the supply cabin had huge double doors in the back, perfect for truck deliveries.

The place looked very well taken care of. From the middle of "The Green," as Pearl called it, I could see Crystal Lake stretching out in front of us, blue-green and glistening in the afternoon sun.

"It's so pretty!" Bree gushed, creeping closer to the window so she could see more.

"Yes. It is," Pearl said, in a warm matter of fact tone. I had to agree.

Pearl pulled the truck up to the back of the Main Office. She hopped out and slid around to the back to grab our bags. She had a bounce in her step and lilt in her voice; she seemed downright giddy. Her manner was so contagious that I caught myself grinning. Bree was beaming, as her wide eyes soaked in her surroundings. It *was* a beautiful place, there was no denying that. The woods around the water made it feel like we'd stumbled upon a secret lake all our own.

We followed Pearl through the side door of the Main Office. Upon inspection, it was mostly just one large room. Standing in the doorway, I could see that there were two doors at the back, one labeled "Washroom," and the other "Storage." At the front of the cabin, there was one large desk sitting in front of a huge window overlooking the beach and water. I figured that it was Pearl's. Beside her desk, there was a door leading outside, to the front of the building and the beach.

"Well Cora, this is where it all happens. You'll be able to find any information you need in this room. My desk is always open to the Leads if they need anything. Over here, will be where you run your team from," she explained, indicating a smaller desk at the back of the room. "You will be sharing your space with our swim instructor. Each desk is assigned to two people. I find that it helps build relationships and team spirit, or just plain tolerance." She smiled knowingly.

I took a look around and counted four desks, meaning that there were eight Leaders, including me. I stepped over to my desk. It was wooden and big enough for one person to sit comfortably at, but not two. I supposed we wouldn't be spending too much time there, anyway. On the desk were some supplies: paper, scissors, pencils, and erasers, all in unopened boxes. Included in the array of new supplies, there was a time table and cabin assignment. I saw no evidence of my desk partner, and I didn't see any schedule either. I hoped that she would be someone I could get along with. As long as she didn't try to get me in the water, we would be just fine.

While Pearl rummaged around her desk, I quickly opened the new supplies and organized them in the desk drawers. I left my schedule on the desk. I wasn't ready to face everything just yet. I looked at my cabin assignment, but all it said was "ORANGE," and listed a bunch of girls' names. *I guess we are color-coded.*

The walls were covered with posters, covering topics from swimmer's itch to fire safety. Bree was busy taking it all in. There were also pictures of kids at camp from years past, and group photos of the Leads and their corresponding cabins. There was too much to catch in one visit. I could've looked at the walls for hours.

"Well, girls, let's get you settled, shall we?" Pearl exclaimed, and with that she whisked up our bags and bounced out the front door, onto the sandy beach. We followed her out and hopped to the ground. My breath caught in my chest and my body went rigid. Open water…

14
Darrien

I HAD BEEN SCRUBBING and painting all day, trying to kill some time, but I was coming to the end of my giant to-do list. Though that felt oddly satisfying, I was also aware that I would have nothing to do once I finished it. I wasn't one for relaxing on the beach, sun-tanning like an idiot, Mer had no use for a tan. I was wandering camp aimlessly, trying to avoid the main beach and the girls' side for the day.

Pearl asked me to stay away from those areas for the evening so that she could let the new girl figure out the area. I didn't understand what that had to do with me, but Pearl was weird that way, so I was staying away. Things had been good between us, and I didn't want to ruin it.

I found myself missing Tyde and wondering how things were going with him. I wished that there was a way we could communicate, but water to surface communication was nearly impossible.

I was hungry, so I decided to sneak to the Hall and get something to eat. Anne was probably starting on supper. I could help her for a while.

Sure enough, I found the old gal in the kitchen, cutting up some veggies.

"Could you use an extra set of hands?" I asked.

"Ones as young and good looking as yours? No thanks!" She joked.

"Oh, just give me that knife and let me help." I shoved her over playfully and took the knife from her hand. She giggled the entire time. I liked her. Anne's manner was like my Mom's, sweet and kind, but in a sarcastic way. I was quick with a knife, and not just in the kitchen, so in no time the veggies were done. I sat on the counter and watched as Anne bustled around the kitchen, concocting her meal for Pearl and the new girl. I hoped that they appreciated it. Anne's cooking was unreal.

"Have you met the new girl?" Anne asked over the pot she was stirring.

"No. Pearl wanted me to stay away for the evening."

"She probably wanted the poor thing to keep her wits about her for one extra day before losing them at the sight of you!" She kidded. I chuckled.

"You flatterer! I doubt Pearl thinks that way. But it's nice of you to say."

"Oh, Pearl…she has had it tough in the romance department. Perhaps one day, things will change for her." Anne put her attention to the pot. I didn't respond. There was something wrong with talking about something so private. If Pearl wanted me to know about that stuff, she would have told me herself. It was none of my damned business what her love life was.

"Have you seen her? I mean the new girl," I asked, needing to change the subject off of Pearl.

"Not yet. They are coming in here in a bit for some supper. I expect I'll meet her then. You going to be joining them?" she asked.

"Nope. I won't be responsible for the loss of anyone's wits tonight, thank you very much. I'll be stealing some of that fresh bread you baked this morning and some cheese, and I'll be hiding in my cabin for the rest of the night, if anyone needs me." I scooped up a loaf of bread as I headed to the huge fridge.

"Too bad, would have loved to see the 'Darrien Effect' on someone for the first time. I never get to do anything fun in here," she pouted.

"Oh, now, don't be like that. I'll come visit you again. You're my favorite gal!"

"Ah, you tease an old lady. But that's okay, I like it!" I chuckled as I headed to the door with my snack for supper. "You just watch yourself, Darrien Locke. One of these days, you will be swept up by someone when you least expect it."

"Sure, sure." I nodded in sarcastic agreement. "Have a good day, Anne!"

"You too, Darrien, dear!" Anne called after me.

15
Cora

MY HEART THRUMMED in my chest and my feet were bolted to the ground. The water. *Breathe, Cora.* Just *breathe.*

There, stretching out in front of us, was Crystal Lake in all her glory. It was breathtaking! It wasn't the biggest lake I had ever seen; it was small enough to swim across. What struck me the most was the color. For a lake stuck out in the middle of nowhere, I felt like I had come upon a tropical lagoon. The water sparked like diamonds dancing over its crystal-clear surface. It might have been small, but the dark green at the center told volumes; one look and I knew this lake was deep, *really deep.*

The main beach was long. Its fine sand stretched out the entire distance, right to the edge of the woods on either side. It looked like velvet from where we stood, and I looked forward to the feel of the soft warm sand between my toes already. If I could just move, I might have been able to test it out.

"Oh, Cor! It's beautiful!" Bree whispered. I nodded stiffly in stunned agreement.

Pearl smiled and then walked toward the path. I let out a sigh of relief. *No water.* That was the key to the release on my feet. I grabbed my bags and followed Pearl, grateful that no one seemed to notice my momentary loss of control. Bree did the same and jogged up next to me, her smile just as big as before, as she dragged her suitcase behind her.

The road was surprisingly smooth for a trail, and just big enough to get a truck through. The same tall trees and thick brush walled the route that we took, so thick that we couldn't see further than a couple of feet in.

"Remind me not to get lost in there," Bree whispered as we walked.

"Don't get lost in there," I whispered back, reminding her. She shoved me and I giggled.

We had been walking for a while when we came to a clearing in the wood. Five cabins stood in front of us, four lined up in a row facing us and one backed the lake. I could see we were almost on the opposite side of the lake from the beach. The cabins were close to the water, but there was no beach here. I liked the seclusion of it.

A small Camp Crystal flag hung above each cabin's door. The only difference I could see between them was that each cabin had a different colored door: pink, red, orange, and yellow. I guessed that the cabin I was responsible for was the orange one.

The first cabin, closest to the road and backing the lake, was for the Leads and was going to be my home. Pearl ventured straight to it. The door was painted white with four squares, in each cabin color. Bree followed me into the cabin. Pearl busied herself checking the water in the bathroom and opening the windows. I just stood there. A wave of disbelief washed over me. I had been dreading being there for so long, and the reality of finally arriving was slow to set in. *Just breathe, Cora. Just breathe.*

There were four single beds, two on either side of the room, and a set of drawers and a night stand by each. All the furniture was left to the natural color of the wood, which matched the color of the logs inside. There was a trunk at the foot of each bed and two closets in the back of the cabin, one on either side of the bathroom. A breeze trickled in through a window Pearl opened, and I could smell the water from the lake. I closed my eyes and drew in a deep breath. My heart slowed. *I think I might be happy here.*

"You get first choice of beds, Cora. Feel free to take whichever you want. There's no seniority at my camp. You start fresh every year here!" She was looking around the room, checking behind the curtain and under the beds, and running her fingers along edges. The room was meticulously clean, and yet Pearl smoothed the bedding. When she smiled and nodded, the room had passed its test. Looking around, I decided on the bed at the back of the cabin, closest to the bathroom, on the right side. I tossed my backpack on the bed. *Home sweet home*, I thought with a sigh.

"Well, kiddo! I guess you're wondering where I put *you*," Pearl said, winking at Bree. Bree smiled and blushed a little, she had been silent since we came in the cabin. Her eyes travelled around the room but her usual cheeriness was gone. Bree and I had shared a room as far back as she could remember. This would be the first time in her life that I wouldn't be right there in the room with her. I knew it scared her. Who was I kidding? It scared me too.

"I didn't think that you'd want to be in Cora's cabin all summer, under your sister's iron fist." Pearl laughed, and Bree absentmindedly nodded in agreement. I curled my lips into a grimace. It was better for our sanity that we were separated, even if it was going to be tough.

"Cora is Lead for the Orange Team. You, Bree, will be close by, as part of the Red Team, when you're not helping in the office with me. How does that sound? If you have any problems with the girls or anything else, your sister is right next door." Pearl sounded pleased with her rationale, and so was I.

"That sounds good. Thank you," Bree smiled and let her shoulders drop. That brought out a brighter smile in Pearl and me too.

"Cora, feel free to stay here and get unpacked if you wish. Half of that closet is your space," she said, indicating the closet on my side of the bathroom. "Don't let the other girls tell you otherwise. No seniority, remember? You make yourself at home! I'm going to take Bree over to her cabin, get her all settled in, and we will be back to get you for supper! Toodles!" And in a flash, she was out the door, with Bree jogging to catch up.

I walked over to my bed and, with a grunt, flopped down on it. I stared at the roof, took a deep breath in and held it for a moment, basking in the pleasure full lungs gave me. Then, slowly, I released the air through pursed lips. I was "home."

It's going to be fine.

I couldn't believe all the storage space that Pearl had for us. Two closets in the back to share, a set of drawers and a trunk. *How much stuff do these girls bring with them?* I only had my backpack and medium-sized suitcase. I went to my closet, opened it up, and could immediately see why I needed the other space. It was full of camp shirts: Pink, Red, Orange and Yellow. I took out the orange shirts and put them on my side of the closet. I went to the other closet and fetched the orange shirts from there, too. Then, my organizational skills took control. *Pink over here, red there…then yellow goes here.* I found colored tape and labels in a box in the back of the other closet, and before I knew it I had the entire room color coded. It took Pearl and Bree to walk in before I realized I hadn't unpacked a thing of my own!

"Excellent work, Cora! I never thought of assigning beds like that! I'll take you over to the boy's cabin after supper and help you do the same there. This is great! You must be starving after all that work. Let's get some food!" Before I could really respond Pearl was on her way to the Hall for supper. Bree stood there and stared at me.

"Cor, you need a life!" She teased. "I'll help you unpack your stuff after supper." She gave me a playful shove out the door, and we ran after Pearl. I *was* starving.

16

Cora

THE HALL WAS BIG ENOUGH to fit eight long tables in it, each with enough seating for twenty people. There was a long hot and cold buffet at the front of the room, with the kitchen doors right behind it for easy access. One small circular table was off to the side of the room. I figured that was where the Leads sat to eat. The rest of the tables were color-coded, according to cabin.

Supper was good, and I mean *good*. Mom wasn't much of a cook, and she didn't instill a love for it in me *or* Bree. We did the cooking, which meant that our meals were simple and easy to make…and yeah, mostly frozen. It would be nice to have someone else do the cooking for a while, especially when it was that delicious.

After we gorged ourselves, Pearl introduced us to the cook, Anne Norris. She was a stereotypical cafeteria cook if I ever saw one: stout, with short grey hair, a messy apron over a white cook's uniform, and a hair net. I guessed that she was in her fifties. Her face was round, with red cheeks from the heat of the kitchen. Her eyes, though, were a beautiful deep green. When she came out of the kitchen, she stopped short and took a long look at Bree and myself.

"We've got to get some meat on those bones! You two look half starved!" Anne had a boisterous voice that seemed to boom inside my head as she spoke. As intimidating as that should be, there was a sweet and sincere sound to it that made me feel cared for. I liked her immediately. Anne smiled warmly. "One summer here, and I'll fix you right up! Right, Pearl?"

Pearl beamed. "Right! Anne, this is Cora and Bree. Cora is one of the new Leads this summer, and Bree is her sister. Cora is Orange and Bree is Red!"

This seemed to categorize us for her, or maybe made us easier to remember somehow. Pearl smiled generously at us, as did Anne. Bree and I cleared dishes and helped tidy the kitchen. Anne was impressed and thanked us many times over. I got the impression that the Leads didn't help out around the kitchen much.

Our mom would have been pleased with us. Good manners were something that she took very seriously. "If you respect others, you will earn their respect in return," she would say on her rare good days. Though, it didn't seem to matter how much I respected the kids at school. They never respected me back. I just wanted to point that out.

Our first day at Camp Crystal was coming to an end, and oddly enough, it wasn't the disaster I thought it would be. But, there weren't any other Leads or kids around. How badly could I have screwed up at this point? After we helped Pearl organize the boys' Lead cabin, she gave us leave to wander the camp until sunset. She said it would be good for us to walk and enjoy each other's company a little before everyone started arriving. Who knew how much time we would get together after that?

Bree and I walked back to my cabin. Keeping exclusively to the path, we listened to the birds and the soft breeze through the trees. There was a gentle song to the sounds in the woods. I'd never experienced that before. The darkening sky warned that we'd better get a move on if I was going to get unpacked.

Once my things were neatly organized and put away, I went to have a look at Bree's cabin. It was about the same size as the Leads'. It had six bunk beds, each with a large set of shelves beside it. There were also two mini lockers and a set of drawers at the foot of the bunk. She had more than enough room for her things. She went to her locker, and discovered two camp shirts in red, her cabin color. I peeked into the two bathrooms, which held toilets and sinks only.

The shower facilities were in a big building on the other side of the road from the cabins. Inside were more bathroom stalls and sinks, and enough showers for one whole cabin to get clean at once. They were all stalled too. *Smart.* I imagined there would have been a few girls that would've rather stunk than showered in the open. *And I'm one of them.* The Leads had a shower in their cabin. I was eternally grateful to Pearl for letting us have that one luxury.

The sun was sinking low in the sky, but there was still enough light out to enjoy the walk back to meet Pearl. I could see some early stars winking just above the towering trees. The air was cooling down, but my sweater kept me perfectly warm. I wrapped my arms around my bunny hug, my Dad's name for a hoodie, and smiled.

When we came out of the trail to the main beach, Pearl was waiting there with a canoe and two lifejackets. I stopped instantly. Bree actually smacked into my back.

"What are you…oh," Bree said, answering her own question the moment she saw the canoe.

"I'm sure that Pearl just wants to take us on a tour around the lake so that you're familiar with it, Cor." There was no movement on my end, not even a breath. She tried harder.

"She's been doing this for many years and I'm sure she knows what she's doing," Bree urged, taking my hand and trying to pull me out of myself, but even that wasn't working. My heart was pounding and my breathing was shallow. I could feel the tightness spreading through my chest, squeezing the sanity right out of me. I was going to have a full on panic attack. Bree swung in front of my face, her eyes searching mine. "Look! She's got a big bright lifejacket for you to wear, too. Nothing to be afraid of."

I feel sick. The blood drained from my face. My legs were heavy, cemented to the ground. I couldn't move them. I didn't *want* to move them.

Bree was now tugging at my hand, but I wasn't budging. Pearl noticed that there was a hold up, and to my complete embarrassment, she came trotting up the beach toward us.

"How about an evening ride around the lake, girls? I want to show you around, Cora. I thought it might help you since you've never been here before." Her smile faded as she noticed my hesitation. "Is something wrong?" She looked at me. I mean, *really* looked at me. Her expression changed from excitement to concern almost immediately. I was trying hard not to let my fear register on my face, but I was doing a terrible job of it.

"Bree, what's wrong with her?" Although Pearl's concern warmed my heart, and I could feel a little weight come off of my legs, I still wasn't moving.

"Cora is deathly afraid of water. She can't swim." Bree looked at me tenderly. She had seen me this way many times before. My cheeks were burning.

Pearl relaxed. A look of relief flitted across her face, and a smile peaked the edges of her mouth.

"Don't you worry, Cora. I'm not going to force you on the boat. I just thought that it would be a relaxing way to end your first day here. I promised that no one was going to toss you in the water, I keep my promises. I'll try to give you as much info as I can from the shore, how about that?" Pearl reached out and ran a soft hand down my arm, effectively relieving the tension in my chest and allowing me to breathe normally.

Her eyes were searching my face, waiting, expecting. I was at a loss for words. My mouth must have dropped open because she leaned in, raised her brows with eyes wide and waited, looking anxious for my answer, but nothing came out.

"Look, I'm putting the lifejackets down and I'll pull the canoe completely out of the water. No one is going anywhere in it," she explained. Pearl dropped the jackets far away from us and took a large step from them, then she pulled the canoe on shore and threw the paddles on the sand further away from us.

I finally found my voice, and the locks seemed to come off my feet. I closed my mouth and willed the muscles in my legs and to relax.

"Th-Thank you for offering, Pearl." *You are such an idiot, Cora!* Embarrassment didn't even touch the way I felt. "I really appreciate you taking time to help me. Sorry I'm making things difficult." I frowned.

"Oh, don't beat yourself up about it, Cora," Pearl said with a flip of her hand. "You're being too hard on yourself." I blushed. I didn't think I was being hard on myself at all. "Come down this way, where we have a better view."

Pearl whipped around and headed toward the shore, making sure she stayed far from the canoe to assure me we weren't going anywhere, and effectively locking herself into the position of one of my all-time favorite people.

"You okay?" B asked.

"Yeah, sorry," I said dropping my eyes to the sand. I hated being that way, *hated* it.

"You know you don't have to apologize to me, Cor," Bree said in her gentle tender voice that always warmed my heart. She squeezed my hand and smiled at me. I gave her a small grin back, that was the best I could do, but she was happy with it.

Bree and I walked silently to the edge of the lake. She and Pearl removed their shoes and stepped into the water. Not wanting to look like I was completely ungrateful for Pearl's kindness, I slid my shoes off too.

My heart raced as I ventured closer to the water's edge. Ignoring the pounding in my chest, and the urge to squeal, I ever so slowly slid a foot into the water. It was like stepping into a warm bath and, *oh my goodness*, I missed that sensation. A wide smile grew on my face as I closed my eyes and allowed my body to relax in water for the first time in a very long time. I stood between Pearl and Bree, all of us looking out across the lake. It was an incredibly calm night; there wasn't a ripple on the water.

The scent of the water drifted across the lake and over to where we were. It smelled sweet, like flowers or perfume or rain. I couldn't put my finger on it, though it was lovely.

"Over on the far side of the lake, you can see our boat house." Pearl's strong voice interrupted my thoughts. "We have enough canoes and kayaks for two cabins to use at the same time. The boat house is in the middle of the boys' and girls' cabins. On the left you can just see the girls' side. To the right are the boys' team cabins. Our swimming lessons take place on the main beach and the dock at the boat house. This year's instructor is a master and will undoubtedly be anxious to get you into the water," she said with a smile and a wink. *Yeah, good luck with that.*

The three of us stood there at the shore of Crystal Lake and watched the sun sink beyond the horizon. I'd never taken the time to do that before. It was beautiful, perfectly beautiful. The sunlight played off small puffs of clouds, changing them from pink to blue against a red-stained sky. As the sun sank below the horizon, the silhouettes of the trees stood out more and more, then blended in entirely with the dark sky. The water on the lake was so still, it perfectly mirrored the ever-changing painting that hung above it. When the moon appeared it was the perfect finishing ornament to the color-washed sky. I wished I could have captured it somehow, but a picture would've never done it justice. When the night lights came on across the lake and down the trails, we stopped watching and proceeded to our cabins.

After such an eventful day I was exhausted. Bree and I walked back to our cabins in silence, enjoying the night time sounds in the woods. We climbed the steps to our cabins. As I opened the door to mine, I noticed Bree was just standing there in front of her door.

"You okay, Bree?" I removed my hand from the door and took a step down.

"No, I mean yeah. I mean…" She chewed her lip and looked at her shoes. I stepped down my stairs and climbed up hers.

"How about if I come in with you for a bit?" I asked, knowing she was nervous about spending the night alone.

"No, it's okay Cor," her voice was small and wavered when she spoke. She wouldn't look at me either, and that was never a good sign.

"You sure? It's not a big deal, I'm sure Pearl won't mind," I added, trying to convince her to let me help.

"I have to grow up some time. I can do this. I can," her eyes flashed to me and I saw the determination winning out over fear as she stood taller and stopped fiddling with the door knob.

"Okay, but I'm right here next door if you need me. You can shout and I'd hear you. I'm right here, so you know you're fine, right?" I wrapped my arms around her and gave her a reassuring hug. She wrapped her arms around me, too, and fiercely held on, nodding into my shoulder.

"You know what, no. How about you come stay the night in my cabin? There's no reason we have to stay alone. We won't be alone the rest of the summer. There will be a cabin full of girls with us the whole time. You stay with me tonight, okay?" She peeked at me, and I could see relief and

66

happiness flood her big blue eyes as her body relaxed in my arms. We closed up her cabin, and she took the bed next to me.

"Good night, Cora," Bree said through a yawn.

"Night, Bree. Love you."

"Love you too," she whispered. I smiled. I'd do anything for that girl. "Cora?"

"Yeah?"

"Thank you." My heart swelled.

"Always, Bree." She was asleep in minutes.

It took me a bit longer than that. It was really quiet out there. All the unfamiliar noises played with my imagination. I was a master at creating creatures and scary stories, and dredging up thoughts of every horror movie I'd ever seen. Well, I saw *commercials* for them, but since I was too scared to actually watch any of them, the commercials were the closest I'd ever come to actually *watching* a horror movie. I'm just as much of a chicken as Bree, if not more.

I shook my head in an attempt to clear away all things scary. I decided a nice hot shower would help…and it did. The warmth from the water loosened my joints and relaxed my muscles. The smell of it was intoxicating, and it was hard to get out into the chilly cabin after that. I changed, then climbed into bed and under the sheets. Thankfully, the bed was warm and welcoming. The covers were soft and smelled amazing. I buried my nose in them and breathed in deep. The weight of the day rested on my eyes as I gave into the blanket of sleep that wrapped around me.

17
Cora

THE BOAT TIPPED.

Swim!

I kicked with everything I had. Expending most of my energy, my head finally emerged, choking and coughing above the water.

"Help! Help! Help her!" Someone was screaming.

I looked around. The boat was leaning sickly to one side. Everyone was yelling, crying. I tried to keep my head above the water. My legs and my arms moved together, keeping me just above the churning waves. I couldn't call for help. Splashes kept hitting me in the face, choking my words as they tried to come out.

Help me! Please!

I wanted to yell, to scream for someone, but every time I opened my mouth, more water would splash in. My words were cut off every time.

I can't breathe!

I got lost in panic, and started falling beneath the surface of the waves. My tired legs and arms waved around me.

Swim!

Then, the water buckled and pulled me down. Twisting and turning, I lost my sense of direction. Gravity didn't matter there. I couldn't feel where the surface was.

Which way do I go?

Exhaustion reached out and wound its way around my limbs, making them heavy and slow. My body was losing its fight. The water was winning. Soon, there would be nothing I could do, and acceptance started to set in.

I'm going to die.

"Swim! *Swim!*" I heard a voice command.

I didn't know where the voice came from. Maybe it was the last bit of self-preservation I had. It didn't matter. I summoned the very last of my strength and thrashed my legs around as best as I could.

"Go! Go!" the voice yelled.

No matter what I did the surface was not within my reach!

Please, air!

I fought every urge I had to open my mouth. My body was screaming at me to breathe! *Breathe!*

I can't give up. She needs me! I need to find her!

No air. No surface.

Time's up.

Dark shadows closed over me. My body no longer fought. Against my every command, my mouth flew open and took a deep breath in....

Ana…

18
Darrien

AFTER I ATE MY SUPPER in my cabin, alone, I found myself wandering well into the night. I still wasn't used to the air up there, it invigorated me in a way I never anticipated, making it really hard to sleep. I paced the beach for a while, trying to get some energy out so I could head back to bed. I decided to head over to the girls' side and check out the shower room. I had cleaned it meticulously the day before, but something told me I forgot something.

The night was cool with a warm breeze. The smell of the water was driving me to the lake. A side effect of being Mer and so near an entrance to Titus; it called to me. I was getting used to it, though, and it didn't affect me that much, just in my dreams.

I had been thinking about the next days' chores when, as I rounded the corner to the girls' cabins, I saw something disappear into the bush behind the showers.

What the hell was that? I ran around to try and get a look at the figure I saw, but it was gone. *Probably a deer.* I shrugged it off and went inside to check the shower room out.

I did a pretty nice job, if I did say so myself. It may have been grunt work, but a spark of pride ran through me to see all that hard work pay off. It had been a long time since I had physically worked hard on something other than military training. It was satisfying.

A rustle in the bushes outside sent my nerve on edge. *Okay, what are you?* I got in a low crouch and headed to the door. I knew how to move without making a sound, but this thing sure didn't. It crashed out of the bush and onto the ground...hard. I jumped off of the shower room stairs and landed next to it...*her.*

Her hair was splayed around her head, full of debris from the woods. I looked at the trees and brush. *How the hell did you make it out of there?*

She wasn't moving. I bent down next to her and pulled back her brown curly hair. "Please be breathing!" I whispered to myself. Her face was white, made paler in the moonlight, but she was breathing. I brushed some mud from her cheek with my thumb. Her features were round yet delicate with a splatter of freckles across her nose and cheeks. I ignored the pull in my gut when I looked at her.

I knew I couldn't just leave her out there. I lifted her up in my arms and carried her back to her cabin. When I opened the door, I noticed another sleeping figure in the room. Carefully, I snuck to the closest bed and gently lowered her onto it.

Where did you come from? I brushed her brown hair away from her face once again and she stirred. My heart stilled and I was suddenly aware that I was standing over her. If she woke now I would scare the crap out of her. I crept out the door and down the walk. I hoped that she would stay in the cabin. I didn't know the girl, but I knew what sleepwalking looked like, and that wasn't it. She should have been startled awake the moment she hit the ground. She was in a trance, and that spelled all kinds of trouble for her.

Good thing she is not my problem.

19

Cora

I AWOKE, AND SHOT STRAIGHT UP, gasping for air. *Sweet, fresh, AIR!* I took several deep cleansing breaths before I was calm enough to assess what had happened.

I wasn't in the water. I was safe.

I closed my eyes again and took another deep breath. *No water.* Willing myself to calm down, I opened my eyes. *Where am I?*

In the moonlight, it was so hard to see. Shadows stretched out from every corner of the room. My bed was hard…really hard, and cold. I reached a hand down and felt a smooth, cool surface.

That's not my bed.

As my eyes adjusted, I could see a hint of ceramic tiled walls. *Is that a drain in the floor?* My brain took a little longer to adjust than my eyes. When it finally caught up, I was shocked into full consciousness. I was in the shower room!

"Cora?" A timid voice called to me from the doorway. "Cora, are you in here?" *I know that voice….*

"Bree?" I whispered.

"Cora? Where are you? What are you doing?" She stepped into the room, flipping on the lights as she went. Her eyes grew wide. She went white as a sheet as she came around the corner and found me.

"Bree, it's okay. I'm fine. I just came for a shower and slipped, that's all," I lied, hoping that my state would help conceal the deceitful look on my face.

"You were planning on showering in your pajamas? And in the dark?" She stared at me with a skeptical expression on her face. Clearly, I wasn't getting anywhere by lying.

"Okay. I don't know what happened. I guess I was sleepwalking." I went to get up but realized that I was wrapped in a shower curtain. It took me a few minutes to get myself out of that mess and put the curtain back up. Bree just stared at me the whole time from the doorway, clearly not knowing what to do or say.

"Hey, what are you doing up? How did you figure out I was in here?" I lifted an eyebrow. She should have been in bed still...sleeping!

"I-I had a nightmare. It seems silly now that I found you in here!" *So her pale face wasn't all my fault.* I felt a little better, though sad that she had such a bad dream, and then couldn't find me.

"I'm sorry, Bree! I must have really scared you. Come back to the cabin, and I'll change into something dry," I just realized that I was cold and wet. "Then we'll talk about your dream."

Bree nodded. I gave her a hug as we exited the shower room. I could tell she felt better being near me, and truthfully, I felt better having her with me too. I focused on her. It was easier than having to deal with my nightmare, and how I managed to get all of the way to the shower room. *I've never sleepwalked before...ever.*

I turned all the lights on in the cabin to scare away any remnants of our nightmares. Bree found me some dry clothes while I went to the bathroom to wash the mud off of my feet and hands. I gave my face a quick scrub, but avoided looking at it. I quickly brushed my hair and pulled it into a messy bun. I changed and snuggled next to my baby sister on my bed.

"So, what was this scary dream about?" I asked, trying to keep the mood light.

Bree hesitated, sighed, and then started. "Well, in my dream, I was standing on the edge of a waterfall. It was so beautiful. I bent down and picked up a rock. But it wasn't a rock, it was like a tile from the ground. I looked closer and the whole ground seemed to be covered in these beautiful blue and green tiles. It was incredible. Then I started hearing voices." She looked up at me, probably checking to see if I thought she was crazy. I didn't.

"Keep going, I don't think you're nuts...yet." I nudged her and smiled. She gave me a little smile back.

"Well, the voices were sweet and musical at first. I didn't understand what they were saying, but I didn't care. I just kind of stood there and enjoyed them. But then they became angry, mean. I felt the air around me change. It got heavy and started moving, blowing hard. It was hitting me and...and pulling me. It was clawing at me. The voices," she started to shake, "were terrifying, Cor. They sounded like someone being tortured, screaming and crying. It scared me. I recognized the screaming too, I can still hear it." Her voice trailed off. I grabbed her in a bear hug and pulled her close to me. She was ice cold and shivered against me.

"It'll be okay, Bree," I said, trying to comfort her. "It was just a dream. I'm here now." I squeezed her tight, rubbing her arms with my hands to take the chill off her skin. She was staring at the sheets on the bed and fiddling with her fingers. I could see wet dots appearing on the bedding. Bree sniffled and wiped her nose with the back of her hand. More wet dots appeared as her tears started to come harder and faster. I couldn't hug her tight enough, or comfort her enough, and it was killing me.

"I'm sorry, Cora." She finally lifted her eyes and looked at me. They were huge and a brilliant blue that only came when she cried. I held her hand and bent down to look her closely in the eyes.

"Don't ever apologize to me for needing help. I will always be here for you, and I will never let anything happen to you. You understand? Nothing is going to happen to you. I won't allow it." She rested her head on my shoulder and let the nightmare seep out of her. When her breathing returned to normal and her tears were drying up, I asked her the question that had been nagging at me.

"Bree, you said that you recognized the screaming?" Her breath caught in her throat and I thought for a second that she was going to start crying again. I grabbed her hand, hoping my support would help her get over this dream.

"Yes." She was focused on the pattern on the bed sheets now, running her fingers over it.

"Who was it?" Bree lifted her eyes. They were full of tears again, and her face was white.

"It was you."

20
Darrien

"WHAT DO YOU MEAN, UNCONSCIOUS?" Pearl yelled as she wrestled with her sweater.

"I found her unconscious, full of leaves and twigs and mud. She collapsed coming out of the woods. Not sure what else you want from me. She looked like she was sleepwalking or in a trance. Either way, she needs to go home," I pressed.

"That's what we're here to do, Darrien!" Pearl's shout startled me. She was racing around the room searching for something and mumbling under her breath.

"What?" Then it dawned on me. "WHAT? You're not saying that- she can't really be..."

"Well, she is!" She threw her arms in the air for emphasis, tossing the couch cushions aside.

"Zale's daughter? How can that be? I mean, she's a Mutt!" I was yelling, not in anger, in shock. I grabbed my hair with both hands and cursed under my breath.

"I'll thank you to stop using that term in front of me. It's offensive, especially coming from someone who has had virtually no experience with humans to know what he is talking about." *Ouch*.

"Fine, I'll watch my language...*mom*." She glared at me, but a half smile cracked the anger. Pearl and I had gotten pretty close since our talk. We chatted a lot after that, both sharing stories of our families, jobs, home...anything. I never really talked to anyone about that stuff, even Tyde. It was cathartic. I respected and cared for Pearl, more than I ever could have imagined when I was sent here. So when she yelled at me, I was shocked because it was the first time I had heard her raise her voice. "Sorry. It's just...I was not expecting that. So, now what do we do?"

"I don't know. We're going to have to set up a watch at night on her cabin. We can't have her wandering into the woods. There are places in there…she can't get to them. It's dangerous." Her frantic search was slowing as her ideas started to form.

"I agree. Well I'm on a weird sleep schedule already, so I'll do it. But that means that you gotta keep an eye on her in the early mornings. I can go on little sleep, I'm used to that, but I'll need a recharge swim and a bit of shut eye." My mind was racing.

"Done. This isn't good, Darrien. She shouldn't be acting like this. She just got here." Pearl started looking for whatever she was looking for again.

"I've never heard of someone doing this. But then, I've never heard of a Mer raised on land either. Do you think it could be the call of the entrance to Titus. It pulls us all to the lake." *Wait that didn't fit…she went straight into….* "She went straight into the woods." I watched Pearl carefully. "What aren't you telling me?"

"I told you, there are things in the woods that are dangerous." I stared at her, waiting. She looked back but finally broke her resolve. "There's a pool, with a waterfall. It belongs to Midira."

"The Siren Queen! Holy shit, Pearl! Why didn't you tell me about this before! That's kind of crucial information!" A large wave hit the beach from the lake. I could see the look on Pearl's face. The first time I released my power in anger, she was scared, but now she looked like a mom whose toddler just threw a tantrum. "I'm sorry. I'll get it together." I apologized and took a breath. The lake calmed. *Get it together, Locke, and do your job.* I started pacing the tiny room too, which was really just shifting weight from foot to foot.

I shook my head, trying to process everything and calm myself at the same time. "I'm sorry. So…the Siren Queen has a direct line to her. That is going to be a problem."

"I don't know. The pool has been stagnant for years. I check on it periodically to make sure that nothing is brewing; but it's been a rotting hole for as long as I can remember. That's why I didn't think of it until now," she said. "There's never been anyone attracted to the woods; the lake, yes, but not the woods."

"What does that mean?" I growled.

"Nothing!" she squeaked. I watched Pearl. There was still something I wasn't getting, something she wasn't telling me. "Maybe she really was just sleepwalking and we got lucky this time." It sounded lame. I rolled my eyes at her. "Look, we'll guard her during the night. It won't happen again, I'm sure. Until then, it might be a good idea to make sure any interaction she has in the woods is supervised."

"Meaning…."

"Once the campers get here, you should go on all her hikes with her. We can't take any chances," she answered.

"Done," I agreed. "Just a little curve ball, right? Nothing we can't handle. Just get the job done and get home. Right?" I eyed her, waiting for reassurance.

"Right. Okay, well we need to check on Cor- Ah ha!" she yelled, bending to the floor and standing up with a triumphant look on her face and a slipper in her hand. "Cora. We need to check on her. She brushed past me and was out the door before I could say anything.

"The rest of the Leads are going to be getting here this morning," Pearl whispered as we headed towards the girls' side. "I should warn you though, Ambassador Sands has sent his daughter up this summer as a Lead, along with her brother."

I stopped in my tracks. *Not Aurelia…*

Avery wasn't bad, her brother, we'd been in training together. He was a decent guy, but his sister…we had some history. Pearl stopped and looked back. She threw an arm out in the direction of Cora's cabin and I started walking again.

"Wow, and the hits just keep on coming. Anything else?" I stared at her. "Is there a kraken in the lake I'm supposed to fight off?" Pearl's light chuckle brightened the mood.

"I know it's not going to make things easier for you, but after everything you've told me about Aurelia, this might be good. She needs to see you moving on, though if you decide to take a shine to one of the lovely ladies here, we may have a problem. I would be very afraid of your ex's wrath." She may have been joking, but she wasn't far off. Aurelia wasn't known for her soft side.

"Well, there's no chance of that happening. I'm here to do a job, and that's it," I stated.

Pearl smiled her all-knowing smile. "We'll see. We'll see." She grinned as we rounded the corner to Cora's cabin. We both snuck up the stairs and peaked in. There was Cora, right where I put her, but she was changed and there was someone else in bed with her.

"Bree," Pearl whispered.

"Huh? What?" I said.

"The other one is Bree, Cora's younger sister," Pearl whispered back.

"Well, she's fine," I said, descending the stairs and making my way back to my cabin.

"For now, yes," Pearl whispered, more to herself than me, but I still heard it.

"I'm going to bed," I said over a yawn. "There's only a few hours until sun rise and I have a feeling that her time in the woods is over for the night."

"True," Pearl replied, following me down the path. "This is going to be an adventure."

"I've had better," I said and smiled.

"We'll see," Pearl grinned and doubled our pace back to the cabin.

21

Cora

I AWOKE TO A FOOT IN MY FACE.

It took me a couple of seconds to figure out where I was, and why there were toes up my nose.

I'm at camp...with Bree. Must be Bree's foot....it better be Bree's foot. What happened?

The nightmare, the water, the shower room...it all came back to me a like a wave washing over me. Then I remembered Bree's dream, how odd it was that we should both have a nightmare on the same night. I realized that we must have fallen asleep together on my bed after our talk.

I shook Bree to wake her. She moaned a little then turned to look, maybe glare at me. Her face squished up as she looked around the room, bleary sleep full eyes took in the room slowly. They were a pale blue which was thanks to the night of nightmares. All the stress and anxiety from last night dimmed the brilliant blue I was accustomed to seeing. Breakfast would help...hopefully.

I stumbled to the bathroom, keeping my eyes down, not wanting to see what a mess I was. I knew it wouldn't be good, and I wasn't prepared to face what I had dreamt last night. My own nightmare hung over me, waiting to snatch my sanity. I grabbed my toothbrush and scrubbed at each tooth like they were coated in toffee.

Bree called from the door. "I'm going to get ready! See you in a bit!" And then she was gone.

I slowly lifted my eyes to my reflection. A bubble of laughter squirmed its way up my throat and out of my mouth. I was a disaster! I still had mud on my face and shoulders. I had the biggest circles under my eyes and the craziest hair I had ever seen. It was going to take me a long time to get myself looking presentable. *Better get at it.*

Bree was waiting for me outside the cabin when I finally emerged. The shower was refreshing and I was finally feeling awake. I actually did my hair, not something I usually do. I could tell Bree was thinking the same thing, she stared open-mouthed at me when I came out of the cabin.

"Good morning sunshine!" I chimed.

"Good morning…umm…have we met?" Bree asked, eyeing me out of the corner of her eye.

"What? Do I still have leaves in my hair? I thought I got them all!" I exclaimed and started tugging at my hair, running my fingers through it.

"No, Cora! You look amazing!" Her eyes were wandering all over me and it was making me uncomfortable. I lifted an eyebrow. I didn't do anything special with my hair. Just washed it and dried it, that was my idea of "doing" my hair. Usually, I just left it wet and let the kinky strands fall, or stand up, where they may.

I had a flashback to the floor in the bathroom, and all the debris that fell from my head when I brushed my hair last night. I must have tumbled through some bushes.

Wait, that didn't make sense, how on earth would I have made it to the shower room if I had stumbled into the bushes? Not only were there none between my cabin and the shower room, but I would have been immediately lost if I ventured in them. *How did that much junk get in my hair?* I *had* thought it was the shower room floor, but thinking about it again, they were spotless, and ready for the campers. My questions were pushed aside as Bree grabbed my hand and pulled me toward the trail.

"Well whoever you are, you look great. I used to have this sister that typically had hair sticking out at every angle. She could use your help with that!" Bree giggled as we walked the path to breakfast. I smiled, glad to see the long night forgotten for the time being, and my bubbly sister start to return to normal.

I could hear my stomach roaring as we entered the Hall to the mouth-watering smell of Anne's cooking. It would be the last meal she would cook for just a couple of people, and she outdid herself. I couldn't see how she would be able to cook like that for over a hundred people at each meal.

"Good morning, dears!" Pearl chirped as she danced through the door.

"Morning, Pearl," Bree and I chimed in together. We shared a giggle.

"Morning, Anne!" Pearl yelled at the kitchen. There was a shuffle and grunt from behind the door, then Anne appeared.

"Morning, everyone!" Anne's eyes were as bright and green as before. She was also carrying the most mouthwatering food. I didn't know if it was the night or the air or what, but I had never tasted pancakes that good! *Heavenly!*

"Excited to meet the other Leads, Cora? I hear we have a great batch this summer!" Anne winked at Pearl and watched me expectantly.

80

"I'm working up to that," I said as gracefully as I could through the huge bite of bacon I just took.

"I can't wait!" Bree piped up excitedly, spitting bits of her toast across the table. The food was having a great effect on her spirits. I was glad to see the stress of the night was gone from her eyes. *Thank goodness.*

"Cora I'm going to need your organizational skills today, getting the office ready for the Leads. There are some schedules that I have yet to make up. One more set of hands will be a great help." I nodded, welcoming the distraction. "Bree, you are free to wander around, or go swimming if you like. I don't really have anything that I need you for at the moment." She winked as she spoke.

"If you go swimming, Bree, can you stay where I can see you from the office, please? And no going out past your waist!" I demanded.

"Yes, ma'am," Bree drawled out. I made a face at her, but she made a better one back.

After Bree and I cleaned up our dishes and helped Anne in the kitchen, Pearl and I got to work. Bree ran off to get her swim gear together. I followed Pearl into the office and opened the blinds on the window to make sure I had a good view of the beach. With the blinds up on all the windows and the doors open, the room was bright and friendly. I could smell the water through the open front door. *What a gorgeous day!*

I watched as Bree returned to the beach with her bag and towel. Throwing them on the sand, she slipped into the water quicker than I figured I ever would again. She didn't go past her knees, she never did.

"You good, Bree?" I yelled out Pearl's beach door.

"I'm fine, worry wart!" She bellowed back and laughed, shaking her head as she let the water creep up over her knees. My pulse stilled for a second before I scolded myself, forced my hands off the doorframe, and walked stiffly back inside.

"Alright, I'm going to start you off with these," Pearl said, slamming down a mound of paper. "The registration forms. I need them alphabetized. I also need all campers with allergies pulled out so that we can photograph them when they get here." I nodded and got to work.

I hated how lame it seemed, but I really did enjoy work like that. It was oddly satisfying. I took out the alphabetizer and got to work.

As I neared the end of the stack, my mind wandered to the water outside. I watched the sun skip off the tiny crests in the water and a part of me ached to get into it. To have the sensation of sliding in, feeling the cool water caress my skin, the weightlessness...*no air*!

And just like that I was reliving my nightmare, right there in Pearl's office! I took an instinctive gasp. Struggling to maintain the smallest semblance of calm in front of my boss, I closed my eyes and gulped in several more breaths before my heart settled down again. But, it didn't really help. Pearl looked up at me.

"You okay?" she asked, sitting up in her chair.

"Where's Bree?" I said more to myself, as I looked past Pearl and out the window at an empty beach. My heart stopped.

"Where's Bree!" I was shouting now. The alphabetized stack of forms cascaded from my lap and onto the floor. I stood up and ran, bursting through the door and down to the beach.

"BREE!" *What have I done? I wasn't watching her!*

"BREE!" I screamed. Tears welled up in my eyes and I rubbed them away with the back of my hand. The beach was empty! Empty!

"Bree! Answer me!" My chest tightened as my panic rose. Though the day was bright, sunny, and warm, the water had become choppy, as if a storm stirred it. I felt the sob coming from the pit of my stomach, as I searched the water, and when it reached my mouth an awful mournful sound came out. *Where was she?*

Pearl came bounding down from the office to me. She was shouting for Bree now, too, looking from right to left and back again, hand over her eyes, searching over the churning lake water.

"I'm here!" a faint, tiny voice responded.

"Cora! Look!" Pearl jerked me around pointing to the water. There, way out on the diving pad, I could see an arm waving at us. *Thank goodness!* A sigh of relief gushed from me. She was okay.

"Bree?" I was so relieved, and *so* angry! *How could she do that to me? How did she even get out there when she can't swim?* "Get back here right now!" I yelled, not caring how "mom-ish" I sounded. She was in BIG trouble.

Another head popped up right by the diving pad. It slipped out of the water effortlessly and glided up next to Bree on the pad. *Who is that?* I looked at Pearl. She didn't look worried anymore, just annoyed. She was shaking her head with a half-smile, and I wasn't sure how to take that.

"I'm coming!" Bree shouted. She jumped into the water, which had gone from choppy to calm in a flash, next to our new addition, and swam...*yes, swam*...back to shore. When she could stand in the water, I raced into the lake and grabbed and hugged her, like it was the last time I would get to do that. Tears of relief gathered in my eyes.

"What were you thinking? You scared me half to death! Don't EVER do that to me again!" *She's safe, she's okay.* I turned to the mystery swimmer. I could feel my anger build and radiate off of me as we all walked onto the sand.

"Who do you think you are?" I barked, turning on him, as soon as I was out of the water. His eyebrows hit the top of this head fast, but I didn't let him speak. *No.* He would hear *me.*

"Didn't it occur to you someone might be looking for her?" I asked, not allowing him to answer. "She can't swim! What were you *doing* taking her out there? Are you insane?" My voice was getting high and screechy. I didn't care. I also didn't care that I was yelling at a total stranger.

I kept imagining the worst case scenario. I could have lost her. My sister. My only real family. My everything. *How could he do that? Why would he do that? What self-centered, egotistical, ass* – I felt the burning sensation rise from my gut and expand through my chest until it filled me with a rage I was not aware I was capable of, and then, to my ultimate embarrassment…I slapped him.

22
Darrien

A SPLASH ON SHORE told me that I needed to keep it together before I blasted the shit out of little Miss Princess. My duty and my need to lash out were battling inside me so badly that I was brought to a standstill. All I could do was stand there and stare at her.

Her eyes were flashing a hatred that rolled off her in hot waves. That's when I realized that I wasn't the one making the water splash on shore…it was her. Her Mer powers were wakening. Not a good time to piss her off. And yet…*she* slapped *me*.

Oh yeah, baby…it's on.

23

Cora

I COULD HEAR PEARL and Bree gasp, then it was silent. Pearl's eyes were about to jump out of her head, and Bree was white. They both stared in wide-eyed horror at me. I didn't know what to do. My hand burned and tingled from hitting him.

Oh...no....I hit him. Like, really hit him...hard. What the hell is the matter with me?

The guy was in shock, he stood still but for the tightening of his jaw. I stood back, not sure what to do from there. I had never hit anyone before, what was I thinking? I didn't take long for his shock to wear off. I watched as the tightness from his jaw spread through his body and recoil, ready to spring. He pulled himself up to his full height and his eyes set on fire.

"What the hell? Are you *insane?*" He didn't even touch his cheek, where a red mark was starting to appear. His glare tore into me and made me take a step back. Something told me I just poked a bear...or rather, slapped one.

"You're lucky I can take a hit and keep my cool," he yelled and jabbed a finger at me. I startled backwards away from him. I wasn't feeling lucky. "You didn't even give her a chance to explain what happened! You just assume I'm out here lurking around for a moment to kill your sister! What the hell do I look like to you?" He demanded.

I blinked and took a step back. For the first time, I had a real look at the person I attacked. He was tall, easily over six feet. He had a swimmer's body, long and lean, with muscle definition everywhere you looked. With no shirt on from the swim, water dripped down and rippled over the muscles in his stomach. His hair was jet back, cut stylishly shorter at the sides and longer on top. It was dripping and stuck out at all angles, which just added to the whole sexy wet look he was managing to pull off flawlessly. He had startling blue-green eyes, which were ice cold now. They were deep set and rimmed

85

in dark long lashes. His cheek bones were high and angular, as was his strong jaw. Top all that up with a long nose and thin lips.

I shamelessly stared.

He took a step toward me and glared, intent on an answer. But I couldn't make my mouth move.

"Um…." *Say something, you idiot!* But I couldn't.

"Okay then." His brooding eyes lifted a little, and a smile was starting to appear at the corners of his mouth. Pearl mercifully stepped in then.

"Cora, this is Darrien Locke, our swim instructor and my troublesome nephew." She gave him a little shove and a playful frown. He smiled back at her, just with one corner of his mouth.

"Huh? Swim what? Huh?" *He is Pearl's nephew?* I just slapped him! I could feel my cheeks begin to burn. *I'm so fired.*

"Cora, don't be mad at Darrien! It isn't his fault!" Bree pleaded, moving between Darrien and me. Her eyes darted back and forth between the two of us. She landed a look on me.

"Mad? I'm not mad!" An awkward giggle escaped my throat, "I'm just…concerned. That's all. About your…life." I glanced at Darrien for a second time and met the icy cold gaze.

"Well, what's done is done," Pearl interrupted. "I do wish your *instructor* would have waited for lessons to begin teaching swimming, though," Pearl chastised. She was glaring at Darrien. He didn't seem to notice. He was looking at me. Actually, it was more like hard staring, maybe glaring. When he spoke, there was an edge to his voice.

"You don't need to be so upset, Cora. Bree is a natural swimmer." He said it like that would make everything better. I tried to stop it but, nephew or not, my wild anger broke free again. I launched myself toward him and tore into him with every bit of my remaining, admittedly misguided, anger. Which really came from my fear. It was always fear.

"Don't tell me how to feel! You have NO idea what we've been through! You don't know Bree *or* me, so don't presume to tell me what is best for *my* sister!" And on that note, I grabbed Bree's arm and stormed off toward the girls' cabins. And that should have been enough…but…it wasn't.

Stopping a few steps away, I turned and yelled again, clearly unable to control the tiniest amount of my temper.

"And by the way, if your first impression didn't leave me thinking that you were at *total* jerk, your second impression upgraded you to *complete ass*!" I could hear Bree sigh and groan at my side. Yanking her arm, I dragged her back to her cabin, spouting insults about my personality all the way, leaving Darrien behind with a shocked and irritated Pearl.

I stormed into the Red cabin like a mother with a troublesome child in tow. "What gave you the idea to do that?" I yelled. I threw her clothes around trying to find a sweater for her to wear to get the chill off of her.

I glared at Bree, in hopes there was a very good explanation coming my way. Bree walked to her locker and pulled out her clothes. She sat on her bed and watched me, waiting for the moment rational Cora would surface again. I could tell she felt guilty for what she had done, but she was also pissed at me for yelling at Mr. Perfect. I sat down, slightly calmer and ready to listen, and waited for her to start. I wasn't going to forgive her that easily this time, whether or not she thought I was being unreasonable.

"Look, I walked out in the water, only up to my *knees*." She eyed me, emphasizing the *knees* part. "I was just walking and enjoying the water, when I saw some minnows swim by and I followed them. I didn't realize that I was getting into deeper water. The water is so nice you can barely feel it creep up your body." I held my breath. Something told me I was about to feel like a colossal ass wipe.

"The water was up to my waist before I realized it, and I decided to go back to shore. When I turned around, I must have fallen into a hollow. The water went over my head and I started to sink." Bree's voice dropped right along with my heart. I couldn't breathe. *Oh my god.* "I kicked my legs, but there was something wrapped around my ankle. I was tangled in something, I think. I managed to get my head above water enough to shout for help, but there was no one around, and then water filled my mouth." The pummeling in my chest was hard enough to see through my shirt and my stomach had headed to my feet. I just stared at her, grasped her hand squeezing tighter and tighter as if I could somehow save her, but I was too late. I wasn't there for her. I had no words.

Bree took a breath, "I was really scared. Every time I got my head above the surface, my screams were cut off by water choking me."

My heart broke. I knew exactly what that felt like, and I never wanted her to experience that. She wouldn't look at me, but she continued anyway. I sat rigid, bracing for what she was going to say next.

"Then, Darrien was there. I don't know where he came from. I never saw him on the beach, but he pulled me out of the water and helped me back to shore." She locked on me with those big blue eyes and I understood why she desperately didn't want me to be mad at Darrien. *He saved her.* My stomach clenched as realization hit me…I *slapped* him! *Oh my god, what have I done?* I groaned, burying my face in my hands. Bree continued her story. I couldn't look at her.

"Anyway, after I stopped coughing and calmed down, Darrien asked if I would like to learn a few things that would help me. So I said yes." *I'm a horrible sister!* I glanced down at the bed and caught a glimpse of her ankle. There were red marks around it. It looked sore. *What on earth happened to her in that water?*

I gathered myself up and willed my eyes to rise to hers. I sagged further into the bed, I was a jerk.

"I'm sorry, Bree. I am an *idiot* and I may have overreacted...*slightly*." I half smiled at her. Bree raised an eyebrow at me.

"Slightly?" she asked.

"Well, that might be an understatement," I said with a sigh.

"Slightly," Bree teased and held her arms out for a hug. I grabbed her and held on tight. I almost lost her. If it wasn't for Darrien, I would have. I sighed knowing what my next step had to be. I need to smooth things over with him. *And that was* not *going to be easy.*

24
Darrien

"SHE HIT ME!" I yelled at Pearl as I trudged up and down the shore line, gripping the back of my neck. Pearl was standing calmly watching me. "I've never been treated with such disrespect!" Waves were beginning to roll onto the beach as my powers called to the water for some revenge.

"No, I suppose you aren't used to someone standing up to you, are you?"

"I- what is that supposed to mean?" I shouted. Pearl smiled, but had the decency to turn her head and attempt to hide it. "You think this is funny?" I hollered.

"Oh, come on! You can't see the humor in it?" I glared at her. "I guess not," she said, still smiling.

"How am I supposed to bring her back to Titus now? She already hates me! All I did was try to help her! I saved her sister's life, you'd think she'd be grateful!" The waves were subsiding as my anger ebbed. I stood by Pearl and glanced at the path that Cora took Bree down.

"She will be, once she finds out that's what you really did. Just give her time."

"We don't really have a ton of that. I'm supposed to work through a decade of water phobia in less than two months. That's not going to be easy. At least she will be more open to learning once we tell her about what's really going on here."

"Um, actually, Zale has asked not to tell her yet." Pearl's voice barely a whisper.

"What? Why the hell not?" I bellowed.

"He's worried that it will be too much to handle and she'll run. She's already been through a lot. He doesn't want to cause her any more pain," Pearl said throwing up her hands in defense. I groaned. I understood his need to protect her, but how was I supposed to do this without explaining anything to her? *She's a damned Mer!*

"Great. That's just great," I spat and continued pacing. "Well this is starting off perfectly. First time I meet her, I save her sister, get slapped across the face, and then called a complete ass." *I can't believe she slapped me.* No one did that. *No one.*

It was *hot, though.* I caught the smile that grabbed the edge of my lip before Pearl saw it.

No one had talked back to me in years, other than Sands. Since I became the youngest king's guard ever, people stayed a respectful distance away from me. Cora was the first female I had met in a long time that didn't turn into an irritating pool of giggles in my presence. It was nice, really nice…even if I *was* getting yelled at and slapped. I could respect that, for the most part. She was just defending her sister, after all. I wouldn't have acted different if it was Tyde's life in danger. The red-hot flaming anger dragon that had awoken in me was sleeping again.

Plus, she's…gorgeous, in a clumsy sort of way. But I liked that. *No! No you don't.*

"We've got all summer to figure this out, Darrien. It's just the first day. Sure, not a great day, but we'll recover. Just focus on what needs to be done. She needs to learn to swim, and she needs to find out who she is, easily and gently. Mostly, we need to protect her." Pearl wrapped an arm around my shoulder, which shocked me back to the conversation. "On a side note, how do you like being my nephew?" She laughed. I smiled. After the last couple of weeks, Pearl felt like family.

"I suppose I could have chosen a worse aunt." I nudged her. She laughed a deep, full laugh.

"I picked *you*, sweetheart. Couldn't have picked better in my opinion." I smiled at her, pride filling me up. That was a compliment I didn't believe I deserved at the moment, considering what just happened, but it meant a lot.

"Thanks. So now what?" I asked.

"Now, we back off and let tomorrow do its magic. There's still a lot to do. The other Leads come after lunch. I think you are about as excited as Cora is about that. Don't worry, things will sort themselves out." She gave me a side hug and shook the doubt out of me. I smiled and my cheek stung. I was sure a Cora-sized hand print was there. I could *respect* that she was standing up for her sister, that didn't mean I *liked* the way she did it. She would have to figure out how to handle that temper, or we would really get into it this summer. As sexy as standing up to me was, there was no way I would allow things to go any further.

At least, that's what I would keep telling myself.

25

Cora

AFTER LUNCH, I HELPED PEARL out with the remainder of the schedules. I was in my element, sorting and organizing and planning and scheduling. I loved it. I just wouldn't let myself think too much about all the things on the schedule that I was terrified of doing with my campers. That was a problem for another hour. My current problem had just waltzed into the office.

Though his temper had simmered, an awkward energy filled the room. I couldn't even look him in the eye, and it wasn't just because I hit him.

It's not like I had never seen a good looking guy before, but there was something different about him. I was attracted to him and that scared the crap out of me. I never found any guys in high school attractive, not really. Cute, maybe…but Darrien…he was something else entirely.

Guilt churned in my stomach, and I thought I might be sick. Staring at him while he was looking elsewhere was no problem, but I couldn't look into those eyes and see his anger. I had made a horrible mistake. My insides twisted thinking about what would have happened if he wasn't there to save Bree.

Okay Cora, you can do this…you have to do this. Darrien mumbled something incoherent to Pearl and strode over to his desk. *Our desk*, I reminded myself. *Great.* He didn't even glance at me as he grabbed for the schedule I made. *Ok, here's my chance, apologize Cora, you can do it.*

"Hmmphmm." *Oh god.*

"What?" Now he *was* staring at me. With every fiber in my being, I willed the words to come out. *I'm sorry. I'm sorry. I'm sorry.*

"Sthhrrry…."

The moment stretched out for an eternity before he spoke.

"Uh-huh. Okay." He looked at me like I was crazy. My cheeks burned with the fire of a thousand suns. *Kill me now.* Darrien picked up his schedule and proceeded to the door.

Ahhhh! Why can't I just say sorry! Sorry! Sorry! Sorry! Oh god, he stopped. Why is he staring at me? Why is Pearl laughing? Why do I get the feeling I said that out loud....

"Did you say something to me?" His eyes were watching me. His lip tipped up at the edge. *He's going to laugh at me!* Part of me wanted to throw my perfectly sharpened pencils at his eyes, but the other needed to set things right. *Come on Cora, you can do this.* I cleared my throat to get my words going. "Yes. I mean...I meant to ap- apo- apologize for what I did earlier. I should have waited to hear the whole story." *Say it!* "So, I'm sorry."

"Yeah, well, thanks, I guess." He turned to leave, but stopped short and twisted around again. I braced for the slap of words I was sure were coming. "You shouldn't be so hard on your sister, you know." *What?* "She just wanted to make you happy. That's all she talked about. How proud you would be of her." The guilt grew again and my stomach churned in response. *Ugh why did he have to say that? Like I wasn't feeling bad enough already.*

I cleared my throat. Why was it so hard to talk? I just nodded and tried to avoid his stare, but failed.

"Well, you aren't my first apology today," I admitted, and started tapping the pencil I was holding on the desk.

Darrien's smile hooked the corner of his mouth. He let out a low chuckle.

"Well, the bus should be arriving soon. See you out there?" That half smile sent a rush of heat straight through me.

I nodded and smiled. At least that was a little better.

What is wrong with me? Get a grip, Cora! I knew how these stories ended. I saw how heartache destroyed people and families. My family, my mom...I never wanted that to be me. I won't do what she did, what he did. *I'm better off alone.* Still, it was nice to look, especially when the view was perfection chiseled out of white chocolate. *Yum.*

When the time came to meet everyone on The Green, Bree and I walked together. Darrien was cool and calm as he strolled up to us. Meeting the other Leads didn't seem to affect him like me, though the muscle in his jaw was working...not that I noticed. Bree waved and screeched "Hi!" when he joined us on behind the office. Darrien chuckled and smiled. My heart jumped into my throat. *Calm down, Cora.*

I still couldn't put my finger on what made him so different. There were a few cute guys at school, but they didn't know of my existence, and I wasn't interested in informing them of it. There was no one like Darrien. None of them came close. I looked away from him, hoping he didn't notice me staring.

With Bree as a buffer, I was able to calm down enough to refocus.

"Thanks again for today, Darrien," Bree gushed and grinned like a cat. *Geez.*

"My pleasure," Darrien replied in a low voice. Then he looked at me. I opened my mouth to say something, but...crickets. He lifted his brows and waited-so did I- but nothing came. Nothing. He tipped his brows again in amusement and looked toward the entrance. *My god, I look like an idiot.*

I shook my head and grimaced at the grass. The bus appeared through the trail, bumped along the road, and finally came to a great creaky stop in front of us. I realized my body was tensed up tight, and I willed my shoulders to relax. I was clearly more nervous about meeting these guys than I thought I'd be. I held my breath and bit my lip as six strangers stepped out and onto the grass.

"Welcome, everyone! Boy, am I glad to see you guys!" Pearl rushed up, giving hugs all around. "I'm sure you're all eager to visit and get your assignments, so let's get to it!" Pearl was beaming. The woman was so incredibly happy that I couldn't help but soak it in a little. I found I was smiling in spite of myself. I looked at Darrien and Bree and they were as well.

After the passengers emptied off the bus and collected their belongings, they headed for the Main Office. The two of the girls were giggling and watching Darrien as he carried some of the bags. He was loaded up, and yet he toted them around like they weighed nothing. I could see his muscular arms tighten as he carried the baggage to the office. *Stop it, Cora!*

The other three guys were chatting with Darrien. They must have known each other from somewhere. The boys glanced over at the giggling girls, but didn't pay them much attention. I have to say, I found a little satisfaction in their lack of interest, especially Darrien's, who didn't spare a look at the girls. However, all at once, the guys turned and looked at me. My face flared red, as I imagined Darrien just told them I slapped him. *Great*

26
Darrien

IT WAS GREAT SEEING THE GUYS again. We had actually gone through training together - okay, so maybe *I* trained *them*. Devin, Avery, and Zach were some of the hardest working guys around. If shit was going to hit the fan, at least I knew I could depend on these guys to help. Zale, as usual, had selected the best.

Aurelia and Jade had been joined at the hip for years. They were essentially the same person, and that was not an attractive thing…anymore. I rubbed my face, trying to work up the patience to talk to Aurelia, but I failed and ended up just walking away from her.

Luckily, she took it as a hint and left me alone. In the meantime, the guys and I had a great time catching up and working our asses off getting the camp ready for the campers. I knew it wouldn't be long before I would have an awkward conversation with Avery, Aurelia's brother. We were sharing a cabin and I had dumped her publicly, and of course she made an epic scene. I wasn't sure if he was going to threaten to kick my ass, or just give me some empty threats. I was wrong on both accounts.

A couple days after we arrived Avery walked into the cabin and sat on his bed next to mine. His stark blonde hair, a direct contrast to his sister's, shone like a halo. Avery was a tall guy, though shorter than me and he carried himself with the authority of a Sands. He was nothing like his sister and father though, he had a good head on his shoulders and I respected him.

"Okay man, we need to talk," he said, watching me carefully.

"Okay," I said, unsure of where it was going. I sat gingerly on my bed across from him, readying myself for whatever was going to be coming my way.

"Look, I know things ended in flames with you and Lia. I just wanted to say," *Okay let me have it, I deserve it,* "thank you."

"What?" I leaned forward, not sure I had heard correctly.

94

"I know you probably think that I'm pissed at you, but I'm not," Avery said, sitting back a little.

"Okay," I answered, drawing out the word. Avery laughed.

"You should see your face!" I dropped my shocked expression and looked at Avery. He was serious. I relaxed and sat back a bit. "I know why you did it. I don't blame you. Lia is a lot to handle." I grinned and nodded, still not completely convinced this wasn't leading to a fight. "I'm glad you dumped her the way you did. Don't get me wrong, I love my sister and I don't like to see her hurt, but she has turned into this nightmare of a girl. You knocked her down a few pegs. I appreciate that, and she will too, one day. She needed it." I smiled then, almost sure he wasn't about to punch me.

"Um, thanks?" I said.

"Just wanted to clear the air," he said with a wave of his hands. He got up from the bed and slowly walked to the door.

"I appreciate that," I said honestly.

"But," He stopped and looked back, "do us all a favor and don't date someone else. Not now. She'll make your life and the girl's a living hell." I nodded, knowing full well he was right. I knew his sister's talents at making people miserable. Avery looked out the door and chuckled.

"I won't survive it, either," he admitted. "She's been an unbelievable monster these last few months. I was so happy to be coming here. But, then she heard that you were sent too and that was that...she was coming." He dropped to the first step. "So much for my vacation from the Queen of Misery." He chuckled again as he started off toward the beach.

I sighed and flopped on the bed. Avery knew his sister better than anyone else. Even though they weren't twins, they were only nine months apart, they acted and looked like it. They knew each other so well, and they were very protective over one another. Avery just had a better, less dramatic, head on his shoulders and understood how to pick his battles. Clearly he wasn't picking one with me. *Smart guy*.

27
Cora

THE NEXT FEW DAYS FLEW by as we prepared for the campers to arrive. There were six new people to share the camp with, three of whom I now shared a cabin with. The boys seemed nice enough. I hadn't really said much of anything to them since they arrived, though. Most of the time, I was with Pearl in the office helping her organize paper work, which she desperately needed assistance with. The boys were in charge of general maintenance stuff, like getting the grass cut, extra painting done, and unloading food into the kitchen. They hadn't spent a moment apart since their arrival, and I hadn't spoken a word to Darrien.

It was a little different with the girls and me, unsurprisingly. Aurelia and Jade could have turned every head in the camp, but they ruined it with their giggling and stupidity, especially around Darrien. Aurelia was the worst, by far. There was something going on between her and Darrien, but it was decidedly one-sided. He didn't watch her or even look at her most of the time, but her eyes were always drawn to him, fixing her hair in case he looked, or shifting for the best angle.

"Darrien, hasn't changed a bit," Aurelia purred to Jade over her porridge and fruit.

Aurelia had the thickest, longest raven hair I had ever seen cascading all the way down her back, to the top of her jeans. She also had huge sapphire blue eyes, rimmed with thick long lashes, and a small perfectly turned-up nose and full red lips. Even though she was short, maybe five-foot-four, she demanded attention. The only look I received from Aurelia was a clear once-over. Whatever test she ran, I could tell that I failed miserably.

"It's only a matter of time before he's begging you to come back. I mean…once you've had…." Jade make a distinct look at Aurelia's lady area and laughed.

Aurelia wailed. "Jade!"

I want to puke…too much information. I really didn't want to know what Aurelia and Darrien had done. I mean I really didn't care. At least that's what I thought; however, the pang of disappointment in my gut told me differently.

The two girls were completely ignoring me. Somewhere, I had failed to impress and now was beneath acknowledgement. Jade's personality was almost the same as Aurelia's. She was just as cutting with her looks and judgments, but her personality wasn't as loud. She was slightly taller than Aurelia, with long dark red hair. She had big green eyes that angled up at the ends. Her long slender nose and small thin lips just added to the pinched look she adorned. Her skin though…her skin was so light, almost as if it glowed. She looked like a burgundy-headed porcelain doll. Sitting across from the pair, I felt grotesque, and decided it was probably best if I just left.

"It's not as if there is anyone here that is going to catch his attention," Aurelia added as I stood.

Jade's eyes ran up and down me, "Nope." The two of them stopped and stared at me. I smiled lamely at them, not knowing what else to do. They burst out laughing. I didn't stick around to hear their commentary on the way I walked or my clothes, so I double-timed it out of there. I was used to it, but I was really wishing to possibly escape it this summer. *Guess that's not happening.*

I was hoping that the cabin would be empty. I'd just grab a book and read, or devour some chocolate, anything to distract me and maybe feel even the tiniest bit better about myself. Unfortunately, as I came up the stairs I could already see Penelope on her bed, sketching.

Damn it, I muttered to myself. I just wanted a moment to myself. She looked up from her work and I hesitated. I didn't want to go in anymore, but I didn't want her to think that I was avoiding her either. I don't know why I cared, but I did. I carried on into the cabin, determined to grab a chocolate bar and flee as fast as I could.

A shiny object caught my attention on the floor.

"Um, you dropped this," I said, bending down to pick up an artist's pencil from the cabin floor. I handed it to Pen as I made my way to my trunk.

"Thanks, I was looking for that!" Pen smiled at me. She was slowly twiddling her pencil in her hand, her eyes on the ceiling.

Penelope was much quieter than the other two. She spent more time in the cabin than they did, but they seemed to include her in everything anyway. Penelope, "Pen" as they called her, had long strawberry blonde hair that hung in big curls down past her shoulders. She was very fair-skinned, but flawless. I was fair skinned too, but more the "see all your veins" pasty skinned. Pen's features were all round, round blue eyes, round small nose, and round lips.

Though she was pretty in her own way, she was a natural with no make-up and no style to her hair. She was one of those girls that was an earthy beauty.

Pen was artistically talented in a way I could only ever hope to be. I had sneaked a peek the last time she had her sketch book out. Anyone that could draw like that fascinated me because couldn't draw if my life depended on it.

"What are you working on?" I asked quietly, opening the lid of the trunk at the end of my bed.

"Oh, just sketching some things that I see around camp. I always feel more inspired to draw up here." She closed her book and packed it away in her locker. "Your sister is here this year, right? Bree?" she asked, turning and looking at me.

"Yes, she is. She's in your team," I answered, my head in the truck still searching for that chocolate bar.

"Yeah, I met her yesterday. She seems really nice." She smiled softly. "She's going to be here all summer right? Must be nice having a sister around." She stood and plunked herself down on my bed.

"Um, sure. I mean, I like it most days," I admitted.

"I don't have any sisters," she explained as she watched the chaos exploding in my trunk, "It's just me and my three brothers. They're all older and out of the house, so I'm kind of the baby. I was so happy to get this job and get out. I love my parents and all, but they swarm around me all the time, like I'm going to break or something. It gets to be too much. How about you?" I froze, not entirely sure how to answer that question. I never really talked about my parents to anyone, other than Bree of course, and even then, the subject of "Dad" was a no-no.

"Um, well, Bree and I live with Mom. She's gr-great. I mean, she's nice and stuff. It's just the three of us." I gave her a half-forced smile. *Where is that chocolate bar?*

"Well, that's good. Must be nice to have all ladies in the house!"

"Uh, yeah, most of the time I don't mind it. So, what do you think of your schedule?" I held my breath. It was a terrible attempt at changing the subject, but I didn't want to talk about my family anymore. I peeked out over the lid of the trunk at her.

"Oh! Uh, it's great!" She forced a confused smile, but was kind enough to just continue. "There's so much to do here! It's going to be a great summer, I can just feel it. Can't you?" Pen let out a sweet laugh, which made me feel the most at ease that I had been at camp so far. She wasn't like Aurelia and Jade; she was actually really nice.

"Sure. I'm glad that you approve of the schedules," I said. "I made them, so it's nice to hear it works for you."

"No, they are awesome. No offense to Pearl, but I gather that she isn't the most organized person. She was smart to hire you."

"Th-thanks. I appreciate that." I smiled into my hands. Wanting to quit before I said something stupid, I decided to go. "Well, I'm off to grab Bree for supper. I guess I'll see you later." I gave her a wave and started out the door.

"Wait!" Pen ran up behind me, "Is this what you were looking for?" and she handed me my chocolate bar. I couldn't help the huge smile that spread across my face.

"Yes! Thank you!" I shouted and took the bar from her. I was about to rip into it but stopped and looked up at Pen, who was kind enough to listen and get to know me better, "Umm, I don't really need it anymore,' I said, tossing the bar on my bed for another time. "See you at supper?" I asked.

"You bet."

28
Darrien

"DARRIEN!" THE SING-SONG VOICE almost made my ears bleed. I slapped on the best, half-assed smile I could muster and turned around.

"Aurelia...it's you." I may have smiled but my tone failed me. She sauntered into my cabin like she owned it.

"Aren't you going to give me a hello kiss, silly?" *I'd rather donate my lips to a leper.* Then she came at me like I didn't have a choice, wrapped her hands around my neck and smashed her lips against mine, effectively tackling me onto the bed.

"Mmm, I've missed you baby," she purred.

I removed her hands from around my neck. Placing them against her chest, I pushed her, gently, off of me and across the bed.

"Aurelia, we've been through this. We. Are. *Over.* It ended months ago," I emphasized. I wanted to tell her she was embarrassing herself, but I also wanted to be nice. I really did. She didn't deserve the hurt I caused her, but it was the right thing to do. The problem was, she was under the delusion that I was still in love with her. Truth was, I never fell in love with her in the first place, and once I realized that, I broke it off.

"Sure, sure. We'll see," she teased and dotted my nose with her finger. I fought to keep my temper, clamping the bedding in my fist. "I didn't force Daddy into getting me a job here for nothing. I'm getting you back, baby. You can count on that." She turned with a flourish and model-walked out of the cabin.

It took everything in me not to scream. How was I going to do my job with Aurelia around? Zale better not have known she was coming. If he did, we were going to have some serious words when I got back, because this just made my job a million times harder.

I skipped eating with everyone that night. I wasn't up for small talk, or Aurelia staring at me while I chewed my food. Instead, I went straight into

100

the kitchen and pulled up a stool to the counter. The smell of Anne's cooking reminded me of my mother's. Anne was bustling over a few pots and was singing to herself. I knew the song, it was a lullaby from home. It told the story of sisters bound to vanquish evil from the seven seas. It wasn't really much of a lullaby, now that I thought of it.

"You hiding, Darrien?" Anne slid a bowl of her homemade soup in front of me, turning immediately back to her pot.

"You mind?" I asked as I grabbed a spoon.

"Do I mind having you guarding my kitchen…never!"

I took a sip and melted right into the bowl. "Anne, what are you doing to me?" Her light chuckle drifted through the steam.

She chuckled again into her pot of soup, turning around to shove a freshly baked bun under my nose.

"Oh my gods, you do things to me. You don't even know!" I sunk my teeth into bread heaven.

"Be good, you! Now, finish your soup!" She bustled out of the kitchen with a serving tray full of soup for everyone else. From the hall, I could hear Aurelia's tinkling giggle. *Like a tray of wine glasses smashing on the floor.*

"Where's Darrien?" I heard Aurelia asking, "Hey! Kitchen lady! Where's Darrien?" Aurelia's voice rose above the others, reaching me all the way in the kitchen. "Kitchen lady! I'm talking to you!" I heard a chair brush the floor, as I assumed Aurelia stood. The chatter around her had stopped.

"Sorry, Miss. I've been in the kitchen all day." Anne was being too kind. Aurelia was being a complete brat. My stomach sank. That was not the girl I dated. That was someone else. I didn't like it one bit. And something told me I was just seeing the tip of the iceberg.

I slipped out the delivery doors at the back of the kitchen and headed to my cabin, after apologizing to Anne. It was just about time for my night shift. I hoped that Pearl was right and that Cora's stint in the woods was a one-night show. *Even if I get to see her in her pajamas again.* A burst of warmth opened in my stomach and made its way south. I bit at a grin, to keep myself enjoying the sensation too much. I was there to do a job, nothing else, no matter how fun it might be.

29
Cora

I WAS RUNNING. The path was rough and hard to maneuver. My feet stumbled over a sharp rock and I crashed to the ground. My hands were cut up, full of dirt and debris from the path, and it was getting harder and harder to see. Sweat was dripping down my face, making me cold and hot at the same time. In my chest, my pulse fluttered wildly.

My eyes struggled to adjust to the inky air, but nothing came into sight.

Have to get out! Have to get out!

My frantic thoughts flitted around in my head. I could feel a scream starting to build in my throat, and it felt like a flapping albatross was caged in my chest.

I'm lost.

Then a fragrance drifted past my nose. Drinking in that savory sweet scent was like feeding an addiction. My body woke and my senses were renewed. I felt really, truly, alive. The fear and anxiety I was locked into drifted away on a fresh-scented cloud and disappeared.

I didn't think about where I was stepping. I just let my feet do the work. I closed my eyes and soaked in that aroma with each step. When I arrived, I could feel a gentle spray of water on my face. A sense of total peace fell on me. I smiled and opened my eyes....

30
Darrien

I HEARD THE DOOR to the cabin swing shut. A shadow descended the stairs and ran full tilt into the woods behind the showers. "Shit!" I swore loudly, jumping to my feet from my hiding place beside the cabin. She moved fast, for someone who was supposed to be sleeping! I dove into the woods right after her.

"Where are you?" I swore to the trees. *Where are you, Cora?* I could hear movement coming from ahead of me. All I could do was walk blindly toward it and hope it was Cora, and not a bear. The further I walked, the less certain I was that I was still following her. I stopped to listen for a few minutes and heard something that made my blood run cold. *A waterfall.*

I ran as fast as I could toward the sound of crashing water. As I burst out of the woods, I saw Cora perched at the edge of the pool at the bottom of a waterfall that didn't fit into the landscape around the camp at all. It was as if it existed in another time and space. Cora lifted her face to the sky. She was smiling.

I froze. She looked so peaceful and...happy. Her skin glowed in the light of the moon, and a sleepy smile graced her face. A slight breeze picked up and her hair swept out behind her, waving her long shirt and lifting it slightly. My heart stilled. She looked angelic...stunning. I found myself holding my breath. I watched as Cora dipped toward the water, her smile still present, but her eyes now open, though unseeing.

And there, in the water, it was...a hand. I gave a start, unsure if I was seeing things. But then it slowly extended out of the water toward Cora.

I didn't give a second for thought, I just sprang at her. Throwing myself at her, I grabbed Cora around the waist and we both went tumbling to the soft ground. Whatever spell she was under left her and she went limp.

I turned on the pool. A slippery figure rose from the water. *Siren.* She opened her mouth, a slick grin spreading across her face. She was in full battle mode. A scream like a saw cutting rusty metal came out of her. A swell of protectiveness washed over me in giant waves, nearly knocking me over.

You're not getting anywhere near Cora, bitch.

My temper flared. I lifted a hand and felt for her blood. I debated how intact I wanted her at the end of this, unsure if I wanted to leave anything. I could pop her like a meat balloon if I wanted to, but first, I'd be a gentleman, and give her a chance to answer a couple of questions.

"What do you want with her?" I demanded.

"Poor helpless guard, doesn't know what he's gotten himself into." She hissed and spat at me.

"Answer the question," I yelled and to get my point across, I pulled at all the blood in her thumb. It popped like a blood-filled paint pellet. She shrieked long and hard, then tried to dive back into the water. But I was ready. I grabbed for every bit of blood and water in her. I could feel all of it and held it firm right where I wanted it, just out of the water, out of safety and strength. She gave an ear-bleeding scream, but I didn't care.

"You have no idea what you are up against! You won't win! She's going to be ours! You'll see!" She screamed in desperation, but the more she moved, the more agony she made for herself.

"What do you want with her?" I demanded again, pulling at the blood in her pointer finger. Her resolve fled for a second, as the pressure in her finger mounted. But just as fast it left, a sinister smile replacing it.

"You'll see!" she sang, and threw a tidal wave at me. I flashed a hand up and stopped it mid-air, but the distraction worked. I had dropped her back into the pool in the process. She was gone.

"Shit!" I yelled. In anger, I blasted the pool. Water shot up into the night sky, well above the trees. There was hardly any water left in it, but the waterfall would work to fill it up again.

I turned to Cora. Reaching a hand gently under her head. Her breath was shallow, but it was there. A relief swept me that was bigger than I wanted to acknowledge, as I lifted her into my arms. I glanced down at her as I made our way out of the woods. Her hair fell away from her face and I could see her features in the moonlight, complete with a splatter of freckles on her nose. My chest expanded.

I hugged her close as I made our way back to camp. The need to protect her had gone beyond just my job; it was something else. The feel of her in my arms made me realize that the Sirens were the least of my worries. This girl undid me.

And that was going to be a problem.

31

Cora

THE SHOWER ROOM AGAIN?

I blinked back the dream and focused on my surroundings. Then a horrible thought struck me. *Did anyone see?* My eyes darted around the room. The floors were damp, but not wet, so no one had been in the shower yet. *Thank goodness!*

"What is wrong with me?" I cried to the empty room. *Why was this happening?* I had never sleepwalked before, well...before I got there. *What was I even dreaming about?*

I scooped myself off of the floor and crept to the door. I peeked out to see if anyone was around and then tip-toed back to the, mercifully, empty cabin.

Sitting on my bed, I assessed the situation. *Okay, another creepy night in the shower room. Why? I don't know.* I also didn't know how to make it stop. All I could do was hope that no one saw me if it happened again. The morning was already not shaping up good, and things were not going to get any better. The campers were set to arrive in a few hours, just after lunch. My pulse spiked just thinking about it.

"Cora?" Bree's light voice came bouncing into the cabin. "You coming for breakf- what happened to you?" She screeched, and a look of deep concern imprinted across her face.

"N-nothing, I just woke up. What are you doing up so early?" I was attempting to look nonchalant.

"Don't give me that! You look terrible! And it's almost *nine*! The campers will be here in a few hours. You're supposed to meet the other Leads for breakfast in ten minutes! They're all in the Hall already!" She ran over to me and started helping me pull things out of my hair...twigs, leaves...again. *Wait...what?*

"Okay! Okay! I'm moving! I don't suppose I have time for a shower, do I?"

"NO! No, you don't!" She shouted and started pulling out clothes for me to wear. Orange everything was glaring at me from my locker. My stomach did a back flip.

"Thanks for helping me, Bree. I just had a rough night, I guess. I don't know what's going on with me lately." A gymnastics routine was being performed by my tummy. I had to take a couple deep breaths to calm everything in me down. I ran my fingers through my hair, to attempt getting a fraction of the tangles out. "Okay, what's the damage?" I said, turning and looking at Bree.

"Uhhh...." Bree was just staring at me, dumbfounded.

"That bad, huh?" I pouted, dropping my arms down to my sides in resignation. *Great.* I ran to the bathroom to make a last-ditch effort on my hair and...*whoa! How is that possible? My hair looks amazing!* While my usual springy brown hair looks like I stuck my finger in an electrical socket, the frizz was replaced by big, controlled curls. *Okay...that's weird.* I didn't have time to wonder about it, though. It was time to go.

Bree and I raced down the path, and through the doors of the Hall. Everyone was sitting, eating a breakfast fit for kings. Anne sure knew how to put on a spread. I plunked myself down at our Lead table, half breathless from the run.

"Wow! Look at you! It took so long to get you looking presentable, you're late for breakfast!" Aurelia chimed in as soon as my rear hit the seat. I didn't respond, as she shared a giggle at my expense with Jade. Pen gave a little wave and smile. The boys' eyes lingered a little too long for my comfort. Avery whispered something to Zach, and they both smiled and glanced at me again. I could feel my pulse come to life and my cheeks heat up. *Guys never look at me like that, never.*

Darrien had a different reaction. He went white. I thought for a second that he was going to be sick. I never felt as self-conscious as I did in that moment. I stared at my food.

Whatever, if he was going to lose his breakfast because of me, so be it.

When he finally tore his eyes off me, he attacked his breakfast like it was the embodiment of his worst enemy. I could feel the furrow in my brow deepen. What was his issue? Bree, who missed the whole thing while running to the bathroom, sat down and started to devour her breakfast.

We were just finishing our meal when Pearl bustled in carrying a box.

"Okay, everyone," She announced. "Today marks the first day of our great summer adventure together! I see you're all anxious to get things started." Everyone around me perked up, excitement vibrating off of them.

I wanted to throw up. "I have your orientation booklets and supplies for your first two weeks at camp. Please take according to your camp color." Pearl was beaming. She had endless energy, I was sure of it. We all walked over and collected our kits.

Mine contained the Camp Crystal Leader Handbook, rules and regulations to go through with the campers, name tags, bandanas in our camp colors, and a duplicate copy of our schedule and camper list. There were lots of things to learn and get ready for.

Pearl began, "Every morning, starting at 7:00 a.m., you will wake your cabin. Give them until 9:00 a.m. to get to the Hall for breakfast. There is a schedule posted outside the shower room, with the shower times for your team. Only one team at a time starting at 7:00 a.m., please. Each team will get a half hour in the shower, and yes, the water is cold by the time the third cabin gets in. That's why it's a rotating schedule. Camp activities run from 10:00 a.m. until 5:00 p.m., lunch is at noon until 1:00 p.m., supper is at 5:00 p.m., and free time is after supper. You all will take turns supervising the main beach and other areas of the camp after supper in pairs.

"Have your team in bed by 9:30 p.m. every night. Quiet hours begin at 10:00 p.m., and after that, any noise violations will result in disciplinary actions." Pearl paused to let it all sink in before continuing. "I know all this information is in your orientation kits, but I want to go through it with you anyway. *You* are in charge of your team. Make sure that they understand the rules of this camp. If there are any problems that you feel you can't handle, let me know immediately. If we have a camper that is nothing but trouble, they will be going home. Are there any questions?" Pearl scanned the table, her eyes serious for the first time since she arrived.

"Just one, Pearl," Avery looked up. "Do we have to do every activity we are scheduled for? Or can we switch with another Lead?"

"You have to stick with your cabins the whole time. It'll help you get to know your campers better, and they you. If you are in need of help in any areas, come and talk to me or talk to another Lead. We are here to support one another, right?" She looked straight at Aurelia with the question hanging in the air. Aurelia stared right back at her, not saying a word. *Yeah, I wouldn't be asking her for any help.* Pearl smiled at me, as if she knew what I was thinking. I was stuck teaching everything, except swimming. I was thankful to Darrien for that. I glanced down the table at him. He was concentrating on his booklet.

"The campers should be arriving in two hours. You have this time to prepare yourselves however you see fit. If you are unsure of what to do, ask around. Everyone here has something to offer." On that note, Pearl walked briskly back into the kitchen to talk to Anne.

Great, now what am I going to do? How am I going to pull this off?

Just thinking about it my body started to shut down. I could feel the blood draining from my face. *Just calm down Cora, calm down.* A soft breeze from the open windows filled the cafeteria and my spirits lifted a little, I closed my eyes. *Everything will be alright. Deep breath.* The sweet scent from the lake filled my lungs, quenching a thirst I didn't know I had. I let out my breath slowly, concentrating on the calm that came over me. When I opened my eyes, I stood and walked out the door.

The fresh air was calling me, and I needed to feel it wrap around me. I sat on the bench, on the beach, and looked out over the water. For the first time in a very long time, I allowed myself to sing. It had been years, seriously. I looked around, but no one was there. I let the first song that popped into my head come out my mouth and was stunned at what forward.

A tune I hadn't thought about for years, many, many years. It was beautiful but one I had tried really hard to forget.

My heart gave an anguished thud as memory flooded in. Dad used to hum it all the time. He did it when he was doing laundry or cooking; whenever his thoughts were occupied, it would slip out. Part of me cursed the memories, but the other welcomed them with open, aching arms.

He had such a beautiful voice, so deep, so calming. I would stay out of sight and just listen to him hum away. He wouldn't sing in front of us, but we knew the song anyway. He didn't realize he sang it most of the time, unless he was interrupted. Oceana and I would hide outside the room and listen to him. *Oceana....*

"Cora?" Bree's voice broke through my memory. The picture of my father and Oceana floated away on the morning air like smoke.

"Hmm?" I said, turning to Bree. "Oh, I'm okay, just needed some fresh air." I straightened my shirt and cleared my throat. Bree was staring at me, arms crossed, her worry clouding her brilliant blues.

"You sure you're okay? You don't look it," she stated, looking me up and down.

"I'm fine, or rather I will be. Just have a lot on my mind today with everything going on. Nothing to worry yourself about though," I assured her. She raised a brow and I smiled. "I promise," I added, to which she grinned.

"You were humming when I walked up. It was pretty. What song was it?" Bree asked, jumping to my side as I stood to return to my cabin. There was no way I was going to answer her question truthfully. I bent down to retie my shoelace so she couldn't see my face.

"Um, I don't really know, off of some commercial probably. Just a tune that I got stuck in my head somehow," I answered to my shoe. She couldn't see my face, which was good, because I wasn't about to start into "Dad" stuff now.

"Oh. Well, it sure was pretty," she replied softly as we walked together back to the girls' side. Her spirits quickly lifted when she saw Pen catching up to us on the path. Pen waved and smiled.

"Hi, Cora! Hi, Bree!"

"Hi, Pen!" Bree exclaimed, I waved a hello.

"I am so excited to have a helper in my cabin!" Pen gushed and wrapped an arm around Bree's shoulder. "We're going to have so much fun! Don't worry I won't work you hard," Pen winked at B.

"I actually have a favor to ask you, Pen. If it's okay, I mean if it's no trouble," I stammered. It had occurred to me that she might be able to help me.

"What's up?" Pen asked and scratched her arm.

"Um, okay. I was wondering if you had any ideas, or suggestions, of what I could do for crafts with the campers. I'm really lost."

She smiled wide. "It's no problem! I have some great books back in the cabin you can borrow. I checked out the supply shed and there's a ton of stuff in there what will work." She grabbed my arm, and we all proceeded back toward our cabin.

"You sure? I don't want to take anything of yours if you're going to be using it this summer," I said.

"I have tons of ideas for crafts, so don't worry about it! You need it more than I do! Oh...no offense!" Pen apologized. She ran up the steps to the cabin and in the door.

I laughed, "None taken!"

It's not like I didn't know I needed all the help I could get.

32

Darrien

SHE KNOWS THE SONG!

After Cora had left the hall, I had followed her out with the intention of talking to her, but I stopped short when I heard her start to sing. Her voice was beautiful and that alone caused me to pause, but it was the song that froze me in my tracks. I hadn't heard it since I was a little boy, when my mother sang it to me and Ty before we would go to bed. I hadn't thought of that song…well I didn't think about anything that had to do with my parents at all. I couldn't. It hurt too much.

When Bree came out I turned to go to my side of camp. The memory of my mother haunting my every step. I needed a distraction, I needed a job.

Pearl was sitting at her desk in the office when I walked in. Watching her head appear and disappear behind the mounds of paper made me wonder how she could stand to be that messy. There were forms and booklets everywhere. Stacks a foot high teetered on each corner of her desk, on chairs beside her desk, and on the floor around her desk. I glanced at the empty file cabinet against the wall and shook my head…classic Pearl. Yet, somehow, in all that mess, if I asked her where a camper's registration form was, she would be able to pull it out. There was order to that chaos, but no one could see it but her. As a result, even though we were all allowed at her desk, we stayed away. I didn't want to be responsible for one of those piles being sent to the floor.

"Pearl, I need help," I admitted as I peeked over the top of one of the paper mountains. Her face lit right up.

"The day has arrived! It's happened! He asked for help!" She stood and raised her arms in a "hallelujah" stance. I chuckled.

"Okay, crazy lady." I brought up a chair to the desk.

"What can I do for you?" She asked, still smiling.

"I…can you stop gaping at me like that? You look insane!" I laughed.

"Sorry!" She readjusted her face to nonchalance.

"Thank you!" I smiled. "I need an excuse to talk to Cora, a camp-related matter. Something that doesn't need me to make up an excuse for visiting her alone." I had decided that I needed to do *my* job.

"Okay…why?" she asked. Her lifted eyebrows at the word 'alone' didn't escape me.

"Why? I have to get to know her better, right? I need an opportunity to talk to her while others aren't around. Try to gain her trust," I insisted.

"Okay…." She wasn't buying it.

"What?" I demanded.

"Nothing. Why the emergency today? What happened?" My eyebrows flicked up. Boy, she didn't miss a thing.

"She sang a lullaby after breakfast that my mother used to sing to me and Tyde. It's the twin song, do you know the one?" I asked.

"Yes, I know it. That's interesting." Her bright face dimmed as her thoughts took over.

"What?" I asked leaning in.

"It's just that I am surprised that Zale and Ce- uh, his wife would have taught the girls that song," she started to chew on a nail, her eyes unfocused.

"What do you mean? I thought that it was just a kids' song."

"Oh no, it's much more than that," she stressed sitting up in her chair. Pearl's train of thought broke and she looked up at me. "Never mind. Apparently, they did teach them, or she wouldn't know it right? No sense dwelling on why." She cleared her throat. There was something off. When I had the time to dive into it, I would figure out what was going on, but not now.

"Well, anyway, I need something to talk to her about that won't raise her suspicions," I added.

"I have the perfect thing. I gave Cora the wrong number of cabins for the schedules. She counted you as a team. Your schedule needs to be redone." She handed me the copy of the schedules and a blank for my new one. I glanced them over and then it occurred to me. Cora really needed help, and, not just with getting into the water to be a Mer princess and all, but she needed help doing her job there at camp.

"I want to do her swim times and canoe lessons too," I stated. "I think that anything that has to do with water, we need to be there."

Pearl hesitated for a brief second, but answered, "Agreed."

"This will do nicely, thank you." I stared at the schedules.

111

"I've already penciled in the other teams' swim times. Hers is the last. There's lots of empty space left on your schedule, so you can pencil in her canoe times there."

"Great, thanks," I said, and headed for the door.

"One more thing, Darrien." Pearl stood behind her desk, and seriousness filled the room. It didn't feel natural.

"Yeah?" I asked, not knowing what was coming.

"Don't fall for this one. Okay?" my brows hitched up high as my eyes widened. "It won't end well. You know that, right?" I paled when she said it. Disappointment and rebellion brewed inside me. Part of me wanted to tell her off for sticking her nose where it didn't belong. The other part wanted to crawl into a ball of shame, for being transparent enough that she thought that she needed to say that to me. Not knowing how to respond, I just waved the schedule at her and smiled as I stepped out the door.

I should have denied it, but I couldn't. *Why can't I?* Cora and I had barely exchanged a word since she got here, and I was acting like an idiot. That put me in a foul mood as I headed to Cora's cabin.

33
Cora

I WAS SITTING ON MY BED, going through the orientation kit and the book Penelope had lent me. I was also enjoying the last bite of the chocolate bar I inhaled.

When I looked down at my lap, there were melted bits of chocolate smashed into my jeans. *Great.* I got up and went to the bathroom. I grabbed a facecloth to wet and dab at the chocolate, but when I turned on the faucet the pressure in the pipes shot the water out and soaked me from the bottom of my bra to the bottom of my crotch. *Perfect!*

I cursed, shut off the faucet, and ripped a towel off the rack. I took off the tank top, not wanting to soak my bra too, and ran the towel over the water on my jeans. *Why do these things happen to me?* I groaned and patted at the wet spot. *Come on! Dry!*

As if it answered my command, the water on my jeans seeped into the towel, soaking it and leaving behind dry, clean, pants. I gasped as I ran my hand over the fabric. *How am I doing this?*

Just then, I heard a light knock at the door. My breath stilled when I saw who was leaning against the door frame.

Darrien.

"Come in?" I said.

"Thanks, I-oh!" and he turned around in a flash. That's when I realized that I was standing there in my bra.

"Oh my god!" I yelled and dove for my closet, ripping a shirt off a hanger, snapping it off the rod, and shoving it over my head in less than three seconds. *Again, why do these things happen to me?*

"You dressed?" he asked, still standing with his back to me. I would have laughed, but I couldn't I was too embarrassed. Though, it was pretty adorable that he clearly blushed before he turned around.

113

My heart started beating fast, and I could feel the rush of heat starting its way to my face. *What is he even doing here?*

"I'm dressed," I said quietly, sinking down on my bed.

He turned slowly, and assessed the room as he did.

I could feel a rush of heat bubbling up from inside me. If this didn't calm down, I was going to burn my face. He was wearing a black Camp Crystal t-shirt that pulled tight across his broad shoulders. His arms were strong, and as he moved, I could see the muscles tighten. I was staring again, but I couldn't help it. I put every ounce of strength I had into my eyes and broke my gaze. I crossed my arms across my chest as if I was still without my shirt and sagged into the bed.

"What do you want, Darrien?" I murmured, trying to sound like he hadn't just seen me half naked.

"I just came to talk to you about the schedule," his low voice stated. He sauntered in and stopped in front of my bed, shoving the schedule into my face. I couldn't tell if he was all business because he was all business or because he was feeling half as awkward as I was.

"Oh," I said. *Okay, I can handle this.* His abrupt manner took me off guard, but I did the schedules so I knew what I was talking about. And hopefully, I could speak properly. "What's wrong with them?" I asked and, looking at him, snapped the schedule from his hand. I eyed it, scanning for an error but I couldn't find anything.

"Pearl wanted me to tell you to add an extra half hour a day of swimming for your group. She noticed that you were short." *What? No way!* I looked up at him from the paper. His brilliant eyes were staring straight back at me.

"I have no idea what she's talking about," I muttered, running over to my schedule. *Red, Yellow, Blue, Green, Purple, Pink, Black and Orange…eight teams…and they were all equal!* I walked over to Darrien to show him the schedule.

"See, here are all eight teams," I pointed to each one of them, "and their times are all equal! I don't know what Pearl is talking about!" I could hear myself getting louder.

"Wow. Okay, you don't need to yell at me. I'm just the messenger." He put his hands up defensively and then put his finger in his ear. *I wasn't yelling,* I said to myself with a pout. Darrien's expression softened slightly. His eyes met mine, and that half-smile snuck across the corner of his mouth.

"I'm sorry, is this amusing to you?" I asked. His eyes widened at the challenge, and a small chuckled escaped his mouth. The smile slid across the rest of his face and dimples came out. *Oh God, no! Dimples? No, put those away!*

"Absolutely not!" he jested, "I take scheduling craft times very seriously!" The sarcasm was not lost on me. I opened my mouth to give him a scathing

114

retort, but he grabbed the schedule right out of my hand and started examining it. "Let *me* have a look at that. Maybe Pearl saw something that you missed."

"Hey!" *Is he serious?* "Give that back! I didn't miss anything! I've checked it a million times over!" I reached for the sheet, but he moved it out of my reach. I was not playing this game with him. I crossed my arms and glared at him. His face was positively beaming. He was enjoying this! My blood was boiling. His eyes searched the paper for a split second before he brought it back down and faced it toward me,

"Here look! You put too many teams in, that's your problem," he declared with a triumphant smile.

"What?" *That's impossible!* "There are eight. Eight Leads, eight teams." I started picturing slapping that perfect smile right off his face. *It felt good the first time. I'm sure the second would be just as sweet.*

"Actually, we only have seven teams this year. I'm not a Leader, remember? I'm only a swimming instructor." Darrien turned to me and spread that smug smile across his face again. *Damn, he's right.*

I sighed, resigning to the fact that my supposedly perfect schedule was now wrong. It pissed me off, especially with Darrien's cocky smile shoving it in my face. I looked up to glare at him and he met my gaze with those gorgeous blue-green eyes. My pulse flopped around like a trout in my chest. I stopped breathing. For a brief second, he looked at me differently. There was a tenderness there that flitted away as soon as it appeared. It frightened me, and scared the fight right out of me. I broke contact and stared back at the schedule.

"Oh. I didn't know that. Pearl didn't tell me. I'll fix it. Tell Pearl I'll bring it to her when it's done." I sat down on my bed, deflated and defeated, and started reworking the schedules for the other Leads.

Darrien plopped himself down next to me. "You don't need to worry about the other teams. Just add yourself in where it works." He handed me his schedule. I cursed myself when I reached for it and saw that my hand shook. I let out a breath. Well, at least I didn't have to rework a bunch of schedules in the hour before the campers arrived.

There were a lot of blank times to choose from. *What is he doing with all this free time? I didn't have any of those times open on my schedule.* Darrien took the sheet back and had a look at it.

"Great! Now your girls will be swimming like Mutts before the summer is over!" he smiled triumphantly.

"Mutts?" I asked, not sure I had heard him correctly.

"Dogs!" he blurted, "I meant dogs...or fish...you know, something that swims well. Ha-ha!" He gave me a jack-o-lantern smile, all teeth and dimples.

I could feel a rush of blood course through my chest. I smiled back, dropping my eyes, and cursing the blush that was raging across my face again.

"Yeah, thanks for taking the swimming. There's no way I would have been able to do that. I'm still trying to figure out how to teach canoeing from the shore." I gave out a little laugh, trying desperately to look like this conversation didn't make me uncomfortable.

I could feel warmth radiating off of Darrien's skin next to mine, and my thoughts started to drift. I tried staring at the floor boards. Not making eye contact made it a little better. If I couldn't see his lips, maybe I would stop wondering about what they tasted like. I could feel Darrien shift on the bed next to me. My pulse halted, and then shot to life.

"Right. I am going to take over your canoe lessons, too." My head shot up and my mouth dropped. "That is, if you aren't opposed to someone else teaching your team how to go out on open water," he said sweeping his arms out in front of him like waves on the lake. His eyes searched mine for an answer, but all I could do was stare at him, mouth open.

"Okay, well I am going to take that as a…yes?" He tipped his head and watched me, his confident smile slipping away. His brow furrowed.

I couldn't help myself, and a huge grin sprang to life on my face. *Mr. Perfect, thank you!* Any anger that I felt for him vanished. It took all my self-control not to launch at him and hug him so tight, it would make his head pop off. I guessed my smile gave him his answer; he continued as I sat there with a ridiculous grin on my face.

"That's why I have so many blanks on my schedule," he went on. "Pearl made sure I had some extra time to help you out. When would work for you?" My jaw was still open and I was staring wide-eyed at him. Was this seriously happening? No water! At all! I wouldn't have to get into a boat. I wouldn't have to get into the water. I wouldn't have to touch water…nothing…no water! NO WATER!

Darrien leaned in closer, placing the sheet in my lap and holding out the pen for me to take. *No water! No water!*

The more I said to myself, the happier and more excited I got. I was near to vibrating when the excitement got to be too much. Unable to keep it together anymore, I could have screamed. I could have jumped up and down on the freaking bed. I could have praised Jesus…but did I?

NO!

Instead, I did the worst possible thing. I grabbed his face…and kissed him.

33
Darrien

THE MOMENT HER LIPS TOUCHED MINE, a burst of electricity exploded in my chest and ran the gambit of veins around my body. I knew I shouldn't be wanting it, or liking it, but I was. Even more, I wanted to press against her and deepen that kiss until she was breathless. It took everything in me not to wrap my hand around the back of her head and bring her in for another one, a good one. I needed to….

You are going to get yourself fired!

From somewhere inside me, in a place I had *never* heard from before, came the most terrifying response.

I don't care.

34

Cora

WHAT THE HELL ARE YOU DOING?

His lips were soft and supple, and I wanted to find out how they would feel if I hadn't smashed my face into his. But, I just threw my lips at his, with no thought of what the fallout would be.

I had no idea what my expression was, but I'm sure it looked something like I had just been slapped in the face. At least, that's what his face looked like.

I pushed away from him as quickly as I could, and just stared in wide-eyed horror. Darrien gained control of himself, but not before he touched his lips with his fingers. It was sweet, even if it was while in a state of complete shock.

"I'm sorry!" I blurted. He was so close to me. I could feel his warmth as his arm brushed against mine. The butterflies in my tummy were exploding through my body. I bit my lips to try and keep it all under control.

I could feel the bed start to vibrate. I raised my eyes to him, and he was laughing! Suddenly, I was on the receiving end of his full smile.

"I'm so sorry! I don't know...I'm sorry!" I blurted again. I wasn't entirely sure what was coming out of my mouth.

"It's okay," he chuckled, shaking his head. "You just surprised me." His one-sided smile tipped higher. "People don't surprise me." He shook his head, grinning.

"Umm," he continued, having lost his train of thought. "I- uh.... right, the canoe lessons? Boat times?" Darrien stammered and chuckled deeply again.

That deep chuckle had sent a shiver up my back, the good kind of shiver. I gave a weak laugh and smile.

"R-Right," I nodded. "Thank you. That's what I wanted to do...I mean, say. I seriously can't tell you how much I appreciate this!"

118

"You don't have to say it. I felt it!" He joked. I buried my face in my hands. He cleared his throat. "Well, I guess I should be off. Everyone is gathering at The Green to meet the buses soon. I'll see you in a bit?" Darrien jumped off the bed and started for the door.

"By the way," he said, turning around at the door, "I caught a bit of your singing on the beach after breakfast this morning. It was pretty. Maybe next time, you could take requests!" he teased. I stared open mouthed, no sound coming from my gaping lips. "See you later, *Humbug!*"

And with a satisfied smile, he was out the door.

35

Darrien

MY LIPS WERE BURNING as I left the cabin. I wished I could've slapped the stupid grin off my face too, but that was a lost cause. Her lips were so soft and sweet, and the thought of getting more intimate with them made an ache grow inside me.

I couldn't believe she just kissed me! And, for doing something so little, so…unimportant. Had no one ever helped her before? That's when it dawned on me. *No one had ever helped her before. She's been on her own.* I stopped mid-stride and turned to look back at her cabin. I felt bad for her.

I knew better than to get involved with Cora, but there was just something about her. She *did* surprise me, big time. I'd never met anyone like her. She was different, in a good way. Stunning in an unconventional manner that shocked me. She called me on my crap, which I kind of liked. She was stubborn and violently protective of her sister, which I respected. And those that I respected were a rare breed. There was something about her. I wanted to know more. I *wanted more*…and that was *bad*.

An epic battle ensued inside me. I'd never been at such conflict with myself.

Zale will kill you. There are rules- laws, actually.

I know, and I don't care. There's something about her. I can't help it.

She's going to be Queen, and you are a soldier. You can't have her.

I know what I am.

Then stay away from her.

I can't do that either. I have to train and protect her.

Then give her a reason not to think of you that way.

That's not who I am. I'm not doing it.

Fine, but you better be careful. She likes you.

No, she doesn't.

Yes, she does, and you know it. And you like it.

120

I don't deserve her, I shouldn't want her, and when it comes down to it, I can't have her forever…but I can for now. Maybe, there are some things that are just meant to be for now, and not forever. Maybe, this is one of those things.

Is she going to feel that way? When does she get to decide that?

She has the power to change everything in her destiny. If she wants me, she can have me.

Careful, that's starting to sound a lot like love. You're not in love are you, Darrien?

This conversation is over.

There were just some things that I didn't want to talk about, even with myself.

36
Cora

AFTER DARRIEN LEFT, I WALLOWED in self-pity for a while. Did I seriously kiss him? I walked around the room, unable to focus on anything other than the humiliating moment I touched his lips.

To top things off, it was my first kiss! My *first kiss*, and I flung myself at a guy in a moment of sheer stupidity. I guess it could have been worse. He could have recoiled in horror and disinfected his mouth right after. But Darrien didn't. He smiled and touched his lips. The memory brought a burst of warm tingles through my chest. Then, I was smiling.

The clock told me it was time to meet the campers. My smile faded as my stomach roiled. My anxiety took over. I pulled myself together as much as I could, shaking off the last bit of that desperate kiss and headed to meet the Leads.

The Green was big enough to have a decent football game in, with grass that was meticulously groomed. Pearl was standing in the middle with a clip board, a whistle, and a big smile. Darrien strode up and stood next to me.

"You'll be fine." Darrien's whisper stopped my heart. He gave me a crooked smile, and then walked on and joined Pearl. A great thump in my chest told me my heart started pumping again. A ridiculous grin pulled at the corner of my mouth.

I just hoped that no one noticed, especially Aurelia. But I would be wrong. I'd like to say that she was calm and cool about it, but that didn't happen. She was glaring so hard I thought her eyes might be capable of shooting lasers. Jade whispered in her ear, and she looked at me and giggled. They both shot me a warning glare, just in case I was oblivious to them marking Darrien as Aurelia's. They should have just gone over and peed on him. I really wanted to give them a one finger salute but I rose above…for now.

"Okay, everyone, the buses should be arriving any minute now. We're expecting around seventy campers! Good luck, and have fun. Let's make this a great summer!" She was beaming and, as if on Pearl's cue, the buses could be seen coming up the road.

Bree came up beside me. "You going to be okay, Bree?" We were together pretty much all the time, so this was going to be a huge change for us.

"Of course! I'm going to miss you, though. This is the first summer we haven't spent every waking moment together." She read my mind. Bree put her arm around me and gave me a little hug. I sighed. She meant everything to me. If I had a miserable summer, it would ruin her summer too, so I wasn't going to be miserable. I was going to make the best of it...*for Bree.*

"You be good for Pen! She's got permission to beat you, you know." Bree punched my arm. I pushed her back and before we knew it we were giggling again. I was beyond caring if others were looking. But when Darrien's eyes locked mine, I couldn't get a giggle out. He looked almost sad as he watched us. I peeled my eyes away, feeling like I had intruded on a private moment. As quickly as the expression came, it went, replaced by a nonchalance and steady gaze. *I wonder what Mr. Perfect was thinking about?*

After getting sorted out, I only had ten girls in my team, and all of them had never been there before. That was great; it meant they had no one to measure me against. I painted on a smile and lead them to their cabin and inside. I took a deep breath and, in a voice that I didn't know I possessed, started orientation.

"This is your home for the next two weeks! Your bed has been assigned to you. Find your bed and have a seat." *Alright, so far, so good.* They seemed to be listening. Some were even smiling. "My name is Cora, and I will be your Lead for Team Orange. There are a few things that we have to go through, so let's get going!"

During the next couple of hours, I went through the Rules and Regulations of Camp Crystal, the shower schedule, and the cabin cleaning schedule. Okay, that last schedule wasn't in *all* of the cabins, but I thought that it would work well to make sure that everyone did their fair share. I handed out their camp shirts, which they were all excited to get and immediately put on. After that, I gave them some time to unpack and get settled in. We still had about an hour to kill until we were due in the Hall for supper, so I decided to take the girls for a walk around the lake. Then, I could show them where all the buildings were and where they would have swimming lessons.

When the loud speaker rang the dinner bell track over camp we rushed for some supper. The other teams had sat down already when we arrived. Pearl was standing at the front, waiting for our team to get settled.

"Welcome, campers! I hope you have all acquainted yourselves with your team, your Leader, and the camp itself. There are many adventures to be had and friendships to make during your time here. For now, though, we will have our first meal together. Our wonderful camp cook, Mrs. Norris, has cooked up a feast for you tonight. It is first come, first served here, so don't be late. Today, though, we will start with our Red, Orange, Yellow and Pink cabins. Sorry boys, ladies first. Enjoy!" Pearl's big smile could be seen all the way to the back of the room. She was really loving this.

The sound in the Hall was incredible, just like my high school cafeteria. I could hear the familiar sounds of girls giggling about boys, and boys doing disgusting things with their food to impress the other boys. The noise level was intense, but I enjoyed it all the same. The only difference from school was that I got to sit at the Lead table, and not in the back corner by myself.

"So, Cora, how was your first day? I see Pearl gave you the easy group of girls. I guess being a family friend has its perks, huh?" Aurelia's voice cut right through all the noise in the room, and buzzed in my ear like a mosquito.

"Lay off, will you, Lia?" Avery chimed in. Aurelia shot her brother a death glare. Avery shot one back. I chuckled. Avery had almost white blonde hair, in complete contrast to his sister's raven hair, but the same startling blue eyes. His eyes were ice as he confronted her. "What's your problem with her anyway? What's she done to you?" My eyes widened. I'd never had someone stand up for me before, especially someone that I didn't know.

"She didn't have to *do* anything, she's *here*. That's good enough." She lifted an eyebrow at me and gave a smug look.

"Give it a rest, Lia. You aren't impressing anyone." Avery glanced at Darrien, then smiled at me warmly. A butterfly took off in my chest.

"Whatever, Avery." She shot him another glare, then turned her long-lashed eyes on me. "I'd be happy to help you manage your girls, Cora. You might have the easy group, but it takes a special kind of person to really lead."

"I'll be fine. Thank you." The words barely made it out through my clamped jaw and tight smile.

Aurelia was wearing her camp shirt, which she clearly asked for in two sizes too small. It was so tight, I wasn't entirely sure she could breathe in it. The girl had a curvy body, and she showed no shame in flaunting it.

She took a perfectly dainty sip of her drink, and I couldn't help but wish her drink would just explode in her face and soak her tiny t-shirt. That's when it happened. Her drink exploded and it soaked her tiny t-shirt.

She screamed and jumped up as her pop ran down her chest, completely soaking her shirt and shorts. I couldn't even get out a laugh. That had to have been a coincidence, right? There was no way I could have done that. No. *No, just one of those cosmic moments. Yeah.*

I looked around to see if anyone had seen me...seen me, what? I only thought it, so it's not like I did anything. Darrien was the only one not

124

watching Aurelia; he was watching me, instead. I smiled and shrugged, not sure what else to do. *It wasn't me. Right?*

Jade took Aurelia back to the cabin to get changed as the rest of us enjoyed a meal Aurelia free.

After supper, I rounded up my girls and we wandered back to the cabin. After the incident with Aurelia, I just wanted a distraction and a good sleep.

"Okay, girls, quiet time starts at 9:30 p.m. every night. Lights out at 10:00 pm. The rule is that everyone is to stay in their cabin after 10:00 p.m. You should know that if you're found wandering around, you *will* be going home. Pearl has zero tolerance for that kind of stuff, and same thing for noises after lights out. Wake up starts at 7:00 a.m.-"

"Aww!" A bunch of objections erupted from the girls.

"I know, but the sun rises early too, and believe me, you'll be up with it. It gets hot in here, fast. Breakfast is at 9:00 a.m. Have a great night, girls. I can see some of you drifting already. See you all tomorrow morning!" I closed the door and dropped down the steps to the ground. As I walked to my cabin I wondered how Bree's day had gone, so I decided to stop by for a quick visit.

I walked up the stairs to the Red Team Cabin and knocked on the door. No one answered, so I opened it up. The cabin was empty. *I guess Pen took them for a late walk.* I'd have to catch Bree later. If I knew my sister at all, she would be knocking on my door soon enough anyway. The cabins were spaced out nicely, so that you couldn't hear everything going on in each, just anything that was getting too loud. The Lead cabin was at the entrance to the girls' side. I wondered if the other girls were in there yet. *Oh please, let Aurelia be out...lost in the bushes, maybe.* I giggled to myself as I stepped through the door of the cabin.

"Oh yay. It's you." Aurelia's unimpressed voice came from the back of the cabin. She had changed out of her wet camp gear, and was dressed up in a low cut top and jeans.

Aurelia was standing beside her bed, right across the room from mine. *Wonderful.* With only four beds in there, I supposed I couldn't really escape her. I glanced at her, but didn't respond to her comment. In my years of experience, when it came to being teased or bugged, saying anything just made the situation worse. Usually, I kept silent...until I lost my temper, then not so much. Unfortunately, silence didn't go over well with Aurelia.

"You know, you took my bed. I always sleep on that side of the room. I don't appreciate someone taking what is mine." A sly smile stretched out across her lips. I didn't like it. This girl really didn't like me, and I had no idea why. This was totally unprovoked. I made my way to *my* bed to start to get ready. Aurelia plunked herself down on hers and turned toward me.

125

"You know, I see the way that you look at him," when I didn't say anything she went on. "Stay away from Darrien. He's taken." I turned to say something, but again my words failed me. I didn't care about Darrien, so why couldn't I just say that to her?

She swiftly stood, turned and strutted out of the cabin, shouldering Pen as she was coming in. "Watch the new friends you're making, Penelope. You're slumming it," she scolded and sauntered down the steps to the road.

"What was *that?*" Pen asked as she came into the room. She dropped down on her bed and started removing her shoes. "Do you *like* poking bees' nests?" She stared at me, eyes wide with confusion. "She stings, you know."

"I came in and she started on me. I honestly didn't say *one word* to her," I explained as I started getting out my pajamas. Pen smiled and nodded.

"Well, you did *something* to set her off. You're in for a rough ride this summer if that keeps up. What did she say to you?" Pen shuffled to the bathroom with her toothbrush and paste.

"Nothing much, just empty threats. Oh, and to stay away from Darrien. Apparently, he is *hers.*" I folded my clothes on the bed and got out my bathroom caddy. I could hear Pen gurgle and spit from the bathroom.

"Don't underestimate Aurelia. She can put on a sweet front when she wants something, but she can back up her threats too," she said popping her soapy face out of the door.

"Well, she doesn't scare me. I'm not interested in Darrien, so she can stop worrying," I replied as I took my toothbrush and paste out and twiddled them in my hands.

"Really?" her skeptical tone not lost on me. She came out, rubbing a warm cloth across her face. "You're not interested in him at all? Not even a *little?*"

I shook my head. She gave me a doubtful look, "I don't buy that for a second. You'd have to be *blind* not to notice him! He's gorgeous!" Pen was watching me closely.

"Well I don't think so. I mean, not all that much," I said examining the bristles in my toothbrush. Pen huffed, and I looked up and shrugged. "Well, okay, maybe he's a *little* good looking. He has nice eyes. But that's all." *Those big blue green eyes that make my temperature rise…and the way he smiles out of the corner of his mouth …and how when he looks at me….*

"Cora? You there?" Startled, I broke out of my Darrien-induced trance and looked wide-eyed at Pen. She had come out of the bathroom and was right in front of me, and I hadn't seen or heard her at all. "If you could see your face! You're so funny!" She erupted in laughter. "No, you're right, I *totally* believe you. You don't think of Darrien that way at *all!*" She laughed her way to her bed.

"Oh god, I never did, I swear! But he came and talked to me today and-"

"He what? Tell me *everything!*" Pen stopped fast and launched herself onto my bed and eyed me expectantly. I sat beside her. I couldn't bring myself to tell her about the kiss. That was just way too embarrassing. So, I told her about the schedules and the mistake I made instead.

"Lucky girl, gets a visit from Darrien! No wonder you have Aurelia so upset! She's *jealous!*" Pen exclaimed. I didn't get it. *Why would anyone be jealous of* me?

Pen gawked at me and shouted, "Why would she be jealous? Are you kidding?" *Damn, I could have sworn I said that in my head.*

"Sorry, I didn't mean to say that out loud. Forget it. Please." I could feel my cheeks burning from embarrassment.

"Have you looked at yourself, Cora? You're hot, and it is *killing* Aurelia! She just can't stand that there might be some competition for the boys' attention around here!" She was smiling triumphantly at me, like I had won some kind of contest.

"Maybe I should just talk to Aurelia and explain that I don't want Darrien, or attention, and that she can have it all! I don't care!" I argued, trying desperately to spin all this in a way that wouldn't cause further damage and ruin the summer.

"Please, tell me you're joking," Pen scolded. "Aurelia would eat you alive if you tried talking to her. Just leave it be. You did the best thing tonight, and that was not saying anything to her. Just keep that up and you'll be fine. Well, you should be, hopefully," Pen said pulling back the covers in her bed and sitting. *Oh sure.* I've always been good at keeping my feelings to myself. Wait, nope, no I'm not. *I'm screwed.* If it doesn't come out my lips, it's on my face. *Great.*

"You think that she'll just…forget about it?" I smiled at the hopeful thought. Pen giggled as she crawled into bed. Well, that gave me lots of fuel for nightmares. Good night's rest? Forget it. But then I thought of a pair of blue green eyes…

37
Darrien

"WHAT ARE YOU DOING?" A slow, cold shiver ran up my spine.

"I'm cleaning the kayaks, Aurelia. What are you doing here?" I stood up and looked at her. She was leaning in the doorway of the boat house, knowing exactly what pose would show off her curves best. Her shirt was cut so low, it was indecent at a kids' camp. She'd better hope Pearl didn't see her in that…or her father, for that matter. I didn't think Sands would be thrilled she was putting that on, especially for me. The thought made me smile, but she took it the wrong way.

"You haven't changed. You're just as handsome as ever." Her triumphant smile was lost on me.

"Aurelia, we've been through this. Please, just let me get my work done." I hung the last of the kayaks up on the rack and locked up the door to the canoes. The Boat House had a water access right in it, so we could launch the canoes and kayaks from the dock inside the house if we wanted to, though mostly they were taken outside onto shore for that purpose. It also had two rooms, one for the kayaks and one for the canoes. The life jackets were kept out in the open for easy access.

"Oh, Darrien. You act like you don't even want me around you anymore!" *Ding, ding!* She was finally getting it!

"Lia-" I warned.

"I love when you say my name like that," she purred.

"Okay. *Aurelia*, we need to talk," I stated.

"Okay, baby, whatever you say." She sauntered over to me.

"When did you start talking like this? This is not you at all. It's not attractive, if that's what you are going for." Her face fell.

"Oh, Darri Bear…that hurt." I rubbed my face to keep from lashing out at her. This was ridiculous. She was making a complete ass of herself.

128

"Stop it, Aurelia. You're embarrassing yourself. We are *over*. I don't know what you thought would happen if you came here, but my feelings haven't changed," I said, half shouting.

"This is about that freak, isn't it?" Her eyes flashed in rage.

"Cora?" I said it before I thought. It was a mistake. I knew I just painted a target right on Cora's back.

"So, you admit it!" she yelled.

"What? No! This has nothing to do with her. You and I broke up a long time ago. What's going on with Cora has nothing to do with you."

"So, you have something going on with her then?" she accused. *What? Shit.*

"No!" *Not yet, anyway.*

"You think showing her some attention is going to scare me away? Forget it! I remember what we had. It was hot. It was *amazing*. You don't just let that go!" She came toward me and I flinched. I'd never seen her like that. A Siren in full battle gear scared me less than she did in that moment. I knew how to handle a deadly fighting machine like a Siren…Aurelia, was another story.

I rallied and came back at her. "You let it go if it's not right! I don't love you, Aurelia!" I roared, my hands turning to fists at my sides.

"We'll see, Darrien. We'll see." Aurelia said, as if a promise had been made and bounced out of the boat house. That conversation went nowhere. *Why doesn't she just get it?* I needed to get my frustration out before I blew something up.

I turned to the water access in the boat house and dove straight in. The feel of it over my skin was like an electric bolt shooting straight through me, filling me with an energy that was almost too much to contain. The stress of the conversation with Lia flowed away from me as I dove deeper into the water. My clothes didn't weigh me down, but I got rid of my shirt and shoes anyway. I'd find them on the way back.

The water was perfect, like a cool bath on warm skin. It was so clean, too. I'd been in other waters where I could barely see where I was going. This water smelled amazing, tasted incredible, and felt better than both. Adjusting to breathing the water was smooth and gentle, easier than I had ever experienced before. The deeper I went, the better it felt. Soon, I could feel the pull of the entrance. It was powerful, but not enough to draw me in. Water had a wonderful way of cleansing you, and not just your skin, but your soul. Immediately, my mind went to thoughts that made me happy, the ones that excited me. *Maybe it's time to get out.*

I streaked to the surface in time to see the sun go down. I'd forgotten how you could lose time in the water. What seemed like moments was actually hours. I'd really need to watch myself. I had a job to do, and I was going to be late for my date.

The date with the bush outside the shower room, that was…hoping to catch a glimpse of Cora in her pajama shirt…that was a little too short. A smile slipped across my face.

38

Cora

IT WAS INCREDIBLY BRIGHT, and really hot. I slowly cracked open one eye, followed lazily by the other. A gush of air poured out of me in relief. I was in my bed, not the shower room!

Instantly, I was in a great mood. A big, sleepy grin spread across my face as I sat up in bed. The girls were still asleep. *Wow, I beat my alarm clock! And the shower is all mine!*

I grabbed my shower bag and tip toed in. I debated pulling a prank on Aurelia, but knew that would just come back on me ten-fold. Besides, I wasn't much of a prankster, though dyeing her hair bright green *would* be funny. Grinning at the thought of messing with Aurelia's hair, I slid into the bathroom and treated myself to a long, hot shower. It felt amazing. Afterwards, I got dressed and slipped out of the cabin without disturbing the girls. Most thankfully, Aurelia didn't wake up.

The water must be beautiful this time of the morning. I was full of energy, and the beach was calling. The air was crisp, but felt and smelled so fresh and pure as I strolled my way down the path. I rounded the corner and looked at Crystal Lake. Just as I suspected, it was stunning.

I walked up to the crystal-clear water, removed my shoes, and stepped in, just up to my ankles. Taking a deep breath, I closed my eyes and stood there, enjoying the sensation of the clean water flowing over my toes. I opened my eyes and glanced across the lake, and my relaxation was broken as I saw something move in the water. I blinked a couple of times, sure that I was seeing things. *No, there it is.*

In the middle of the lake, something was swimming…and it was big. *Too big for a fish.* I walked forward to get a clearer look, but it disappeared into the water. The more I looked, the less sure I was that I saw something in the first place. I just couldn't shake the feeling that there was something odd about that thing. I didn't realize how long I had spent trying to find it, but when I saw the sun rising higher above the lake I figured that I had been out there a long time and it was time to get the girls up. It wasn't until I turned to go back that I realized I had wandered out into deeper water.

Oh, God! No!

Now that I could see how deep the water was and feel it up my legs, I panicked. I raised my feet above the surface of the water as I leaped and ran back to shore, cursing as I went. Water splashed up my chest and back as my feet stomped through the calm surface. Just as I was almost on shore, I tripped, falling and soaking myself. There was water everywhere. I stood, panting, and walked, soaking wet, to the shore. I felt like a complete idiot, and very grateful that I was alone.

"Wow. That was graceful." An amused chuckle came from behind me.

Oh, no. Please. No.

I turned around and feigned a smile, "I-I was just...well I didn't rea-...I'm sc-...what are you doing up so early, Darrien?" I asked, as I desperately tried to sort myself out.

He stood there in shorts, sandals, and a black zip up hoodie that was open. His hair was wet and stood out at odd angles, and yet somehow looked carelessly styled. Those turquoise eyes danced and sparkled with laughter as he looked my soaked body up and down. He brought the only warmth I had straight to my cheeks.

"I just got done with a morning swim. I usually come out here for some quiet time before everyone wakes up," he explained, crossing his arms over his broad chest. His smile was slightly smug, but more mischievous, having caught me in a moment of insanity.

"I was looking for some quiet, too, before I had to get the girls out of bed," I said, trying to maintain some dignity. It didn't work as I squeezed at my shirt, attempting to get some water out of it. I looked across the beach, praying no one else was coming out. Darrien moved his hands to his hips. His confidence always radiated, but this morning it was subdued. It was more comforting than cocky, and I was liking that side of him. I was also liking the fact that he wasn't wearing a shirt under his unzipped hoodie. My eyes followed the dips and planes of his stomach, down to the divots by his hips, the ones that angled and disappeared beneath his shorts. *Look away, look away!*

"Um, I thought that I saw something in the water. Did you see anything? It was out there, in the middle of the lake." I pointed and tried wringing out a little more of my shirt.

"Nope, nothing." He shrugged and looked at the sand. "You looking forward to your first day of activities?" He looked me up and down again. I wasn't oblivious to the change in subject, but I was starting to shiver from my cold, wet clothes. I crossed my arms, realizing what the cold was doing to my chest. If I had warmth left, I would have blushed profusely. The water was warm, but the early morning air was not, and it was time to get back to the cabin and change.

Darrien's smile faded, and a concerned look deepened his eyes as his brow furrowed. "Hey, you're shaking! Here, put this on." He took off the black zip-up sweater he was wearing and draped it over my shoulders. It was still warm. I couldn't help leaning my nose close to the fabric; it smelled like fresh spring rain. Even though we were standing close, I couldn't resist staring at his bare chest. My heart was starting to race just looking at him. I swallowed hard and reluctantly tore my eyes away from him.

Darrien tucked the sweater around me tighter, either oblivious to my staring or graciously letting me get away with it. His hands ran up and down my arms, warming them under the pressure of his strong hands, but then slowed down to a stop when our eyes locked. Speechless, I was flooded with an attraction that nearly consumed me. I couldn't think, couldn't move, but was stuck there, terrified of what would happen, and yet excited for it in a way I never understood before.

I could hear his breath hitch, and a muscle tightened in his jaw. A tingling sensation streaked through me, sending my heart into frenzy. His face was so close to mine, the warmth of his skin caressed me. When he dipped his head slightly, I watched his eyes flick to my lips. He reached out and swept a stray hair away from my face, tucking it gently behind my ear. The touch of his fingers sent warm bursts through my body, as he softly trailed them down my jaw and behind my neck. He raised the top of the hoodie around my neck and carefully pulled my hair out, so it wasn't cold against my back. My breath drew short and my lips tingled, as I was pulled closer to him. He smelled like rain, and I desperately wanted to know if he tasted the same. But before I could find out, from somewhere deep inside, a promise I made to myself surfaced.

"You...uh...you don't have another shirt on. You'll be cold," I mumbled, knowing full well I had just ruined the moment. Disappointment coursed through me with surprising ferocity. I *wanted* to kiss Darrien, *badly*, but I promised myself that I'd never *want* to do that. I shouldn't like this, him...any of it! But I did. *I can't be like Mom. I can't.*

I tried desperately to stop staring at him. His skin was so smooth and flawless, except for two moles, just inside his arm, above his right elbow. Despite his looks, there was something else about him that drew me to him. A glimmer in the way he looked at me at times, there was more to him than I was seeing, and I wanted to find out what it was.

His eyes broke away, and he cracked a wistful smile. His hands slowly loosened and he placed them in his pockets, his muscles rolling and flexing

133

as he moved. Clearly not ashamed of his bare chest, he made no attempt to cover up as he backed a step away.

Darrien rubbed his neck and cleared his throat. "You take the sweater. I insist. You need it more than me. Besides, the air doesn't bother me here. I won't freeze." He smiled genuinely, his adorable dimples getting deeper as he spoke. I hugged the sweater tighter around my shoulders, grateful for its warmth.

"Thank you." I didn't know what else to say, so I just stood there awkwardly. The seconds stretched out between us, and finally, it got too much for me. "I guess I should head back to the cabin to change. Thank you for the sweater." I took it off and held it out for him.

"You keep it, for now. Stay warm. You're still wet, no sense getting a chill on the walk back." He gave me a kind grin and draped the warm sweater around my shoulders again. I felt the butterflies in my stomach flutter as he touched me. His eyes latched onto mine again and his lips cocked in a crooked smile, revealing one dimple. "I'll see you later at our canoeing lesson, anyway."

"Right," I replied, a stupid grin spreading across my face.

"See you later, Humbug," he teased. I blushed and watched as a shirtless Darrien jogged down the beach and out of sight. I snuggled the huge sweater around me, threading my arms through the sleeves, and enjoyed its warmth. The scent of rain rose from the fabric and sent a warm flutter through me. I had drool-inducing thoughts of him slowly coming out of the water, water rippling down his muscular stomach, running in slow rivulets down his perfect, tight skin. I was smiling as I stepped lightly into the cabin for a change of clothes.

39
Darrien

I WAS FLOATING in the middle of the lake, enjoying the smell of the water and the feel of it, when I heard her step in. My hearing was enhanced in the water, and though she thought she was a panther, she was like a herd of elephants to me. When I surfaced and saw exactly who it was, I quickly dove deep and made my way to the bushes.

Why her? Why now? I was bare-assed naked and cursing myself for being too lazy to go to the cabin to get shorts to swim in. I stepped carefully out of the water and grabbed my clothes, then made my way back to the beach.

I *should* have just gone back to the cabin and gotten some sleep after watching Cora all night, but I couldn't. I wanted to see her.

When I got to the beach, I saw the most hilariously uncoordinated girl clamor her way out of the water to the sand. It was funny, and I had to keep a grip on my laughter, so as not to embarrass her more than I was already planning.

For my first words, I opted for the sarcastic, backward compliment. It worked, and totally flustered her. She was so adorable when she had no idea what was coming out of her mouth. I could have pushed the act, but didn't. As soon as her teeth started to chatter, I was done. I didn't stop to think as I took off my sweater for her. I just wanted to see her warm.

When I got close to her though, feeling her warmth under my hands, an electric pulse exploded in my core again. I stopped, frozen, watching her cheeks turn a lovely shade of pink. Her heart was slamming in her chest and that was almost enough to undo me. I'd been with other girls, but I'd never felt anything like that before. Her lips were full and begged to be kissed. I teetered there. I was unsure if I wanted to make that move, but also uncertain if I would be able to stop myself if it happened. She made the decision for me, pulling back slightly and changing the subject.

I was grateful. I needed to think. I needed to get my mind straight.

Cora, what have you done to me?

Whether it was her temper or her innocence that got to me, I couldn't be sure; but I did know that I wanted to find out.

40
Cora

"WHAT ARE YOU *WEARING*?" Aurelia screamed at me, and ripped Darrien's sweater right off me, as I reached into my locker for dry clothes.

"Hey! Give it back," I yelled, reaching for it, but she dodged out of my reach. I crossed my arms, refusing to get sucked into a game of tuck of war with her.

"It's not *your* sweater, is it?" she yelled back. "What are you doing with it? Where did you get it?"

"Darrien lent it to me this morning when my clothes got wet. I was cold. Can I have it back now?" I glared at her and held out my hand.

"You're *lying*! You totally stole it from him!" her voice screeched and my blood was starting to boil.

"What? I did *not*!" I shouted, and snatched the sweater out of her conniving hands, hiding it behind my back. Pen and Jade were now sitting up in their beds, staring wide-eyed at us. Jade was slightly smiling, I got the feeling that she was enjoying this, and Pen still needed to pick her jaw up off the floor. Neither of them would be any help. I needed the screaming to end quickly.

"Yes you did!" she launched at the sweater again, but came up short. *This is ridiculous.* She refused to see the truth, and there is only one way to deal with someone like that.

Summoning all the self-restraint I had, I rationally and calmly spoke. "Okay, you're right Aurelia. I admit it, I'm completely obsessed with Darrien. I just don't know what to do anymore. I took his sweater, stupidly hoping that he would notice me. I really don't know what I was thinking," I pouted and for added effect, covered my eyes with my hand, "You should return it to him." Looking as sad and dejected as I could, I just stood there staring at the floor, holding out the sweater for her to take.

"You are so *weird*. Why did you even come here? No one likes you." She paused for effect, waiting for me to respond, but I bit my lip and prayed for that to be the end. My prayers never get answered.

Aurelia took a step towards me, seeing that she wasn't going to get the reaction she wanted. I backed away, now pressed against the locker by my bed. "You're worthless, I'll bet your Daddy even thought so." A wicked smile stretched across her lips as she leaned in. My stomach dropped. *How did she know that? How did she know Dad left? How does she know that!* When she saw that she had hit the right button, she drew her hand back and I braced for the hit, but she snatched the sweater out of my hands and started toward the door instead. She never looked back as she left.

It took me several moments to calm myself down. After her comment about my dad, I was struggling to keep my tears at bay. I've always blamed myself for him leaving, but I never told anyone that, not even Bree. *How did she know that?*

I walked over to my bed and plunked down. Pen came over and sat next to me, while Jade went for a shower.

"I can't believe that you stole that sweater, Cora! What were you thinking?" she exclaimed. I guess I was a better actress than I thought.

"I *didn't* take the sweater! Darrien really *did* lend it to me, but do you think that Aurelia would have accepted that? Not a chance. I wasn't going to win that argument, so I just told her what she wanted to hear. Maybe she'll leave things alone now." I traced the lines in my hands with my fingers, something that I often did when I was upset.

"Look, she's just jealous-"

"Jealous of what?" I shouted in exasperation, standing and pacing the floor. "I have *nothing*! I *am* nothing! What could she possibly be jealous of?" I didn't mean to yell, but it just came out that way. Pen's mouth dropped open like I had just slapped her. My stomach twisted. I sat back down and dropped my head into my hands, grabbing my hair. "Sorry, Pen. I didn't mean to yell. I'm just upset. Sorry." I ran for my trunk, threw open the lid and dove in.

"It's okay. She upset you. She's good at that." Pen bent down and picked up the chocolate bar I was looking for from the mess I had strewn across the floor. "You're a good person, Cora. I may have only known you for a few days, but I can see that much." Her smile was warm and friendly as she handed me the bar.

"Thanks," I said, taking my salvation from her hands. "That's nice of you, especially after I yelled at you." I gave her a half smile, full of chocolate.

She was being so kind. I wasn't used to being treated like that by anyone other than Bree. I never really had friends. I guess I never saw the need to have one because I always had Bree. Let's face it, girls weren't exactly lining up to be friends with me either. After the accident and Dad, I focused on being there for Bree. She's the only real friend I've ever needed. But it was nice talking to someone my own age for once.

Pen walked around to her locker and started pulling out her shower things and clothes for the day. "Well, it will all be worth it to see the look on her face when Darrien tells her that you didn't steal his sweater. Can't wait!" Pen giggled. She was right. It would be good, and at that thought, we shared in a laugh and finished getting ready for the day.

41

Darrien

SOMETHING SLAPPED ME IN the face. I reached up to remove it. *What the…my sweater?*

I peeked out from under it. Aurelia stood in the doorway of our cabin, with a triumphant look on her face and her body angled in a model pose. I moaned and flopped over in bed, pulling the covers over my head. *I am not in the mood for this….*

The blankets were ripped off me and Aurelia stood there, shamelessly gawking at me. I glared at her as she put on her "prom queen" smile.

"You're welcome!" she chimed.

"For what?" I grunted and grabbed for the sheet, wrapping it around me.

"For returning your stolen goods, of course."

"It wasn't stolen. I gave it to Cora to wear because she fell in the water and was freezing," I answered. Her face went red.

"What the hell were you doing with that weirdo so early in the morning?" she demanded.

"She's not weird, and it's really none of your business what I was doing, Lia," I answered, sitting up in bed and rubbing the sleep from my face with my palms.

"It sure as hell is my business what my boyfriend is-"

"I'M NOT YOUR FUCKING BOYFRIEND, AURELIA!"

She stopped, momentarily taken aback by my roar. But I knew this girl, and she loved a fight…this was just foreplay to her.

"Temper, temper," she chided. *Oh, she really knows how to push my buttons.*

"Lia…." I warned at a low growl.

"Whatever you think you have with that…*girl*," she said it like it left a bad taste in her mouth, "it is nothing compared to what we had." I was seriously starting to wonder about her sanity. There was something else going on here with her. This was not the girl I dated. She wasn't this one-track minded.

140

Strong willed, yes. Bull headed, yes. But not stupid about it. She knew when to concede to save face. This…this was something different. She was obsessed. I didn't get it. I also didn't have the patience for it, either.

I grabbed her arms and yanked her toward me, getting down on her level and looking directly in her eyes. "Now, you listen to me, Lia. We are *through*. I don't love you. I never did love you. I never *will* love you. I don't want to have anything to do with you. I have lost all respect for you. So, for your own sake…*give…it…up*." I stressed every syllable before letting her arms go. Her eyes were wide. I saw the moment that it sunk in, the initial hurt and then, finally, the rage that replaced it.

"You son of a bitch!" she screamed and lunged at me.

Poor Zach came out of the shower while she was standing over my bed, screaming at me. He nearly took a header into the toilet, back-peddling so fast. *Hilarious.* It would have been funnier if I didn't have a deranged woman beating me with my clothes. I managed to say something ungentlemanly at her, between her swinging my sweater at my head, and piss her off even further, which caused her to toss my bed.

Then, once she was done ineffectively beating on me, she made it to the drawers next to my bed, and started yanking them out. I wrestled with my sheets, trying to untangle myself and stop her, because she was actually emptying Devon's clothes all over the place, not mine. I would have to apologize to him later and…apparently, replace the shirt she just took scissors to. *Where the hell did she get the scissors?*

Zach had recovered and was standing in the bathroom with the door open, now in boxers, watching the whole scene with a wide-eyed stare. He only broke when she went for his stuff too. That was when we both grabbed her and hauled her to the door. She was scratching and fighting the whole time. She even bit Zach in the arm, thinking it was me. I had a lot of apologizing to do. I held on to her as tight as I could, until she calmed down. When her breathing returned to normal, I let her go. We glared at each other for a stretched-out moment.

"What the hell do you have to say for yourself?" I barked at her. "You've trashed our cabin, you nut case!" She looked around, assessing the damage. Her shoulders sank for an instant, and in that moment, I thought I saw regret in her eyes. But the moment passed.

"Fuck you, Locke!" With that lady-like retort, she slammed the door so hard the handle came clear off and the frame cracked. I was beginning to wonder what I saw in her in the first place.

"Dude, what the hell did you do to her?" Zach asked as we cleaned up the room.

141

"Don't ask. It's a long story. Sorry about your stuff, man. I'll replace what she broke, or tore, or shredded." I meant it. He'd get a replacement, and more.

"No worries. Most of it is Devon's anyway. Oddly enough, she managed to avoid her brother's stuff completely." I stopped and looked around the room.

"Holy shit, you're right," I said, picking up a dresser off the floor. Here I was thinking that she just went on a blind rage, but she cased the room and went after everyone's stuff...but Avery's. *Clever girl.*

"She's not always like that, though. Right? I mean...there's a nice side to her, right?" Zach's question raised a flag for me.

"She's capable of better, that's for sure," I said and stopped, looking at him I raised an eyebrow, "Why?"

"Oh, no reason," he shrugged and shook his head, now focusing on the mess in front of him. That's when it dawned on me. Zach had a thing for her. My jaw dropped. *Seriously, man? After what she did? Good luck with that.* He was a nice guy, too nice for Lia.

I smiled to myself as I cleaned up the guys' stuff she had tossed around the room. Lia tended to explode when things were at their worst and then she settled down again. The destroyed room was a sign that things were going to get better. At least that's what I thought.

42

Cora

I HAD MY GIRLS IN THE HALL at 9:00 a.m., sharp. Pen and I were disappointed to find out that Aurelia gave Darrien his sweater back in private. We didn't get the show that we wanted over breakfast, but to my satisfaction, Aurelia had never looked so determined to massacre her hash-browns. Aurelia was radiating rage and if looks could kill, I would have died a million deaths over my omelet.

Darrien didn't say a word to me. He was busy talking with the boys. When I sat down, he did give me a half smile. He pointed at Aurelia behind his hand and whispered "Stop stealing from me." I stifled a laugh. His morning must have been as interesting as mine.

As always, the food was great, and I was stuffed as I shuffled my girls out the door. I made sure that each day, someone from the team went into the kitchen to thank Anne for their meal. She deserved some recognition for all the work she did. Not just anyone could whip up the quality of food she did for so many people.

The team and I paraded around the lake to our canoe lessons. The giant boat house was between the boys' and girls' cabins. Darrien was standing at the end of the long dock when my team arrived. He was wearing shorts and the sweater that he lent me that morning.

"Good morning, girls. I'm Darrien, and I'll be your boating and swim instructor this summer!" The girls were giggling to themselves, and several were blushing. I laughed to myself watching them.

Darrien strolled down the dock to shore, where we were standing, and took us on a tour of the boat house.

It was huge. There were enough canoes, stored in giant shelving units, for at least two teams to be on the water at once. Plus, there were enough kayaks to do the same. Pearl sure had a great collection. It was Darrien's job to maintain all the boats and the boat house. There were two rooms, one for

143

kayaks and canoes, and the open room for the life jackets. There were jackets in every size, and tons of them in all those sizes. Darrien asked the girls to grab one. I did too, even though I had no intention of going in a boat.

We exited the boat house and went onto the floating dock. As I neared the end of it, I peered over the edge to get a look at the depth of the water. It was deep, but the water was so clear, I could see pretty much to the bottom. It was still calm out on the lake, and I could see my reflection staring back up at me from the water.

Movement in the water had me focus my attention back on my reflection. My face looked the same as mine, at least I thought so until it turned its head all on its own. A burst of adrenaline exploded in my belly. *Did that just...move on its own?*

My reflection stared back at me with eyes that were not my own. I blinked. *Am I really seeing this?* Its mouth opened and, in a voice that wasn't mine, whispered *"Cora!"* from the deep. My blood fled my body.

The last thing that I remembered was a sparkling, beautiful deep green coming for me.

43
Darrien

I WAS LOOKING FORWARD to canoe lessons. My plan was to get Cora into a boat with me. I was hoping that, just maybe, she might trust me enough for that. But before I could even talk to her about it though…SPLASH!

All I saw was the tip of a foot and a lot of water up in the air. I didn't think. I just jumped in. When I hit the water, something was different. The temperature was off. It was cold, like ice. The smell was off, too; it stunk. And Cora…*my god….*

She was floating in the middle of the water, eyes open, staring straight ahead of her. A glow was coming from her eyes as she looked on, unseeing, into the water. Her mouth was slack and open. Her skin was a sickly looking shade of grey-green. My heart was beating so fast, I thought it might work its way out of my chest. It was so terrifying I was struck immobile. I just stared at the haunting sight in front of me.

Then, she coughed.

She was out of air and was trying to breathe the water. I flew to her and grabbed her around the waist. At my touch, she went limp, just like when she was sleepwalking. The glowing eyes returned to her normal green, and then closed. I sighed in relief. Hopefully, she would be okay. I nestled her head gently against me, as I sped to the surface.

I got her on shore as quickly as I could, and carried her up on to the dock. The girls were all screaming. My heart was on hold until I saw her eyes flicker. Her first cough finally let me breathe again.

My god, what is happening to you?

44
Cora

"CORA! CORA!" A MILLION LITTLE flies were buzzing around my head. *I didn't know flies could talk. Buzz, buzz. Cora, Cora.* They were talking to me. *Funny little bugs.*

"Cora! Cora! Wake up! Come on!"

Slowly, I opened my eyes. Darrien was crouched over me; his eyes were wide and his face pale. He was also soaking wet and dripping on me! "Why are you so wet?" I wanted to ask, but all that came out was a huge cough and a ton of...water?

My eyes darted around. *What happened?* Water was trickling from Darrien. He was wet from head to toe, and was panting, staring wide eyed at me.

"What happened?" I asked, staring at him. My voice sounded rough and rusty. My mind was fuzzy; my eyes were watery and my throat burned from the water.

"You tell me! One minute you were fine, and the next second you fell face first into the lake!" *Oh, that would explain why I feel like I've been slapped.* I rubbed my cheeks with my hands.

"Then, Darrien jumped in and rescued you! He's a hero!" The girls were all aflutter with coos and sighs, and gazing adoringly at him.

"Th-thanks," I managed to stammer out. My lungs and nose were burning from inhaling water, and I was still trying to get the buzzing out of my ears.

"Uh...maybe...I should just...sit on the shore for now. I'm ok, I'll just...be over here." I stood and wobbled heavily, a pair of strong arms wrapped around me. I turned and looked right into Darrien's eyes. He cleared his throat.

"Let me help you," he said. I nodded. He wrapped an arm around me and held my hand to the end of the dock. I sat on the hard, safe, secure *ground.* He knelt in front of me, looking me over. "You okay?"

"I'm fine. Really, I am. I'll just be here…drying off," I mumbled, my voice getting slightly stronger.

"Okay. You sure you don't need anything?" he asked and left me wishing I did need something to keep him next to me. *No, stop it Cora.*

"Nope. I'm good," I said instead. Darrien nodded once and got up.

My clothes, for the second time that day, were completely soaked, along with my hair and shoes. I was a complete mess. As Darrien took over the lesson, I laid back, gazing at the sky, and decided to just let the sun do its work and dry me. It was a good thing the canoe lesson was just starting, I had over an hour to dry up. I removed as many layers as I could without getting indecent. I noticed Darrien's eyes drifting over to me as I peeled off the wet clothes. That caused a bloom of warmth to seep through me.

By the end of the lesson I was mostly dry. I realized my shoes would be a lost cause for another day. When I picked them up, and turned them over, lake water ran from them.

Great, they're my only pair.

I turned them upside down to dump what water would come out and a gush of it streamed out and onto the ground. *I thought I already dumped these things.* I paused, watching the water run into the lake.

No. There's no way…

I put my hand inside my shoe, testing the theory I was hatching. When I felt the dryness I gasped and shot my hand out of the shoe, slamming it right into something hard behind me.

"You know, you really need to stop hitting people." His deep chuckle was enough to draw me out of the insanity that was building in my mind. But still…

"You alright?" Darrien asked, easing himself to the ground next to me.

"Yeah. At least I think so," I uttered picking up my shoes.

"That was quite the dive you took, you sure you are going to be okay?" *Dive?*

"Huh? Oh! Right! Yes, the fall…into the water. No, I'm fine. I'll be fine." I assured him, but he looked skeptical. "Really, I'm fine," I smiled and stood. I slipped my shoes on, thankful for whatever powers that got them dry for me, and yet freaked right out that they were.

The Yellow cabin was making its way to the dock, so I gathered my girls and set off for our next activity. When I turned to look behind, Darrien was watching.

Luckily for me, craft time went by splendidly, thanks to Pen's book. We made pinecone bird feeders, and the girls were loving it. Before we knew it, we could hear the dinner bell track ringing from the loud speaker, so we packed up and trekked off for something to eat.

Lunch was amazing. I took the first seat at the Lead table, since none of the other teams had arrived yet. I watched my girls talking and laughing; they were having a good day. Seeing all of them enjoying themselves so much cheered me up.

"How are you feeling there, Humbug?" Darrien asked as he sat down beside me. "You really know how to flex my life-saving muscles. It must be a family trait." It hit me hard that he had now saved both my and Bree's life.

"Um...by the way, I didn't get a chance to properly thank you for what you did for Bree. I was so wrapped up in the thought of losing her, I didn't say it right. I'm very sorry about the way that I treated you." A warm smile slid up the side of his face, his dimple winking into existence. That was enough to make my heart leap into my throat. I cleared my throat and looked away.

"Anyway," I continued. "I'm sure Bree would thank you for what you did today, too." *That didn't come out right.* "Not that *I'm* not grateful for today. I'm just saying that she would be grateful if you asked her. You don't have to ask her, but- what I mean is...thank you." I tried not to look at him, so I concentrated on my sandwich.

"It was my pleasure," his voice warm and kind, making my heart pound in my chest. "The girls were really scared for you, by the way. You're doing really well with them, I told you that you'd be fine." A small laugh escaped my mouth as a smile crept its way across my face.

"Thanks for saying that, but I'm sure they think I'm nuts." I watched Darrien bite into his sandwich. He smiled at me, mouth closed, cheeks full and mustard from ear to ear. My mouth dropped open and a laugh bounded out.

"What? Do I have something on my face?" He grabbed a napkin and swept it across his face, leaving just the smallest drop below his bottom lip. He was chuckling to himself now, too. "Did I get it all?"

"Um...there's just a little, right here." I pointed to myself where the mustard was and watched him wipe the last of it off his perfect lips. Humor danced across his beautiful face when our eyes connected. My heart stalled. And just like that, all humor was gone.

This was something else. The way he looked at me made me feel like I was the only person in the room. I didn't know how to process that. I finally tore my eyes away from his, lowering them to my fingers and smiled at the heat that rolled off me. My heart raced to catch the beat it lost. Darrien seemed unaffected, his playful spirit still going strong.

"Oh, by the way, you should really reconsider the way you return borrowed items. It was quite the...thing, getting my sweater back this morning," he joked, a sly grin appearing on his face. I could only imagine how that scene played out.

"I'm sorry." I giggled as I said it. The thought of Aurelia returning his sweater was just too funny. "Really, I am, but she took it from me. She really wanted to return it to you so you would know I *stole* it." Darrien frowned to himself.

"You know, she doesn't like you," he pointed out, as if it was new information. His lips curled at one end, the shadow of his dimple sending my heart into a spasm. He lifted his eyes to meet mine. "She's jealous of you." My stomach lurched. It was one thing for Pen to say it. It was a complete other for Darrien to.

"She hasn't made a secret of the fact that she doesn't like me."

"Well, she knows that you didn't steal the sweater now, though I can pretty much guarantee that won't be the end of it." Darrien was finishing up his sandwich. "So, what exactly happened to you today? How did you end up in the water? I had my back turned for a second and then, splash, girls screaming, Humbug missing...what a mess!" He was smirking. At least *he* found humor in it, because I certainly didn't. It scared me. The image of my reflection sent chills up my spine.

"Um...I must have gotten dizzy, I guess. I don't really remember much of what happened right before." I remembered, but I wasn't going to tell him that. I didn't want to think about it.

"Okay, that's vague." He flashed me an easy smile. "Why are you are so afraid of water?" My stomach lurched.

"I'm really not comfortable talking about it," I said, surprising myself with the amount of restraint I showed. I faked a half smile. That was the best I could muster.

"Well, when would be a good time for you?" he asked pointedly, looking at me. "Cora, you realize my goal this summer is to get you in the water." He smiled like a fox. I looked down. There was no way that I was stepping close to the water again. He'd be lucky if I got out on the dock again. That was a disaster already. I couldn't begin to go into the weird water moving thing. And, even with the weird hallucination aside, just being close to water that deep resurfaced thoughts I had worked hard at locking away.

"I'm not taking you now, Humbug. Breathe!" I hadn't realized that I was holding my breath. Darrien moved so fast, I barely saw him. He had his hands on my face, gently sweeping his thumbs over my cheeks, bringing me out of myself. The warmth from his hands penetrated through my skin and relaxed my muscles. His face was so close to mine, I could feel his hot breath on me.

149

With those clear eyes staring intently into mine, I couldn't look away, and now I couldn't breathe for a different reason.

The moment stretched out between us before he lifted his hands slowly away, his eyes staying on mine. My heart hitched as his hand reached out and gently tucked that stray hair behind my ear again. His touch sent electrical shocks through me. His keen eyes watched me for a reaction. I held my breath again, but this time it felt glorious. His lips were so close...*no!* I backed away from him, breaking whatever bond that had tied us in that moment, and gave him an uncomfortable smile.

"Um, thanks." I willed my pulse to slow down. I struggled to remember what we were talking about. *Oh, right, he wanted to get me in the water.*

"It's nice of you to make some summer project out of me. But, you won't be seeing me in any water. I can guarantee that." I smiled triumphantly at him. I knew I was right. He just hadn't realized it yet.

"We'll see, Cora. We'll see." His dimples deepened as his smile spread across his face.

Aurelia didn't make an attempt to hide her anger when she came over and slammed her tray down. Darrien and her had an epic stare down, and, after awkward silence stretched beyond even my comfort, I decided it would be a good time to leave.

I left my girls to finish their lunch and went to the beach for a few minutes of silence. It was deserted, since everyone was now inside, eating. I sat on the bench, closed my eyes, and hummed the tune I was becoming familiar with all over again. It was relaxing, it was beautiful; it was Dad. It was all Dad.

He was wonderful, and I missed him. It was my fault that he left. If I could have just saved her, he wouldn't have gone. We'd all still be together: Mom, Dad, Bree, Oceana, and me.

Oceana...things would be so different if you were still here. I stared out at the deep green waters of Crystal Lake, and let my reluctant memories flow over me.

Dad called us "twin fish," because we spent so much time swimming. I wasn't afraid back then. I lived for the feel of the water wrapping around my body, and Ana loved it just as much as I did. Mom wasn't a swimmer, not like Dad. Dad was like a fish; he could swim for hours and never get tired. Mom could swim, but she was wary of water, only getting in for a short time and never more than once a year. She wouldn't even bathe, just shower. Ana and I always tried to get her to swim with us, but she wouldn't.

I remembered one summer, when we were really little, we all went to the fair. Even though Mom had Bree in the stroller and two twin girls to watch over, she looked like it was the best day of her life. Dad had his arm around her, holding her tight; it wasn't in a possessive way, but with pride. He stood tall and handsome, and pressed a tender kiss to her forehead as she smiled peacefully. Ana and I giggled and grinned up at them. I was so incredibly happy that they were my parents.

The last happy memory I have was the morning that Ana died. We played on the beach and in the water all morning, and ate lunch there too. When evening came, it was time for our first boat ride. It took all my Dad's special powers to convince Mom to get on the boat that day. She was always worried around water, and being out on the lake was terrifying for her.

For a while, it was a great time. Even Mom was enjoying herself. But then, the storm hit. Dad was steering the boat, and I could see, by the look on Mom and Dad's faces, that something was wrong. The storm moved so fast, it was as if it had a mind of its own. I remember Oceana leaning over to me and grabbing my hand. I was a stronger swimmer than she was.

"I won't let anything happen to you," I said to her. "Just hold on to me." I made a funny face. She laughed. We had the same laugh, my Ana and me.

But suddenly, Ana wasn't laughing anymore, and the boat was listing from side to side. We were all soaking wet from the rain and waves.

Everyone was staring wide-eyed at the churning water around us. Mom was clinging onto any handholds she could with one hand, while wrapping the other around Bree. Poor Bree, she was only four. She was crying and screaming, terrified of the water surrounding us. I remember Mom hugging her as tight as she could, kissing her forehead and telling her it was going to be okay.

Mom stared in horror out at the water. She was mumbling to herself. Dad was cursing into the wind. I couldn't hear what he was saying as he tried desperately to get the boat to do what he wanted. Their eyes darted from the water to us, as they yelled at us to hold on.

The wind was strong. It whipped around us, stinging our eyes and throwing light objects around the deck. Then, out of nowhere, the boat lifted and tipped. Teetering on its side, it shuddered, as if some unseen force was shaking its contents loose. Ana and I were the only ones that fell into the churning water; everyone else managed to hold on and stay in.

We were pulled deep under the surface. Ana's hand still firmly in mine. *I've got you, Ana.*

There was no telling where the surface was. Even in our life jackets, we were twisted around like contortionists. Then, the water stretched and sliced between us, as if something fought to separate us. My hand felt like it was going to come out of its joint as we were being pulled away from each other. I watched Ana's eyes fly from our hands to my eyes and back. Panic settling in for us both, as my grip faltered.

I cried as her hand slowly slipped from mine.

151

Her face was full of fear and panic. I'll never forget it. When her last finger fell from my grasp, I screamed into the dark water as I watched Ana's fighting figure disappear from my sight. She was gone.

I reached out, searching for her in the darkness, but I was alone. Paralyzing panic set in when I couldn't hold my breath anymore. I was still being knocked around by the water and couldn't find air. I couldn't find Ana. *Ana, please, come back!*

I was ready to give up.

With no strength left, my body resigned itself to its fate. That's when I felt something grab me. I flailed, trying to get away from it, but instead of pulling me under, it propelled me up.

I broke the surface, choking and coughing. I was nowhere near the boat anymore, but Mom and Dad saw me and came for me.

The storm had dissipated as fast as it had swarmed in. The boat was in an uproar. Dad was yelling for me, shouting orders to anyone that was listening, but no one was. Mom was sobbing, utterly beside herself with panic and grief. Bree was screaming.

I was silent.

Ana was gone. I had failed her. I let go.

The next day, Dad left. He just *left*. We had just lost Ana and he abandoned us!

Was it too much for him? Was it me? I knew he couldn't look at me. Ana and I were identical twins. He couldn't see me and not think of her. It was my fault. I let go. Everything was *my fault.*

Nothing was the same after that. Mom slipped into a deep depression; losing her daughter and then her husband was just too much for her. They were supposed to mourn together, to deal with it together. But Dad abandoned her and tore Mom apart, completely.

At the heart of it, Mom *disappeared* the day Ana died, and *died* the day Dad disappeared. I'll *never* forgive him for that, but I *hate* myself for causing it all.

I should have saved her. I should have held on longer. I should have been a stronger swimmer. I should have been braver for her.

She would still be here if I didn't let go!

I was sobbing. Mournful, loud sobbing. Sounds came from me that I didn't even know I was capable of making. Tears trickled down my cheeks and landed with little splashes in my lap. I watched as the salty water slowly spread into wet pools on my jeans. It just made me cry harder.

Letting go felt satisfying and weak at the same time. I had spent so much energy locking away those thoughts from Bree, and myself, that I felt like I had failed to some degree. I wiped at the tears with the back of my hands.

Taking a deep breath, I exhaled deep and long through wobbling lips. *You are a mess, Cora.* That's when I felt a soft hand on my shoulder.

"Cora?"

Startled I jumped and turned. Darrien's concerned eyes gazed back at me. The ruffle of his brow made him look more distinguished, somehow. *He came to check on me, that's so sweet. He-ugh no.* That's when I realized what a mess I was. My eyes were swollen and red, my face was wet, and there was snot running from my nose.

"Yeah?" I asked, wiping away as much of the tears and snot as I could with my sweater sleeve, in a losing attempt to look presentable.

"Are you okay?" He looked at my face and a darkness came upon him, as anger flashed in his eyes, "Aurelia." He grunted and stood to go.

"No!" I yelled, holding up my hands for him to stop.

"This thing with her has *got* to stop," he forced through a tight jaw.

"I'm fine," I said, not believing it myself, but trying to show him it was the truth.

He didn't go, but dropped beside me. He pulled a stray hair behind my ear and made my heart kick in my chest. My eyes met his as his hand lightly touched my cheek. I forced my eyes away and out to the water.

"I couldn't care less what Aurelia thinks of me. She's annoying and mean, you're right, but she didn't make me cry." I knew it looked pathetic, and maybe humorous, considering my red and puffy appearance.

Several moments passed before I broke the silence. "I'm okay, Darrien, really. I just...want to be alone. Okay?" I appreciated that he was concerned, but I just needed some time to myself.

"Is there anything I can get for you?" he asked. I shook my head. He shifted uncomfortably at my side, and a huff of air came out of him. "You've been through a lot today. I'm going to ask Pearl if I can take your team for the rest of their activities. You look like you're about to fall over." He stood up to go.

"No! Please don't!" I shouted, clamoring to my feet. He stopped and turned. His shoulders were stiff, and his muscles flexed tightly. "I-I don't want her to think that this job is too much for me. Really, I'm fine! You don't need to do that." Darrien raised an eyebrow at me. I recognized that question immediately and smiled to myself.

"Yes, I'm fine...really. Thanks for coming and checking on me." The way that he looked at me...

My face burned and I threw my eyes to the ground. I cleared my throat, "I'd better get back to the team. We have to be off for outdoor survival." The thought made my stomach drop.

"Cora, you look sick," Darrien argued and made a move for Pearl's cabin.

"No! Stop! I was just thinking about the outdoor survival class that I have today. I'm not really-outdoorsy. I honestly have no idea what I am doing." I sighed, admitting my short comings to him.

"No problem," he smiled and shrugged. "I'll come along with you. There's tons of trails to hike and walk. We'll do one today, and I'll show you where the others are tonight. Then you'll have an activity for your team to go on almost every day," he waited and watched to see if I approved of his help this time. My mouth dropped open. Was he really offering to save me from this too? It was too good to be true!

And when things seem too good to be true, they usually are. So I should say 'no'. Say no.

"Okay!" *Ugh…*

45

Darrien

I WATCHED CORA tirelessly attempt to be graceful down the path. The girl was hopelessly clumsy, but somehow, that was endearing. She was a disaster, and yet she was perfect at the same time.

After the day that Cora had, I was relieved to be able to help her. Her team was great, though a little too interested in my personal life. I was excited to be able to show the other paths to Cora…alone. The thought gave me a bounce in my step, and a pang of yearning that was terrifying.

We made our way around the trail and back again in no time. I told Cora as much about the trails as I could, even though I had no intention of letting her go on her own. With the Siren falls around, there was no way I was chancing it. Plus, I had something special planned for our private hike.

46

Cora

"WELL, THAT'S IT for today, girls," Darrien announced as we came to the end of the trail. He was met by a resounding and loud wail by my team. I giggled. *They* weren't afraid to show how they felt about him.

"Ladies, I will see you all at your canoeing and swimming lessons tomorrow!" Darrien's smile was bright and full of humor.

"Yay!" The girls replied in chorus. I laughed again. I really enjoyed the hike, even if it resulted in a bruised ankle and shredded knees.

I watched as Darrien fielded more questions from the girls as he started to slowly venture away from them. He was smiling, dreamy dimples and all, but he answered every question, being just as kind to each girl in turn. My heart swelled watching how great he was with them. I would think, with all the attention he got, his head would be inflated, but I hadn't gotten that impression of him at all.

It was glaringly obvious that all the girls on the team had huge crushes on him already, and yet, he didn't seem to react to it at all. He was confident, but not arrogant, and, *damn it*, that was attractive. Darrien caught up to me, and walked beside me as we set out for supper.

"You still interested in some of the other trails tonight?" he asked standing too close to me.

"Sure! That would be great!" I squeaked, losing the attempt to sound nonchalant. But when his arm brushed mine, my knees nearly buckled.

"Perfect. I'll meet you by the trail we did today. There's a branch-off I want to show you, say, at seven?" His eyes were a deep, dark green-blue, so kind and gentle. How could I say no to that?

"Seven! It's a date!" My face dropped the second I said it. *Date? No!*

I opened my mouth to correct myself, but nothing came out and then I tried again…nothing. I was starting to breathe heavily when Darrien chuckled. He stopped walking and reached for my hand. His strong and

156

gentle fingers threaded through mine. My breath hitched in my throat as he leaned in closer to me. His deep blue-green eyes focused on mine.

"It's a date."

47

Darrien

"OKAY, WHAT'S GOING ON, Darrien? Is it about Cora?" Pearl's smile suggested that she knew more than she was saying. I had showed up at her door unannounced. I was confused and worried about lots of things I didn't want to talk about, yet, there I was.

"Yes...it's about Cora," I admitted and dropped into the over-stuffed chair in her tiny living room. I couldn't look at her.

"What did you do?" She demanded, stepping into the cabin from the door. I snapped my head up.

"Nothing! Well, kind of...I don't know." I played with an empty cup, moving it from hand to hand.

"Okay." She sat down across from me, on the couch and eyed me.

"I-," I started but didn't finish, instead I looked for something at the bottom of the cup.

"So, you *want* to do something. Is that what you are trying telling me?" She hinted, gingerly taking a sip of her coffee that I had interrupted.

"No. Yes...both, I guess," I mumbled.

"I'm guessing this has nothing to do with your job, but is on more of a personal level?" She quipped, and sat back against the chair. She was eyeing me, reading me as best as she could.

"Perhaps." I grinned, or I tried to.

"Okay, well I guess you should probably pack up and head home then," she declared and stood brushing her pants. My heart skipped a beat.

"What?"

"I can't have you here messing this up. It's too important. I'll let Zale know you did your best, but that for personal reasons, this isn't the job for you," she retorted, and stood up as if dismissing me.

158

"Are you shitting me right now?" I shouted. "Zale sent me because I'm the best person for the job, the *only* one," I yelled and stood up, too. *There's no way I'm going anywhere. Not now…no.*

"Is that so?" she challenged, looking entirely unconvinced.

"Yes," I said with more confidence than I'd had before.

"Then do your job," she warned. I cursed under my breath. She was so cut and dry about this. It was just not that easy.

"I have feelings for her, Pearl," I uttered. Admitting it felt like a release and a death sentence at the same time.

"You've been in relationships before, Darrien," she pointed out.

"I have. But they were arranged, and they all ended in a disaster."

"So, this time, you think going after the *one girl* that you absolutely *can't* have is going to make this work out for the best? Your logic is flawed. You see that, right?" she argued.

"Oh, I *see* it. I just am starting to *care* less and less," I admitted. "My logical side has taken a flying leap off a cliff."

Pearl eyed me, working out something in her head. "I can't say that I miss the stick up your butt, however, this new Darrien is a little too devil may care for me. Have you forgotten that she is Zale's daughter? What is he going to think of all of this?"

I couldn't say that I had given that much thought, I hadn't. But, she was right. What was I thinking? This was my boss's daughter. I dropped my face into my hands, and scrubbed it.

"Yeah, I know," I grumbled into my hands.

"As much as I am usually an advocate of following your heart, I really don't want to see you get hurt. Like it or not, I feel responsible for you." Her eyes sparkled over the rim of her mug.

"Thanks, Pearl. I like you too," I said with smile. I could've sworn that made her blush. She was the closest thing to a real aunt that I was going to get.

"Darrien, you are an amazing person. You truly are. I want you to be happy. I just can't see how being with Cora will do that for you." Her face went sad and serious quickly, her tone melancholy as she rested the coffee mug gently on the table between us.

"She is incredible, Pearl. I wish you could see that," I pleaded.

"I'm not disputing Cora's attributes. I *know* she's amazing…it's in her blood. I'm saying that her position, the future queen, will put a spike right through the heart of this. She is going to get hurt, and so are *you*." *That can't be the only way this goes.*

"She has the power to change all that crap if she wants to. She can *do* whatever she wants."

"She's betrothed, Darrien." My heart froze. *No. Please no.*

"Who? To who, Pearl?" I asked, my heart thumping back to life in anger and a sadness I was not prepared for.

"I really don't want to say." She was hesitating.

"I don't give a shit. Who?" I demanded, the anger taking over.

"Look, what are you doing to do? Threaten him? He has just as little control over all this as she does. Their families made the arrangement a long time ago. They were *promised* to each other. It's binding, Darrien. Nothing short of a god's intervention will change that." She was pleading with me to understand, but I couldn't.

"How can she have no say over who she is supposed to be with? How could a family do that? *Why* would they do that?" I could hear the demanding whine in my voice. I hated it, but there it was. I was acting irrationally in the face of the inevitable truth.

"Zale didn't sign up for it. It was his father. Calloway signed over Zale's children in a peace treaty with another Mer family. Zale was sickened when he heard," she answered.

"But *now*, he's defining her life *for* her. He's locking her into a future she has no say in, and doesn't even know exists! How is that *fair*? How is that *right*?" I fumed.

"That's not our place to say, now is it?" Pearl said so matter of factly I stopped. I put my head in my hands. "Look, Darrien. Your feelings can't be that strong. You just met the girl, for goodness' sake. You have a crush. It will go away! Just do your job, get her home, and then everything will be fine." She looked like she had come up with the perfect answer. *Is it just a crush? Maybe it is. Maybe....*

"Right, do my job. Do my job," I mumbled, but my frustration mounted again. "All I have ever done, is do my job. Do what's right, what's best for everyone, *but me*! I'm tired of it! When do *I* get to be happy?" I asked, knowing the answer. Pearl's eyes shone. She reached across and took my hand.

"That is the sacrifice we all made when we chose a life of service. We send our happiness into the world for others to find, and we keep none to ourselves. In that sacrifice, you must find your happiness, if not contentment," she confided.

"I don't think I can do that," I blurted.

"Darrien, please don't do this," she begged.

"I haven't done anything. I haven't hurt anyone. All I have done is offered to help, to gain trust, to do my job and bring home a princess. That is- SHIT!" I hollered.

"What?" She jumped, releasing my hand.

"I just saw Aurelia in the window!" I was off my seat in a flash.

160

48
Darrien

I BLASTED OUT THE DOOR and down the beach. Aurelia was running, but not nearly fast enough to elude me. When I grabbed her arm and swung her around, the smoothest smile slid across her lips.

"Oh, Darrien! What's up?" she chimed.

"Don't give me the sweet-as-candy routine. What did you hear?" I demanded.

"Oh, nothing much," she said licking her lips and straightening her shirt.

"How much!" I yelled as I shook her. Fear registered on her face, but was quickly replaced by that smirk I hated.

"Oh, just a little something about a job, and returning a- now what was it-oh yeah...*princess*." I could feel the blood drain from my face. Aurelia grinned like a cat with a mouse. "Who is it, Darrien?" She pressed. I glared at her.

"I'll bet I can guess...." she sang. "Jade?" she looked in my eyes, "Hmm, no, you haven't paid her any attention." She pulled her arm free of my hand and circled me as she spoke. "Pen? Umm...no. Not Pen." If I could kill her with my eyes, I would have fried her in her sandals. "*Cora*," She whispered and trailed a finger down my chest.

"If you-"

"If I *what*?" She looked at me with doe eyes. I grabbed her hand and tightened my grip. "Darrien, I would play nice with me now if I were you," she lilted.

"Don't. Threaten. Me," I seethed.

"I wouldn't dream of it. But I can't promise that I won't talk in my sleep. Who knows what I might say?" She threatened.

"What do you want, Lia?" I forced the words through a tight jaw.

"You know what I want," she whispered in my ear.

"Me?" *You've got to be kidding me.*

"Oh, please. You think I'm so desperate that I would blackmail you into a relationship with me? I don't think so. But, that doesn't mean that I am going to sit idly by and watch you start one with someone else."

"Are you serious?"

"You've made yourself very clear, but I don't give up easily. I'll step back, but I won't step away. I know you. The *real* you. You'll come around. We were *meant* for each other, Darrien."

"I have a job to do Lia. Cora is a job, that's it. You are overreacting."

"Am I? I don't think so. I've seen the way you look at her."

"I'm telling you there's nothing going on!"

"And you're lying! But, whatever, keep telling yourself that. I'll help you out. Stay away from Cora, or there's a chance that my lips will loosen." She smiled at me triumphantly.

"This is insane, Lia, even for you." I gripped the back of my neck and paced the path.

"You might think so, but I do this with you in mind too. Your job means more to you than anything, Darrien. I know you, you won't do anything to jeopardize that. You'll do your job and nothing more. *That's* who you are. *That's* who I love."

Her sincerity stilled my heart. Lia wasn't one for vulnerability, but there she was, bearing it all and there was nothing I could give back to her. I didn't love her and I wouldn't, especially not now.

"Lia…" and just like that the soft girl was gone, replaced by a hardness that was startling.

"Don't," she barked, holding up a hand. "Remember, this isn't just about you. You have a precious princess to protect too. You wouldn't want anything happening to her would you?"

"No," I answered, as a massive wave swept onto the shore.

"Good." She pressed a tiny kiss to my cheek and then sauntered away.

"Shit. Shit!" I cursed into the trees.

What am I going to do?

49
Cora

BEFORE I KNEW IT, the day was gone and I found myself sitting on my bed, with Bree and Pen.

"What happened to you, today?" Bree asked. She had a big grin on her face and was leaning over her knees, painting her toenails. She looked at me through inquisitive blue eyes.

Pen had just changed out of her camp gear and took a place at the end of my bed next to Bree. She grabbed another bottle of nail polish and started on her own.

"I love this stuff!" Pen exclaimed then looked at me. "I don't suppose you know what has Aurelia so wound up?"

"I might have an idea. Possibly," I hinted.

They both leaned in closer, their eyes off their toes. "I'll tell you, but you can't tell *anyone*! Promise?"

"Promise!" The two rang out.

I stumbled through a retelling of my entire day, careful to leave out the part about the massive breakdown on the beach at lunch, and the face in the water, and, yes, the moving water. They both were excited to hear the part where Darrien pulled me out of the lake, and even more excited when I told them about the "date".

"No wonder Aurelia is so mad!" Pen was beaming.

"You two are the only ones that know, so I would really appreciate it if you wouldn't say anything right now. I don't want anyone making more out of it than there is." Then, it dawned on me. Was *I* making more out of it than there was?

In my excitement, I forgot that I swore I didn't want to get involved with him, with anyone. Thoughts of Mom were swirling in my head. She was destroyed when Dad left. I *never* wanted that to happen to me. Then, another thought occurred to me. He never really asked me out…*I* said "it's a date!"

What if I was blowing this all out of proportion and this was nothing more than a hike through a trail? *Did I totally misinterpret this whole thing so badly?*

"You're so lucky, Cora! All the girls in camp would *kill* to be in your shoes!" Bree's smile was so huge, it broke through my dark thoughts for a brief moment.

"Guys, what if it's really *not* a date? Am I making more out of this than there is? I mean, look at me. I'm not exactly Darrien's type."

A sarcastic scoff radiated from the door. *Aurelia.*

50
Cora

"MIND YOUR OWN BUSINESS Aurelia," Bree's voice sounded from the bed. I glanced over and saw the fire behind her eyes. It had been awhile since B had stepped in when it came to a bully and me. Though, it made me inwardly smile that she wanted to defend me, I knew it was just going to make the situation worse.

"Oh no, don't send your attack dog after me," Aurelia feigned fright and glared at B.

"You're just jealous!" Bree pointed at her.

"Jealous? Me? Of what? He doesn't actually care about her," she flicked a finger in my direction. I placed a hand on B's shoulder, I didn't want Bree to become Aurelia's next target, and this was heading there. But Bree shook off my hand and stood her ground.

"He asked her on a date," Bree crossed her arms in victory and smiled. That didn't faze Aurelia at all.

"Date? Sure. I'll bet that Pearl put him up to it. Those two are as thick as thieves. Don't be surprised if he's not just doing his *job*." She saw the look on my face as it sank in. "Have fun on your 'date' though, by all means. Make sure you get as much out of it as you can, because he won't feel sorry for you all summer."

She turned and sauntered away.

My heart dropped with each stair she hit. *She's right.*

"Cora, don't you believe one word she says. She's just jealous," Pen stated pleadingly.

"You're a wonderful person! Darrien would be lucky to have you!" Bree insisted.

"I'm not going," I uttered. Aurelia was right. It made perfect sense. He's been helping me do my job better all day! It made sense that Pearl would ask him to make sure I knew what I was doing.

165

"Yes, you are!" Bree argued.

"No, I'm not," I stated loudly, glaring at B. "Pen *you* can show me the trails, right?" I tried not to let the disappointment I felt affect me. *You're not Mom,* I repeated to myself.

"Not a chance. You're going with Darrien if I have a drag you there myself!" She and Bree exchanged a knowing glance. *Why don't they get it? This is embarrassing.* But the determined look on their faces made my choice for me. I was going whether I wanted to or not.

"Fine! Fine. I can see when I've been beat. But, I'm going under protest." What better way to make sure things were running smoothly than having Darrien take over things so I didn't look so incompetent. How could I have fooled myself into thinking that I had a chance with him? *I'm such an idiot!*

Pen left to go for a walk, after saying she was coming down with a headache, and Bree went to chat with the girls in her cabin. I was left to get ready for the big "date" alone. I threw on a t-shirt, and stuffed a sweater and water bottle into a backpack. This took all of one minute. I'm not one for make-up and fancy hairstyles, so getting ready takes me literally all of five minutes, if that. Though, my hair somehow managed to look like I had spent hours styling it and my eyes looked like I was wearing bright green contacts. I hoped the t-shirt and jeans would make me look less like I was making an effort. I didn't need to embarrass myself further.

When it was time, I grabbed my backpack and trudged out the door. Aurelia's words hung like a little black cloud over me. *Let's just get this over with.*

51
Darrien

I STOOD IN THE PATH on the way to the girls' side. Just stood there. Indecision and frustration making it impossible to move. What was I going to do? I needed to meet Cora right away, I had to tell Pearl what happened and I had to do something about Lia. But what?

"Darrien?" A quiet voice interrupted my thoughts.

"What?" I screamed.

"Whoa…sorry!" Pen yelped, looking offended and scared.

"Sorry, Penelope. Sorry. I'm just…going." I started to storm off to Pearl's; I was sure she was anxious to know what happened with Aurelia.

"Wait, can I talk to you for a second?" Pen asked. I'm sure that she was summoning all her courage to talk to me, but she picked an epically bad time to do so.

"I really have to go, Pen. I'm sorry." The resignation in my voice bothered me. I had never felt so defeated.

"No, it's okay, I understand…it's just about Cora," she said quietly. I should have kept walking, but did I? Nope.

"What about her?" I replied, and tried to put on a nonchalant expression, but I wasn't sure it was working. I was too upset.

"I had a vision," she revealed. Pen was like an oracle, clairvoyant, or seer. In our world we called her kind a Claire. She was born with the ability to see the future.

"A vision? What kind of vision?" My voice betrayed me and wavered.

"Well, I would like to say it was good, but…it wasn't. I'm worried about her." Her brow furrowed and her lips tightened.

"I don't understand, why Cora?" I asked pointedly.

"Look, I know she's different from the rest of us, unique. I don't know why. That wasn't revealed to me." She eyed me. "I really like her, Darrien.

She's my friend. I don't want to see her get hurt. But I can't tell you what the vision was about. There are…rules." Her voice was weak.

"So why are you telling me this, then, Pen?" Frustration stormed out of me.

"Because I sense a struggle in you, and I just wanted to tell you to…this is embarrassing for me to say to you." I leered at her. "Okay…just…go with your heart, Darrien." She could barely look me in the eyes.

"What?" My jaw dropped.

"Your heart is right, whatever it's telling you. It's right. I've seen it," she pressed.

"I don't know what you're talking about, Pen. What does this have to do with Cora?"

"You know *exactly* what it has to do with her. Don't try to pass that off. You know what I am," she warned, pulling herself up to full height.

"I'm sorry. I've kind of had a day," I apologized.

"Yeah, I can sense that too. I didn't want to upset you. I was just hoping to ease your mind a little, I guess. There's something inside you that's trying to guide you. Call it what you want, fate, destiny, heart, all I'm saying is that you should listen to it." She watched me. I was so unbelievably lost.

"Great, that's great. Thanks," I said tossing my hands in the air.

"Sorry. I guess that wasn't the relief I thought it would be, she apologized, and stared at her fingers.

"It just complicated things a little more," I admitted.

"Or simplifies it," she said. I looked at her, and a sense of relief did come over me. *Did it simplify it? Maybe.*

"Thanks." I smiled. *I might have a direction, now.*

"Hey, that's what I'm here for. At least, that's what I'm here for *now*." I liked Pen. She was a kind soul and, I would guess, a great friend to Cora.

"I guess I'd better get ready for my-"

"Date?" She filled in.

"Yeah. Date." A smile crept across my face.

168

52

Cora

DARRIEN WAS SITTING on a log at the entrance to the trails. He had a walking stick in hand and a backpack on. He was wearing a plain black tee that pulled tight across his chest and blue jeans.

"Hey, Humbug! You ready to hit the trail?" He smiled at me and stood up. His eyes squinted at me through the setting sun, but I could still see the powerful green-blue swimming behind. "Everything okay?" I faked a half smile, surprised by his perceptiveness.

"Sure. Yeah, everything's...great. So, was Pearl happy you were taking me on the trails tonight?" I tried not to make eye contact, hoping it would help me keep my nerve a little longer.

"I didn't tell her, actually." He lifted his eyebrow and gazed at me. "What's up? You look upset." Anger, disappointment, and humiliation all settled in a sour ball in my stomach.

"Come on, Darrien."

His smile faded. He stood up straight and blinked in mock confusion. "What's going on, Cora?" *Like he didn't know.*

I cleared my throat to gain the courage I needed.

"I know what this really is. I know that this is some *job* you've asked to do. You don't need to waste your time helping me out, fixing me, or whatever." The more I thought about it, the more upset I got. I didn't want to admit that I was hurt that this wasn't a date, or at least that I was pretty sure it wasn't. I was mad at him *and* myself. "You think just because you have everyone drooling over you that you have the right to step in where you aren't wanted."

His mouth hung open. I had him. He knew he was caught. When he collected himself, he stood tall. I watched as his face went from shock to anger.

"What are you *talking* about, Cora? What gave you an idea like that?" he shot back.

"I'm not stupid! There's something more going on here. I-"

"No, there's *not!*" He bellowed. His eyes were flaming and his voice was harsh. For an instant, I forgot why I was mad and I actually felt guilty for what I said. The fire was gone. I just stood there with my mouth gaping wide.

"Cora, I asked you to come here because I knew you needed help! That's it! I just wanted to *help!*" He was gesturing wildly, the flame in his eyes burning as his gaze scorched me.

I found my voice again and turned on him.

"Why do you think I *need* help? I never asked for it! Why are you *so* interested in helping me?" *There's more to this than he's telling me, I know it!*

"You're kidding, right? You DO need help, Cora! You can't teach swimming lessons because you have a phobia of the water. You can't get into a boat for the same reason. You need HELP!" He was upset now, voice raised and loud. His expression was dark and heavy, never breaking his hard gaze at me.

"I don't *need* help! I don't *want* help! I'm not a charity case! I can take care of myself. Always have, always will. What makes you think that I need *you?*" I would not back down from him. He was going to hear me.

"Cora," Darrien took a deep, slow breath, clearly struggling to calm himself. He closed the distance between us in a stride, staring hard into my eyes. "Cora, I am not here to fix you. I don't want to fix you. You are the way you are for good reasons. I like *you* the way *you* are. When I look at you, I see someone who is struggling with a fear they have no control over. I don't feel sorry for you, and you aren't a charity case for me. I just want to help you."

His eyes were suddenly gentle and kind, which threw me off. His body seemed relaxed and calm now, and he stood there with a soft, yet intense, expression on his face. My heart ached and wanted to give in, but my head kept telling me otherwise.

Were there things wrong with me that I'd like to fix? Yes, of course. I wanted to fix them really badly. I didn't like being so clumsy, awkward, and fearful. I wanted to be confident. I didn't want to be a freak. I wanted to be normal. I really wanted to swim again. I used to love it. So, *why* was it so hard to ask for help? He was right. I *needed* help.

"Darrien, I-um...I don't know what to say." I couldn't look at him anymore, I was too embarrassed. Again, I was yelling at him when he was just trying to help.

"I'm sorry for yelling. You don't deserve it. But, it's hard for me to ask for help when I've been let down every time I did." My eyes widened, that truth bomb came out of nowhere. He was standing too close, and I was starting to lose my thoughts. "I-uh-just don't know how to trust your intentions, I guess."

I shouldn't have let my feelings run away. I should've known better. I sighed and dropped my shoulders, "I'm sorry for jumping to conclusions. I really am sorry. You have been extremely kind to me, and I owe you more than I can repay. And now I owe you more, because I just yelled at you...again," I admitted, and bit at my lips.

"Maybe it's best if I just head back," I proposed. "Thanks again for your help, and sorry again for...well, all this." I turned and slunk back to my cabin. *Way to go Cora. Way to stay out of your head.*

"Cora, wait!" I paused in my tracks, turned and peered over my shoulder at him. Darrien walked slowly up to me. With every fiber of my being, I struggled to keep my heart in check. *No more.* I won't invest anymore thoughts or feelings...no more.

When Darrien caught up to me, I could see the anger was gone. His gaze circled the trail entrance and fell back on me, the muscles in his jaw working. "Cora, it's a nice evening. It would be a shame to waste it. I would still like to help you out with the trails, if you're up to it."

My heart gave a solid thump in my chest. I couldn't believe that after the things I said, he would still do me a favor. It was kind, *too kind.* I didn't deserve it.

"Umm, no. That's okay, I-are you sure you want to be alone in the forest with a crazy person? I did just yell at you for nothing...again." I tried to smile, but failed.

He lifted a shoulder. "Meh, I can handle your brand of crazy. I will insist that all sharp objects be kept at arm's length from you though, you know, for my safety" A dimple appeared and my resolve weakened. "You ready to head in?"

"Sure, ready." I smiled.

53

Darrien

THAT WASN'T EXACTLY the way that I imagined the start of the night going, but Cora was full of surprises, and she didn't disappoint. I had never had anyone accuse me of being too nice before. If someone would have told that to my brother, Tyde would have laughed in their face. I wasn't known for my soft side back home. I was slightly more militant. I was a soldier, so it came with the job, or at least it was a convenient thing to blame my personality on.

The thing that killed me the most was lying right to her face. I *was* on a job. She had that part right, but I wasn't asked to take her on the trail, so I kept my peace knowing that bit was still the truth.

I couldn't let her know the whole truth. Not yet. I needed her to trust me. I also had to be with her whenever she was in the woods. But, what she didn't know was that I *wanted* to be there. I found myself thinking about her all the time and wanting to see her. The hike was merely an excuse to spend the evening with her alone, one that Pearl wouldn't balk at, and one that I could justify for myself, too. I was *technically* helping her with her job and guarding her at the same time. I was also taking her to my favorite place at camp, and hoping to spend some time alone with her. Pearl probably wouldn't have agreed to that last part.

It didn't help that Cora also looked incredible. Even in her obvious attempt to look casual, her shirt and jeans hugged her in all the right places. My thoughts were anything but pure as we made our way down the trail.

54
Cora

IT WAS A BEAUTIFUL EVENING. The sun was sinking below the tree line, setting off a sky painted in warm pinks and oranges. The clouds looked like cotton candy against the sunset, spun sugar good enough to eat. The sweet scent from the lake floated through the evening air, perfuming the summer sunset perfectly. I had honestly never seen such a sight.

Though, the start of the evening was far from perfect Darrien was in good spirits. I was plodding along behind him, as we ventured down a trail into the forest. Thick brush ran on both sides of it, similar to the trail we were on earlier that day. I could see the sky through the tops of the trees above us. They reached up with all their might, their tips pointing out the stars as they winked into sight.

"This trail is a bit longer than the others around, but there is a fantastic site at the end of it I want to show you," Darrien said, his voice unaffected by the hike. He smiled warmly, and then turned to venture further down the path.

"Thanks," I said, my breathing heavy. A ball of guilt churned in my stomach, sending a sour taste into my mouth. I thought of all the stupid things that I had said to him, and made a promise to myself to keep my temper under control. Darrien was such a great guy, and if I didn't get a hold of myself, I'd never be able to keep him as a friend, much less anything more. *No! Nothing more, damn it!*

The sky was beginning to darken. The cotton candy turned dark blues and purples as the last hints of pink disappeared with the sun. The night air slowly crept across my skin, leaving a trail of goosebumps in its stead, and I was forced to retrieve the sweater from my pack. The sky seemed to open as we neared our destination. The stars looked so close, I felt like I could reach up and touch them.

Just then, Darrien led me around a sharp corner in the trail. I could feel the grin spread across my face as I looked over the place he had taken me to. In front of me was a clearing with a pretty little stream running through it. There were thick trees and bushes all the way around it, and the ground was covered in grass and wild flowers. Larger rocks stood in the stream, causing a lazy trickling sound. In the evening light, the water sparkled like thousands of tiny diamonds dancing over the rocks.

"Oh, *wow*! It's beautiful!" I gushed. My eyes scanned the area around me as I followed Darrien into the clearing. There was so much to see, even in the thinning light. Darrien took off his pack and pulled a blanket from it. He spread it out over the ground by the stream and sat down. He looked up at me expectantly. I hesitated a moment and then sat down on the blanket too, making sure to keep a distance from him.

"Thank you so much for bringing me here." I took a deep breath in. The smell of the wild flowers was intoxicating. I had never experienced a perfume like that before, both sweet and fresh. Darrien stirred next to me, getting close enough that I could feel the warmth from his skin even through my bunny hug.

"I discovered this place a few weeks ago. I thought you might like it." His dimples deepened.

The moon was glowing bright now, and it lit the little clearing with a shiny light. Its silvery rays shone on everything bringing an otherworld feel to the place. Darrien's eyes twinkled in the moonlight, and his skin glowed, as if he somehow absorbed the moon's light and shone it back. I wanted, more than anything, to be close to him, but at the same time I kept my distance. *You don't want him*, I reminded myself.

Darrien's eyes were far away. He stared up at the sky with a look that suggested his mind was elsewhere. I followed his gaze. The stars were twinkling brightly. I wished I could reach out and take one for myself. We sat there in silence and watched them. A couple shot across the sky, and I made a wish.

The night air got a bit cooler, as a breeze picked up. I shivered slightly.

"Are you cold?" Darrien asked. His eyes had shifted to my own.

"No, I'm fine. Just a little breeze, that's all." I ventured a smile, not allowing the calm I felt to escape through my goosebumps. I wasn't ready to leave this spot because of a little chill.

"No, you're cold, Humbug. Here." He pulled a jacket out of his pack and wrapped it around my shoulders. He moved closer, making sure the jacket was snug against me, and he didn't move away. My body tingled the closer he got to me, and yet, somehow, he made me feel calm and relaxed enough to just be. Be myself, be calm…just to sit and be. I never had that with anyone before.

"Darrien, I wish I had the words to describe how much I needed this, and how much I appreciate you bringing me here." Our eyes met and my heart kicked at my chest. My head and my heart were in obvious conflict about Darrien until…he wrapped his arm around me and pulled me closer. I could feel the warmth from his body penetrate my chill. My heart pumped new life into me, as I felt blood rush through my veins. I shivered again, but this time it felt good.

I struggled between my logical side, which knew that this was just going to lead to me getting hurt, and the part that knew that I wanted this anyway. I wanted to be close to someone. Never, in my wildest dreams, did I think I would be facing this problem. Darrien was not part of the plan, but I liked it.

Why is this so hard for me? Why did I push people away, when really, deep down I just wanted someone to care about me? Darrien, may or may not care, but it shouldn't matter. I should be willing to give it a chance. Right?

"I'm really glad you like it here. I hope you'll come back with me." Darrien's eyes flitted to mine. My heart pounded so loud, I thought for sure he could hear it. He shifted his weight and I felt his warm fingers thread through mine. I bit my lips to keep myself under control, to ignore the sharp pang of need that was running through me. "Cora, I know that we got off to a rough start…"

"Uh…." was all I could choke out. I tore my eyes away and stared at the stream.

"I'm glad I was able to show you this place. It's nice to share this with someone." I felt new heat rush to my cheeks, grateful for the dim light so Darrien couldn't see.

"I…ah…am really happy you chose me." The fluidity of my words surprised me. I gasped as his arm pulled me closer and his eyes connected with mine, and I mean *connected*. His dimples deepened as his smile spread. My heart was officially out of control now, and I didn't care one bit. It was like nothing I had ever felt before. I loved it. He felt warm and safe and scary, all at the same time. I let my head fall and rest against his shoulder. I could feel the wall of excuses fall.

His warm breath fell on my face as Darrien rested his chin on my head. I could feel the unsteady rise and fall to his chest. Knowing that he was just as affected by our closeness as I was, was a rush. I didn't understand it, but I liked it. I turned my face up to look at him. He lifted his head off me and gazed down. I could feel the pull to him, like a magnet. He wasn't breathing, and neither was I. I wanted to feel his lips on mine more than anything. He slowly lowered to me, moving so that I was pressed closer to his chest. His

175

heart was beating as fast and hard as mine. An ache I'd never known before filled me. I wanted him. I needed him. But, suddenly, he rocked back away from me.

"It's getting late. We should probably be heading back to camp," he whispered. In Darrien's soft words, I could hear a mixture of sadness and excitement in his voice as he stood from the blanket.

"Okay...sure. I suppose you're right." I smiled halfheartedly. I wasn't prepared for the hangover from all the anticipation. My body felt weighed down and monumentally disappointed. My mind was relieved that someone had sense not to start anything. I was disappointed in myself that it wasn't me. My body was at war with itself. I wasn't prepared for that, either.

Darrien put out a hand to help me up. *Such a gentleman.* He pulled me against his chest as I stood. I fit perfectly into him, like we were made for each other. His arms were warm and strong as he held me. I didn't want to move, or to let go.

He pulled away, just enough to look at me. His hands ran up my arms, leaving fiery trails across my skin.

"You know, you're nothing like I expected." He smiled at me as his hands slowly crept off my arms and to my hips.

"I'm not?" I was getting lost in the sensation of his- "Wait. What do you mean?"

"I mean, well...the first time we met wasn't exactly the best first impression. That's all." He looked at his feet and shuffled the grass with his toe.

"Oh, yeah, I suppose not. Well, you weren't what I was expecting either, then, I guess. I thought you were a total jerk for the Bree thing. I guess you've turned out better than I thought." I smiled, "What were you expecting? In me, I mean." I lifted an eyebrow at him.

"Oh, I don't know. When I was told to help you, I was expecting someo-"

"Whoa! What do you mean, you were *told* to help me? You said you did this all on your own! That's what you said. Right?" My voice got slightly shrill and angry at the end there. Aurelia's mocking voice came rushing to my ears. *"I'll bet that Pearl put him up to this. Those two are as thick as thieves. Don't be surprised if he's not just doing his job."*

Darrien was staring hard at the ground. I pulled away from him.

"I did say that," he started and nodded. I stared hard at him, waiting. "Uh, okay. I was asked to watch out for you. But-"

"You *lied* to me! All this time I was feeling guilty for the way that I yelled at you, that I had jumped to conclusions! But I was right!" I yelled.

176

"No! It's not like that. It's not as bad as you think." He grabbed the back of his head and pulled on his hair.

"Just take me back." I grabbed my pack and started walking in the direction of the trail. I'd had enough. I knew this was coming, and I totally ignored my intuition. Sure enough, I got hurt.

"Wait, Cora. Please let me explain," he pleaded and ran to catch up with me.

"There's nothing to explain, Darrien! Were you asked to help me out?"

"Yes, but-"

"There's no 'but' here. I thought…that you *wanted* to help me, not that you were being *forced* to! I don't get it. Why the charade? What's the point? Why not just be honest?"

"It's not easy to explain, Cora," he plead. He wouldn't even look at me!

"Whatever, Darrien. Just take me back." *I'm done.* I felt betrayed and hurt, but most of all, I felt *stupid*. I knew it would happen and I fell anyway. Darrien was rubbing the back of his neck as he started down the trail. He was silent all the way back, and so was I. I wasn't interested in an explanation anymore. It really didn't matter what he said. He lied to me.

I didn't say anything to him when we arrived at the end of the trail. I strode straight for the cabin. I didn't turn around for second, even when I heard footsteps coming up fast behind me.

"Wait, Cora." I would have kept going, but he grasped my arm and turned me around. I stared at him. There was a lot that I wanted to say, but I kept my mouth closed. Darrien started, "Okay. Yes, I was asked to watch over you. And in the beginning, I did it because I was told to, but things have changed. I…I started to get fee-"

"Stop right there! You expect me to believe that? How am I supposed to trust you? I should have known better. Thank you for reminding me why I don't trust people, and why I'm better off alone. Thank you for the walk, the info about the trails, and for taking on my water lessons. I appreciate that. I really do. But from here on in, that's as far as it goes. I'll see you tomorrow. Goodnight." I turned and walked into the cabin without sparing him another look.

Have you learned your lesson yet, Cora?

55
Darrien

THERE WAS SO MUCH that I wanted to say to her, but I couldn't get the words to come out right. After watching her stumble up the path and slam the door in my face, I resigned myself to the fact that it wasn't going to happen that night. I let her sleep on it and hoped that things got better in the morning. I had something more important to do in the meantime.

There was a reason that I was so anxious to get back to camp. When we were out in the woods, I sensed something out there with us. I couldn't put my finger on it then, but now that I was back at camp, I knew what it was. *A Siren.* I sensed the blood in her. They have a different feel to them; it's not like regular blood, but thicker and stronger somehow. I should have known that out there, but my mind just wasn't on lookout when Cora was around. She...distracts me. I ran my fingers through my hair and gripped tight. *Idiot.*

I made my way back to the stream to see if there were any traces of the Siren there. Nothing that I could see in the fading light lead me to believe that my hunch was right. Frustration drove me to seek out the falls again, where Cora nearly was lost to the Siren the first time. I knew what I sensed, but I needed proof.

As I approached, silence met me. *Why don't I hear anything?* When I approached the pond, I was astonished. It was as if it had been abandoned decades ago. Stagnant water filled the hole. Where the falls should have been, a trickle of filthy water dripped into the mucky pool.

I didn't understand. I was there a few days ago, and there was a whole pool and waterfall. It was beautiful. Looking around now, there was no way that this place could have looked like that. Decay was built up on the ground. The odor in the air was acrid. I was looking at years of neglect.

What happened here? The only way a pool could manifest itself, like it did that night, was if it was calling to a Siren. There was a Siren there that night, but she was already in the pool. Instead, the pool called Cora. Why? Or more disturbingly...*how?* Mer were not susceptible to Siren calls; only humans and other Sirens were.

Then, I asked myself a question I never thought I would have to.

Cora was Mer, wasn't she?

56
Cora

IN THE MORNING, I woke with a headache and a sinking feeling that something bad had happened. Then, I remembered my "date" with Darrien.

I pulled myself out of bed and to the bathroom. My shower felt amazing; the warm water seemed to revive my drowsy senses, fully waking me. The other girls were still asleep when I came out, so I decided to go for a walk. Maybe it would bring me some clarity, or distract me, at the very least.

Out the cabin door and to the beach I walked. The water just seemed to call to me. There was a part of me that wanted to be close to it. I didn't remember feeling like that before, even when I loved swimming. It was strange that, with the phobia I had, I would be drawn to water. But, strange as it was, I found myself standing at the edge of the lake anyway. I took a deep breath in, and let the calm fall over me.

"Good morning, Cora!" A friendly voice interrupted. Pearl stood on the front porch of her cabin, coffee cup in hand and bathrobe on.

"Morning, Pearl!" I said, happy it was her voice and not Darrien's.

"What are you doing up so early? Everything okay?" She waved me over to the porch. I smiled at her and walked over.

"Everything's good. I just woke up early, that's all." A half smile crept across the corner of my face. Pearl's smile faded as she looked at me.

"You sure? If you need a chat, my door is always open." She gave me the kindest smile. It made me want to talk, but I bit my lip instead.

"Thanks, Pearl, but I'm fine. I'd better get going. I've got to wake the team." I smiled and turned to go.

"Oh! Cora? I was wondering if you would like to take Bree into town tomorrow. I know it's your day off. Bree was talking to me about the shops, and she said something about a gift for your mom?" *Right.* I had completely forgotten about that.

"That sounds great. Thanks! Tomorrow, you said?" I was already looking forward to some sister time with Bree.

"Tomorrow, right after lunch. Darrien will drive you in!" I froze. *Oh, no. Not Darrien.*

"Darrien?" I didn't mean to screech. My mind raced for an excuse not to have to go with him.

"Oh, uh, that's not necessary. I don't want to bother anyone. We can wait until you or Anne run in for something. It can wait. It's no problem. No rush!" I wanted it to end right there, and even though I started backing towards my cabin Pearl wasn't about to let it go.

"Nonsense! Darrien has some things that he needs to get done in town too, it works out perfectly! I'll hear no more! He'd be glad to do it!" And with that, she glided back into her cabin and closed the door. *Great. Now I had to spend an hour in a closed space with Darrien.*

The rest of the day was…awkward. I had to break the news to Pen and Bree about the "date" last night. They were confused and sympathetic, but most importantly, they were just as mad at Darrien as I was. Then, I had to spend two lessons with him and the girls.

During our canoe lesson, he tried to talk to me, but the girls were a great diversion and he never got the chance. I couldn't see what more there was to say. I mean, if he was told to help me, whatever, but why lie about it? And why let me think there was something more going on between us? That's what hurt the most.

The day dragged on and on. Every time I let my mind drift, it was on Darrien. It made my heart pound hard when I thought of how close we were to kissing. I really thought- it didn't matter what I thought. *It's over.*

At supper, I sat down at the Lead table alone, and was about to dig into yet another amazing meal by Anne, when the smell of rain invaded my senses. *Darrien.*

"Can I talk to you for just a minute? Before anyone gets here?" Darrien's voice was low and urgent.

"Fine. Get it over with," I grumbled. Whatever he had to say was not going to change my mind about him.

"Look, I know you're upset with me for not telling you the truth about *why* I was helping you out. I did start to do things to help because I was asked, but I kept doing things for you because I *wanted* to. If I didn't *want* to, I wouldn't have." And with that, he got up and left. I wasn't even given a chance to respond.

Something still wasn't sitting right with me, though. I couldn't put my finger on it, but there was something he wasn't saying. I could see it in his eyes. When he was confident about what he was talking about, he looked me in the eye. He couldn't maintain eye contact with me when I called him out on being told to help me.

The rest of the day went by with no interruptions from Darrien. Even at swimming lessons, he left me alone, thank goodness. My thoughts were confused and my feelings were...well, they were all over the place, too. I needed some help...and the only person that knew me better than myself was Bree. So, after supper, Bree and I went for a walk together. I was in desperate need of some sister time.

"I'm really sorry about your date with Darrien, Cor," Bree said, watching the path in front of us closely. I decided to take her down a trail, and familiarize myself with it before taking the team down. I figured if it was still light out, we'd be okay. The path looked clear and easy to trek.

"Bree, I'm just mad about it. I mean, I thought he was being genuine with me." I tripped over a root and stumbled a bit. Bree caught my arm and tried to steady me, but ended up falling on me instead. We landed in a heap on the ground, giggling.

"Well, thanks for the save!" I teased and laughed as I got to my feet.

"Sorry, I tried! I'm just no Darrien, I guess." She laughed to herself, then stopped when she saw me glaring at her. "Sorry, it just slipped out."

My shoulders sagged, "It's fine. I'm just frustrated that I got duped, that's all. I thought after everything Mom went through, I was smarter than that." I grabbed Bree's hand and helped her off the ground.

"You're not Mom, Cora. So Darrien is a jerk. No big deal. It's not like you were in love with him or anything." She shrugged and looked at me.

"No...not in love, of course not! How could I be? We barely know each other." Bree said nothing, but I couldn't stop talking for some reason.

"I mean, I did like him. I liked his company and the way he made me feel. He looked at me differently last night, but that was what he was told to do, right?" I sighed. What did love feel like? My heart sank a little, wondering if I'd ever know.

"You sure he wasn't telling you the truth? You know, he *did* help you get out of doing things that you are terrified of- which is great. I could see Pearl asking him to help with that. But, taking you to that place with the stream...I can't see Pearl asking him to take you on a romantic walk like that. That would just be creepy." She made a grossed out face and looked at me with those big blues. My mouth dropped open. That never occurred to me, not once.

Bree was right. I could understand Pearl wanting Darrien to help me out with camp stuff, but not taking me to that spot in the woods, at night...alone. So, was Darrien honestly interested in me? *I'm really confused now.*

182

I moaned. "Now, I don't know what to think." I scrubbed my face with my hands. "I'm tired. Can we sit for a second?" There was a fallen log on the side of the trail. I plunked down on it and patted a spot next to me for Bree. She sat herself down next to me.

"Well, all I know is that whatever Darrien is doing with you, is *really* ticking off Aurelia. I didn't tell you this, but I was heading back to the cabin this afternoon for some sunscreen and I ended up overhearing a conversation." I lifted an eyebrow. She raised her right hand and put a serious face on. "Honestly, I stumbled on Aurelia and Pearl talking." I felt my eyebrows hit my hairline. "Yeah, I didn't let them know I was listening, so it was a bit sneaky of me, sorry, I'm not sorry." I chuckled lightly.

"Anyway," Bree continued. "Aurelia was saying something that was really ticking off Pearl. No surprise there, but they mentioned your name a couple of times- and Darrien's."

"What? Like how?" *What would Pearl be saying to Aurelia about me?*

"I'm not sure. I didn't catch most of it. But, there was something about Aurelia not telling anyone about something. And Pearl said the word 'blackmail'." *Blackmail?* "Aurelia talked about Darrien like they used to date. She's super mad that he's spending time with you."

"You didn't hear anything else? Something a little clearer?" I asked.

"They were talking really quietly and checked around a lot to make sure they weren't seen, so I missed a bit of what they were saying. I did catch Darrien's name a couple times, though, and something about a 'job.' That's it. What do you think it means?"

"I have no idea. I'm just as confused as you are. Nice spy work though, B. I'm impressed!" I smiled at her and nodded my approval. I *knew* there was something going on. Darrien wasn't telling me everything, and it seemed that Aurelia and Pearl were in on it, too. I'm not going to get any answers out of them though.

"It's getting a bit late," I turned to Bree. "We should head back." I was looking at the sky; the clouds had rolled in a thick blanket of grey. Once the sun was low, it was going to get dark fast.

"Aww, I don't want to go back yet. Can we go a bit further?" Bree pled. She had her hands clasped under her chin, with a big grin and puppy dog eyes. It worked a lot better when she was little, not fifteen, but still... *how can I say no to that?*

"Alright, just a little further. I don't have a flashlight with me, and we won't be able to see our way back in the dark. I don't want to be stuck out here all night...do you?" I stared pointedly at her.

"Nope, not at all." She grinned at me and took the lead on the path. The evening air filled me up with renewed energy as we ventured further into the forest. But soon, night crept quickly through the woods, and it was catching up to us.

"Bree, we need to turn around. It's getting dark." I called up the trail. "Bree?" *Where is she? She was just here!*

"Bree! Don't play, this isn't funny!" I scolded. My heart gave a frightened thump and fell to my toes. She wasn't on the path anymore.

"Bree! Answer me! Bree!" I shouted.

"Yeah! I'm right here! Jeez!" She appeared out of the woods right behind me.

"Don't DO that! What's the matter with you? Where were you?" I demanded.

"You won't *believe* what I found! Look at this!" She opened her palm and revealed a little tile. It was green, but when she moved it around, it changed to blue. "Isn't it pretty?" Her face was beaming.

"It is...I guess. It looks familiar. Where'd you find it?" I asked. *I wish I could remember where I've seen it before.*

"There's a trail of them back here! Come, look!" She scampered back up the trail to where she came out of the bushes. She pulled back the bush and pointed. There it was, a small trail of shining green tiles, running like a mosaic river through the bushes. It was beautiful, but strange.

"How did you even see this?" I wondered out loud, as my eyes followed down the stone path.

"It just caught my attention. Want to follow it?" *Whoa.* I knew her excitement was going to get away from her. A trip through the woods searching for who-knows-what couldn't end well.

"I don't think so, Bree. I bet there used to be a building around here at one time, and that's why these are here. Plus, just in case you still want to find out, it is getting too late. We won't be able to see these tiles for very long, anyway- and then we'll really be lost. We should head back." I turned around to go and I heard it....music. I froze. I knew that tune. My heart leapt into my throat. Bree was humming it. She was humming Dad's song.

"Bree...how do you know that song?"

"What song? What are you talking about?" She looked at me with innocent eyes. They changed to pleading ones in a flash.

"I really want to follow the path," she begged, "just for a little bit. It's not getting *that* dark out. Look, the sky is even clearing!"

The song was getting louder. But how could that be? I turned around. *It has to be Bree.* But when I looked at her, she was standing there waiting for my answer, and she wasn't humming.

"Can't you hear that?" I questioned. Alarm bells were going off in my head. My heart was racing.

184

"Hear what? Can we go?" She was vibrating with anticipation.

Where was it coming from? *It can't be*...I walked over to the tiled path and pulled the bushes back. The melody wound its way down the path and all around me. The music was coming from whatever was at the end of that mosaic. The sound reached inside me and pulled. I felt something in my core tug, and my body moved forward. I leaned into the bush, trying to get closer.

"I don't...know...Bree." It was like talking through a fog. The words were coming out, but they weren't registering with my brain. Part of me knew that we needed to get back to the cabins, but the other part of me needed to follow the sound.

I need to know what's down there....

I pulled the bushes back further, stepped off the trail and onto the broken tile floor.

Everything seemed to glow in the evening light. The music got stronger, enticing me to follow. The sound was like nothing I had ever heard, like a thousand ethereal voices working as one. I felt another tug. It was getting forceful. Somewhere inside me, a cord was being fastened, and as the melody grew louder, the cord grew and pulled harder.

B had to be hearing this.

"Wow, this is so cool, Cora! I can't believe we're doing this!" She was loving this. I wished I could be happier for her, but the melody was getting so loud, it was hard hearing her. But, she didn't seem to be affected by it at all.

It can't just be me.

The pull was so strong, I gave into it and went down the path, floating on the melody. There was nothing but the music, nothing but the song...then floating through the woods came the words:

Together they're born, in beauty and grace,
To save all our souls from a malicious race.
Our salvation rests in their loving devotion.
Together they stand, to save our ocean.

I remembered then. The words to Dad's song. He rarely sang the words; usually, he just hummed the tune. How did Dad's song find its way into the middle of the woods?

Bree was wandering down the mosaic path further and further. I could feel myself yelling for her to slow down, but I couldn't hear my voice because the music was so loud.

"Bree, come back!" My lips moved, but no sound came out. The song beat inside my head like a bass drum, pounding and vibrating. The pressure and the pain was reaching a point I couldn't manage anymore. I collapsed on

185

the ground, unable to take another step and threw my hands over my ears. It didn't matter, because it was *inside* my head.

My blood chilled. *It's coming from inside me.*

I couldn't see Bree anymore. Ice cold blood rushed through my veins. I forced myself off the cold mosaic floor. Where was she? I was stumbling. My head was pounding, and I was seeing stars. I was so dizzy, it was difficult staying upright.

"Bree? Wait for me!" I knew I was saying it, maybe even yelling it, but I couldn't hear anything but the song.

"Bree! Come back! Come back!"

I started running in a desperate try to get away from the music. *Bree come back, please.* Finally, the sound overwhelmed me. My dizziness amped up, the stars closed in, and the beautiful mosaic came fast and hard for me.

57
Darrien

CORA WOULDN'T TALK to me all day. She barely looked at me.

Maybe this is the out that you need. Make a clean break.

I don't want a clean break. I care about her. I don't want her thinking I'm dishonest.

You are dishonest.

Thanks.

This is a good thing. You can go about your job and get her home, with no feelings involved.

How am I supposed to do my job if she doesn't trust me? I have to get her to swim. How am I going to do that if she won't come near me?

You could just drown her, you know. That would do the trick.

Yes, it would, but it would also destroy any kind of trust that I have built up with her.

I thought we just established there was no trust left. Nothing to lose!

Zale said to teach *her, not to drown her.*

He also didn't say to fall for her.

True.

So, what are you going to do, then?

Try again. She doesn't deserve for one more person in her life to betray her like that. I'll figure out a way. I won't drown her.

Good luck with that.

I decided that it was time to try to talk to Cora alone. Besides, it was dark, which meant that it was time for my guard duty, anyway.

When I got to the girls' side, I saw Bree coming out of a trail. Her eyes were glassy, her face was expressionless, and she was walking as if in a trance. She went straight to her cabin and closed the door. I watched around to see if anyone else came out of the bush, but there was no one. I was just about to go and see if she was okay when I overheard a couple of girls from Cora's team talking.

"Was Cora at supper?"

"Yeah, but I haven't seen her since. Have you?"

"No. She said she was going to meet us at the beach later, but she never showed up."

"That doesn't seem like her."

I didn't stay around for the rest of the conversation. I dove down the trail Bree came out of.

Damn it! She went into the woods without me!

There wasn't a doubt in my mind that she went with Bree, and something happened.

My heart was pumping as I crashed through the bushes. *Where is she?* I raced as fast as I could, listening and watching for any sign of her. The trail didn't lead to the falls, but that was no guarantee that she wasn't heading in that direction anyway. Maybe that was the safest bet. That's when I heard it. *The lullaby. That can't be good.*

My first instinct was to follow it. My instincts were rarely wrong, so I went with it. I broke off the path and into the thick bush. In a few seconds, the ground changed from broken branches and dead leaves to a sea of turquoise and teal tiles. *What the hell?* The lullaby was louder here, and I followed it. It wasn't long before I found her.

"Cora!" I bolted up to her and gently lifted her head off the ground. She was out cold. "What happened to you?" The lullaby was staggeringly loud, and almost unbearable. I fought the urge to plug my own ears, and raced away from there as quickly as I could with Cora cradled in my arms.

I pressed Cora close to my chest. Her rapid breathing slowed down as we got further away from the song. I stopped and checked her when her breathing returned to normal. Her eyes were pinched closed, as if she were in pain, but I couldn't see anywhere that she might be injured. I sat down, keeping her against me, not wanting to wake her. Her hair was wet with perspiration, likely from pain, I realized. I gently tucked it behind her ear.

I've got you, Humbug.

I picked her up and carried her back to camp as quickly as I could. As luck would have it, as I stepped quietly and carefully out of the woods, Pearl was doing an inspection of the shower rooms. I discreetly called her over.

"What happened?" She screeched.

"Don't wake her! I found her like this. She went down a trail with Bree, I think."

"Let's get her into the cabin. The others girls are doing some work for me in the office, so they won't be in there." She ran for Cora's cabin, opening the door for me.

"Alright." I lifted her up the stairs and into the cabin. We set her gently on her bed.

"What are we going to do now? She's going to wonder how she got back here," I said, watching Pearl.

"She doesn't know you found her?" she whispered.

"No. She was out when I got to her," I said in a low voice.

"You go, I'll take care of her." She started taking off Cora's shoes.

"What are you going to do?" Concern filled my voice, more than I wanted to show Pearl.

"I'm going to get her into some clean clothes, and there's no need for you to stay and watch. Now go!" she insisted. I wanted to stay. I wanted to make sure she was okay, but Pearl was right.

"I'll wait outside." I headed for the door.

"Fine," she said, as she busied herself over Cora.

"This isn't good, Pearl," I stated.

"I know, Darrien. I know. Now go." I stepped out of the cabin, into the night air. Pearl would take care of Cora. My head buzzed. I needed to know what I was dealing with. I couldn't protect her against an enemy I didn't know. I needed to get to the bottom of it. *Now.* So, I headed back down the lullaby trail.

I followed the tile mosaic, past where I found Cora, and deeper into the bush. There was no lullaby now; it was quiet. Further in, I could hear it before I could see it…a waterfall. *No, it can't be.*

There it was, fresh and luscious like before. The pool was full of clean water that cascaded into it from the waterfall. The putrid sight I saw before was gone. I went to the edge of the water and looked down. It looked harmless enough, but I knew it wasn't. The last time Cora was there, she was almost taken by a Siren.

This was a dangerous spot, very dangerous. I gazed into the deep center of the pond, and out from the depths came a figure. I jumped back from the edge, as she rose to just below the surface. When I looked again, it was as if we were two sides of a mirror.

"Midira," I spat.

"King's Guard," she said, her deep voice sounding as if it came from far away, like an echo inside my head.

"What do you want, Siren Queen?" I demanded.

"I want…what you want," she teased. *Cora.*

"You can't have her," I growled.

"Neither can you, my dear," she hissed. My anger flared red.

"I won't let you have her," I threatened. *There's no way I'm losing Cora to this monster.*

"Oh, my dear, sweet boy, I already have her. I have something she wants, something she'll do *anything* to get back. It's only a matter of time." Her voice rang out inside my head. It almost hurt, though I wouldn't let her see that.

"What do you have?" I demanded.

"I've already said too much. I have to leave some of the work to you. It's not very fun for me to just *give* you everything," she sang.

"This isn't a game, Midira." I wished I could reach into the water and strangle her with my bare hands, but it wasn't my territory, and her power was potent there.

"Oh, it's a game for me." She smiled her sharp-toothed smile.

"Stay away from her."

"Now, there is nothing you can do to make me stay away from her…she's family."

"What?"

"Oh, you don't know?" She was enjoying this. "Oops, I guess I've said too much, then."

"You're lying! She's nothing like you!" I was bellowing now.

"Maybe not…yet. But I'll change all that."

"You're going to have to get through me, first," I threatened.

Midira rose out of the water. Her long lithe body was slick with the water. She looked Mer in that she had a build similar to a human, but that was it. Her skin was a sick green and she wore a tight dress that barely covered anything, that clung to her body. Her sea weed colored hair hung down almost to her toes in long waves. Her angry eyes were pits of darkness unlike anything that I had ever seen. Even though she was a stunning dark beauty, it was lost on me. She was the reason my parents were killed and I would not stand by and watch anyone else I cared about be taken from me because of her.

Midira smiled and flicked her finger. Water shot out of the pond like a spear, and hit me square in the chest. Throwing me hard against a tree, I banged my head against its thick trunk. It stunned me, but not before I got off a shot myself. I reached for the water in the pond and pulled it up as high as I could.

Midira fell from her watery perch and landed on the side of the pond, *hard*. She lifted her head and screamed at me. Rage-filled black eyes glared at me from behind her deep green hair. I ran for her. A deadly anger consumed me. My power was humming in my veins, aching to be unleashed. I could feel every bit of water around me, and all of Midira's blood, too. I smiled and summoned it to me. She felt the pull, and her eyes hit me hard. She screamed, a blood-curdling sound.

From out of the water sprang three more Sirens. They were in full battle gear, and were ready for a fight. A Siren's battle gear consisted of a tunic made from the skin of a kraken, and was nearly impenetrable. They had a hard helmet that was pinched and sharp from front to back, capable of slicing through bone. One of them held a long spear; its tip glinted in the night light. I knew from experience that all their blades and weapons were poisoned. The second Siren was whipping around two small blades, and the third, a long sword.

They hissed and spat through their needle-like teeth. I smiled. The guard with the spear came at me first. I dispensed of her hand in a bloody burst before she reached me. She screamed, but kept coming. Unable to hold her spear, she dropped low and launched herself at me. Her full body flew through the air, right at me.

In poor form, as I should have expected, the others came around to attack me from behind. I held on to Midira fast. I wasn't letting go of the Siren Queen. If I could end this tonight, I would. I reached for the first guard's blood, and pulled it from her in one movement. Her body shuddered mid-air, as a red mist lifted from her skin. She dropped like a dead fish, her battle cry dying on her lips. *One down, two to go.*

The other two hesitated for a second after seeing what happened to their sister. I turned my eyes on them and grinned, making sure they knew their fate if they wanted to continue this.

Midira screamed, which woke them both up again. I was expending a lot of energy on holding Midira. I knew I couldn't take out both guards at the same time. I searched the area for something to help, *anything*. When my eyes landed on the tree I crashed into, I had a plan.

When the second one jumped for me, I threw out a wave of water from the pool. It crashed into her and sent her spinning toward the tree. Her head knocked hard against it. *Two down, one to go.* But before I could turn to find the last one, she was already on me.

She jumped on my back, and as I swung to knock her off, the tip of her sword cut deep into my arm. I cried out as the pain made its way up my arm. I tried to hold on to Midira, but the guard on my back took advantage of my moment of weakness and stabbed me in the leg. When the second stab came, I lost Midira. The guard tumbled off me and turned to come back and finish the job. With the last bit of energy I had left, I pulled enough water and blood from her that she fell unconscious. She hit the ground with a loud smack.

"She'll be mine, King's Guard, and there nothing you can do to stop that," Midira's voice teased from the water. I summoned the water and blasted the pool with the last remaining energy I had. Darkness grew from all sides. My last thought was of Cora.

58
Cora

CORA? CORA? *Buzzy bugs, buzzing around me. Buzz. Buzz. Wait, not bugs. There are no bugs.*

My eyes opened slowly. Hovering above me was a set of bright eyes.

"Cora? You okay? It's time to get up. You'll be late!" As if Pen's voice wasn't enough, she was shaking me, too.

"Hmm? What?" Sleep was still wrapped tight around me. I tried to think through the thick fog. *What time is it?*

"It's almost eight! You need to wake your team up in, like, five minutes!" *My team? My team! Crap!*

I shook off my dreamy state and sat up in bed. *Wow, last night was a mess! What happened? Wait, how did I get back here?*

I didn't remember how I got to bed, but I was dressed in my pajamas. The last thing I remembered was standing on a tile path- and there was the song! It was so loud, it hurt. That's all I remembered. I must have passed out from the pain. *I need to talk to Bree*, now.

I hurried through getting my clothes on, and bolted out the door to the Orange cabin. I threw open the door, yelled a quick and loud "Get up! Shower! Dress! Let's move!" at the girls, slammed the door shut again, then raced to the Red cabin for Bree. I didn't bother knocking on the door; I just tossed it open. The cabin was clear. Pen must have had them up and ready early this morning. *Where are they?* I ran to the shower room, in hopes they were still getting ready, but no luck there. *This is crazy. Where are they?*

"Bree! Bree!" Panic and desperation overruled the impracticality of just yelling her name. The chances of her hearing me were-

"Yeah? You okay?" Bree came walking up the path to the cabin.

"Are *you* okay? What happened last night?" I demanded.

"What are you talking about?" she questioned, staring at me like I'd gone crazy.

"What do you *mean*, what am I talking about? We went for a walk in the woods. I don't remember getting back to the cabin, and yet, I wake up this morning in my bed and dressed in pajamas! How did that happen?" I asked. Bree looked at me with her mouth open.

"Cora, you're scaring me! How can you *not* remember getting ready for bed?"

"I don't know, okay? I don't remember anything after we started following that mosaic pathway in the woods. What happened?" I ran my hands through my hair, my breathing was shallow and fast, I knew what a panic attack felt like and I was seriously close to having one. Nothing was making sense.

What can't I remember?

"What path? Are you sure you're okay? You look a little…frazzled." Her eyes went from scared to concerned in a flash.

I'm not crazy! I'm not!

"What do you mean, what path?" I shouted. "*You* found it! You're the one that wanted to follow it so badly! Remember? *Please* tell me you remember," I pled and grabbed her arms. This was not at all what I was expecting.

What the hell is going on here?

"Cora, you need to calm down. Take a deep breath. Listen to me," she said, releasing my hands from her arms and now gripping them in her hands. Bree's expression was serious as she looked intently into my eyes.

"There was no tile path," she said in calming tones. I opened my mouth to protest, but she clamped a hand over it. I glared at her over her palm, but allowed her to continue.

"We went for a walk down the trail. The sun was setting and it was cloudy. You said it was going to get dark quickly. We didn't have a flashlight and were worried about getting lost, so, we went back. We said goodnight and went back to our cabins." Bree was completely serious.

What? No!

The song…it was so loud, how could she not remember that? Then, I remembered that Bree couldn't hear the melody at all. But that still didn't explain why she didn't remember the tile mosaic. She was the one that discovered it!

Her hand loosened around my mouth, slowly removing itself from my lips. Bree watched me carefully. I tried to calm down, but frustration was getting to me.

"But," I interjected as soon as her hand was clear of my face, "there was this tile mosaic on the ground. You found it! Remember?" I searched her eyes.

Please remember! Remember!

"Sorry, Cora…no mosaic," B said sadly, shaking her head. "That would have been cool, but no tiles…no."

I knew my expression looked desperate, but that was the way I was feeling.

"You're freaking me out a bit here. You sure you didn't just have a really vivid dream?" she asked, her brow furrowed as she watched me carefully.

No! It happened, I swear.… But how could it have been real if Bree didn't remember it?

"I'm not sure anymore," I admitted. "It seemed so real. It must have happened. You sure you don't remember any tiles…none?" I asked, now grasping at straws, but I had to try.

"None, sorry," she apologized, looking disappointed.

"And we came back here, and you saw me going into the cabin, to bed?" I asked, trying to call upon that memory. Nothing came. There was a big, blank drawn over the night.

"Yup," she nodded. Bree grabbed my hand and led me to the path. "I think you need something to eat. It might wake you up a bit…maybe some chocolate?" she teased.

I wasn't in the mood. I was disturbed, truly disturbed. Half of my night was gone, and replaced with a story that no one would believe. And the only person I was with had no memory of it at all.

Am I going crazy?

"Yeah," I nodded, "I guess I need to eat."

Bree shook her head and wrapped an arm around my shoulder, "Let's go get you some breakfast."

"Right, breakfast," I said and let myself be lead away.

59
Darrien

"DARRIEN! DARRIEN!"

My eyelids wouldn't work. They were glued shut. I went to reach up and rub the sleep out of them, but a searing pain cut into my arm. I yelled out, my eyes flying open in the process. I looked around the room. Pearl, Pen, and Avery stood above me.

"Where am I?" I asked in a voice I didn't recognize.

"You're back at camp. You're safe." Pearl's voice was warm, and felt good to hear. Another shadow moved in the room. My eyes went to the other figure, and my heart nearly leapt out of my chest when I saw who it was.

"Ty?"

"Man, you are so lucky your baby brother has some serious healing skills." Avery's voice answered my question for me.

"How-" I was cut off as a yelp escaped my throat, from whatever Ty was doing to me.

"We called for him," Pearl explained. I looked at Tyde. He was concentrating, but he was pissed. I could see that much, too. I felt a wave of guilt. I never told him what I was really doing, and this was not the way that I wanted him to find out.

"I'm sorry," I said, trying to get Tyde to look at me.

"Save your energy," he barked at me. I wanted to press further, but whatever he had done had sent a wave of exhaustion over me. My eyelids slammed shut. I didn't wake again for hours.

It was like coming through a thick fog. I was walking, though unaware where I was or where I was going. When the mist finally dissipated, I realized that I was inside the military academy that I grew up in. The blank, sterile walls of the academy brought back a swell of memories inside my dream state. That's when I realized that I was standing in front of my room.

The door opened, and there was Tyde, all of eight years old, playing on the floor. He looked up at me, or rather, *through* me. Behind me, a twelve-year-old Darrien strolled through the door. Looking at the two of us, I realized just how young we were then.

Even though we took to military training considerably well, being orphaned at such a young age made us grow up too fast. We missed being kids. But we were lucky; it turned out that we had exceptional gifts, which caught the attention of commanding officers early on. Tyde could heal others, an ability that no Mer has *ever* had. I have an exceptionally strong ability to control water. This gives me the ability to see things made of water even through walls, almost like heat signatures.

My powers helped catapult me up the ranks of the military. I was top of my class every year, even though I was at least five years younger than everyone else.

That didn't help me get any friends. Turned out, the guys in my classes didn't like being showed up by a kid. It was one of the reasons that I discovered I could sense water through a wall. I had to start to watch out for the older officers in my classes hiding in my room, ready to ambush me.

*Oh no...*my dream warped, and that's when I realized I wasn't in a dream at all. It was a memory.

Not this day. I don't want to see this again.

But I was stuck, watching a day I wish never happened, the day I discovered I could summon someone's blood.

I watched in silent horror as a younger me came home from classes to hear a commotion behind my bedroom door. I focused my power and reached through the door, sensing four bodies bigger than myself, and one smaller.

I can't explain the rage I felt when I opened that door.

Tyde was on the floor, in a pool of his own blood.

Four large Mer were standing over him with satisfied looks on their faces. All were from my classes. They were a lot older than me, and were always being showed up by me. I knew they didn't like me, but never in my wildest dreams did I think that they would take things *that* far.

Tyde was badly cut up from the beating he took. His face was barely recognizable, a large gash on it being the source of most of the blood. I thought he was dead.

I lost all control.

Letting out a scream, something inside me snapped. The room pulsed and, for the first time, I could feel the water in blood. I focused in on the four Mer towering over my brother and pulled. *Hard.* Blood streamed from their eyes, nose, and ears. Their screams were satisfying, but not enough.

This ends now.

I summoned every bit of water in their bodies, lifting them off their feet. They screamed in pain. One of them passed out from it. I suspended them there and watched the fear grow in their eyes. I wanted them to know pain. I wanted them to suffer.

I could have killed them right there, but I didn't. As much as that would have been satisfying, I reigned in my anger enough to leave them alive. Instead, I sent them crashing through the window and down a couple of stories.

I didn't look to see if they were still alive. I didn't care. I didn't see anything but my little brother in a heap on the floor.

The memory washed away as my younger self crouched beside Ty.

He lived, thanks to his ability to heal. He still has a couple of nasty scars from that day on his back and face. He has no memory of that day, but I haven't forgotten, and I *won't* forgive.

I went to a dark place after that. I stopped holding back my powers. I let them rage during sparring classes. I made sure that I squared off against Tyde's attackers. I tested my abilities on them.

Could I control just a little bit of water? Say, just the tip of their finger? Yes, I could.

It was satisfying to watch them have to beg Ty to heal them after they lost their finger. If it wasn't for Zale and Ty, I'm not sure if I would have come out of that.

The fog thickened, and the faces of the attackers swarmed me. The guilt that I felt for not protecting my brother swelled all over again. Then, the faces changed and morphed into something else. *Someone* else.

Midira.

"You're going to lose her," her voice hissed.

"No!" I shouted into nothingness. Her smiling face faded as I tried to get to her. The fog swirled, and I was lost to it once again.

Cora....

When I opened my eyes again, the room was empty, except for Ty. He was sitting on Devon's bed and reading a book. I grunted as I tried to change positions. I was already feeling the effects of Ty's healing skills in my arm and leg. I had mobility again. I was lucky.

"You stayed," I said in a gruff, sleep-soaked voice. I shook my head to get rid of the remnants of the dream.

"Not that you deserve it. Ass wipe," he reprimanded.

"Look, I'm sorry I didn't tell you why I was leaving," I began.

"You think I'm pissed about *that?*" he barked at me.

"Well…yeah," I admitted.

"You're such a self-absorbed ass sometimes, you know that?" he grumbled. I shrugged.

"What is it, then?" I asked.

"You almost *died*," he said in a smaller voice than I was accustomed to hearing from him. I wasn't expecting that. He knew what the risks were in this job. Hell, he chose the *same job*.

"Hey, you know it's part of the job, Ty-"

"Taking on a Siren, alone, is *not* part of your job description," he said in a low hard voice.

"Four."

"What?" he shouted.

"There were actually four. And one was Midira," I answered, maybe making too light of the situation. That's when Ty stood up and punched me straight in the cut in my leg. I screamed out in pain.

"What the hell was that for?" I bellowed at him.

"You're seriously trying to tell me that you took on three Siren guards and Midira…alone? *Are. You. Insane?*" he yelled, smacking me in the head with each word.

"I didn't have a choice," I tried to explain, and fend off his attack.

"That's not how I see it," he said, backing away and sitting on Devon's bed again.

"There are others here that you could have enlisted the help of," he pointed out. "You could have taken Devon or Avery…*anyone*, to have a look at that pool. They didn't need to know anything about Cora to do that. A Siren pool is enough of a reason to go."

I stared back at him. I never thought of that. Not once did it occur to me to ask for help.

"You're right," I admitted after a moment.

"What?" he blurted.

"You're right," I repeated. "I should have thought that through more. I'm sorry."

"Uh, okay," he said, his voice going high as he shifted on the bed.

"What?" I asked, not missing the odd inflection in his voice.

"You don't apologize, like, ever." He eyed me. "I think your injuries are more serious than I realized." Ty's light chuckle eased my pain a little and I relaxed into the bed again.

"So, you can heal Siren poison now? That's handy," I commented, knowing how hard it was to heal.

"Yeah, I guess so," he shrugged with a smile. "I don't exactly know how I managed to do that. I was in a bit of a panic when I was called up here to heal you. I didn't expect that, especially having been under the impression that you were here to spy on the humans," he glared at me and I gave him a guilty smile.

"Well, I'm feeling about a thousand times better," I said, easing up higher on the bed. "How did I get here, though? Last thing I remember was falling unconscious at the Siren pool."

Tyde leaned back on the bed. "Pearl went looking for you. She thought she knew where you had gone. When she found you out cold, she ran back for Avery, who helped carry you back here. Penelope called me when she realized that your injuries were beyond even *her* Claire skills. The rest of the guys are cleaning up the Siren mess you made at the pool."

Damn.

"Thanks for coming," I uttered, lifting my gaze to Ty.

"I would punch you again, but then I would have to heal you again. I'm getting tired," he complained.

I looked outside. It was pitch dark. He had come a long way, and left Zale to do so. My injuries must have been really serious.

I shouldn't have gone.

Cora wasn't the only one that needed to learn how to control their anger. Tyde laid down in the bed next to me and closed his eyes.

"How are you doing?" I asked him, hoping to shift attention off me.

"Fine. The job is demanding, but I like it. I was just thinking I didn't want to give it up, but I wasn't willing to let you die so I could have your job." He looked at me out of the corner of his eye.

"I appreciate that." I smiled. The pain in my arm and leg had subsided. I was starting to feel sleep coming for me. "Will you stay for breakfast?"

"No, I have to get back. I don't want to be gone long."

"I understand. Thank you for coming and- you know- not letting me die," I chuckled and a yawn escaped me.

"Sure, sure. You should be better by morning, but, please, don't push it today. You aren't a god, you know."

"Sure, sure." That made him smile, and me relax.

Soon, the sound of night crept into the cabin and lulled me to sleep again.

60
Cora

EVEN THE SMELL OF Anne's cooking couldn't cheer me up. I sat at the Lead table and stared at my food, unable to eat it.

I was totally preoccupied with my thoughts, when Darrien sat down next to me.

"Oh, thank the heavens you are alright!" Anne's voice boomed from the kitchen door. She bustled right over to where Darrien had just entered the hall and threw her arms around him.

"Now, you get that handsome face in the kitchen this minute! I made you some of my special breakfast tea." She put both hands on Darrien's back and shuffled him into the kitchen. He smiled and chuckled as he let her guide him in.

I didn't know that they were that close. Anne sure seemed worried about him.

I wonder why?

Several minutes later Darrien came out of the kitchen carrying a thermos and a large mug of tea. He was moving slower than usual and lacked the grace he normally had.

"So, I hear you and Bree are quite the adventurers," he said as he slowly lowered himself into the seat next to me. He was smiling, but the dark circles under his eyes betrayed the easiness that he was attempting.

"What?" I asked, distracted by the way he looked, and not in a good way.

"Pearl told me that you two are heading into town today to do some shopping," he said and lifted an eyebrow at me.

"Right, yeah," I nodded absentmindedly, relieved he wasn't referring to the walk on the trail.

Wait. *Going to town?*

My eyes flashed to his as what he said sank in.

200

"That's right," I said in a small voice. "We're going into town…with you…today." I planted my face in my hands.

I had completely forgotten. And, on top of that, I didn't ask Bree if she wanted to go. After the night I had, I wished I could put it off, but I really needed to get Mom something for her birthday. As much as Bree and I wanted to be out of the house for the summer, we missed her and wanted her to know that we were thinking of her. When we left she was so upset. Hopefully a gift would cheer her up a little.

"Ugh, sorry. I forgot until just now," I admitted to Darrien.

"Oh. You don't want to go, then?" He looked and sounded disappointed.

"No, I'll still go. I just forgot to tell B, and I don't know if she'll be able to or not," I said and concentrated on my scrambled eggs. The look on his face was almost enough to melt my resolve, and start to feel for him again.

I can't. I won't.

"Oh, okay," he said, a half smile winked a dimple to life. "Well, I'm still heading to town, and I hope you can come. Bree too."

If I wasn't mistaken, a hint of pink showed on his cheeks. He cleared his throat, "I know all the shops. Anything you're looking for, I can find. Well, almost anything. It *is* a small town."

He smiled at me. I wanted to believe he was a genuine guy. I wanted someone to talk to. I was so confused about my night and Bree, but I was sure I would just end up looking completely insane. And then, there was the whole thing with *him*. It seemed like it had been ages since our date/non-date fiasco.

"I'd better go ask her." I stood to go and knocked over my juice glass, spilling orange juice all over the table.

"Crap! I'm sorry!" I grabbed for a napkin, but before I could put it on the spill, the juice ran towards my hand and pooled under it. I gasped and then quickly smashed the napkin on it, hoping Darrien didn't see. When I looked up his eyes were wide and he was staring.

"I-"

"Well, well, don't you just look perfect this morning, Cora. I love your hair!" My mouth dropped open as I looked between Aurelia and Darren. *Did they see? Did she just compliment me?*

"How do you get it to come out of your nose like that?" she sneered.

There it is. Aurelia slithered into her seat beside Darrien.

"Some of us don't need to spend hours getting ready in the morning. It just comes naturally," she chimed.

I'm so not in the mood for this.

"I just woke up ten minutes ago, Aurelia. And I've seen your mountain of make up in the bathroom, so don't preach to me about natural beauty." I almost slapped my hand to my mouth.

I can't believe I just said that!

I probably shouldn't have said it, but it felt good. I grabbed my tray and left, while shock kept her tongue silent.

I need to talk to Bree.

By the time I found Bree, she was just starting her swim lesson. Pen was instructing the lesson, filling in for Darrien. Pen was having a great time and so were her girls, especially Bree. By the time I finally got her out of the water to talk to her, and explain about the shopping trip, there was no point trying to convince her to come. Pen was making great progress with her in the water, and Bree didn't want to stop.

I heaved a sigh. That meant a long truck ride alone with Darrien, which I had mixed emotions about, and shopping alone, which I hated.

I met Darrien behind the main office. We were taking the old green truck, with no seat belts and holes in the floor. The safety of the truck bothered me, but it seemed I was the only one. Pearl was unaffected by it, as was Darrien.

I guess they're used to it by now.

Darrien was leaning against the hood of the truck, arms crossed and looking ridiculously…yummy. When I walked up, a huge smile spread across his face. It was sweet. I couldn't help but return it as my heart did a little jig.

"So, ready to hit the great metropolis of Stenen?" he asked with a chuckle, then looked over my shoulder. "Where's Bree?"

"No Bree," I shrugged. "Pen is giving her an amazing swimming lesson right now, and I couldn't get her to leave the water. You might have some competition for your job!" A grin crept across my face. It felt good, but unnatural, considering how my morning had started.

"I'll have to watch my back, then," he chuckled. "Well, if it's just the two of us, we should get going."

He moved around to the passenger side and opened the door. It took me a second to realize what he was doing.

He's holding the door open for me!

I never thought about it before, but I guess I liked that sort of thing; it was so…*respectful*. He closed the door for me, too, and then ran around to his side of the truck and hopped in. I knew I was staring open-mouthed again, but I was just so shocked. I'd only seen that in movies!

Pearl came running out of the office just as we were about to back out. She came over to the driver's window and leaned in to talk to Darrien. Clearly, she didn't want me to hear what they were saying, but I caught a few

202

words. It was something about "job" and "be careful." The information that Bree told me when she was spying jumped into my head. Something was going on with Darrien, and that peaked my curiosity. How much was Pearl involved?

"Have a safe trip! Good luck finding a birthday present for your mom, Cora! And don't worry about your girls, I'll take good care of them!" She smiled and waved.

Darrien didn't acknowledge her at all; instead, he stared intently at the road ahead and drove away. He didn't seem to be in a good mood anymore. His eyes were clouded, thoughtful, and a little angry.

"Um, thanks for driving me, Darrien," I muttered. He jumped at my voice.

"Yeah, no problem. I was going anyway. It's nice to have some company, though." He gave me a half smile, his eyes still on the road.

"I know it's none of my business, but is everything okay? You seem...upset."

"No, everything is just fine," he answered. I lifted a brow and looked at him. He smiled and nodded slightly. "Pearl and I just had a disagreement on something," he shrugged. "She's worried about me, but she's being a bit ridiculous about it. I'm a big boy and can look after myself." He smiled to himself, his eyes seemed to come to life again.

"Oh. I guess that's what aunts are for, keeping you in check. I don't have any aunts or uncles; both my parents were only children. The only family I have left is Bree...and Mom. How about you? You have any family?" I asked wanting to get off of the topic of my family.

"Yeah, a younger brother. It's just the two of us." His face lost its laughter.

"What happened to your parents?" The question spilled out of my mouth before I could stop it. "I'm sorry, it's really none of my business," I apologized.

"No, it's okay. They died in the, uh...in an accident, when we were young. We don't have any family either, so it's been just the two of us for a long time." I could relate.

"How old is he?" I asked.

"He's sixteen, four years younger than me," he answered.

That made Darrien twenty, two years older than me. I was surprised, because he seemed a lot older than that.

"He must have been pretty young when you lost your parents then?" I asked, watching the furrow in Darrien's brow deepen.

"Yeah. He doesn't remember my parents much." He gave a sad smile and a one shoulder shrug. I recognized that look immediately.

I knew what it was like to lose your parents. Although, mine were both technically still alive, they were just completely absent from my life. Bree and I had basically been on our own for years.

Darrien and I had more in common than I thought.

"I'm sorry to hear that, Darrien. It must have been really tough for you." I struggled not to think about how tough it was for Bree and me.

"Well, as long as we're together, we're okay. Anyway, change of subject?" He offered. *Yeah.* I didn't want to dive further into that, either. It brought up too much for me, too.

"Yes, change of subject." I stared out at the road ahead, not sure what to say.

"So," he said, sitting up taller, "how many boyfriends have you had?"

WHAT? My face flamed, and I could feel my jaw drop open. *Seriously?*

"I...what? Why are you asking?" I blurted. "How many boyfriends have *you* had?" *Jeez!*

Darrien's throaty deep laugh was loud and hard and filled the cab of the truck.

"You're funny, Cora." His smile was endearing.

"Well, who asks questions like that? Really?" I laughed to myself.

He was funny too, in a charming way I wasn't expecting. It irritated me, because I didn't want to like him.

"I haven't had any boyfriends," I said, answering his question, though unsure why. "Guys just aren't interested in, well, me." I smiled half-heartedly and shrugged.

It never bothered me before. I didn't *want* to date anyone. But now, it seemed like something I should have been embarrassed of.

"Well, don't worry about it. I haven't had any boyfriends either." He chuckled and nudged me with his elbow. "Besides, *clearly*, those guys have no taste."

I thought my skin was going to melt right off my face and drip to the floor of the truck. I had never had someone say something like that to me before. My body reacted to Darrien in ways I had never experienced: sending my heart into spasm, causing blushes that scorched my skin, and uncontrollable grins that looks half crazed. Speaking of, I forced down a huge grin that was fighting its way to my lips. I had to look away from him to hide my face.

My heart was thumping hard in my chest, no matter how much I willed it to stop. That stupid grin won the fight for my lips and wasn't surrendering.

Ugh...what is going on with you, Cora. Seriously.

When I managed to sneak a peek at Darrien, he had one arm on the steering wheel and the other propped on the sill of the open window. There was a half-grin on his lips.

Why does he have to look so freaking good?

My window was open and I stuck my hand out, riding the wave of air rushing by. The sensation reminded me of swimming, the way the water felt against my skin. I thought of Dad and all the fun we had in the water. Then his song sprang to my head and I found myself humming it.

"So, Humbug-"

"You know, I hate that," I said, cutting him off.

"I know." He paused. "So, Humbug," he smiled defiantly at me and I elbowed him, "what song were you just humming?"

I swallowed hard unsure what to say, finally shrugging. "Just a song my Dad used to sing around the house. He wouldn't sing it in front of the two of us, though. I don't know why."

"The two of you? You and Bree?" Darrien asked, as his eyes went restlessly between me and the road.

"No, me and Ana." I felt a stab of sadness settle on my heart, just saying her name.

"Your sister," he stated.

"Yeah, my sister. My twin sister," I nodded. "Wait. How did you know that?" I asked, my surprise keeping the tears momentarily in check.

"Oh, uh…lucky guess. What happened to her?" Darrien's smile was gone.

"She, um…she died in a boat accident," I said, my voice cracking. The part of my heart that had never mended tore open again.

"I'm sorry to hear that, Cora," Darien said, his tone gently and kind. "Losing a twin…that must be tough."

He wasn't looking at me anymore. I didn't blame him. I tried desperately to stop the trickle of tears, but I failed. I was just glad that his concentration was on the road, and not me. I wiped my eyes as much as I could, until my tears slowed down a bit.

"Sorry, I just miss her," I sniffled. Darrien, looked over at me. I met his gaze, red eyes and all. He smiled reassuringly to me, then reached across the seat and took my hand.

"You must have been really close. I'm sorry." He looked almost guilty for a second. As his thumb rubbed the top of my hand, my heart thumped to life and butterflies erupted in my chest.

"Thank you," I whispered. The touch of his skin was sending electrical bursts through my body.

No, no, no.

I gently pulled my hand away from his and wiped at my face, not wanting to offend him, but needing to break the connection my heart was starting to form.

205

"Sorry I'm such a mess. I don't talk about her…to anyone, really," I admitted.

Somehow, he made me comfortable, like I could spill all my secrets to him in a second. No one has ever done that. I wouldn't even talk to *Bree* about Ana.

"Alright, enough about that," I said with a shake of my head and a sniffle. "Want to hear about a crazy dream I had?" I blurted out.

Darrien's eyes perked up, and he looked intently at me.

What are you doing?

61

Darrien

"WHAT DREAM? TELL ME," I said, willing myself to calm down. Finally, I might be able to get an idea of what is going on in her head when she sleepwalks.

"Okay, well…it's weird," she warned. I lifted an eyebrow. I was expecting that, but I needed more.

I sat in silence as she recounted her whole dream: song, tile path, and all. There were no real surprises, seeing as how I found her on the path and I heard the song myself.

"Cora, I don't think you should be going into the woods alone anymore," I stated, gripping the wheel tighter. "If you want to go, I'm coming too. Okay?" I eyed her, hoping she understood the gravity of what I was saying.

"It was just a dream!" She laughed.

My mood was dipping. My arm was aching from my Siren wound and my leg was starting to as well. Her dreams were causing more trouble than she realized, and I wasn't seeing the humor in the situation.

"Hello?" A hand waved in front of my eyes. Frustration flared.

"I'm serious, Cora. Don't go in the woods without me," I barked.

"What do you know? You know something! What is it?" she demanded. I could feel the tightness in my jaw, as my teeth worked over one another. This was not the conversation I wanted to have.

"Just promise me you won't go into the woods without me anymore." She looked like I was asking the impossible. I calmed down, forcing away the overwhelming need to protect her. "Please, Cora." I watched her drop her guard. Her face softened, the fight gone.

"Okay, I promise," she uttered, watching me. "Now, will you tell me what's going on?"

"Nothing, it's just…I just don't want you to go without me, that's all. It's not safe." I had never had problems lying to get my way or to do my job, but for reasons unknown, I couldn't lie to Cora.

"But *you* told me to take the girls on the trails! It was *your idea*! What's changed? You're not telling me something!" Her voice was getting louder with each word. She was mad, and I felt bad for being the cause of that, even if it was for her safety.

"I know what I said and I know what I'm saying now. Stay out of the woods," I said in a stern voice.

"I want to know what's going on with me. You know. I know you do," she pushed, but I wasn't budging. I couldn't.

"I just don't want to see you get hurt."

The words were useless and empty. I knew that, but what else could I say? She looked hurt and disappointed, which was a lot worse than facing her anger. But I didn't have long to wait for that. Her posture stiffened, arms crossed, and face turned away; I could sense the tension starting to roll off her.

"Ugh! Fine! But this isn't over," she pointed at me. "You're not getting away with silence forever." She smiled sarcastically, with a glare thrown in for emphasis. I mirrored it back to her.

"We'll see," I said. Silence. So much silence. I wasn't bothered by it. I wasn't much of a talker, and I didn't read Cora as one either. So, I was interested to see who would break first.

"So, where are you going?" *Me*. It was me.

"I'm not sure. You can just drop me off at the end of Main Street. I can browse through the shops myself." She huffed and refused to look at me.

Cora just sat there with her arms crossed and stared out the window. I smiled to myself. She was cute when she pouted.

"Sounds as good a place as any, I guess. I have a few things to do for Pearl, so I'll catch up to you later. There aren't too many places you can hide here." I laughed, indicating the five shops on Main Street.

"Okay, see you in a bit then," she said and barely waited for me to stop the truck before she hopped out. She didn't look back as she slammed the door.

62

Cora

I WAS STILL MAD I wasn't getting any answers. What was he hiding? I shook my head, in an effort to put it on a back burner.

Okay, focus Cora. Mom's birthday. Don't think about whatever Darrien knows, or doesn't know. I nodded and strode off.

Birthday gift, here I come.

Looking at the lack of shopping choices, I figured it was best to start from one end and make my way through them all. I had enough time, and I didn't know what I might find in a small town shop. I decided to go to the book store first, Rusty Readers.

The store was ancient, and smelled of old paper. It was the scent of knowledge and adventure, life and death, and love…first love, true love, unrequited love, eternal love…*what is my obsession with love, all of a sudden?*

I wandered around, scanning the shelves for something that would catch my eye.

The room was filled to the brim with books. The shelves reached for the roof and had stacks of books on every shelf that was at least two deep.

There were stacks on the top of the shorter shelves all across the front of the store. By the register, a trolley acted as an additional shelf that, even though it had wheels, you couldn't move if you didn't want a tower of books to come down on you. I was nervous just walking around, one wrong move and I would be the cause of a catastrophic book avalanche.

I wouldn't find a gift there for Mom. She'd never been a reader. But, by the till, I spotted a young adult fantasy book that I heard was really good. It had everything in it: vampires, fairies, werewolves, and angels…and a lead male who was to die for.

Who wouldn't want to be swept off their feet by a super human hottie?

I ended up with a nature book for Bree (she loved them), and I spotted a beautiful journal for myself. The itch to write was getting to me, especially since I had forgotten my writing journal at home. I paid for the three items, to the great excitement of the elderly owner, and walked out the door.

Next to Rusty Readers, was a store called Artsy. A chime of ceramic birds and the smell of vanilla welcomed me as I entered. Shelves of hand-crafted and painted birds were off to the right, and hand-made pottery dishware to the left. Some brightly colored and patterned furniture were sprinkled throughout the room, in every available nook and cranny. There were splashes of vibrant colors here, there, and everywhere. Everything was friendly and bright.

Mom would love this place.

In the back of the store, there were little hand-sculpted figurines. They were shaped like people, but lacked details like facial features and fingers. They were beautiful in their simplicity. A smile slipped across my face. *Perfect.*

I looked for one that Mom would like. When I saw the two sisters, one with brown hair and one with blonde, I knew I had it. It was the perfect gift.

I smiled with satisfaction as I paid and left the store. I felt good doing something that I knew would make her happy, even if it was just for a moment.

There was still lots of time to kill, so, for fun, I wandered across the street to Fresh Fashion.

I could smell the place before I even opened the door. A flowery and fruity scent gushed from the door as I opened it, nearly choking me.

As I stepped inside, my eyes were met with a sight unlike anything I had ever seen before. The store was full of an odd collection of clothes, some new and some secondhand, some for the young and some for the elderly. Hats, shoes, bags, and boots were scattered everywhere. Everything I could imagine, from seemingly every fashion era, hung from each wall, shelf, and hook.

My eyes didn't know where to settle, and I stood there just gawking for a few minutes, until a rack of bunny hugs caught my attention. I found one in a pretty shade of blue, and was inwardly celebrating at my great find when a voice startled me.

"That's a nice color, but I think this one is better," Darrien said and held up a neon pink hoodie that was so bright, it was creating sun spots in my vision.

"I'd need sunglasses just to wear that. Put it down. I'm getting a headache," I chuckled to myself. I hadn't even noticed him come in the store.

"Okay, you're not a pink girl...got it," Darrien commented. He roamed around the next few racks, fingers touching the shoulders of the clothes. "How about this one? Totally you."

I laughed as he held up a purple colored t-shirt. "The Little Mermaid? Maybe when I was seven. Actually, it *is* one of my favorite movies," I admitted and shrugged.

"Of course, it is," he said, matter-of-factly.

"Anyway, I was going for something more like this." I held up a teal-colored bunny hug.

"And I was thinking something more like this!" He held up a red bikini.

"Ha!" I yelled! Heat bloomed on my face. I couldn't even look at him. "Good luck with that! I'm not getting into that thing...ever."

"You? Who said anything about you? It's for me!" He chuckled and held it against himself. I dropped my jaw on the floor, then started to giggle. "What, not my color?" he asked.

"Not your gender!" I laughed.

He's in a weird mood. But I liked it...a lot.

"Ouch," he feigned pain. "Well, then you're going to have to wear it. We can't leave it here! It's *lonely*," he pouted.

"Not happening, Darrien," I said, seriousness creeping back into my voice.

"Can't blame a guy for trying." He resigned with a shrug and hung it back up.

It was a nice suit, I'd give him that, and it just happened to be my size. But, if I was ever confident enough to put on a bathing suit and go swimming, I never would have chosen one like that.

"Chicken," he mumbled just loud enough for me to hear. I huffed, and open mouthed stared at him.

Fine, two can play at this game. I searched for a way to get back at him and found perfection on the rack next to me.

"I think you should get this!" I declared, holding up a tiny black pair of speedos for him. The look on his face went from shock to determination.

"I'll put on *those*, if you try on *this*," He challenged, pointing to the bikini. I thought about it a second.

There was *no way* he was coming out of the change room in that tiny thing. No way was he *that* confident. If he didn't come out then I wouldn't have to worry about showing mine.

"Deal," I blurted before I could stop myself.

Five minutes later, I was tying the last of the strings on that red triangle mess when I heard the door to his room unlock.

No he didn't.

"I'm waiting!" His voice rang out from outside the change room. I watched the blood drain from my body in the mirror as I went increasingly

211

paler. I felt completely naked. Literally my underwear was bigger than that swim suit.

I can't. I can't.

"Hello?" Darrien called.

Oh, grow a pair Cora! I bit my lip, threw on my new bunny hug, and slunk out.

Oh god, this is such a mis-

My jaw hit the floor, and drool may have rolled out.

Darrien was standing there in practically nothing. I mean I didn't look at…I couldn't look…down…there. But if I happened to…

If I thought he was defined before, I really had no clue. He was chiseled and defined with deep valleys between his muscles. He was strong…there was no denying that, like someone that knew how to fight.

My favorite were the indents right by his hips; they dipped deep and out of sight, even in that tiny suit. He stood there with his hands on his hips, no shame in the way he was dressed, with an incredulous look on his face.

"I'm out here freezing my nards off, and you're wearing a hoodie? That's not the deal that we struck, Humbug. I'm disappointed," he tutted and shook his head.

Oh, my god. I can't do this! It's like stripping for him! I can't. I can't. I can't. I can do it…I'm going to do it. No, I'm not. Why did I agree to this?

Darrien closed the space between us quickly, and I had to avert my eyes to stop from looking him up and down. My face was flaming hot.

"Hey, I was just teasing," he said, in a soft gentle voice as he rested his hands on my arms. His dimples winked into existence, and he pulled the hood over my head.

"I like the hoodie. It leaves something to the imagination," he said with a smile as he tugged at the hood strings. My heart sang. He leaned in closer, levelling his eyes on mine.

"And I have a *great* imagination," he whispered.

I turned about fifty shades of red as the mischievous smile on his face deepened his dimples. *My god…*

I swallowed hard as he sauntered back to his change room.

Once we got dressed, I paid for the bunny hug and bathing suit…*yes, I bought it!* I didn't let Darrien see, though. I didn't want him to think that there was a great chance of me getting into the water. There was a little chance…just a little one!

What I *did* want, which I made me sick and excited at the same time, was for him to see me in that suit. The look in his eyes when I came out in just my bunny hug was pure *hunger.* I wanted to see it again, and if that meant I had to wear the suit…well, I might just be okay with that.

212

"How'd you make out? Find something for your mom?" He asked, looking around me, searching for a bag.

"Yeah, I found these great figurines that she'll love." I was smiling as I looked in my bag from Artsy.

"We have tons of time before we need to be back," he said. "You have your gift and I have all my errands done. What do you want to do to kill time?" he asked as we walked down the street, side by side.

Our hands were so close to each other, the urge to reach out and grab his was almost too much for me. I switched my bags to my other hand, filling it so it wouldn't be tempted to grab his. I was so attracted to him- I mean, I'd have to be blind not to be. But there was more to him than just looks. I wanted- no, I *needed* to know more about him.

"So, tell me more about *your* dating life, Darrien. You asked me about mine, so you owe me!" I joked, but only half-heartedly. I realized too late that maybe I didn't really want the answer to that question. His dating history had to be lengthy. A slight pinch in my gut made me realize that, maybe, I cared about that too much.

"Oh, um…." Darrien looked at the ground as we walked. To my surprise, there was a hint of blush on his cheeks. "My dating history is…complicated. I've been out with a few girls, but nothing worked out…obviously."

"Oh…" that was not the answer I was preparing for.

"I'm picky," he said, and smiled at me.

"What about Aurelia?" I had to ask.

"What *about* Aurelia?" he dodged.

"What's her deal with you? Why is she so…you know?" I watched him. He stared at his feet, then sat down on a bench and patted the seat next to him. I sat down, making sure to leave a little space between us.

"Aurelia is the way she is because of me." He lifted his eyes to mine, and there was regret brewing in them. I lost my breath.

What did he do?

Darrien looked away and cleared his throat. He ran a hand through his hair and started.

"It's hard to explain. After my parents died, I was an angry guy…a really angry guy. *That* part of me got along with Aurelia, really well. I had a huge chip on my shoulder, and I took it out on everyone. Aurelia, if you hadn't noticed, is kind of the same." I lifted a brow. *Humph, yeah. I noticed.*

"I went to a military school, and I was really dedicated to my education, not relationships. But, back then, we had a lot in common, and everyone around us really wanted it to work. So, I gave in. Aurelia was different then, too; not as harsh, just passionate." I shuffled in my seat, so did he. This was

213

not a comfortable conversation and yet it was necessary. I needed to know and he seemed to agree with that.

Darrien peeked at me from the corner of his eye and continued, "I liked her, and we did have some good times. But, I didn't…uh…love her. I wasn't open to that, at the time. I figured that out and ended it. It wasn't right being together when my feelings didn't match hers." He watched me, ready for my reaction. But I wasn't ready to respond just yet, so I looked back at him. He sighed and went on.

"I got my job and loved it. I ended up coming up here, and getting to know Pearl better. I started opening up about myself and…uh…feelings." He shivered and stuck his tongue out. I chuckled. "Pearl's got a gift for getting people to do things that they really don't want to do. So, after a few weeks of Pearl pushing every emotion out of me, including raging anger, I'm in a better place."

I couldn't help the smile that came across my face. He spoke so warmly about Pearl. It must be nice having an aunt like that.

Darrien sighed and ran his hands through his thick, black hair.

"I was not expecting Aurelia to show up here, thinking that she could force her way back into my life. She has *not* forgiven me for ending our relationship. It was embarrassing for her. I tried to do the right thing, but she's not the kind of person that lefts stuff go. Unfortunately for her, I'm the same way. When I set my mind on something, I'm kind of an ass about it," he chuckled to himself.

I was astonished and tried really hard not to let it appear on my face. I never expected him to open up so much.

"I don't regret being with Aurelia. I learned a lot in the end, but I wish it hadn't come at the expense of her pride. I never wanted that."

"So, Aurelia wasn't always like this, you just bring out the best in her." I nudged him and smiled.

"She's always been an…*intense* person. I didn't change that. But yeah, her anger towards you is probably, mostly, because of me…just a little, tiny bit." He smiled apologetically.

So, Aurelia was the victim of unrequited love. A part of me actually felt sorry for her.

"Well," I began, "I don't get why she's so angry with me. I mean, it's not like we're dating or anything."

I regretted it the moment it left my lips. I wasn't hinting at anything, I was just stating the obvious. But, it didn't sound like that. I bit my lip. *Maybe if I pretend I didn't say it, he will do the same.*

"I told you. She's jealous of you," he stated.

I opened my mouth to protest, but he put a finger on my lips to stop me. He looked at me, watching my expression. My heart started racing. Darrien's eyes were intense as he slowly removed his finger from my lips.

"She doesn't like the way I look at you," he said, his voice just above a whisper and his eyes intent on mine.

The thundering in my chest was almost deafening. Darrien picked up my hand and ran his fingers slowly over mine, sending a wave of pleasure dancing through my veins.

"While we haven't, officially, been on a date...*yet,*" he began, "she sees that I've moved on. So, yeah," he nodded as the corner of his perfect lips tipped up, "that's why she doesn't like you."

He entwined his fingers around mine and grabbed my chin between his finger and thumb, bringing my face closer to his.

My heart felt like someone was playing basketball with it. Just the feel of his skin on mine was sending pulses of pleasure shooting through my body. I watched his lips when he licked them, wishing I could feel them on mine. I could feel his need, his want right there along with mine.

But then, Darrien bit his lips and sighed a remorseful sigh. He dropped his hand off my chin. I blinking not understand what just happened, but relieved just the same. Darrien stood, still holding my hand.

I had never felt disappointment to that degree before. My whole body felt hung over from the rush of sensations that had nowhere to go. I didn't know what to do with that. What was he waiting for?

With Darrien's hand in mine, we walked up and down every street in Stenen, all five of them, for the rest of our time.

We chatted and laughed about all sorts of things, staying away from any heavy family subjects. We just talked and walked, side by side, hand in hand, and enjoyed being in each other's company. It was glorious! I put my brain on hold and just let myself be. It felt good, even exciting, being with Darrien.

When it was time, we walked slowly back to the truck. Again, Darrien held the door for me, then ran around and hopped in himself. The afternoon had been amazing, but there were some answers owed to me.

"So, I'm not supposed to go back into the forest alone...why?" I asked, now that he had nowhere to run to.

"Because I said so." And he smiled triumphantly at me.

"You know, that just makes me want to go to find out what would happen." I smiled at *him* triumphantly. His cocky grin dropped off his face.

"Okay, okay. I'm just worried about you going at night, mostly. The woods are different at night, and you don't know your way around them. If you want to go down a trail, just come and get me and I'll come with you. I know my way through those woods blindfolded. Better?" His smile never reached his eyes, but hung there, unsure of itself.

"Okay, that's reasonable under normal circumstances, but you were freaked out about my *dream*. What does that have to do with the woods?" I watched him. His eyes were on the road, but I could tell they weren't focusing on his driving.

"I shouldn't have reacted like that. I'm sorry." He made a face that looked like he surprised himself. "I'm just worried that you might get lost, that's all. You aren't the most rational person at times, you know. You tend to blow up and do things you later regret." He winked at me and rubbed his cheek. I opened my mouth to say something sarcastic back, but he was right.

"Okay, you got me there. I'll stay out of the woods at night." He eyed me. "I promise." Darrien looked relieved. There were tons of questions looming in my head, but it was hard for me to focus.

That afternoon completely changed the way I felt about him. I couldn't believe he really liked me. I mean *actually* liked me! It was like a dream I never realized I wanted.

And yet, there was something that he was keeping from me. *How can I trust someone that is keeping secrets?* I looked over at Darrien and realized that I couldn't. If I couldn't trust him, where did that leave me?

"Darrien, I have to be honest with you. I can't completely trust you when I know you are hiding something from me. My mind wanders, thinking of everything that it could be. The more I think about it, the worse it gets. I can't believe that I'm saying this, but I *want* to trust you. I just don't know how when there are secrets involved," I admitted.

Knowing my words would probably hurt him didn't make them easier to say and made it that much harder to tell him. Nothing about this felt good, but I hoped he would understand.

Darrien's smiled faded. His eyes darkened and his lips turned down. *Ah damn, that was the look I was dreading.*

"I understand," he mumbled, then looked at me. "I really do. I wish-" He stopped, struggling for words. He gave me a half grin. "I wish things were different." I could feel the weight of that in a way I didn't totally understand.

Saying I didn't trust him was the truth, but that didn't make it easier to admit. It didn't make it easier to deal with, either.

I had many more questions bouncing around in my head, but my need to ask was deflated.

He said that he understood. Why do I feel so guilty? In that moment, the answers I sought seemed shallow and unimportant.

What a crazy day. When we started out I would have never guessed that the day would include connecting with Darrien the way I had. I certainly wouldn't have though that he would share that he like me.

Like. It wasn't love. I wasn't ready for that.

I don't ever want to be ready for that. Love is dangerous.

There was something about Darrien, though, something that made me feel comfortable, safe, home.

Is that love?

Soon, we were pulling up to camp. It was past supper, so everyone was on free time until lights out. There wasn't anyone around when we drove up. Darrien raced around the truck and opened my door for me.

"Humbug, I'm glad we got to spend the day together. I know that you would have liked it if Bree was with you, but I'm selfishly happy she wasn't able to make it." He smiled guiltily at me, but I knew what he was saying, I felt the same. The day would have been very different with Bree there.

"I had a good day, too. Thank you." I smiled at him and stepped out of the truck. We stood there awkwardly for a moment, not knowing what to say or do.

"Well, I guess I should head back and make sure my team is settling in for the night," I said finally, breaking the silence. I turned to go, but felt a hand grab mine. Darrien's fingers were gentle and warm.

"Cora, would you go back to the brook with me?" he asked, his eyes wide and waiting. I liked that he wasn't completely confident in my answer. It was endearing.

"Sure...yes, that sounds good...great," I answered, fighting the urge to giggle and knowing that the ridiculously huge smile on my face was making me look happy enough. There was no hiding my feelings from him. I did like him. *Damn it!*

"Great!" He grinned big at me. He leaned in closer, still holding my hand, and in a low voice said, "It's a date, then...for real, this time."

His smile was so sweet, and the way his lips parted into their perfect formation, I wanted to lean into them. My heart was beating fast in my chest as he lowered his lips to my hand and kissed the top of it. They were smooth and hot, and sent an electrical shock wave through my body.

"Good night, *Humbug.*" That name was starting to grow on me, and so was Darrien.

217

63
Darrien

I CAN'T BELIEVE I kissed her on the hand! All day, I wanted to kiss her. *All day!* That was all I could think about. It took everything in my willpower to *just* hold her hand. What was wrong with me? I'd never been that crazy for a girl before.

*And that bikini today…*I'm actually glad she didn't come out with it on. Those tiny speedos she picked out would not have hidden my excitement at all. That would have added a whole new level to embarrassing myself, one that I was not thinking about when I came up with that challenge.

Pearl came out of her cabin just as Cora disappeared towards hers.

"How was the trip? Get everything?" she asked, as she sat on her deck chair.

"Uh, yeah. No problems." I walked up the stairs and sat across from her, on the other chair. Our knees almost touched, the deck was so small.

"Did Cora get her mother a gift?" she asked, looking out over the lake.

"Yes, she found something," I said, as nonchalantly as I could.

"Good. Did you kiss her?" she asked.

"No…wait. What? Why are you asking me that?" I asked in a higher voice that just screamed a guilty conscience.

"Just making sure you aren't endangering yourself. Remember what we talked about. This won't lead anywhere good," she pressed.

"Look, Pearl, I respect you a lot. But, I'm sorry, this is none of your business," I pointed out.

"The hell it's not! You *and* Cora are my business!" she said, fighting to maintain a discreet tone.

"No offense but I can handle myself. I can protect Cora," I said pointedly.

"You can't protect someone's *heart*. It doesn't work that way. And you both are going to suffer." She was raising her voice, something she rarely did.

"Enough! Enough with the doom and gloom. Jeez, you sound like the world will come to an end! We haven't done anything. I kissed her on the hand, if you must know, and that is as far as it has gone." Her eyes went wide.

"You kissed her on the hand?" She squished up her nose, like it smelled bad.

"Yes," I groaned, placing my face in my hands.

"Who does that anymore?" she asked.

"I know, okay. I know," I whined.

"No...it's sweet, Darrien. It's really sweet." She was smiling at me. Her tone changed.

"Oh, well...thanks." *I think.*

"Okay, I concede. I'll stop with the doom and gloom. I'm just worried, that's all. I just want everyone to be happy," she said and patted my knee, watching me.

"Or no one to be happy," I said sarcastically and hated it the moment it came out. I didn't agree with Pearl, but I didn't want to hurt her.

"Now, that's not fair. I don't want *anyone* getting hurt," she emphasized. She looked pained by what I said.

"If you are too afraid of getting hurt all your life, you'll never experience anything worth living for. That's no way to go through life, Pearl," I argued.

She shrugged. I stood and descended the steps, leaving Pearl to think over her life choices.

I didn't want her life. As much as I respected it, I wanted more.

64

Cora

"SO, HOW WAS YOUR TRIP to town? Did you find something for Mom?" Bree was sitting on the end of my bed. Her hair was wavy from drying in the sun.

"It was good...great." A smile crept across my lips, then I realized what I looked like. I shook my head and cleared my throat, "I'm sorry you couldn't come, though."

How am I going to explain today to her?

"Good? Great? Okay...I thought you didn't want to spend any time with Darrien. The drive there and back must have been awkward after the other night." Those big blue eyes examined me.

"It wasn't that bad. We talked. We have a lot in common, actually. He's not as bad as I thought. He's...different." I was trying to keep myself busy, sorting through my clothes and cleaning up around the cabin.

"Different? How is he different? I'm so confused. Do you *like* him now?" She was perched on the edge of the bed, eyeing me.

"I think...I *do* like him. There's something about him. I don't know how to explain it." I ran out of clothes to sort, and without the distraction, the truth came pouring out of me. "Oh, Bree, I like him...like, I *really* like him. What am I going to do?"

I plopped down on the bed and ran my hands against my face. I did have feelings for him, and it was killing me. I let my guard down. This was the end. I felt free and full of dread at the same time.

"That's so exciting, Cora! That's huge for you! What did he do to change your mind?" she gushed.

I smiled and told her what he said to me as we were walking around town. His explanation of why Aurelia didn't like me made Bree sigh. She was genuinely happy for me, and it made me smile even more.

"I don't know what I'm doing! When I'm with him, all I think about is how great it is to be with him, but when we are apart there are all these questions!" I admitted.

"What do you mean?" Her eyebrows furrowed as she watched me.

"It's nothing. I just…you know me, I question everything," I shrugged. I didn't want to talk about the dream to Bree anymore. It was my problem. I would deal with it on my own.

"She doesn't like the way I look at you," he had said. My heart beat excitedly in my chest just thinking about it. I loved feeling it come to life like that; it was a sensation I had never experienced before. I never wanted to be without it. Luckily, all I had to do was think about him and there it was again, tiny electric butterflies fluttered through my veins.

"I'm in trouble, Bree." I started laughing. She smiled at me and rested her head on my shoulder. I loved having her there. I felt like I could think better with her around.

"He asked me on an official date. I said yes. Should I have done that?" I asked.

"Yes! Of course, you should have! Are you *kidding* me? I've never seen you like this before. You're beaming. Every time you say his name, you smile…it's crazy. You have to go. You *have* to," she plead, grabbing my hands. Her smile lit up her face.

"Jeez, B! Tell me how you really feel!" I laughed. She was right. I had to go. But more importantly…I *wanted* to.

"Alright, I'll go!" I stated. "What would I do without my baby sister to counsel me? Goodness knows, I need it!" I smiled at her.

For two hours, we chatted in the cabin, and decided after that we would walk down to the beach to wander in the water.

It was early evening, and the sun was just starting to sink under the trees. As we walked, we talked and caught up. Bree told me she was having a great time at camp. Pen told her that she was improving in her swimming and was getting much more confident in the water. I was proud of her, though I was nervous about her being in water so much. But, I didn't want to project my fear on her more than I already had so I said nothing.

When we reached the beach, there were a few campers here and there. Some were swimming, and others were playing games. Bree had her swim gear on, so she slipped into the water and I could see how much Pen's lessons had taken with Bree. She was confident and graceful, just like I used to be.

I held my breath as I stepped lightly into the water. With each step my breathing hitched a little, as I felt the water creep higher on my legs. I had on shorts, so I wandered freely in the water, up to a drastic mid-calf, keeping a watchful eye on Bree as she swam around me. The water was almost empty of other campers by now. Bonfires tended to draw them at this time, and there was a big one by the Boat House.

"It's like a bath," I gushed, as I moved my legs around in it, feeling the warmth against my skin. The water felt incredible. I moved my feet around, just to feel the water rush between my toes, and hummed as I walked.

The words to the song echoed in my head, as I thought of Dad and Ana: *Together they're born, in beauty and grace, to save all our souls from a malicious race. Our salvation rests in their loving devotion. Together they stand, to save our ocean.*

What did it mean? *Dad, why am I hearing your song in my dreams?* I thought of the intensity of it, the sound of the song, the tile path, and Darrien. The dream scared him, I could tell. *But why?*

The water felt great on my legs, so smooth and soft. The sand between my toes massaged my feet with each step I took. A kind of calm washed over me. I closed my eyes, and remembered what diving into water used to feel like: the rush of water across my face, the way the cool liquid trickled through my hair, making my scalp feel alive, the weightlessness of my body. Swimming was the only time I felt graceful, powerful.

"Cora! Wow!" Bree was right beside me…swimming.

What?

It took a moment for it to register with me that I was in the water up to my neck!

No, I don't want to do this. I'm not ready!

Whatever my body had been doing to keep afloat the way it was, it stopped doing the moment I realized what was happening. I started to sink.

No! NO! Not again! Help!

"Help!" I thrashed my arms and legs around as best I could.

"Cora! Stand up!" *What?*

I concentrated on calming myself and putting my feet down. *Oh, no.* My feet met the ground and I stood, lifting myself out of the water. The water was only at my arm pits. People on the beach were staring at me.

Oh…my…god, I'm going to die.

"Are you okay? What happened? You were swimming!" Bree beamed and clapped.

"Stop it! I wasn't swimming. At least, I didn't mean to. I don't know how that happened," I stressed to Bree in a loud whisper. I cursed myself silly in my head, as I turned to leave the water.

"I'm going to go and dry off now," I muttered, and trudged to shore. Anger and frustration were storming though me.

What was going on with me? How can I be so oblivious to what my body is doing?

"I am so proud of you, Cora!" Bree loudly whispered after me.

222

"Thanks, but I didn't do anything!" I sang. When I got to the sand, I squeezed out the bottom of my shirt, the evening air bringing out goose bumps across my wet skin. I shivered against the cold and my mood dipped even further that it was before.

"You looked about as graceful as a beached whale out there."

Perfect timing...as usual. I turned and leveled a glare at the face of the voice. Aurelia.

Aurelia and Jade had just come around the corner, from the path to the girl's side. Of course, they would appear just as I was squishing up on shore.

I was more empathetic toward Aurelia after learning about her infatuation with Darrien. I guess I understood her better. It would have been hard, knowing that he was finally interested in having a meaningful relationship, but that he had no interest, whatsoever, in having one with her. Right then, though, being dripping wet and embarrassed, my empathy was in short order.

"Aurelia...."

My temper was bubbling over, and I wanted to tell her off more than anything, but...*ugh*...was I going to sink to her level? I looked over to the water and saw Bree watching the whole scene unfold. Would sinking to Aurelia's level really achieve anything? *Nope.*

"Never mind. Have a good night." I waved to Bree and walked toward my cabin.

"Oh, come on, Cora! That's all you've got?" she called to me, as I moved away from her. I kept walking.

"How was your time in town?" she teased, running up to catch me. I turned and glared at her.

"Oh, yeah. Everyone knows you and Darrien were gone to town all day...alone. I can just imagine the wonderful time you had with him." She was circling me, her eyes sharp and her face tight. "He's quite the charmer, isn't he?"

Don't say anything, Cora, don't give her the satisfaction. Keep walking. And I did...for two steps.

Aurelia's hand came down on my shoulder and stopped me in the path. She circled around me, looking me hard in the eyes.

"I don't like you," she stated. "I haven't made that secret, but I'm going to do you a huge favor right now." I gawked at her. *Is she insane?* I didn't want any favors from her.

"I don't know what Darrien is doing, going after you," she began. "He's lost his mind. It's completely inappropriate and he knows it. It won't last long. See, he's always been more concerned with his job than anything or *anyone* else. He's ambitious, and cares about only himself. Don't get sucked in...*he will hurt you, Cora.*"

223

My anger shut off, like a bomb diffused. The crazed look in her eye was gone, replaced by a sincerity I didn't think she was capable of. But just as I saw it, it was gone. Her eyes hardened, and she was back to the Aurelia I knew. She leaned in and whispered, "Stay away from him if you know what's good for you." Then, she shouldered me out of her way and went back toward the beach.

After hearing about Darrien's history with Aurelia, I took her words more seriously than I would have yesterday. She was hurt by him, and she *did* know what he was like, or at least what he was like before. But, Darrien said he had changed.

I gazed in the direction Aurelia went. The girl was unhinged, but there was clarity there for a second and in that second I saw the hurt she had. Would that be me if he decided that he didn't feel for me what I did for him? Was that my future too?

65
Darrien

SLEEP WEIGHED ON ME like a cement drape, and didn't crumble away until my hot shower. As I stood under the steaming water, I thought about the dream that I had. I didn't typically dream, *ever*. I never remembered them, at least, if I did. It took me by complete surprise when I started to recount what I dreamt.

The water was murky and smelled of waste. I could barely breathe in it. I could barely see in it. I was searching for something- no, *someone*. It didn't matter which way I looked, I couldn't see where I was or who I was looking for. Then, I heard the song, the one from the path. My pulse shot. Where is she? *Where's Cora?*

Immediately I started swimming in circles, panic slicing through my calm. *Where is she?* The sound was getting louder, banging around in my head like a medicine ball. Then, from a shadow, I saw her. *Cora.*

But at the same time, it wasn't Cora. She looked the same, but there was something about her that didn't fit. The eyes...they were violet. *Ana!*

I knew then- I *knew*...Ana was alive. She was a Siren.

The water had long since gone cold. So was my blood. I stepped out of the shower in a daze.

Dreams are a doorway. They are a kind of communication that Mer have- and Sirens have it, too. Mer can communicate through thoughts; this has lent itself easily to travelling through thought to another Mer. On the other side, though, Sirens have manipulated that power. There have been a few cases of Mer being possessed by a Siren, which is an absolutely terrifying thought.

Was that what I was seeing? An attempt at possession? Or was it an attempt at communication? Why was she trying to talk to me? Or was this a warning?

Whatever the answer, it started my day off terribly. I was anxious to see Cora. Even though her night was uneventful, after the early morning dream I had, I was wary. Something was going to happen. I could feel it.

At breakfast, I sat next to Cora. I'm sure if Aurelia could have castrated me with her spoon, she would have hummed a merry tune while doing it. There was no mistaking her feelings about my interest in Cora. It didn't scare *me*, but it made me worried for Cora. Lia wasn't the girl I knew and respected before. I was constantly watching for her tipping point.

But that's all I did…for days.

I watched and waited for the other shoe to drop.

Almost a week went by before I relaxed slightly. I decided not to share the dream with anyone. Nothing had happened, and Cora hadn't sleepwalked in a long time. I was starting to second guess what I thought the dream was about. Maybe all the doom and gloom I was anticipating was just in my head.

So, with that in mind, I decided to finally ask Cora on a real date. I had mentioned to her that I wanted to take her back to the brook, the day we went to town. I didn't follow through for fear of something happening while we were away from camp. At least here, there was help if we needed it. Thoughts from the last time that I encountered Sirens sent pain shooting to my arm and leg, right to where I was stabbed. My wounds had healed, but they left savage scars. Even Tyde's powerful healing skills couldn't hide them. The Siren poison in the wounds wouldn't allow for it.

I watched as Cora dipped her feet into the water, as we stood on the main beach. Her slender legs were powerful, and graceful beyond what she realized. When she wasn't thinking about it, she was a stunning beauty, full of grace and agility. The moment her head took over…*boom*…her body went out of control. It was really a sight to see. The Mer in her was begging to come out. She just had no idea what was going on.

"Cora, would you let me teach you how to swim?" I wanted her to learn about who she was. Being Mer was incredible, and I couldn't wait to show it all to her. I watched for her answer. Her body moved nervously.

"Um, I don't know. I don't really need swimming lessons. I know how to swim. I just don't want to anymore." She swirled the water around with her feet. As much as it pained me to admit it, there was also a part of me that *didn't* want to tell her who she was. If she never knew, we could continue like we were, and the politics of Mer would stay away.

She sighed loudly. "Okay, so there's a part of me that wants back in. But, if we're doing this, we take it really, really slow…and on my terms, got it?" she demanded.

I was pretty sure that my jaw hit the floor for a second. It took a moment to process that she was actually agreeing to do this.

"Alright!" I yelled, maybe overcompensating a bit. "I mean, that's great." And it was. She should know who she really was. I needed to be less selfish and help her do that. Yes. I would be less selfish.

"I was wondering if, after supper tomorrow, you wanted to go back to the brook with me." *I'll start being less selfish next week.*

"Yeah, that sounds good." Her sweet lips inched high. I reached out for her hand as she turned to leave the water.

"I'm excited to get you in the water. I'll finally get to see you in that bikini you bought." The look on her face was everything. She elbowed me and blushed. I fought every impulsive thought in me, except one. I grabbed her arm and turned her to me, pulling her close. Her blush deepened as her breathing became quick.

Instantly I wanted more, much more.

I could see the pounding of her heart in her throat, and my heart matched hers. A blossom of yearning opened in me, just feeling her so close. She smelled like freshly cut flowers. I leaned into her, and her eyes flashed to my lips. I almost gasped with the pang of need I felt.

Without knowing where it came from, I broke the hold she had on me and took a step back. Clearing my throat and breaking out a stupid grin, I spoke in a rough voice I had never heard before.

"I think that- I mean, we should get ready for supper."

"Yes. Right. Of course," she said, her voice shaky, and there was a flash of disappointment on her face that made me feel like a total ass.

Get it together, Locke.

66
Cora

THE DAY OF THE DATE was a blur. It felt like I woke up, then it was time to meet Darrien. I didn't remember sessions. I knew they were in there somewhere, though. Instead, I found myself sitting in the cabin, just after supper, my heart trying desperately to leap out of my chest.

I was so nervous, I had dug into my chocolate stash. Two chocolate bars later, I was feeling a little bit better.

Pen and Bree were sitting with me, chatting about events of the day. I was absent from the conversation. My mind was elsewhere…on Darrien. And then, as if on cue, he appeared in the doorway. With a gentle knock, his smile was all I needed to calm my nerves. I grabbed my backpack and ran out the door, giving a small wave to a giggling Bree and Pen as I left.

We arrived earlier to the brook than we did last time. Wild flowers on the banks of the stream were open, splashing colors around us that were absent last time. I could see butterflies and bees zig-zagging from flower to flower. Darrien opened his pack, pulled out a blanket, and spread it on the ground for us. We sat on it for a while, just enjoying the view.

Darrien leaned back on his hands and stared at the sky. His eyes squinted in the bright sunlight, making the cutest wrinkle on his nose. I took a deep breath in, and leaned back on my hands, shaking my hair loose and letting the breeze flow through it. I could hear Darrien's breathing slow down, and I watched his eyes close. He was clearly relaxed.

I did the same. When I leaned back onto my hands, I realized our hands were so close, I could feel the heat from his skin on mine, but they weren't touching. I shifted a bit more so they did.

I snuck a look at Darrien to see what his reaction would be. His eyes stayed closed, but a smile crept across his face. Then, he snuck his finger over and wrapped it around mine, like a Darrien ring. My heart leapt into my throat. It was a small move, but it was just right. I couldn't help it; a big, goofy smile spread across my face. I bit my lip to try to keep it under control.

"Tell me about your brother. You know all about my sister," I asked, the question just popping into my head and out of my mouth. He never said much about his brother on our trip into town, and I was curious. Darrien's eyes opened and glanced at me.

"Well, my brother's sixteen and his name is Tyde. We look a lot alike, but we're very different people, even though we get along great. He's working in my position back home while I'm here, actually." He looked at me from under his long lashes. "He's the only person who understands me, really gets me. You know?" *Oh yeah, I know.* Bree's the same for me.

Darrien continued, "We've been through a lot. He was young when my parents were…umm, when they died." He shook his head, as if shaking away those thoughts, and continued on.

"He's actually very quiet, and more of a bookworm than I am. But he's ambitious and smart. I'm proud of everything he's done. But I think I'm going to have to talk to him about taking it easy when I get back home."

"I'd love to meet him. He doesn't go to camp?" I asked. I was sure I would have noticed a young Darrien wandering around by now.

"No. He's too old to come to camp, and too young to be a Lead. His job back home is really important, so he can't come and visit, either." I could hear the pride in Darrien's voice as he talked about his brother. It'd be fun to meet someone that knew Darrien's true self. *Too bad he can't come up this summer. It'd be nice for Darrien if Tyde could visit.*

I sighed. "I would be going crazy if I left Bree for the summer. I don't know how you can stand being away from your brother this long. It must be tough," I said, and smiled at him, squeezing his finger in mine.

"Sometimes, it's hard not having him here. I miss talking to him, but there's been this distraction I've had, which has occupied my mind…it helps." He gave me a half smile that deepened one dimple.

I was shocked with an electricity that almost knocked me over. I lost my breath, he was just that gorgeous and genuinely sweet. I wanted to know everything about him: his favorite color, song, sandwich, season…everything.

And so, my questions started. We sat on the blanket, watching the sun slowly set, and asked each other questions…many, many questions. By the time the sun was completely gone, and the stars were shining brightly, we had learned so much about each other. The only thing that I desperately wanted to ask Darrien was what he was hiding from me, but I didn't want to ruin an otherwise perfect night.

The air cooled, and a chill set into my skin. I knew it was getting time to head back to camp. Desperate to take advantage of the quiet and calm out here, I closed my eyes again and just let it all seep in. When I opened them, Darrien's eyes were on mine.

"You tired?" he asked.

"No, not even close, just...happy," I admitted, surprising myself. A sweet smile spread across his lips and he turned toward me. I returned the smile, grateful for him bringing me there.

But, the look on his face changed and suddenly I was really aware of how close we were. The mood changed in that instant. He reached out and tucked my hair behind my ear, letting his fingers trail over my skin. He shifted on the blanket to face me. My heart leapt into my throat and I swallowed hard when his eyes met mine.

Placing his hand gently on my face, Darrien rested his forehead against mine, his breath warm on my skin. His nose touched mine, awakening a butterfly in my chest.

"Cora..." he whispered and shook his head against mine. "What you do to me..."

I held my breath.

My heart gave a great thud, sending a shot of pleasure through me, and I trembled.

His eyes shifted, that hunger appearing in them again. I bit my lips to keep myself under control. That's when he lifted his hand to my face and traced a delicate line from my cheek to my jaw with his thumb. The rest of his fingers wrapped around the nape of my neck, drawing me closer to him. I couldn't breathe. I was frozen, locked in his gaze.

He watched me as he slowly lowered his head towards me. He hesitated just as our lips were about to touch, as if he wasn't sure of himself. I saw a flash of hunger just before he closed the tiny distance between us.

When his lips touched mine, an explosion of sensation burst in my chest, racing through me. The light brush of his lips was enough to undo me and I felt the world around us disappear.

It was a gentle kiss. It was perfect. His lips were soft and hot, and I wanted more.

He pulled back the smallest bit, and his eyes locked on mine. I could see in his eyes that it wasn't enough. We had held back so long, letting moments like this break. The hunger in his eyes burned and matched what I was feeling. The moment stretched out and then, somehow, at exactly the same time, we closed the space between us.

This time, his lips weren't gentle. They were on fire. He was firm and possessive, taking everything that he wanted. His mouth worked against mine, eliciting a breathy gasp as he broke away and trailed hot kisses down my neck.

Oh, my god.

There was no space between us anymore. I could feel the muscles in his arms rolling and flexing, as his hand trailed up my back and into my hair. I moaned against his lips and a deep groan came from him, sending shivers down my back.

I didn't know what to do with my hands, but they had somehow found their way to his chest. My touch made him tremble. I had no idea I could do that to someone. It felt powerful to know I could.

Darrien's hands moved to my hips, pulling me into him. I could feel everything; countless emotions coursed between us. I wanted it. I wanted it *all*. His kiss deepened, as I felt a flick of his tongue on mine. I moaned again, and that sent him off the deep edge. He crashed into me as we slid to the ground.

Whoa. My body was on fire, but this was moving fast. Suddenly, the weight of Darrien was off me. He hovered above me, holding his chest off mine. His eyes were an icy fire, the hunger still stirring.

"You okay?" asked, his voice a heavy whisper.

"I'm okay," I squeaked, suddenly aware that the rest of his body was pressing against mine. His eyes worked between mine, and I could see the struggle he was having. I was having the same one. He dipped down and placed a warm, gentle kiss on my swollen lips, then he rolled to the ground next to me.

A pang of disappointment rang through my body, but my brain sighed in relief. My heart was struggling to come back to normal pace as we laid there side by side.

I turned and watched Darrien's chest rise and fall, until it maintained its normal rate. I couldn't stop my heart racing. Even having him that close was too much for me. There really was no doubting my attraction to him. I was like a moth to a flame. I just hoped I wouldn't get burnt.

"Wow," I whispered.

"Yeah…wow," he whispered back, entwining his fingers in mine and turning to me. "Was that-"

"Incredible? Yeah." I smiled at him. He would never know, but it was *everything* I could have ever hoped for, and much, *much* more. He turned his body toward me and placed a hand on my waist, pulling me closer to him.

"I was going to say- I don't know what I was going to say." A deep chuckle came from him. A tightness in my abdomen called me to him again. I needed to settle down. I took a deep breath and tried to get myself under control again.

"Darrien, I-" I heard something. It came from…from the woods. I looked at Darrien, who was staring into the trees too. His brow furrowed, and the muscle in his jaw was thrumming. He crouched, looking dangerous. He could hear it, too.

Suddenly, the song came with a ferocity that took us by surprise, which caused us both to shoot to our feet. Instead of sounding pleasant and pretty, it was intense and harsh. It started to remind me of my dream. I looked at Darrien, and his face was a mask of worry. *That can't be good.*

Darrien pulled me behind him, keeping his hand on mine. His body was tall and strong, and I got the distinct impression that Darrien knew how to handle himself. Whatever was going on, he felt a threat.

Then, I felt a pull inside me and, without thought, I started walking towards the melody. I couldn't control my body. I willed my legs to stop moving, but nothing happened.

"Cora?" Darrien's voice was anxious. It was then that I realized that I couldn't speak either. *What's happening to me?*

"Cora!" He was yelling.

Darrien! Help me! Please!

The music was getting louder, and a thick fog was starting to collect across my vision. Soon, I wouldn't be able to see at all. Darrien came into sight. He was saying my name, but I couldn't hear him anymore. He placed his hands on my face. I wanted to stop. I wanted….

Fog drifted across my vision completely. I was blind to the woods and water…and Darrien. But, something *else* took form in front of me.

Like smoke, it wafted into focus, getting thicker and finally coming into full form. I recognized it right away. It was the face from the lake, but this time, it was in full body. This time, I knew what I was looking at, but I couldn't believe it. If it was true….

"Ana?" I called, but I could barely hear my own voice.

"Cora!" Her voice echoed in my head.

Oh, my god…

"Ana!" A rush of excitement coursed through me. Her beautiful face was shining back at me. I wanted to run to her, but I couldn't make my body move.

"Cora! It's you!"

"It's me! It's me! I can't believe…Ana. I've missed you so much." Tears were starting to form in my eyes.

"I missed you, too," she said, her voice was warm and smile bright, just the way I remembered it.

But then something changed. She started to look around. Her smile faded.

"Cora? Cora?" Her figure was starting to go out of focus. She was disappearing...I was going to lose her again.

"I'm here! I'm here! Don't go! Don't leave me again!" I demanded that my body move, but it wouldn't. I needed to get to her! I needed her!

"Cora!" Ana's voice was no more than a whisper in the wind. A guttural sob escaped my lips. I was losing her all over again.

A scream came out of the fog around me that made my blood run cold. I might not have been able to see her, but I knew that voice. It was Ana's. The sound of it was like nothing I had ever heard. My heart was fluttering like a frightened bird caught in a cage.

And then, there she was, standing before me.

A woman.

She was beautiful and terrifying at the same time, with flawless pale green skin and long flowing seaweed-green hair. Her eyes were completely black. She was stunning...but with one look, I knew she was deadly.

Her ebony eyes locked on mine. She said nothing.

I didn't know what to do. I stood there, frozen in fear. Darrien...I couldn't see him or hear him anymore. I didn't know if he was still with me or not.

The woman reached out toward me. My heart spiked, watching her razor sharp nails getting closer to me.

She placed a finger between my eyes. A wicked grin broke out over her face, and a searing pain shot into me from the spot she touched. It felt like someone was slowly piercing my skull with a red hot needle.

My skin was burning. I screamed and screamed. The sound came from the deepest, darkest part of me.

I didn't know I could make a sound like that.

I didn't know there was pain like that.

I just stood there and screamed, until my throat was raw and she released me. She smiled at me, then.

"You're mine now," she whispered in my ear.

Then, she was gone. The cord inside broke, and I crumpled.

67
Darrien

CORA!

She wasn't moving. She just stood there.

Her eyes were glassed over and glowing, just like in the water. *What do I do? What do I do?*

I grabbed her face, hoping to break through to her. She just looked on, unseeing. Usually, when I touched her, she snapped out of it, but not this time. When she started talking, my heart went to ice.

"Ana?" she called. *Her sister.*

"I'm here! I'm here!" she yelled.

My heart was breaking. She was seeing her dead sister! Then, she threw her head back and screamed. My skin nearly crawled off me. I had never heard anything like that. It was the most terrifying sound, made worse because it came from *her*. I was near panicking.

"Cora! *Cora!* Stop! Please! Come back! *Please!*" I was shouting, running my hands up her arms, trying to bring her back to me.

She looked unseeing at the sky, mouth still open, as her scream slowly died on her lips. Her voice was ragged.

"Midira! Stop it!" I cursed into the night air. "I swear, if you hurt her...."

"It's too late, King's Guard. She's mine." I couldn't breathe. The voice had come from the night air. There was no one around.

When Cora's screaming finally stopped, she collapsed into my arms. Her eyes were closed, and her skin shone from sweat. I held her against me.

A blistering fury built inside me that I couldn't contain. If I lost it, it would be devastating.

I lost it.

I could feel the power surging through me, pulling me into it and taking over me. For the first time ever, my powers took over. I let them consume me, use me to do their bidding. I was adrift in the wash of power I felt.

When it released, my rage went with it. The explosion was…well, I could see the trees snapping around the brook, as if a tornado just tore through. The rocks in the stream were tossed away, and the water just flowed into the hole I made in the ground.

I felt like a hurricane, the destructive power in me calling out to do more damage. I ached for revenge.

But I had to look after Cora.

I turned my attention to her.

She was white. Dark circles appeared under her eyes. She was nearly lifeless; her breathing was so shallow, I could barely make it out.

My heart broke looking at her. I didn't protect her. I didn't save her. Midira was right. I couldn't do anything to help Cora. I felt like a colossal failure. This was the one job I had to do, and I couldn't do it.

My blood was on fire. I thought about what I would do if I could get my hands on Midira.

I didn't think that I could kill in cold blood before, but now, I was positive I could…and I'd do it with a smile.

68

Cora

I WOKE UP IN HIS ARMS. I woke up to his beautiful eyes. I woke up.
What happened?

His hand was delicately placed on my cheek and pressed harder as I started to come around. He took a deep breath, as if he had been holding one. When he spoke, there was a desperation to him that startled me.

"We need to get you back. You need rest." He was starting to stand but I reached for his hand to pull him down to me. I was weak, but he sat anyway.

"No. What happened, Darrien?" I asked. *Something went wrong.*

"Let's not worry about that now." When I made no attempt to move he sighed and spoke again, "You…you fainted," he said, avoiding my gaze.

"I did?" *I felt fine before.*

"Yes. I've got you. Don't stand," he said, and put his arm under me.

"I can walk," I said and tried to stand, but I fell right back down again.

"You *cannot* walk," he stated, his voice calm but authoritative.

Darrien bent down to lift me into his arms. I squirmed and he hesitated.

"What? Did I hurt you?" he asked, checking me over.

"I just…I'm heavy, Darrien." I was embarrassed. I didn't want to see him trying to carry me, and then collapsing under my weight half way down the trail. I wasn't fishing for a compliment, I *was* heavy. I am tall…it comes with the territory.

"Don't be ridiculous, Cora. You're not heavy. Now just lean on me." I did as he asked, leaning against his chest as he threaded an arm under my legs and around my back. I held my breath and grimaced when he went to stand. *Oh this so isn't going to work.*

He picked me up as if I weighed nothing. His smile was triumphant, and I couldn't help the flood of relief that filled me. And, sue me, it was sexy as hell. I leaned against his warm chest and inhaled his sweet, rainy scent. Grateful for the help and the closeness. I closed my eyes, suddenly exhausted.

"I've got you," he whispered. He didn't stop until we were back in sight of my cabin.

"Darrien, you can put me down. I'm sure I can walk up the stairs to my cabin." I smiled at him. I wanted to talk to him about what happened, but I was feeling so tired, I could barely keep my eyes open.

When we reached the bottom of the stairs, he put me down and pulled me in for a warm embrace. I took a deep breath in. He smelled incredible.

His hands were running the length of my back as he held me. He lifted a hand from my back to my face, and tucked away a bit of hair behind my ear. He softly brushed my cheek with the back of his fingers, leaving an electrical tingle along my skin.

"You are so beautiful," he whispered.

My heart jump-started again, and thumped loudly. His fingers lingered on my skin. They were so gentle and soft. Darrien pulled me closer. I was sure he could feel my heart beating wildly, because I could feel his. I could feel the warmth of his skin against my face, his breath now coming a little faster.

I could feel my pulse in every part of my body. I was sure that no matter how much we kissed, my body would react like that every time. He moved his fingers along my jawline, onto my neck, and into my hair as he pulled me into him.

"Oh my, look at the cute little love birds." *Aurelia.*

I instinctively pushed Darrien away from me. We weren't doing anything wrong and yet I felt guilty. I looked at Darrien, not knowing what to do or say.

"Go inside, Aurelia. It's late," shot Darrien. He was staring hard at her, and stepped in front of me, as if he was going to block me from an attack.

"Oh, Darrien. If you want your little alone time, by all means…take it!" She gestured wide with an arm and slammed the door behind her. Her face appeared in the window a second later, though.

"I don't know about you, but I don't like being spied on," he grumbled, grabbed my hand and moved me around to the side of the cabin with no windows. "This is better," he said with a smile. My heart started beating hard against my chest again.

How does he do this to me?

"How are you feeling?" Darrien asked, as his eyes took me.

"Tired and not sure that you are being honest about what happened in the woods just now," I admitted.

"Don't worry about that. I'll-you just get some rest okay?"

I wanted to argue, but my eye lids were slamming slut as we spoke. I wasn't sure if I would even make to my bed before I fell asleep.

237

"Darrien, I had the most amazing night, truly. I- you are…well, you've surprised me," I said and couldn't look him in the eye anymore. My feelings were running away and I was struggling to keep them in check. The night was amazing but things almost got out of control, and that scared me. I don't know if that registered on my face, or what but Darrien tipped my chin up and looked hard into my eyes.

"Cora, I would never make you do anything you weren't comfortable with. I hope you know that you can trust me," he said, his voice soft and genuine. He held both my hands and looked intently into my eyes.

"I do trust you," I whispered, surprising myself. But, it was true. I did trust him; completely.

"I'll see you tomorrow for breakfast, okay?" His hand caressed my cheek and for a moment my worries disappeared.

"That sounds perfect." I couldn't help the big smile that broke out on my face.

"Good night, Humbug. Get some rest." He leaned in and rested a soft kiss on my forehead. It was gentle and tender. It was perfect.

"Night, Darrien." He guided me back around the front of the cabin, and waited for me to go inside before he turned and walked back to his cabin.

What a night.

69

Darrien

I WASN'T GOING ANYWHERE.

I wasn't leaving her.

Cora brought out something in me…this animal urge to protect, and yeah, some serious romantic emotion, too. My feelings for her were terrifying *and* exhilarating. I had never felt anything remotely close to that before.

I would do anything for Tyde, but that was different. I knew he was a fighter and could take care of himself if things got hairy. Cora couldn't. The protectiveness I felt for her was…consuming. I didn't think I was capable of wanting to fight *for* someone like that.

Midira had no idea what she was getting into. She would regret it. If she hurt Cora in any way….

I could feel the surge of anger ride on a wave of power. I had to take a breath to calm the rage.

Cora was special. She was important to me, and it didn't matter that she was going to be queen.

This was bigger than her title.

My thoughts were scrambled. Memories of our kiss mixed with Cora's glowing eyes. Then, there was the song. Cora wasn't the only one who was affected by it. My memories of my Mom surged forward as soon as I heard it. I hadn't thought of my Mom in a long time; it was too painful.

But, hearing that song again tonight, I realized that in not remembering, I had forgotten what I had learned from her. She always told me to follow my heart, to trust it. She was an amazing mother. We were lucky. I wish that Tyde would have had more time with her. It didn't seem fair that he doesn't remember her as much as I do. Cora reminds me of her. She's kind and so sweet. She is so much more than she thinks she is.

What is she going to think once she finds out that you have been keeping who she is a secret from her?

My blood ran cold. That thought was haunting my days, and my nights. To say that I dreaded her finding out was an understatement. My chest tightened just thinking about the look on her face when she realized that I had been keeping a colossal secret from her. One that was going to change her life. That would be the end of us. That would be it. She wouldn't trust me at all after that.

She'll hate me. I'll lose her.

That thought erupted a heartsick panic I didn't know what to do with.

70

Cora

I WOKE WITH A SCREAM. At least, I thought I was screaming. My mouth was open, but nothing came out. A searing hot pain was radiating from my head. I pressed the heels of my hands to my eyes hard enough to see stars, but still the pain persisted. White hot tears started running from my eyes.

I ran to the bathroom, tearing at my emergency kit for a pain killer. I had migraines before, but this was different, searing and hot and everywhere in my head. My eyes, my ears, even my teeth hurt. I turned to the toilet and threw up, my stomach roiling and churning acid.

The pain wasn't subsiding, when a flash flitted across my mind of two black eyes. That's when I remembered I had passed out last night. I had a thought of a woman in the woods with us. She was terrifying, with the black eyes. Did she cause this?

I thought of Darrien. He had been there. Didn't he see any of it? Why wouldn't he tell me?

I rushed through my shower, partly because I wanted to see Darrien, but also because the hot water actually made the thundering in my head worse. As much as I wanted to look good for Darrien after the night we had, I could barely move from the pain. Another pain killer and a bite of chocolate and things were starting to settle down to a bearable throbbing.

I ran to the beach to see if I could catch Darrien swimming. He needed to answer some questions. My head ached severely, stabbing the backs of my eyes with every step I took. A constant reminder of the darkness that took over our date.

When I got to the end of the path the beach was empty and so was the water.

Damn.

I sighed and sat down in the sand. The water was calm and the morning bright. It would be a beautiful day, but it held no excitement for me. I took off my shoes and dug my feet into the sand, feeling the cool slide between my toes. Somehow, being closer to the water eased the ache in my head.

There was a bang on the beach that caused me to jump. Pearl stood, stretching on the front step of her little cabin. She had a cup of coffee in one hand and was wearing a fuzzy housecoat. When she brought her arms down, her brows flew up.

"Cora? What are you doing?" she chuckled.

"Uh, good morning Pearl." An awkward laugh escaped my mouth. "I was just enjoying the quiet, but I'm done now and I'll be going." I stood and turned to go back to my cabin.

"Hold on, Cora. Come and sit." She grinned wide at me and waved me over to the step.

"Sure, okay," I stammered and awkwardly smiled back. I hopped up the steps and sat across from her on the little deck.

Pearl's short brown and silver hair was tied back in a lazy, low pony this morning. Even in her fuzzy housecoat, she looked beautiful. She reminded me of my mom.

"Am I in trouble?" I laughed a little, but stopped when I realized I might be. My smile faded.

"No! No, not at all. Just wanted to check in with you, that's all," she said; her tone friendly as always. It put me at ease. She grinned over her coffee cup.

"How was your trip to town?" she asked taking a long sip. Her eyelids closed as she swallowed and a lazy grin slipped across her face. *Wow. The lady loves her coffee.*

"It was great!" I exclaimed, focusing my attention back on the conversation. "I mean, I got Mom a nice gift so I was happy."

"I'm glad to hear that, your mother will appreciate that. Have you talked to her?"

"I haven't, but B called a while ago to check in on her. She sounded good, which was a relief." I cleared my throat, not wanting to talk about Mom.

"Thanks for letting Darrien drive me in for that gift," I added, hoping to change the subject.

"Oh, well, he had some things to do in town anyway; it was no trouble. Did he behave himself?" My eye brows shot up. How was I supposed to answer that?

"Yeah," I answered, drawing the word out. I watched her for a hint that she didn't approve, but I didn't get a sense of that.

"Good. That's good," she nodded and smiled as her thoughts took her attention. That was my cue to go.

"Okay. I should get going, though. I have to get the girls up. See you later, Pearl."

I was already half way down the path when I remembered that I had left my shoes on the beach. I turned around and jogged my way back, bare footed. Just as I rounded the corner to the beach, I heard raised voices.

I came to a stop just out of sight, not wanting to intrude on someone's argument, but yet close enough to overhear it. I'm not going to say that I was exactly proud of myself for being so sneaky, but my curiosity won out over my conscience.

What I heard next made me wish once and for all that I wasn't so nosy.

71
Darrien

THE NIGHT HAD LEFT ME exhausted. I needed to recharge, badly. After the sun came up, and I was sure that Cora was safe, I took off for the beach. A swim was just what I needed.

I dove deep, feeling the weight of the water pressing around me. The lake was so clean and clear my skin came alive in it. I can't explain just how much water cleanses the mind and soul. It rejuvenated my senses, and I could feel the stress of the night seep away from me. All I needed was a cat nap, and I would be good to go.

As I was coming out of the water, Pearl called to me and invited me into her place for a chat. My heart shuddered. I had a feeling this wasn't going to be about boat care, but rather about Cora.

I really didn't want to have that conversation with her. I lifted the water from me, drying my skin and hair instantly and walked into her cabin.

I sat down in her tiny living room, on her couch, while she bustled about, making a cup of coffee for me

"Look, Darrien, I need to talk to you about Cora," she confided over her bran muffin. *I knew it.*

"Why?" I groaned.

"It's getting serious," she said.

"Again, Pearl, it's none of your business. I'm looking after her the best that I can. I need to be close to her to do that. You have no idea what is going on with her. You don't know what danger she has already been in. Just let *me* decide what's best," I stated.

"I want to but I don't trust your judgement anymore." Her voice just above a whisper.

"What? How can you say that?" I yelled.

"You can't see beyond your feelings. This is a disaster waiting to happen! Why can't you see that?" she yelled.

She just didn't get it, and she never would. My hands balled in my lap. I bit my lips, and closed my eyes against the pain. But, none of that stopped the torrent of words that burst forth from me.

"Damn it, Pearl! You're really testing my patience! This isn't just a job to me anymore. I *care* about her. A lot."

"And that's why you need to separate yourself from her," she reasoned.

"What?"

"I'm relieving you of your camp duties going forward."

"What!" I yelled. "This is a joke."

"I wish I was."

"You can't tell me to stop doing my job," I reminded her.

"Maybe not the job *Zale* gave you. But this is *my* camp. As far as your job as the swim instructor, boating instructor, and trail guide...you're fired." My heart stuttered.

"Why are you doing this?" I demanded.

"You need space. You won't listen to me, so this is the only way I can get through to you! You've left me no choice!"

"You think this is going to stop me from seeing Cora?" I challenged.

"No, but it will distance you; which may be the break you need to figure all this out. You have a job to do, Darrien! Zale sent you to get her to swim and she isn't. You haven't even tried!" she accused.

"But I-"

"But *nothing*! You aren't doing the job you were sent to do! Cora is going to rule Mer and you are too caught up in puppy love to realize what that means for the two of you. It has to stop!" Pearl's voice was louder than I had ever heard. Her face was red, and her lips tight.

I wanted to disagree, but she had a very sobering argument. Cora was going to be a queen and I was just a guard. No matter how much I wished it differently, we would never be accepted in Titus Prime.

I sagged down into the couch. I knew when I started having feeling for Cora that I was venturing into an impossible situation; it's just that, the deeper I got the less I cared. But, I realized that I was only taking *my* feelings into consideration, not Cora's.

How would *she* feel about all this? Would she even want a relationship with me once she knew what she was going to be? Was it better that I just end everything now?

I didn't know the answer to any of those questions and I didn't really want to.

"Cora isn't just a job to me anymore," I uttered.

"I know that and believe me I wish that things were different, but they aren't. Mer is the way it is; unchanging and stubbornly so."

Pearl stood and went to the door, I was being dismissed. She opened the door and held it open for me.

"Just do the job you were sent to do and soon," she uttered. I walked to the doorway and Pearl placed a gentle hand on my shoulder.

"She's just a job," she said.

I nodded as I exited the cabin.

"Thank you, Darrien," Pearl said in a relieved voice.

"Don't thank me yet," I said and wandered down the beach to my cabin. I needed some time to think.

72

Cora

"JUST DO THE JOB you were sent to do and soon. She's just a job."
Pearl.

There was a pause as someone came out the door and then Pearl spoke again.

"Thank you, Darrien."

"Don't thank me yet," he muttered. My heart raced. *What?*

Darrien walked down the beach. He was wearing a big bunny hug and sweat pants. It could have been any of the male Leaders, but I knew immediately it was him.

I waited until he was gone before I grabbed my shoes and walked in stunned silence back to wake the girls.

She's just a job? What does that even mean?

I carried on with my morning routine in a fog. Words from Darrien's conversation with Pearl rolled around in my head, trying to make sense.

"She's just a job." Over and over, those words played. I couldn't get past them.

Between the head ache, that was on its way back to epic, and hearing that conversation my mind was buzzing. There was so much…too much, that had happened in the last twelve hours. I was going to go insane.

First, we had the hottest make out session ever. Sure, I had no frame of reference, but to me, it was *unreal.*

Second, I have a blank drawn over what happened for hours last night. I just remember something about a woman with black eyes and searing pain in my head.

And third, I found out that Darrien is supposed to treat me as a job…whatever *that* meant.

How was I supposed to process any of that *with no explanation?* I wanted to scream at him. I wanted to hurt him. I really did.

But I didn't get the chance to, he didn't show up for swimming lessons.

73
Darrien

"DARRIEN, YOU GOING FOR lunch?" I woke to Avery's eyes watching me.

"It's lunch?" I yawned.

"Yeah, man. You've been out to the world all morning. You missed your lesson with Cora," he said, leaping out of the way as I jumped up out of the bed.

"Damn it!" I yelled, searching for something to wear.

Avery stood aside and watched as I dove into my drawer for a shirt and started pulling it over my head.

"You guys are close, huh?" he asked quietly.

"Yeah," I said, stopping with my shirt hanging around my neck. I turned my attention to him.

"She's nice, Darrien. You're lucky." He half smiled.

"Thanks." I slowed right down. There was something in his tone.

Does he have...feelings...for Cora?

I could feel anger stirring. I shook my head; my jealous streak was something I had never felt before. I had just got my first taste.

Sour.

"I need to talk to your sister," I said, pulling the shirt over my head. Avery's eyes widened.

"Really?" he asked. "What about? Pretty sure she has made her intentions abundantly clear," he warned.

"That she has; but she needs to have some things spelled out for her."

"Alright. Go easy on her, Darrien. I get where you're coming from, but she's still my sis, okay?"

"I can promise you, I *have* tried to be delicate. I've tried to be honest. And I have been blunt..."

I fell over, trying to get my pants on.

"But, it's not working," he added, leaning over the bed and finishing my thought for me.

"Precisely."

"Alright, well, let her have it then. She needs to get it through that thick skull of hers; for everyone's sake."

"Thanks," I said. I had to talk to Aurelia. If she revealed who Cora was, Cora would be in more danger; she would also be the center of social buzz that didn't need to happen. But, I really needed to do it alone, no one else needed to know about Cora. I looked at Avery.

"Can you do me a favor?" I asked.

"Sure," he said, handing me a shoe from the floor.

"If you see anyone heading this way, could you just redirect them away from the cabin? I need to talk with Aurelia and I don't want anyone getting the wrong idea." Avery was a good guy, dependable. Though, his questions about Cora left me wondering about his motives.

There was a knock at the door and we both turned to see who was there. Pen.

"Hey," I said, looking around the room for the hoodie I had earlier.

"Hey, I just wanted to see if you were okay," she said and stopped short when she saw Avery.

Avery looked between Pen and I, and, like the great guy I knew he was, excused himself from our conversation.

"No problem," he said, answering my earlier question. He nodded with a smile, and jogged down the stairs.

"Thanks, Avery!" I shouted after him and he waved.

Pen stepped further into the room, her watchful eyes on me. It was rare to have any interactions with a Claire; they were usually held up in their residence. I admit I was unnerved by her. There were ancient powers in her, ones she didn't fully understand yet. I felt like she could read me just by looking at me, and that made me uncomfortable. I started tossing my bed, looking for that hoodie.

"No offense, Darrien, but you look like crap" she warmly commented as she took another step into the room.

"Yeah, well…I've had a rough couple of days," I said, tossing my sheets to the floor.

"Really? By the way that Cora was acting when she got in last night, I thought that you would be all smiles. What happened?" She picked something up off the floor and handed it to me. My hoodie.

"Thanks," I said and took the sweater from her hand.

"So? What happened?"

"Um…not sure I want to talk to you about it, Pen. Sorry," I apologized. I pulled on the sweater and gave her a weak smile. I didn't want to hurt her feelings.

"I get that. I just wanted to extend an olive branch…you know. You seem like you could use a friend. You don't strike me as someone that really talks to the other guys here. They aren't the most…supportive bunch. Except Avery, but that would be awkward."

"Why, because he's Aurelia's brother?" I asked.

"No, because he's betrothed to Cora."

No.

74
Cora

I FIGURED THAT I'D FIND Darrien at his cabin. So, I watched my girls grab their food and settle down at our table at lunch, and then I took off.

I needed to talk to him, even if he didn't want to see me, which I was worried was the case.

He had missed swimming and said nothing to me about it. Compounded with the whole "job" thing I had no idea where that left us. But I was only halfway to his cabin when Avery cut in front of me, blocking the path.

"Hey, Cora, you lost? The girls' cabins are the other way, you know," Avery teased and laughed sincerely.

"Right. I know," I said smiling and moving around him.

"Whoa wait!" he moved in front of me again.

Avery was nothing like his sister. It wasn't just the startling difference in their hair, his being bright blonde and hers like a raven's, but his eyes weren't cruel or judgemental like Aurelia's.

He stopped laughing, but didn't lose the humor in his eyes; even when I shot him a death glare. I really didn't have time for this.

"Ouch, now that look could kill" he said, throwing up his hands in defense. I couldn't help the half grin that slid up my cheek as I rolled my eyes.

"Sorry," I chuckled, "I'm just looking for Darrien. Have you seen him?" I cleared my throat not wanting to sound too desperate. "Um, he just wasn't at swimming today." Hopefully, that sounded a little better.

Avery got a little awkward, looking down at his shoes.

"No, haven't seen him. I'm sure it's nothing. He'll show eventually." He gave an uncomfortable smile. *Hmmm.*

"Oh. Okay, thanks. I think I'll just go check to make sure he's not sick or something. Thanks, Avery." I stepped around him to go down the rest of the path.

Avery dashed around me and threw his hands up. "Whoa, whoa! You can't just walk into the guys' cabin area. You're a girl, it's not allowed. Besides, he's not in the cabin anyway; I just came from there."

I didn't remember reading that Leaders weren't allowed in each other's camps. But I didn't want to get in trouble, and I didn't want to get Darrien in trouble, either.

"Okay, Avery, relax. I won't go. Thanks for the info. If you see Darrien, though, can you tell him I need to see him? I…uh….have to rebook our swim time he missed today."

I turned and walked back towards the Hall.

No use fighting Avery to get to the cabin. I can sneak back once everyone's eating.

Apparently, Avery read my thoughts, because he bounded up beside me.

"I'll walk with you," he chirped. "So, what do you think of the camp so far?" he asked in a cheery voice.

"It's been good. I'm enjoying it," I said, attempting to be friendly, even though I just wanted to shake him so I could be on my way. From what I knew of Avery, he was a cheerful person most of the time. The guys liked him and so did the girls. I liked him too, even though I really didn't know him well.

It wasn't in my nature to be a jerk to someone that was being kind to me. He seemed genuinely interested in what I was saying. I summoned all my self-restraint, and attempted to be a bit more invested in the conversation.

Avery smiled and continued, "That's good. We've all liked our time away from things here. It's so peaceful." He was sincere; the anxiousness gone from his face now that we were turned around. He smiled with ease.

"Yes, it is peaceful. So, you're Aurelia's brother, huh?" *Wow, Cora Reed, the great conversationalist.*

"Yeah, though I really don't like *that* to be the way that people recognize me," he admitted. I lifted my brows. He grinned and went on, "Everyone assumes we are the same person, and we couldn't be more different," he insisted.

"Yeah, I could see why you wouldn't want to be slotted in with her." I regretted it the moment I said it. "Sorry, she's your sister. I shouldn't have said that," I looked away, feeling guilty. It was true but still. *Poor guy.* He didn't pick his family.

"No worries. I know she's been rough on you. She's got some Darrien issues," he stated with a shrug.

"Yeah, I heard." I nodded.

"Um…I know it's none of my business, but you two seem to be spending some time together. You and Darrien, I mean." I raised my eyebrows. Avery chuckled. "Come on, you haven't exactly been hiding it. It's pretty obvious something is going on between you."

I couldn't look at him. Of *course* I didn't realize it was obvious, I was *oblivious*! This was a first for me and I hadn't taken a second to think about how it was coming across to everyone else.

Avery was watching me, but I wasn't sure what he was hoping to see. I just kept walking, keeping my eyes focused on the path ahead, not knowing what to say. Avery ran in front of me and came to a halt. I almost smashed into him. The set of his jaw was serious and intent.

"What? You think there's something going on with us?" I gave an unconvincing "Pfft!"

Avery looked at me, doubt written all over his face. "No, really," I pushed.

"Just…be careful, please," he added. "If you have real feelings for him, you might want to know that he can get in a lot of trouble being with you. Is that something you want for him?" He seemed so genuine, but it all made no sense to me.

"Wait, if you are talking about Pearl, I think Darrien can handle his aunt," I scoffed at Avery. He was making a bigger deal out of this than there should be. Darrien knew what he was doing. I wasn't going to get him in trouble. At least I was pretty sure I wouldn't.

"It doesn't matter who it's from. I just thought you should know, so you can make an informed decision." Avery stared deep into my eyes, his brow furrowed and his mouth turned down. It was the most serious expression I had seen on him.

Why were things getting so complicated?

"Okay…thanks?" I said, not knowing what else to say to that. "Look, Avery, it's nice of you to walk me back, but I know your sister would flip out if she saw you talking to me. I don't want to get you in trouble; I'm not in the mood to be the source of another scene involving Aurelia." I smiled and tried not to look too desperate to be done with the conversation. It had gone from awkward to just plain weird, fast. Avery seemed like a nice guy, but his sudden interest in my love life was…odd.

"I'm sorry if I stepped out of line," he apologized. "Believe it or not, I don't want either of you getting hurt. I know we haven't really talked, ever, and my sister doesn't help my trustworthy case, but I'm a good guy. I promise." He held up his hand in a Boy Scout manner. It was incredible how different he was from his sister.

"I trust your sister less than a rattlesnake, but you're doing a good job of fighting for your case," I laughed.

Avery seemed like a decent guy. His sister could take a few notes from him.

"Aurelia," he started and then hesitated, "she's a little high strung. She doesn't like people when invade her territory. Especially in the romance department. She sees you as competition, and a target. Plus, you don't fit in with the other girls."

I rolled my eyes. Avery shifted from foot to foot.

"I'm not sure why," he contemplated. "You're just as pretty…even more, I think." He seemed to realize what he said too late. His face got red as he stared at the ground. I felt like I had stuck my face in a bonfire.

"Um, anyway," he said, clearing his throat and pushing through the awkwardness. "I love my sister, but we disagree on a lot of things. You, would be one of them."

He looked up from his shoes and smiled at me. To my surprise, my heart gave a flutter. Avery's words were so kind and unexpected. I didn't know what to say.

"Um, thank you for walking me back," I stammered. "I should go meet my team now." I took a couple of steps. Avery's hand touched my shoulder, and I turned to look at him.

"I know it's none of my business, but if you ever need anything, please, let me know." He smiled warmly, his big blue eyes lingering on mine.

I stood there, frozen, as he walked inside the hall. My heart gave a quiver. Avery Sands, Aurelia's brother, was….flirting with me?

I shook off the barrel of crazy that conversation was, as I walked into the hall. There was still no Darrien. I debated risking going to the boys' camp. Would anyone notice me missing? *Avery would.* So, I stood in line for food. Avery smiled at me as I set my lunch tray down and took a seat at the Lead table.

"Not taking a walk around the lake, then?" he winked at me.

"No, I decided lunch would be better for me." I smiled. "Um, has anyone seen Darrien?" Everyone at the table shook their heads and stared at their lunch. That was the biggest response I got out of anyone, even out of Aurelia.

"Okay, thanks, guys," I answered to the silence. We ate our lunches quickly and quietly, that's when I realized that Pen was missing too.

After lunch, the team was scheduled for canoe lessons. My heart leapt as we headed for the boat launch, hoping Darrien would be there. But it sank low when I saw Pearl standing on the dock; ready to greet us with a big smile.

"Hello, everyone! I know you were all looking forward to seeing Darrien, but he's unable to make it out. So, I'm taking over your lesson today. Shall we begin?" The girls, though noticeably disappointed Darrien wasn't there, ran to get their paddles and boats for Pearl.

Once they were out of earshot, I asked Pearl, "Where's Darrien? He missed my swimming lesson today, too. Is he alright?" I was getting more concerned.

"Oh, uh, he's fine, Cora. No need to worry. He's just doing some errands for me in town, and he'll be gone all day. He may not be back until tomorrow, even. I'm not sure." She smiled quickly at me as she walked away.

I would have followed with more questions, but I didn't want to raise Pearl's suspicions that there was more going on between me and Darrien than I told her. Darrien's absence was just so *odd*. How could Pearl not know when he would be back from town if he is running *her* errands?

None of this makes sense!

"Today, ladies, we are going to be taking these canoes out on the lake for a try. What do you say to that?" The girls gave an enthusiastic "Yeah!" in agreement.

Darrien usually went through safety stuff with them first, but Pearl allowed the girls to get in their canoes and figure things out for themselves. I plunked myself down next to a tree and took out the book I stashed in the boat house. I turned to my marked page and tried to look engrossed in the story.

As soon as all the boats were out of eyesight, I took off.

75

Darrien

"I SHOULD *NOT* HAVE SAID THAT! Please don't tell anyone! Oh, I could get into so much trouble!" Pen begged.

I just stood there and stared at her. *Avery was betrothed to Cora? Avery?*

"How do you know? How do you know about her?" I finally managed to say.

"Well, as a Claire, I can see things. I can see a future for Cora. I can see a past for her, too. I know she's King Zale's daughter, I have seen that." I opened my mouth to correct her, but there was no point. "I've known that for a while. It makes *way* more sense why you're here now. *However,* that really, *really* complicated what I told you about your heart and stuff. I swear I didn't know who Cora was when I said that to you. I'm sorry."

"Yeah, whatever...what do you know about *Avery?*" I demanded.

"The Claires are the ones that put together the betrothals. To have one done in recent years was noteworthy, so we all know about it. I thought you knew!" Pen whimpered, wringing her hands.

I couldn't believe it. Avery and Cora were to be *married.* They were going to join their feuding families. It would bring so much happiness at home. It was the oldest rivalry in our history, the Reeds and the Sands. The two oldest families in our world.

The Sands have had their eye on the throne for centuries. While Zale might have the throne, Alastair Sands has a strong hold in policy and politics on Titus. Their views have never meshed and while Zale has maintained a cordial friendship with Sands, there is a tension there that goes back generations. Cora and Avery would finally bring an end to it. They would bring unity to our people. And suddenly, I was in the way of that.

"I might be sick." I sank down on my bed.

"I'm *so sorry,* Darrien!" Pen cried. "I didn't know who she was when I told you to follow your heart. I swear, I didn't know," she started to pace the floor. "I'm so confused by my visions. They so clearly point to you as the one for her, yet this betrothal…it doesn't make sense. But I see her happy in it, too. I don't get it," she said running her hand over her strawberry blonde pony-tail.

"She's *happy*? She's happy with *him*?" That can't be true. *But it is true.* And that's good, right? I want her to be happy. I just want it to be with *me*, and not Avery.

"I shouldn't have said that…but, yes. I think I should go. I have just upset you. I'm very sorry." She turned to go.

"No, Pen, it's okay. You are the only one that knows about her. Correction, Aurelia knows," I admitted.

"What? How did that happen? She's so dangerous! You don't even know what she's capable of! How did she find out?" she said, her voice tight and high.

"Pearl and I were talking-"

"Pearl knows too?"

I raised an eyebrow.

"Oh, yeah, I guess that makes sense. She did hire Cora, and brought in you. Yeah, I should have figured that one out," she admitted.

"Aurelia doesn't know Cora is Zale's daughter. She just knows she's royalty. She's also threatening to tell everyone who Cora really is, unless I stay away from Cora."

"Oh my goodness." Her brow furrowed.

"Yeah. I need to talk to her. Things have gotten more complicated, and Cora is in real danger."

"Midira," Pen said.

"Yes. How did you know?" I asked, watching Pen carefully.

"Um, I wanted to talk to you about that. I have this sense that there's a growing danger here. No matter where I sense it coming from, it all centers around Cora. I really think we should be watching her at all times," she said.

"I'm outside your cabin all night…not to sound creepy." I smiled.

"Ha! I'm more relieved than creeped out, trust me." She laughed.

"Has something happened that makes you so worried?" I asked.

"Well, now, *this* may sound creepy. The other morning, while she was showering, I noticed she had been in there a really long time. I knocked on the door and peeked inside to make sure she was okay, but she wasn't responding." I watched Pen's face cloud in worry. "She was standing in the shower; her eyes were glowing and she was talking to the wall."

"Shit! How long ago was that?" I yelled.

"Yesterday morning, I think. Maybe the day before. I don't remember! It scared me! I tried to talk to her, but she wouldn't look at me." Pen's eyes were wide.

"What happened?" I asked, half knowing the answer.

"I touched her shoulder, and she collapsed on the floor of the shower," Pen said.

"Was she hurt?" I pressed.

"She was bruised up, but otherwise okay. I got her standing up and wrapped her in a towel. She was so groggy. I left the bathroom to get her some clothes. When I came in again, she yelled at me to get out because she was showering. She was right in the water again; fully awake and completely unaware anything had happened." Pen sat on a bed and looked to the ceiling.

"What was Cora saying when she was talking?"

"She kept saying 'Ana' and 'don't leave me.' It was sad. She was whimpering. Do you know who that is?" Pen asked, trying to make sense of everything.

"It's her twin sister that died in a boating accident when they were young," I said.

"She has a twin sister?" Pen perked up. Her eyes widened.

"Yes," I said, unsure of what she was onto.

"Do you know what that means?" She was practically vibrating.

"That it was really hard on her!" I pointed out.

"No! It's *The Prophesy!*" She was jumping now.

"What prophesy?" I was confused.

"Haven't you heard it before? It's been passed down for generations. It was made into a song so no one would forget! *Together they're born, in beauty and grace, to save all our souls from a malicious race. Our salvation rests in their loving devotion. Together they stand, to save our ocean.* Don't tell me you've never heard it?"

"No, of course I have. My mother sang it to me all the time." She told me that it would mean more to me when I grew up, that I would be a part of it. It can't be....

How did Mom know?

"All the pieces fit." Pen's logic worked for *her*, but my mind was spinning.

"But her sister is dead. The Prophesy is about twins, together, saving our home. Cora is alone," I stated. Then I remembered my dream and the pieces were starting to fit a little clearer. Though, until I could be sure, I would keep that to myself.

"Hmm, you're right," Pen answered. "But everything fits so well. Has she said anything to you about her sister? Have you heard her talking to her?" Pen asked as she started to pace the room.

259

"Yes, I have. I did last night…there was an incident," I said, watching Pen.

Pen nodded, "Okay, well, during my training, I learned a lot about Sirens. They are telepathic. They can reach into your mind and talk to you just like we can, but *unlike* us, you don't *have* to be in water. But you have to be a Siren…so that doesn't work." She stopped pacing, hitting a wall in her logic.

"There's something that we're missing. Someone hasn't been honest about whole story here, and if we don't find *all of it* out, we're going to lose Cora to Midira," I determined.

A piece that had been missing was starting to formulate, but I needed more information.

"I agree," Pen stopped pacing, placing her hands on her hips. "If she's reaching into Cora's mind already, that isn't good. And the scariest part is that Cora has no idea. None," Pen said, sharing my fears.

"We can't tell her, not yet. Not until we have all the information we need. She deserves to know it all. We need to know it all, first," I stated.

"But how are we going to do that? And by *we*, I hope you know I am including myself in this now. There's no way you're excluding me. Cora is my friend. I haven't had any friends; Mer don't like my kind. You fear us. Cora is the first person to treat me with kindness. I don't want to lose her." Pen's eyes shone with emotion.

"I know the feeling. Come on, we have a camp owner to talk to." I stood up to go, and that's when Aurelia stepped into the cabin.

260

76
Cora

I DECIDED TO START WITH Pearl. She said that Darrien was doing some errands for her in town. The only way that he could get to town was to drive. The buses were only out there for pick-up and delivery of campers every two weeks, and the supply trucks for food came on Mondays, so that left the green Ford truck of death.

I jogged down the path quickly, slowing down when I passed Team Yellow, Jade's team. I didn't want her wondering where I was going in such a hurry.

Just look casual.

It took a lot of concentration to keep a slow pace, but I managed to do it. Once past Yellow Team, I ran to the back of Pearl's cabin where she parked the truck.

It was there. *I knew it!* My excitement faded quickly when I realized what that meant. Pearl was hiding something. And so was Darrien.

I crossed the beach and speed walked towards the boys' cabins. There wouldn't be a lot of time to get to the bottom of this. The girls would be all done with their canoe lessons in half an hour. Pearl was a punctual person; she would have them back on time, if not early. I needed to be quick and quiet.

Soon, the boys' cabins came into view. It felt weird being there. Everything was exactly like the girls' side, but a mirrored image. I slowly walked up to the Leaders' cabin. It was the same as ours, but had blue, green, purple, and black on the door.

Now that I was there, my courage was starting to fail.

What if he doesn't want to see me?

I straightened my back and summoned my courage. *Get up there!*

I cleared my throat and walked up the steps. Knocking lightly, I opened the door.

My heart froze. Aurelia was wrapped around Darrien and her lips were on his. They were kissing. Freaking kissing!

Darrien shoved at Aurelia, but she turned and smiled at me. I didn't say a word as my heart started to crumble, I just turned and left. I heard a scuffle and Darrien calling my name, but I didn't stop. The world was closing in, or maybe I just wasn't breathing, I wasn't sure.

My body was breaking down. I just wanted to crawl into the back of my closet and never come out, so I ran. All I knew was that I wanted to be as far from them as possible.

How could he do that? Why?

My stupidity made me angrier than Darrien's betrayal. I knew this was coming, maybe not the part about Aurelia's lips, but the hurt.

I *knew* it. *Stupid!*

I was such an idiot for thinking that this was going to be different than Mom and Dad.

Sure, we had only been on one date, but he made me feel like it was serious. That it meant something. Why? What was he getting out of it?

I struggled to keep my tears in check as I trudged back to the boat house. It didn't matter how hard I tried, I felt the familiar trickle of them gliding down my cheeks. My eyes were glued to the ground in hopes no one would see.

Mercifully, Pearl was late. One of my girls' canoes tipped, and it took them a long time to get them back in the boat. By the time all the boats were properly put away, we were way beyond our regular boat time and well into outdoor survival. I decided we'd go straight for a hike. I needed to get some energy out. I gathered the girls at the cabin and we started out.

77

Darrien

"WHAT ARE *YOU* DOING HERE, Penelope?" Aurelia spat her name like it was poison in her mouth.

"We were just going for lunch," Pen said.

"Get out," Aurelia demanded.

Pen's eyes flicked to me. "I'll come find you after I deal with this," I said, eyeing Aurelia. Pen nodded, then left the cabin.

"What do you want, Lia?" I grunted.

"I came to see you. After out last talk, I thought that I made it clear that you were to stay away from Cora," she sang as she ran a finger up my arm.

"I'm not leaving Cora alone, Lia," I said flatly.

"You're kidding me, right?" She stopped and looked at me.

"No," I stressed. "If you want to go ahead and blab about Cora, go for it. The only damage will be to your family. Once her family gets wind that you exposed their daughter to the dangers they were trying to hide her from, there will only be bad press in it for you. I'm sure your family would just love to be wrapped up in yet *another* royal conspiracy." I smiled like a fox. *I have her.*

"I'll do it, Darrien. Don't threaten me." She barked, but was struggled to maintain the high ground.

"No, you won't. And you know why?" I challenged as she stuck out her chin. "Because you are not this person. You are better than this. You have been hurt, by me, and I'm not proud of it. But it was for the best. I'm sorry, but this is bigger than you. You don't know what you're getting into here. Now, get out of my way. I have work to do." I brushed past her.

"Don't walk away from me!" She yelled.

"I don't have time for this, Lia! Go!" I was yelling.

"No! I'm not going anywhere until you explain to me what is going on! What has happened to you?" She raced up to me and placed her hands on my face. I pulled my head away from her and glared down at her.

"It's none of your damned business!" I scolded; my anger dangerously close to taking over.

"The hell it's not! You are going to destroy everything you have worked for!"

"I don't care. Now leave me alone!" I bellowed.

"I can't. I can't watch you do this-" and before I could answer her, she grabbed my face and kissed me.

When the door opened, I knew who it was before could even see her.

Cora.

I pushed on Aurelia, but she was holding tight. The look on Cora's face snapped my heart in two. She turned and ran from the cabin before I could get Lia off me.

"Cora!" I shouted, but she ran on. "Cora, please stop!" I ran out the cabin door, but she had already disappeared down the path to the beach. A swell of anger expanded inside me. I felt it bubble up from my gut to my throat. It was like I was choking on it. Lia came down the steps and stood by me.

"It's for the best, Darrien," she said. I turned slowly to her, restraining my temper and power as best as I could.

"Get out of my sight," I whispered.

"What?" she asked, genuine shock in her voice and across her face.

I turned to her slowly, looking her in the eye. My jaw clenched tight and my eyes narrowing.

"You have *no idea* what you have done. Leave. Now." I didn't yell. If I let myself go that much I would lose all grasp on my rage.

Lia backed away from me, a mixture of hurt and anger in her face, and left. I walked through the bush and dove into the lake. The moment I hit it, I let my anger flow.

The water swirled around me, gaining speed the deeper I dove. I felt release as I let the power consume me, and the cyclone of water envelope me. It whipped around my body, ripping at my clothes and skin. I didn't care. The pain was part of the punishment.

When my anger ebbed, and sadness kicked, the hurricane of water dissipated. Cora was hurt and I needed to set things straight.

I lo- liked her. I mean, I *really* liked her.

78
Cora

I HAD NO IDEA WHERE the trail led, but I didn't care. I had the handbook with me in case I needed some directions, anyway. I was sure I could figure out where we were if I had to. At least, I was hoping I could. The girls were happy to be out of the boats and moving around. They didn't ask too many questions; it seemed that most of them instinctively knew something was up with me, and they stayed away.

I kept a good pace this time. I wasn't tripping over rocks or fallen branches and roots for once. This trail was thicker than the one Darrien had taken us down before. The trees seemed taller and the forest darker, or maybe it was just my mood. It was quiet.

Too quiet.

I stopped and turned around. My breath drew sharp and short in my chest; my blood stilled in my veins.

Where are the girls?

I didn't see one. Not one.

Not good. So NOT GOOD!

Where were they? I thought they were right behind me!

"Girls? Hello? Where are you?" I shouted into the trees.

Oh, please don't be gone.

I ran down the trail, pulling back branches and limbs to see better.

"Girls? Hello?"

Nothing. Silence.

I'm in trouble...deep, deep trouble. I'm fired, for sure!

I wandered further back the path, as fast as I could. My eyes searched the bushes ahead of me, as I picked up speed.

Where the hell did they go?

My chest was starting to tighten and my breathing became quick.

"Girls? Girls!" I could feel panic high in my throat, clenching my breath. "This isn't funny!" I picked up speed, yelling as I went.

A root reached up and grabbed my foot; I went crashing to the ground. My knees and hands were all scraped up, and they were throbbing. When I stood up, a shooting pain ran from my ankle up my leg. I gasped and collapsed back down, grabbing my foot. It was twisted.

Shit. Now what?

I stood precariously for a second, and then hobbled down the path further. That's when I realized...*the path is gone.* I pulled back bushes and branches, searching for the path, but I found nothing...*nothing!*

"Hello!" I called, knowing no one would be able to hear me, but unable to stop myself anyway.

"Help! Someone? Anyone!" *Nothing.* Again and again, I tried, but there was nothing.

I was wandering freely in the bush, calling, yelling, and, when panic got the best of me, screaming for help.

Lost. I am so lost!

I slid down against a large evergreen tree. I knew that I should just stay in the same place, so that I'd be easier to find.

But who's going to come looking for me?

I hoped that the girls made their way back to camp without getting lost, too. It was better for me to be alone than ten girls wandering about, too. I took a deep breath in an attempt to clear my mind.

This is not the time to panic. Think. What are your options?

I knew I missed supper. The sun was setting and it was starting to get dark out.

When did that much time pass?

The air was slightly chilly, and would get worse through the night. If I didn't find some shelter soon, I was in danger of hypothermia. *Shelter*...now I had a goal.

I stumbled around the bush, looking for somewhere big enough that I could crawl into and be protected for the night. Hopefully, there would be nothing wild living in it.

After about an hour of looking, I was able to find a small cave. Something had burrowed out the dirt on the side of a small hill. So, I would be sheltered from any rain or wind, for the most part.

This will have to do.

My stomach growled. I wasn't going to chance gnawing on random plants out there; I'd get sick for sure. There was no use in making the situation worse by poisoning myself. I would just have to get used to being hungry for the moment.

266

The forest was getting dark, and I couldn't see well anymore. It wasn't the smartest idea to be walking around the forest at night. So, I huddled down in my new home and tried to get as comfortable as I could in the cramped, cold space of the cave.

How did I get myself into such a mess?

Darrien.

It was like he was two completely different people. On one hand, he was sweet and caring, and my heart skipped a beat just thinking about him. But on the other, he was mysterious and secretive. Then he kissed Aurelia...

I wasn't interested in relationships at all, until Darrien showed up. I never wanted to get involved with someone that would just end up hurting me, and look where I've gotten myself!

I had...strong feelings for Darrien, and I didn't even know if he genuinely cared for me, or if there was something else going on. He got me to fall for him and I fell hard.

I never thought I'd be able to do that, ever.

Right then, stuffed into a dirty, muddy hole in the ground; I wished I'd never met him. None of this would have happened if he wasn't in my life.

Thanks, Darrien.

After a few hours went by, reality hit. I had no hope of being found. My breathing started to get fast, and I was having a hard time getting enough oxygen. I started gasping for air.

I closed my eyes, and forced my lungs to take a slow, deep breath in.

Calm down. Calm down.

I let a concentrated breath of air out through my mouth, and allowed the calm to wash over me. In through the nose, out through the mouth; until I could breathe calmly through just my nose again.

Silence in the woods entered the cave and I felt, for the first time, truly alone. A snap of a twig, a rustle in the bush, had my heart piking and my adrenaline pumping. If I couldn't get my imagination under control, I would end up in a full blown panic attack. I needed a distraction. The first thing that popped into my head was the first thing I did.

I sat in the dark and hummed my Dad's tune. Though the song had been tainted by the bad events in the woods, in the darkness of the cave it was comforting.

I hummed, letting myself get lost in the sound of my voice. The melody washed over me like a gentle breeze, and I floated away on the song. Somehow, the forest didn't seem so scary anymore.

It was then that I realized the music wasn't just coming from me. I didn't just hear it in my little cave, but all around me. I stopped humming for a moment, but the melody kept going.

It's coming from outside.

I unfolded, stood, and moved out into the night air. It was chilly, but tolerable. The song out there was stronger and louder than mine. It was beautiful, soft and sweet. I knew that I was supposed to stay in the shelter of the cave. That was the smart thing to do. I wouldn't be able to find another like it for the night.

But my curiosity got the better of me, and I started to walk toward the source of the music.

I hummed as I limped through branches and brambles. The roots and stones at my feet magically made my way smooth. Somehow, somewhere along the way, the pain in my ankle subsided.

The music called to me in a way I had never imagined possible. It felt as if it had reached into my chest, grabbed my heart and was pulling me by it. I followed blindly, not knowing why, just knowing I had to. I wasn't afraid this time. The melody was welcoming, kind, and beautiful.

Below my feet, I suddenly caught a glimpse of stone. The moonlight bounced off of the little pebbles. *Wait, not pebbles…tile! It's the mosaic path!* It wasn't a dream. It *was* real! A huge smile slipped across my face.

I knew it!

The air was thicker, softer and humid. I could hear something a short distance away.

Water?

Yes, it was water, and a lot of it.

I pulled back some branches and stepped through them into a clearing. There was a thick mist floating just above the ground; so thick I couldn't see what was before me. The smell was unmistakable, though. It was a perfume made for water, made *from* water.

A soft breeze picked up and guided the mist into the bushes, like a herd of cloudy sheep escaping into the trees. Revealed in front of me was a stunning waterfall.

I took in a startled breath. *Amazing!*

It was tall and wide, and the water cascaded down from the top of the falls into a pool at the bottom, spraying mist into the air. The air here was fresh and soft, like a blanket right out of the dryer. It felt nothing like the air outside should feel on a cool Saskatchewan night.

This place seemed to exist in its own space and time. Nothing fit into the natural landscape around there. It all felt too tropical to be in the middle of the prairies. Even the color of the water was that deep green-blue only found near the equator.

Even though I was lost, the panic and fear of not being found had somehow disappeared. I felt happy and relaxed. The rational part of me knew that wasn't right, that I should be worried about getting home. But I wasn't listening to the rational part of me. There was something instinctual, animalistic, about the way I was feeling. It was like I was made for this place, like I was home.

I've been to waterfalls before. They were loud. This one wasn't. *Actually….*

I listened closely…*yes*, the melody was coming off of the water. As the water splashed gently into the pool, it created the song. How was that even possible?

I walked around the outside of the pool, careful not to disturb anything. The ground was so soft; covered in a thick green moss, I couldn't resist the urge to touch it. I bent down and took off my shoes. The feel of the moss between my toes, as I walked around the edge, was incredible; like stepping on a carpet of stuffed animals. I hummed to the tune of the waterfall as I wandered.

The breathtaking beauty of where I was, was unchallenged by anything I had ever seen before.

I could stay here forever.

I walked to the edge of the pool and sat down and I ran my fingers through the moss-covered ground. The edge of the pool was lined with beautiful green rocks. They were so smooth, as if each was individually polished. I picked one up and rolled it around in my hand. It was cool and smooth, and heavy. I sat there and hummed, moving the rock around absentmindedly in my hand. I was completely relaxed.

The light from the pool…wait…*light from the pool?*

I swung my feet under me and peered over the edge, into the water. There was barely a ripple in it to disturb my reflection. My skin was brighter; my hair, tamed and wavy brown. It was me, but a much better version of me. I turned from side to side, staring at my reflection. The change was unreal. I looked…*good.*

I bent closer to the water to get a better look, but my reflection didn't move. It looked from side to side, as if it was searching for something. That's when I noticed the eyes were different. Violet.

I froze.

Was this really happening…again? Or had the day finally gotten to me, and I was hallucinating?

I thought when I had seen the face in the water, the day I fainted into the lake, was a freak accident; maybe, a reflection of me that my imagination took for a wild ride. Either way, I thought I would never see it again! I closed my eyes and shook my head.

Snap out of it, Cora!

My reflection came as close to the surface as it could and stared at me. It smiled and reached a hand toward me, but realizing it couldn't touch me, drew it back.

"Cora?" A watery voice, my watery voice, came bubbling out of the water. "Cora, it's me."

"Ana?"

79
Darrien

I FOUND PEN, AND WE took off to Pearl's cabin together. The swim had dampened my anger, but didn't rid me of it. Pearl was in for a mouth full and she only half deserved it. I didn't knock this time. I just threw open the door. I was in no mood for misdirection and lies. I wanted the truth…all of it.

"What are you not telling me about Cora?" I demanded as we entered the room.

"Hello, Penelope. Darrien, maybe we could have this conversation at another time," Pearl urged, eyeing Pen.

"She knows. She's a Claire," I said matter-of-factly. Pen just waved sheepishly and smiled.

"Oh, I wish someone would have told me that." She made a face. "I've told you everything I know about Cora, Darrien. I don't know what more you want," she said as she concentrated really hard on her dishes. She wouldn't look at me.

"There's something you haven't been saying. I know you. I can see it every time we talk about what has happened with her. There's something you're holding back." I stared intently at her, hoping that I wouldn't have to *make* her talk.

"I don't know what you are talking about," she said as she buried her face in the cupboard. She was playing hard ball.

"Midira has been talking to her, Pearl. How is that possible?" I just laid it out there, bluntly.

"What? How? When?" Her calm was broken as she whipped out the questions.

"It's happened a few times. Even Pen has seen it," I explained, my voice tight.

"Really?" Pearl was shocked,

"Yes. I'm worried, Pearl. If there is something you know, please. Now's the time," Pen pleaded.

Pearl hesitated, her eyes going wide and back and forth from Pen to me. She sighed, nodding.

"I suppose so," she relented. "I didn't think that Midira would reach out to her. I was hoping that she wouldn't know about her, that we had kept the secret well enough all these years. I underestimated her." Pearl sank into her chair. Her face full of guilt and sadness.

"What is happening to her, Pearl? Other than for the obvious reasons, why is Midira interested in her? I get the feeling that this is personal to Midira; it's more than just messing with Titus Prime this time." I pushed.

"She's the heir to the Siren throne," Pearl blurted.

"What?" Pen's voice and mine screeched together.

"That's not possible. Mer and Sirens…it's never happened. It's not allowed," I sputtered.

"It *has* happened," Pearl said. I stood there, shaking my head. No. Cora wasn't part Siren.

No, it's impossible.

Pearl turned her eyes on me, her face pained.

"Remember how I told you that I smuggled Celia and her husband out of Titus after Celia's mother killed my sister."

"Yes," I said, remembering the terrible story of her sister.

"Celia is Cora's *mother*," Pearl said. My mouth flew open, and I gaped at Pearl. "Zale and Celia met each other and fell in love. It was unprecedented, and it was illegal, but they were so incredibly in love that it didn't matter. When they found out they were having a baby, they knew they had to leave. I helped them escape." I was stunned. I was *horrified*.

We had been raised to believe that it couldn't happen, that a marriage between the races would result in a monster, a horrendous thing that would destroy Mer as we knew it. I thought of Cora…she wasn't a monster, she was just a girl.

"You're telling me that Cora is a Mer and Siren hybrid?" I couldn't believe I was even saying it.

"Yes," Pearl said.

"What are we supposed to do?" I asked. This was beyond anything I was trained for.

"You are going to do your job, and bring her home to her father before any of this gets worse! If Midira is already reaching out to Cora that means that she's aware of who Cora is. If she gets Cora under her control, Midira will end up ruling Mer *and* the Sirens. Cora must return to her father. It's the only place she'll be safe," Pearl emphasized.

"Really?" I answered, astonished. "You think when people find out what she really is, and that Zale had children with a Siren, there won't be problems? Our people aren't above murdering Sirens, even ones that are half Mer. They *hate* Sirens, and definitely won't tolerate one on the throne. I'm not taking her home. She won't be safe there." I was starting to panic.

How do I keep her safe now?

"Zale will keep her safe!" Pearl insisted.

"Zale can barely keep himself safe! He's had three attempts on his life this year!" I yelled.

"What?" Her voice was barely a whisper.

"That's why he's so anxious about getting Cora back to Titus. He needs to make sure his heir is there, in case something happens to him," Pen's voice rang out. I had forgotten she was even there.

"This could *not* be more of a disaster!" I ran my fingers though my hair.

If I take Cora to Titus, she'll be in more danger, and I will lose her to the political chaos there. If I don't, Midira will get her influence into Cora more and more. And I'll lose her to that witch!

"What do we do?" I looked at the two of them. They looked at each other, clearly as lost as I was. "Great. Just great."

Bree burst through the door.

"Cora's missing!" She gasped through sobs and tears.

"What!" The three of us rang out in unison.

"She took her team on a hike, and the girls all came back, but she didn't!" Bree was almost inconsolable. She was shaking and in full panic.

I looked a Pearl and Pen. Pearl went straight for Bree and took her under her arm. Pen and I ran as fast as we could to the trails.

"It's already dark! How will we find her?" Pen asked.

"I have a pretty good idea where she is. Get the others together and get them to search anyway. We can't take any chances."

I dove into the woods on the girls' side. My instincts told me that she would be at the waterfall. Midira would have taken the opportunity to contact Cora, or worse.

I needed to find her...*now*.

80

Cora

SHOCK EXPLODED IN MY chest like a bolt of lightning.

"Ana?" I whispered. It wasn't my reflection, and it wasn't my voice. It was Oceana, my twin sister.

I looked back down at her. She was beautiful. She had grown so much. My heart sank. I wished she was real, and not just a trick of the light or something. She died a long time ago, because of me. I would give *anything* to see her again.

"Ana? I'm sorry…I didn't save you." The words bubbled out of my mouth, straining against my tight throat. I had said them to myself a million times over, but it felt good to say them to her now, even if it wasn't really her.

"Cora, there was nothing you could have done."

I didn't know what to say, I just stared at her.

Was this real?

"I need your help, Cora." She looked startled, and started glancing nervously around.

For a moment, I couldn't move. I *wanted* to believe that she was okay so badly. I ached to have my sister back. If she was in trouble, and that's why she never came home…a fierce anger started to burn.

"What happened to you? Where have you been?" I shouted to the water.

"I wish I could explain." Her violet eyes were bright and gazing deep into mine. Her eyes…they were different. Those weren't my sister's eyes. A chill slithered up my back.

"You died, Ana. You're dead. This…is all in my head." Ana smiled at me. It was my smile too, but she wore it so much better than I did.

"It's me! It is! I've waited so long to be able to talk to you! Years of trying to get through and finally I did it! She's going to be so proud – I mean…never mind. You're here, that's all that matters right now." Her voice sped up and pitched higher.

"What are you talking about?" I asked, who was *she*?

"I didn't die in that accident. I was taken by Midira. She's the queen of the Sirens!"

"Taken?" I blurted.

"Yes!" Ana confirmed.

"I thought…all this time. Wait…Siren?" *what is that?*

"You don't know? Haven't you ever wondered why you're such an amazing swimmer?" she asked.

"I haven't been swimming since the accident, Ana. I couldn't." I gulped down the guilt I always felt when thinking about that day.

"You have to, Cora! You *have* to!" she stressed.

"I don't understand what's happening! Where are you? Let me come get you! I can call the police and tell them where you are! They'll help us!" I shouted.

I wanted her back! I *needed* her back!

It would fix everything, Mom wouldn't be depressed anymore. Dad would come back. Getting Ana…I'd have my family again.

"Oh, I wish it was as easy as that, but it's not," she grimaced.

"Why not? I don't understand what's happening!" I said, slumping down.

Suddenly, Ana's expression changed. She shook her head hard and stilled; her brow furrowed and her eyes working back and forth as if they searched for an answer.

"Are you okay," I asked, leaning in closer.

Her expression softened as she turned to me. Her eyes widened, as if she was seeing me for the first time.

"Cora! You're in danger," she said in a harsh tone.

"What?" I whispered, not sure I heard her right.

"She wants you!"

"What wants me?" I asked, watching her closely. She was acting completely different.

"Midira!"

"Who's Midira?" I asked.

"She's the one that kidnapped me. You must be careful. She's powerful and-" she shook her head again.

"I don't have long." Her voice just a whisper.

"What's going on?"

"She's-

"The woman in the woods," I uttered, putting the pieces together. "That was Midira." It was starting to come back to me. The night I went with Darrien, the lost time, the woman, and…pain. A lot of pain.

Ana nodded, "You must be careful, Cora. Did she touch you?"

"Yes." I said, bringing my hand to my forehead, the source of all the pain that night.

"She's trying to open your mind to her. Be careful. You don't know what it's like to have her in your head." Her face went pale.

"What do I do? How do I stop her?" I asked, my voice high in panic.

"I don't know. She's worried about you. I know that much. She wouldn't be so desperate to find you if she wasn't," she admitted.

"What about you? We need to get you out of there!" I ordered.

"Cora, listen to me. Midira…she's been doing things to me. I don't- you can't trust me after this. Okay?"

"What?"

"She can get inside me. Like, control me." She dropped her eyes. My heart cut deep. "I find myself having these thoughts that I have never had before. Since she found out that you were alive, she's been diving into my mind. It's like she can take over it, force her thoughts into mine, and change the way that I think."

"How is that possible? That- that's *not* possible."

"She's looking for something. I don't know what, but-" her eyes darted away, looking somewhere I couldn't see. "I have to go."

"No! Let me help you! Tell me where you are! Let me get you!" I protested.

"You can't, Cora. Please, just promise me you'll be safe. Dad must have sent someone to protect you. Figure out who that is," she persisted in a whispered voice.

"Dad?" *What?* No, there was no way he was involved in this too.

"Jeez, you know nothing about our family." Her voice sounded like it held pity for me.

"What is going on?" I pleaded.

"Find the guard. There's got to be one. Dad wouldn't bring you here without one. Find him. He'll help you. He'll protect you."

"Guard? Dad?" I couldn't think straight. This was all too much.

"I have to go," she whispered urgently.

"Ana, please, no. Stay. I've miss you so much," I begged.

"I've missed you, too!" She smiled a sad smile I knew too well. Then, it dropped. She turned, and that's when I saw the hand come across her face.

"Ana! Ana!" I was yelling into the pool. The look on her face…she was terrified. Ana flashed once more in the water as she fought off the figure attacking her.

"Find the guard!" she shouted, and then she was gone.

"Ana! Ana!" I scanned the pool to try to find her.

I won't lose her again.

A hand appeared in the water. I grabbed it, breaking the plane between my world and Ana's. It was too late by the time I realized that it wasn't her hand I was grasping.

The sickly green skin shot me back to the night in the woods and the searing pain in my head. I gasped and tried to release the hand, but it tightened its grip, digging its long nails into my skin. A scream erupted from my throat, full of pain and shock.

As I pulled hard to get away, a figure slowly raised out of the water. Her hand gripped tight around mine. Her eyes were polished black stone, her skin green and flawless. Her hair was deep emerald, long, and wet, hanging down her strong back. She was as stunning as she was terrifying.

I knew in an instant that she was the one that had taken Ana…Midira.

She took Ana. And now she wants me.

I tried to pull from her hand, but her grip just intensified, pulling me towards the water.

"No!" I yelled as I twisted my arm.

She stared at me, and held on as if she were controlling an obstinate toddler. Her nails dug deep into my skin, piercing it, and leaving long deep scratches as they sliced down my arm. I shrieked in pain.

She smiled, revealing a set of teeth that looked like they had been filed to a point. My stomach turned sour.

"Ana's not here, anymore. She's been a naughty girl." Her voice cut through the calm of the waterfall.

My heart was beating fast and furious. I was shaking.

"She'll pay for her betrayal, but, then again, she brought you here. She called to you as only a sister could. I guess I should give her points for that." Her head tilted as her bulging eyes took me in. Blood trickled down my arm and dripped into the pool.

"Where's Ana? What did you do with her?" I demanded, some strength appearing in my voice. I glared hard into the ebony eyes of the creature in front of me.

"Oh, you needn't worry about her. But, *you* are a different story! What to do with *you?*" Her mouth opened into a sickly grin.

"There is a connection between you and your Ana that I just cannot seem to break. Even after all these years, she still can get away from me to get to

277

you. It's astonishing and troubling." I watched her, saying nothing. "You understand that I can't allow you to keep being a distraction for her. She's come so far, having you around will only jeopardize all the work we've done. It's nothing personal."

"What?" Tears were welling in my eyes.

"You have to die, of course," she replied flippantly. "I've been trying to get inside your mind all this time, but you are stronger than I imagined, so I'm just going to have to get rid of you the old fashioned way."

She yanked on my arm, hard. I fell forward and almost lost my balance, but somehow managed to stay out of the pool.

"Why are you doing this?" My voice lost its calm. I was screaming now, losing control.

"The time of the Siren is coming. Mer has run its course. Just ask your *father.*" *What?*

Her grip was excruciating as it pulled me slowly and steadily toward the surface of the water. The moment my fingers touched the water, another figure rose from the surface and grabbed my other arm. This one had blue skin and scars all over her arms and face. I screamed hard. She pulled steadily on my arm again, sending new pain searing up my arm.

"NO! No! Let go! Let *GO!*" As I tried to pull back, long deep gashes were left in my skin. The pain was sending stars to my eyes.

So much blood.

The once calm pool was now thrashing, tossing Midira and the blue creature around. Their faces were determined, but the new one looked around as if searching for someone.

A cunning smile cut across Midira's face, showing her shockingly sharp teeth. A piercing scream erupted from my throat, as I released the fear and pain I was feeling. I had never made a sound like that in my life, I was sure of it.

Water shot from the pool, like a geyser erupting, sending the two flying away from me. I tumbled back onto the ground, gasping and staring in awe at the pool and breathing heavily.

I did that. I knew it. I felt a surge of something within me and the release of it. I stared at the water, too shocked to move.

It only took a second for the two to rally and come for me again. I called to the water to help me, but I had no real idea how I made the first explosion happen and this time there was no response from the water.

The blue girl shot out of the pond and landed on the soft ground. She looked ready for battle and I knew I was hopelessly out matched. When she charged at me I threw a hand up in defense and a wave of water slammed down on top of her, washing her into the pond again, but it took out my feet too and I slid toward the pond.

I screamed, flipping and trying to get a grip on anything as I came closer and closer to Midira and the other monster.

My hands came up empty. I fell, screaming, into the pond.

Not water! Not again! No, no, no!

I struggled against the blue one with everything that I had, but I was already exhausted; no amount of kicking and punching released her grip. Midira was nowhere to be seen. She had left me to her deadly helper.

"Come on, princess…you know you want to go for a swim," blue woman hissed.

Her voice invaded my mind, spiking a will to survive that I didn't know I had. I kicked at her, landing a good one on her shoulder and casting her back, just enough to be free from her grasp for a moment.

I managed to break the surface, followed immediately by her, and grab for the rocks. When my hand wrapped around a larger one, I swung it with all my strength at her head. A satisfying, sickly thud and the release of her hand told me that I had made my mark.

I flipped around, holding onto the side of the pool with one hand and shoving her off me with the other. Her violet eyes stared into nothingness, as black inky blood seeped from her wound. I kicked her further away from me and watched as she sank below the churning water.

I pulled myself out of the pool on shaky arms and legs. Blood ran from the deep cuts Midira sliced into my arms. A sob rose in my throat, and I swallowed it over and over to keep it from escaping. If I gave over to it, I might never be able to stop.

I took several deep breaths to calm my heart.

It's over. It's over.

I needed to get back to camp, but I had no idea where I was going; any place was better than there.

As I stood to go, a whisper came out of the woods.

"You're not leaving, already…."

The wind picked up, tossing my hair around my head. I turned slowly back to the pond and watching in horror as a hand reached out of the water. Lightning quick it took hold of my foot.

I shrieked and fell to the ground, as it pulled my foot out from under me. I kicked at it, scraping at the fingers with my feet.

Idiot! Why did you take off your freaking shoes!

I could hear Midira's laugh as she pulled me steadily into the water. I grabbed at anything, everything, around me; there was nothing but loose stone and pebbles, nothing to hold onto.

When my feet and legs splashed into the pond, I cried out.

I threw my arms around, searching for anything to get a hand grasp on. The water splashed and trashed as I did, but it didn't loosen Midira's grasp. She wasn't letting go.

"Help!" I screamed as the water travelled up my back, to my shoulders. She was going slowly; making sure she prolonged my fear, so that I felt every moment of terror before I inevitably drowned. I thrashed around with the last bit of energy I had, kicking, and hitting with my one free hand. Nothing helped.

I managed to keep my head just above the rippling pool for a moment, my hands gripping the side of the pond, but she was stronger.

As my grip lost and my face sank under the water, I didn't make a sound. Instead, I thought of Ana. She was alive, and I wouldn't even get to see her.

The last thing I saw was a shadow from above, closing over me. I didn't even try to hold my breath this time. I opened it and welcomed oblivion.

81

Darrien

WHEN I CAME THROUGH the clearing at the waterfall, I saw Cora go under.

I didn't stop. I didn't think. I dove in after her.

When I hit the water, I knew Midira was there. The water was cold and smelled like sewage. Cora was deep, deep underwater, and going fast. Her face was calm, serene, and haunting. An explosion in my chest erupted when I realized that she wasn't conscious. If I didn't get her out of the water right away, she wouldn't live.

I sped up, breathing in the stale water. I saw the shadow below Cora and recognized it immediately...*Midira*.

Her eyes flashed to mine and she hissed, swimming faster. I matched her speed, and reached for Cora. I didn't want to hurt her, but I had to get her out of there as quickly as I could. I grabbed Cora around the waist and held tight.

Midira's gasp was on her foot. It was harder for me to feel for Midira's blood when there was water everywhere, but I focused on her hand as best as I could. I summoned her blood to me, but nothing happened.

A terrible chuckle rolled through the water the harder I tried to pull from Midira. I could feel the flutter of panic building in my chest. I looked at Cora. She was losing her color. If I didn't get her to breathe right away, I would lose her!

I cleared my head, focusing on the hand that held Cora. I focused on the fingers first, then bones and tendons. I felt for any water in the bones I could, and expanded it. I heard the cracking and snapping before I even opened my eyes. A wild shriek came from below me, and the hand that had once held Cora released its mangled fingers.

Midira let out a scream that felt like hot pokers being stabbed into my skull, and shot toward us. This time, I was ready. I grabbed a wall of water and threw it at her, knocking her off course. Still holding Cora, I rode an undertow to the surface, willing a wave to bring us up, out of the water. We landed in a heap off to the side of the pool. When Midira broke the surface after us, I used the opportunity to pull as much blood as I could in that moment.

Black ooze dribbled from her eyes and ears like paint from a sponge, but she didn't stop. The smell was like raw sewage and sulphur together, almost enough to make me wretch, as I pulled more and more from her. She still came closer. I was done running, and done taking it easy on her.

Everything I had in me, every droplet of water I sensed in the area, I pulled it all to me. I looked at Cora, her lifeless body nestled beside me. Rage ignited in me, rushing through my veins and setting me on fire.

What the...

Radiating from my skin were blue-green flames. I watched, in stunned silence, as they spread up my arms and through my body. A pleasant tingle trailed through me as the flames rose higher. A pulse radiated from me when the flames finally consumed me whole. There was no pain, just my anger, and the satisfying knowledge that shit was about to go down. I took a breath and stood.

Silence.

Every frustration I had felt, every fear I had about Cora, about myself and about admitting my feelings for her, I focused it all on Midira. I felt the new power engulf me, humming in my veins and licking across my skin. Whatever had awakened in me was powerful, and made a smile spread across my lips.

Then, a rush, like a tornado wind, came out of me. I could feel the fire blast from me, crashing into everything it encountered. Midira was hit hard, right in the chest. She screamed in shock, as a deep gash ripped into her sick green skin. She turned her black eyes on me, surprise and fear brewing in them. She opened her mouth to shriek and I released...all of it.

A great rush of blue-flamed energy exploded from me, laying waste to everything around us. Midira was torn into and fell into the pond with a sickly cry.

Trees snapped; huge trunks tossed into the air and crashed down into the bushes below. Leaves and twigs fell around us. Water from the pond was blown sky high, and then rained down in large droplets, soaking into the scorched ground. The falls crumbled, collapsing in great boulders and dust into the empty pool.

When my rage let go, the flames subsided and went out. I was left gasping and stumbling. I nearly fell and dropped onto Cora, who was still unconscious on the ground. I sat in a lump next to her and looked at her; really looked at her.

My heart stopped. There was so much blood.

What did she do to you?

I ran a hand up her arm where deep gashes wept blood. A shudder rang in my chest, and the rage I thought I expelled swelled again in me. She needed a healer. There was only so much I could do for her. I needed Tyde, but that would take too long. It was up to me.

I reached out across her chest and felt for the water within her lungs. Carefully, gently, I drew it out. I opened her mouth as the water was drawn to my hand in small rivulets. Cora's chest shuddered and she coughed. My heart leapt. She would be okay. She would be okay.

I trailed a hand down her face and heaved a sigh.

What you do to me…you just have no idea.

82
Cora

MY EYES OPENED LIKE RUSTED hinges. They felt like gravel had been poured into them. My head was swimming; dizzy and clouded. The room was spinning and I couldn't focus.

Where am I?

My head was pounding. It felt like someone was in there, hacking and picking away to get out. I closed my eyes against the pain, willing it to subside. Behind them, I saw a face, a terrifying, beautiful face…with black eyes.

My eyes flew open, and I wasn't sure if I wanted to close them ever again. My heart leapt as I felt something warm shift beside me. I turned my face toward it, and saw the most gorgeous set of eyes staring at me.

Darrien.

"Cora, are you okay? How do you feel?" His voice was full of concern. He had his arm around me, and helped me to sit up. I could feel the warmth of his hand in mine and the heat of his body pressed against me. If it wasn't for him holding me up, I wouldn't have been able to sit at all.

"What happened? How did I get here?" My words were like knives plunging into my brain. I lifted a hand to my aching head.

"I found you, and brought you here to make sure that you're okay." He was searching my eyes. Worry furrowed his brow and turned down his lips. My heart fluttered, sending much-needed heat to my body.

"But how? How did you find me?" My thoughts were still so fuzzy.

"Don't worry about that. I'm just happy I found you!" His smile was genuine, but it quickly was replaced with frustration. "I told you not to go in the woods without me! Why don't you listen?" He was fussing with my hand and my sleeve. A searing pain stabbed me when he grabbed my arm. I looked down and gasped. Four long cuts ran the whole length of my arm. They were bloody and dirty.

"Shit." His voice was almost a whisper, and his eyes were wide. His fingers were gentle as he examined the deep gashes.

"I don't know…I must ha….." I saw black eyes and heard that laugh I would never forget. I bit my lip and looked at Darrien, I could feel the blood drain from my face.

How could I explain what I saw? *He'll think I'm insane.*

"I must have fallen…into a bush…or something. I don't remember." I couldn't look at him, I didn't want to lie to him, but I couldn't tell him the truth, either. I stared at the wounds on my arm.

He looked up from the gashes and eyed me. The question was written all over his face. I didn't need to hear it, but I answered anyway.

"No…no, nothing happened. I mean, other than me getting lost and….oh my goodness! The girls! Did they make it back? Are they alright? Are they lost?" Panic slapped me. I cursed myself for my selfishness. I was so focused on my own problems that I forgot what my responsibilities were.

Please, let them be okay!

"Yeah, yeah! They all made it just fine! They managed to make their way back up the trail after you disappeared into the forest. They were scared, but they stayed together and came back to report you missing," he explained, reaching out a hand to calm me. I sighed a huge sigh of relief.

"Thank goodness! I was so wrapped up in my own prob….never mind, you wouldn't care anyway," I said, remembering what brought on this mess. A flash of pain crossed his face.

"Why wouldn't I care, Cora? I care about you…a lot," he said and I could feel his hand tighten on mine. My stomach sank and a burning anger flooded me. Even after everything that had happened, there was still so much hurt in me about what I had seen with Aurelia. Apparently, hell hath no fury like a woman scorned, even if she *was* just attacked by a green sea-lady and almost killed.

"Right…okay." I took my hand out of his and stood up. I stumbled and fell into his arms.

"You're not going anywhere without my help, whether you like it or not." There was a glint of mischief in his grin, as he threw his arms around me and scooped me up. I gasped in surprise and crossed my arms. I didn't like being man handled.

"You're very concerned public awaits, my lady." I frowned as he walked us through the grass, toward the trees. I could see now where we were. He bought me to the brook, his favorite place.

Without a breath catching in his throat or any signs of labored breathing, he started into me.

"What were you thinking, going into the woods that late? I told you not to go without me."

"I was mad....at you." I couldn't say it looking at him, so I watched the path in front of us.

"Oh…" He gently set me down on a fallen log on the side of the path. He paced in front of me, rubbing the back of his neck and pulling on his hair.

His kiss with Aurelia took my breath away, just thinking about it. Darrien was staring at me, unsure what to say. I wasn't at a loss though. After everything I'd been through, my patience was gone, and through the exhaustion and pain I managed a level of anger I was impressed with, granted it wasn't much.

"You were kissing her, Darrien! Kissing her! What the hell? You don't show all day and then when I go to find you, there you are, totally fine and locking lips with *her*! I can't believe you would do that to me! Why?" My anger broke and – damn it - sadness took over.

Darrien's eyes were on me, full of guilt and then fear. He stood there, frozen, not moving and not speaking. I lifted an eyebrow to him and glared. He started pacing like a caged lion.

"I can explain-"

"Explain what? You told me there was nothing between you! You said you had no feelings for her! Why was she kissing you, then? Why? You think you can see two girls at the same camp and they won't figure it out? No *wonder* she hates me so much!" Was he really this stupid and unkind? I tried standing up, but my body wouldn't allow it. All my energy was going into yelling at Darrien.

"Aurelia and I are *not* seeing each other. I told you all that, and it's the truth." He reached over to me to steady me on the log, but I pushed his hands away.

"Then why are you hiding from me and seeing her in your cabin? And again…why is she *kissing* you?" My voice hit its limit and broke. Tears swelled in my eyes, my anger was replaced by resigned sadness.

"Look, I told you before; Aurelia wants me to be someone I'm not anymore. In case you haven't noticed, she doesn't give up easily. That's why she came to see. She still thinks I'll change back; that this is all some phase I'm going through, I guess. And I didn't kiss her, *she* kissed *me*. I know that's a terrible excuse, but believe me, there was no lip action from my side."

He bent down in front of me and gently took my hand. When his eyes met mine…my heart, oh, my heart.

I was hurt and angry, and I wanted to lash out at him and hate him and hurt him right back, but one look into his eyes and I couldn't do it. I couldn't be angry anymore. He was telling the truth. I knew it.

"I...I just don't know, Darrien. I don't know what to think anymore," I admitted, not looking at him. He sat back on his heels, his shoulders dropping. A thought struck me.

"Why did you tell Pearl that I was a job?" Darrien lifted his brow.

"Yes, I overheard you this morning," I said, answering the question in his look. "How am I a job?"

Darrien broke his gaze and studied the air with a concentrated furrow to his brow. He held my hand with both of his.

"I...ugh. Damn it! You aren't a job, Cora. Please believe me. I'm here to help you. I'm not here to hurt you...and it isn't a job to be with you." He raised a hand to stroke my face, wiping away the tears I thought were hidden from him. My heart started thumping in my chest. I shook my head.

"I don't know what to think, Darrien," I mumbled, moving away from him. "I- I need some time to think, it's been quite a day."

I reined in all my strength, slowly lifted myself off the log, and stood facing Darrien. But my knees were weak; they buckled under me and I toppled over. A pair of strong arms caught me and lifted me upright, as if I weighed no more than a feather. Then, Darrien pulled all of me into his arms.

"You're too weak, Cora. Please, let me help you back." I reluctantly nodded. He helped me walk the rest of the way down the trail, nearly taking on all of my weight.

Darrien's eyes drifted over me, locking in my gaze. His green-blue eyes were penetrating. They made my heart flutter like a trapped butterfly. He gave me the most, tender kiss on my forehead. My heart leapt into my throat.

Why can't you just tell me?

All I could do was give him a small smile back and rest my head against his shoulder, as we navigated the path through the woods. When we got to the edge of the trail, he set me gently on the ground. I wobbled like a newborn deer, barely able to support my own weight on my exhausted frame. Darrien's arms were quick to grab me and hold me up. I was in his embrace when Pearl came around the corner.

"Oh! Thank goodness, Darrien! You found her!" She ran straight for us. "Cora, we've been worried sick!" She threw her arms around me in a tight hug. "She's here!" She shouted.

Then, out of the shadows, seven figures appeared: Devon, Zach, Avery, Aurelia, Pen, Jade, and Bree. They were all out of breath. Bree bolted straight to me and launched herself at me, tackling me to the ground. She was laughing and crying at the same time.

"Hey! Missed me?" I said, gripping her as tightly as she did me. My tears were coming hard now, as I hugged my little sister. A hug from Bree was the best medicine out there.

"Cora, I would kill you if I wasn't so happy you're alive!" Her blue eyes were swimming with tears, but they were smiling at me.

"I'm sorry!" I said, leaning in a pressing my forehead to hers. Darrien crouched down on the ground and held out his hands for me. I took them. He lifted me gently off the dirt path and put his arms around me, strong and safe. This seemed to make everyone but Pen and Bree uncomfortable. I noticed, but Darrien didn't seem to; or if he did, he didn't care.

"I'm so sorry for worrying everybody," I said in a timid voice. I was embarrassed for having put everyone through so much. They looked exhausted and frazzled. "Thank you. I'm...." My head swam and I saw stars. Darrien caught me just as I was about to hit the ground.

"You're exhausted!" Pearl proclaimed.

"Just a little." I smiled at everyone. I couldn't believe it. Even Devon and Zach, whom I had barely exchanged a word with, came out to help. And Aurelia, she was even there. She nodded when she saw me, seemingly satisfied that I was okay. Avery was smiling at me.

"Okay everyone, it's been a tough couple of days for all of us. Head back to your cabins and get some rest. Unfortunately, we still have camper activities today. Take it easy, have fun today, and don't overdo it. Thank you everyone, for your help!" Pearl was smiling at me. She looked relieved and exhausted.

She flagged Darrien over to her with a flick of her head. Darrien gently released his hands from me, making sure I was able to stand on my own first, then walked over to her. He smiled reassuringly at me as he went.

"Cora, let's get you cleaned up and in bed. Okay?" Pen was at my side, and Bree was on the other. They had my arms around their necks, ready to steer me to the cabin.

"Thanks, um...." I looked for Darrien, but he had disappeared around the corner with Pearl. I wanted to thank him for everything that he did.

I guess I'll have to wait until later to talk to him.

"Okay, let's go." I smiled at the girls.

I was escorted back to my cabin, the boys headed back to theirs, and Pearl and Darrien were nowhere to be seen. All I wanted was a hot shower and a soft bed.

Bree and Pen brought me inside and helped me to my bed. I took a huge breath and cleared my head, willing all the questions I had to stay away so I could relax and just get some rest.

It was really dark out, must have been an hour before dawn, if had a guess. Bree and Pen ran around preparing everything that I needed for the night. They started the shower for me, got pajamas out for me, and Bree even brushed everything out of my hair. Aurelia and Jade made no effort to help further, and I was happy with that. They sat together on Jade's bed, and quietly talked to each other. Every now and then, they threw a glance my way. I knew they were talking about me, but I didn't care. I was too tired to.

My shower was heavenly. Washing away all the dirt and salt from my night felt amazing. The hot water on my face opened my pores, and the smell that came out reminded me of the scent of the waterfall. But, that just made the memory of Midira flood back into my head.

The woman that took Ana from me, and who was now after me, would haunt my thoughts for weeks to come. I didn't know who she was or where she was from, but I knew that she was not from here, so Ana was farther away from me than I could have imagined. A Siren, Ana called her.

What is a Siren?

By the time I got out of the shower and crawled into bed, Aurelia and Jade were in their beds, asleep, and so was Pen. She was sprawled over her covers, clearly having fallen asleep waiting for me. I tucked a warm blanket around her and walked quietly to my bed, where Bree was waiting for me.

"Hey, B," I whispered. "You must be exhausted. Why don't you go and get some sleep? You need it." I smiled at her and patted her knee. She looked terrible.

"I'm okay. I just wanted to make sure that you were," she said, her eyes had dark circles under them and were rimmed in red. My heart hurt, she looked like she had been crying for days.

"I'm fine now that I'm back," I said and gave her a reassuring smile.

"You were gone for *two* days, Cora. We were going crazy! I thought you weren't coming back. I don't know what I would have done if you didn't come back, Cora!" Tears started streaming down her face. Guilt and sadness hit me, hard.

"I'm so sorry, Bree!" I cried, my heart breaking. "I'm here now, and that won't happen again. I'm not going to leave you, I promise!" I gave her a bear hug, and waited for her sobs to come to a stop.

"Sorry," she apologized into my shoulder, "I know you must have had the worst couple of days...."

"It hasn't been a couple of days, Bree. I've only been missing since supper." I gave her a gentle smile.

"You've been gone since supper two days ago, Cora! You think I would make that up?" She was staring intently at me, clearly trying to drive her point home.

That can't be true.

She must have caught on to my confusion. "You really thought that you were gone just a few hours?"

289

"It's strange, but it seemed like no time to me. I was deep in the forest trail when I got lost. Maybe I passed out or something."

But, deep inside, I knew what caused time to pass so quickly...the falls. There was something about that place that made me want to stay there forever. Time stood still there. That made sense...even though nothing about that made sense, or at least, none of it seemed real.

I wanted to tell Bree everything, but I didn't. It was right there on the edge of my tongue, but nothing came out. We told each other everything, but I couldn't bring myself to explain what had happened, even though it involved our sister.

"I have no idea how Darrien found me," I said, dodging the time difference.

"When your team came back, they ran straight to our cabin, crying and yelling that you were gone. It scared us. I took off to get Pearl. Luckily, Darrien and Pen were in her cabin. They bolted from the cabin and I stayed with Pearl. The rest of the campers were sent to their cabins and told to stay there and all the Leaders were sent to look for you.

"When night fell and you still weren't back, I stayed with Pearl. I think she was afraid I was going to do something desperate. She didn't leave me alone for a moment. She was scared for you, Cora. I mean, *really* scared. Everyone was...all of them, even Aurelia." I raised a brow.

"I know, I was amazed too," she said. I had a hard time believing Aurelia was concerned for my safety, but Bree wasn't prone to lying to me.

"I didn't think I would ever find my way back, to tell you the truth. It was scary," I yawned. My eyes were so heavy. I yawned again, deep and wide. Bree did too. I settled myself down; Bree laid next to me and shared my pillow.

"You've been through a lot. Why don't you stay here with me, you could use it. I could use it too. I'm sure the other girls won't mind," I said to Bree.

"Thanks, I'd like that." She smiled and closed her eyes. "Cora?"

"Yeah?"

"What's going on with you and Darrien?" Her eyes were still closed and her breathing was getting heavier.

"Tomorrow, B. Good night." My eyes closed and sealed, finally giving up the fight to stay open.

"Night," she whispered back.

83
Darrien

"MIDIRA HAD HER," I spat.

Pearl and I were in her cabin. Pearl was pacing the floor, and I was trying my damnedest not to crash right there on her tiny couch.

"Is she okay?" Pearl asked.

"She will be," I nodded. "Midira tried to take her, but I got there just as Cora went under."

Pearl's face twisted up in an anger I didn't know she was capable of. Then, I remembered what her sister had gone through and I understood.

"I managed to mangle one of her hands and injure her. She's alive, but she's hurting," I offered. Pearl's lip tipped up slightly. It wasn't much to ease her pain, but it was something.

"I blasted the pool, too. It won't be a problem anymore." I thought of the blue flames trailing up my arms, and the feel of that power surging from me. I had no idea where that came from or why all of a sudden it had appeared; but I liked it.

It was nothing like my water power, there was an all-consuming nature to it, something that called to the very center of my being. I didn't know if I could summon it again, but I hoped that if the occasion called for it, it would be there.

Midira didn't expect me to do that and it caused more damage to her than my water powers could. She would be wary of me the next time we met.

And we will meet again.

"Let's let Cora rest," Pearl said, finally settling into her over-stuffed chair, "but I think the time for subtlety has run out. We need to tell her who she is...*now*. When she gets up, Darrien. We *have* to. It's not safe to keep her in the dark. She won't understand what is at risk without knowing who she is. She's got to be half crazy with questions right now. We owe her an explanation," Pearl insisted.

"I agree," I nodded, but then sank into the couch. "I just don't *want* to tell her." *I don't want to lose her.*

My heart ached thinking about it. Everything would change after she found out, everything.

"You have to. It has to be you. She trusts you." Her voice was tender and true.

I knew it had to be me. I just wished with every fiber of my being that it wasn't.

"I know," I grumbled. "Can we just wait another day? Let her have one more day as herself before her life is completely torn apart. Let her have one day as a normal girl, before I destroy it."

Every shred of confidence in my ability to do this job was fading fast. The only thing that kept me on track was that I knew she would be safer once she knew what was really going on.

"Fine," she conceded. "One day, Darrien. That's all we can afford."

"Okay," I agreed. I was going to make the most of that one day with her, before I lost her.

84

Cora

SUN SHONE IN MY EYES. The room was hot and my blankets needed to come off. With eyes still glued shut, I thrashed them aside, just to find there was something blocking me...Bree. She had stayed the whole night.

I cracked my eyes open, just a little. I didn't have nearly enough sleep, but something inside was urging me to wake up. I looked at my clock.

5:30 a.m. Really? I didn't have to be up for hours!

It was super early, but the sun didn't seem to mind being awake; it made our cabin feel like an oven. I sat up very slowly, trying hard not to disturb Bree's rest. A million questions were waiting in the shadows of my mind for their opportunity to ambush me. I needed a distraction, quickly. I pushed my thoughts back as far as I could.

I need to walk.

I put on a pair of flip-flops and grabbed a sweater. Even though I was still in my pajamas, I snuck out of the cabin for the beach. Who was going to see me that early, anyway? Everyone was still in bed, since I kept them up so late.

My lack of sleep hadn't hit me yet and I was feeling oddly refreshed. It was a gorgeous morning, with a clear blue sky and no breeze. I threw on my sweater and walked silently down the path.

The beach was as beautiful as I'd imagined. The trees and sand had an orange glow to them, as the sun's early morning light kissed the tops of everything it touched. The lake was still and silent but for a couple of ducks that were enjoying the peace and quiet. Birds were starting their morning routines and sang out their chirping songs, accompanied by the rustle of leaves when a slight breeze picked up. The air...it was so clean and fresh that I inhaled deeply to fill myself as full of it as I could.

I walked slowly down to the edge of the sand, took my sandals off, and buried my feet. I took a deep breath in and filled my lungs again. I could see why Darrien enjoyed his morning swims so much.

Taking my time to walk down the beach, I dug my toes into the sand with every step. I faced the water, sandals in hand, and closed my eyes. It was more relaxing than I could have imagined. Then, a tingling sensation crept up my neck.

I opened my eyes and scanned the beach. Nothing. I couldn't see anyone, but that tingling sensation persisted, unnerving me. My eyes searched the water and the edge of the woods, but still nothing.

Nothing is there.

Come on, Cora. It's a beautiful morning, and the lake is so quiet and serene. Don't let your paranoia ruin this.

I stood and walked up to the edge of the water, dipping my feet in. My heart beat a little faster, as it always did that close to open water. I willed my legs in one more step, until water filled in over my ankles.

One more step?

I went in a little further, allowing water up to my mid-calf.

"Wow, I never thought I'd see you standing in water so confidently."

I never saw him coming, and I didn't hear him either, but I knew without a doubt that it was him I had sensed watching me.

Darrien glided around beside me. My body tensed up immediately. He must have noticed.

"I'm not going to throw you in the water, Cora. I'd never do that to you," he scolded. "When I saw you standing here, I wanted to make sure you were okay. I didn't get a chance to talk to you much this morning before Pearl needed me." He smiled his perfect smile at me. This time my face didn't light up the way it usually did in his presence.

"I'm doing alright. I'm sure I'll be exhausted later today," I shrugged and looked out over the water. I dropped my eyes to my fingers and felt the furrow of my brow deepen as I spoke, "Um, I didn't get to thank you earlier for saving me."

"My pleasure," he answered, taking a step closer to me. My heart did a little dance in my chest, but my head was in control now.

"How did you find me? I was far into the woods, and off the trails. How did you know where to look?"

"I *didn't* know where you were. I took a lucky guess and it ended up being right. You were a mess when I found you. Don't you remember?" He was looking sideways at me, while we stood facing the lake.

"No, not really. I remember being carried, and then I was at the brook with you, but getting there is still fuzzy." I was looking straight at him now.

"Oh, well, it's normal not to remember things when you're in a traumatic event, I suppose. I'm just glad I found you. We were all looking for you, and everyone was worried. Especially…"

294

"Bree? I know. She stayed with me last night. I spooked her, badly. I feel awful," I said, my eyes now across the lake. I felt Darrien switching his weight from one foot to the other and then clear his throat.

"Actually, I was going to say…me." He was focusing on his feet in the water, and…*no! He was blushing!*

My heart thumped in my chest, and all the doubts that I had about Darrien's feelings for me started to lift away.

Deep down, I knew the whole thing with Aurelia wasn't his fault. I believed him when he said she kissed him. I did. But, there was still something he was hiding from me.

This time, *I* reached over and grabbed his hand. He looked up at me and smiled.

"Cora, I care so much about you," he said, his breath unsteady.

He grabbed my other hand and pulled me toward him, taking both my hands in his. My mind was racing and my heart was thumping wildly in my chest as Darrien drew me in closer.

"I never thought I could feel this way about someone, but you've changed that. You've changed me. I can't stop thinking about you." He rested his forehead against mine and whispered, "You drive me crazy, *Humbug*."

He reached his hand across to my face. Gently, with his thumb, he traced a line from my nose, under my eye and to my ear, tangling his fingers in my hair. He brought his face down level with mine, and our eyes met.

I could feel his heart beating fast against my hands, which were resting on his chest. I could feel my pulse racing in my veins, as they ignited.

How could I deny how much he meant to me? Why should I fight my feelings?

I was drawn to him. I wanted to be with him, to be held by him, to feel him close to me. He pulled me in harder against his chest and, with the gentlest touch, tipped my face up to his. My eyes closed instinctively.

When our lips touched, my body exploded with pleasure. Soft rivulets of warmth spread through me, filling my veins with heat. His kiss was gentle, but strong and commanding, too. I melted into him.

What started as a delicate kiss became more urgent as we pulled each other closer. My hands wrapped around his neck and dug into his hair. He groaned against my lips at my touch.

His hands were on my face, pulling me into him. His tongue flicked across mine, and an explosion erupted deep in my chest. I gasped against his lips, which elicited another deep groan from him.

I felt the moment he lost control, because I was lost just the same. Our bodies crashed into each other, hands pulling and pawing. My breathing grew ragged against him when he moved his hands to my hips and pressed against me.

I want him. I had wanted him from the first time I saw him.

My self-control was gone, but Darrien must have had a remnant. I knew he wanted me. I felt it. When he gently pulled away, there was a painful look on his face, like it hurt to separate from me. That just made me want him more.

I'd never felt anything like that before, and I was certain I would never feel it with anyone else. His face stayed close to mine. He was smiling. I was smiling, too.

"Wow," he whispered.

"Yeah...wow!" My speech was breathy and excited. My heart was pounding against the inside of my chest, like it wanted out, like it no longer belonged to me. I realized that maybe, it didn't belong to me anymore. It belonged to Darrien.

Darrien smiled big, laughed, and picked me up in his arms. My feet dangled off the ground. Face to face again, I couldn't resist it. I grabbed him and kissed him again. Heat ignited somewhere deep in my chest, and flaming butterflies raced through me. It was the most amazing feeling!

When he dropped me gently to my feet, we sat on the beach together. Nothing mattered but Darrien. Nothing mattered but *us*. Sitting there together, it seemed like a spell settled over the beach. We were the only two people in the world.

The day went by in a sleepy but lovely haze. After our early morning on the beach, we had to pry ourselves away from each other to get ready for the day. Even though it was only for a few hours, it was still tough. All my thoughts were absorbed by Darrien...and his lips.

Oh, those lips.

My heart kick-started at the thought of them pressed against mine, and the feel of his hard body against me. There was nothing in my life that compared to that, nothing real or dreamed that could compare to how amazing that was.

Darrien was mine, all mine.

I got dressed and showered for breakfast. The others had left the cabin to me, and I enjoyed the calm and quiet as I hurried to get ready. When I stepped out the door, there was Darrien, leaning against my cabin, waiting for me.

"Hey, beautiful."

His smile went from ear to ear. Mine felt like it reached every part of me. When I got to the bottom of the stairs, he leaned in for the softest kiss. My heart burst open and begged for more when he pulled away. But, he was a gentleman, and took my hand, turning us toward the hall. We walked slowly and silently to breakfast, hand in hand.

We were stared at when we arrived, and were glared at when we sat down, but that didn't put a damper on the way I felt. All day went like that. We stole kisses every moment we could, each getting more urgent and intense. He was a new drug, and I was happily addicted.

Darrien and I went to the brook that night. He brought a picnic, and we spread out on a blanket under the stars. We talked and kissed, then talked and kissed some more. I couldn't get enough of his lips, his face, his body. The more intense we got, the more I felt the urge for more than just a kiss. I felt his urge, too.

Before, that would have scared me, but now, it excited me. Everything about him was exciting. I felt safe with him, protected with him. I didn't worry with him. I was in lo.....

Careful, Cora.

85
Darrien

"I DON'T WANT TO DO THIS!" I yelled.

"You have to!" Pearl was fighting just as hard as I was.

"I can't do this to her!" I plopped down in Pearl's chair.

"I know, but it really is the only way," she implored. "She needs to know, and it has to be now."

"I know…I know. Tonight, then. I need more time with her."

"You *want* more time with her," she slid in.

"Of course, I *want* more time, damn it! I want every last second I can squeeze in with her. After this, I'm going to lose her. Give me the afternoon, at least!" I was losing it.

"Trust her. After she knows why, she will understand what you had to do."

"Yeah, right." It didn't matter what she said. I didn't know how I was going to bring myself to drown my girlfriend.

Why me?

86

Cora

IT HAD ONLY BEEN about twenty-four hours since Darrien found me in the woods, but it seemed like a lifetime ago. Somehow, in that time, Darrien and I had gone from being a huge question mark to solidifying our relationship, and I was on cloud nine about it.

Every look, every kiss, every touch set me on fire. I had no idea that it would feel like this. I knew I was leaving my heart right out there to get hurt, but for some reason, Darrien didn't make me feel like I had anything to worry about. My heart was safe with him.

I wonder if Mom would like him. Would Ana? Ana...oh, my god, Ana!

How did a *boy* manage to cloud over the fact that I saw and talked to my supposedly dead twin sister? Where the HELL did my priorities go?

That night in the woods had seemed like a nightmare, not reality, but I couldn't dismiss it. I knew it was all real, as crazy and insane as it was, it really happened. I talked to Ana. I was attacked by a green woman who rose out of a pond. I was lured there by the song my dad used to sing. Yes, that about sums up the insanity of that night.

To top it all off, Ana made it seem like there was something about our family that I didn't know and she was really upset that I wasn't swimming. Why on earth would she care that I didn't swim? Of all the things that she could be upset about, why that? There was no logic in it. In any of it!

She wouldn't even tell me where she was, or how I could help her! After all these years, she's really alive. Alive! But, how was I supposed to tell Mom that she had been taken by a Siren, whatever that is, named Midira? If Mom wasn't already teetering on the edge that might just put her over. *No.* I couldn't tell her.

Suddenly, the happiness that I had felt all day started to feel selfish and stupid. I had no right to feel like that when Ana was somewhere with that *creature.*

It was my fault that she was there in the first place. If I wouldn't have let go that night in the water, she would still be with me! I was filled with an urgency to *do* something about it, but I knew the first step that I needed to take was going to be the worst.

"Darrien?"

There was a swish, and he was right beside me. We had been at the beach that evening, since shortly after supper. Darrien was swimming and I was standing in the water. A new record for me, mid-thigh.

"Yes?" He stood up in the water, and I watched it run off his body, down his muscular chest and arms.

"Oh, wow...uh. I was...uh...I was just thinking about that night in the woods." Water trickled down his abs, and I couldn't help watch the droplets curve around each muscle and disappear down into....

"You feeling okay? You look...distracted." He ran a hand through his wet hair, messing it up.

"I...uh, can you stop being so sexy for a minute, so I can concentrate?" I giggled. Darrien picked me out of the water in his arms, and kissed me generously.

"Oh, well...wow. Okay, what was I saying?" Darrien's dimples deepened, and his smile outshone the sun.

"The night in the woods?" he reminded me.

"Right...that night. Anyway, I...uh...I'm ready- well, at least I think I'm ready- to get into the water more...I think...maybe."

"Cora, that's great!" he shouted and smiled.

"Yeah, I just think that it's time I challenge myself a bit more...I guess."

"You're doing just about the worst job convincing me. But that's not going to stop me. You say you're ready to go, that's good enough for me, even if you haven't convinced yourself yet." His smile made my legs weak, but it gave me a boost of confidence.

"Alright, so we'll start tomorrow. Okay?" I gave him a big smile and turned towards the beach. His strong hands wrapped around my body and turned me back toward the water.

"Oh, no, you don't. We're starting right *now*. You've had an epiphany, and we're not going to waste it!" His smile was brilliant and contagious, and one was slowly starting to sneak its way across my face. "It's time to get back in the water, Humbug." My heart was racing now.

"You know what? This was a bad idea. I don't know what I was thinking. I'm not ready yet! Maybe in a couple more weeks...by the end of summer, for sure...I know it."

Did I sound as unconvinced as I felt?

300

I looked at Darrien, pleading with my eyes, but he just smiled his perfect smile and grabbed my hands.

"You're ready, Cora. There's a part of you that is aching to get in. You dream about it. What more do you want? I know you're scared, but I'm right here. Would I let anything happen to you?"

Damn, he has a point. He'll keep me safe. I knew that with every fiber of my being. *Maybe he's right. Maybe it's time.*

"Um, this is all a lot to digest right now. How about you finish your swim, and I'll try to get deeper. We'll start tomorrow…maybe?" I smiled as sweetly and innocently as I could. He didn't believe me. I could see it. But, for some reason, he chose not to fight me. I could tell it wasn't over, though. He was a stubborn guy, and I would be hearing about this every day until it happened.

Darrien's smile faded as he took a step away from me and dove seamlessly into the water, with not even a splash. My heart fell. I hated disappointing him. Guilt was eating at me. He was so invested in me getting into the water that I felt like I was failing *him*, and not myself.

I wasn't like him in the water. I could never hear him swimming; there was no sound. He was so graceful, like he belonged to it. It reminded me of watching Dad swim. He was the same way. He glided around effortlessly. Darrien loved it; I could see that. His energy never seemed to run out when he was swimming; he could be in the lake for hours, and it didn't seem to bother him.

I watched as Darrien swam great laps around the beach area. He wasn't afraid of going out too deep in the lake; he swam to the center and returned several times. He barely made a splash as he travelled. It was relaxing watching him swim. I took a deep breath and allowed myself to relax. It was later in the evening, and we were the only ones out there. It was incredibly peaceful.

The lake was like bath water. I could barely feel it on my skin. I stood and walked in the water. Concentrating on each breath helped me relax and occupied my mind. I closed my eyes and just breathed.

I searched my memories, to recall what it felt like to dive into water. Ana was always right there with me. I was more daring in the water than she was. I pushed myself harder, swam further and faster, and held my breath longer. I loved it. Ana did too, but not as much as me. We would race in the water with Dad. Mom and Bree would sit on the beach and watch, often giggling at the crazy games we played.

The water was a safe place for me, then. I knew what to expect in it. I knew what the rules were. I was confident and graceful. That all changed, the day of the accident.

Sometimes, when I stepped into a shower that wasn't quite warm enough, I got that sensation of being in water again, and I missed it. I missed the feeling of it slowly working its way up my body, and my body becoming lighter and lighter the deeper I went. There was nothing like it. I could feel the water on my skin, cool and wet, inviting me in. A sadness spread over me with the realization that I was far from experiencing that again. My memories gone, I opened my eyes.

Panic slammed into me. Every sensation I was remembering was actually happening! I was floating, somehow, close to the middle of the lake. A scream erupted from my throat as I sank under the water. I knew how to swim- or at least, I used to- but my limbs refused to move. They froze, stiff, next to my body. I knew I was sinking, and fast. My body wasn't fighting against it at all. The air in my lungs was gone, spent by my scream. I knew I was running out of time. My eyes opened.

Think, Cora. You can do this.

The lake went from a beautiful blue-green to a dark green as I sank toward the bottom. I was going down. There was nothing stopping that. I resisted the urge to open my mouth.

Move, Cora...move!

My ears started ringing. It was a sweet ringing sound, getting louder and louder.

Wait... it wasn't ringing, it was singing! I turned, looking in every direction. It was my Dad's song!

My eyes scanned the water around me.

Where is it coming from?

At the sound of it, my body thawed and my arms started to move. But the melody was louder than before, and I could feel it course through my veins. It drew me in, and down, down, down.

My lungs were burning, but the melody seemed to override that, somehow. I was stuck, unable to rise or sink. In that instant of indecision, my mouth did the unthinkable, and opened for air.

I took a deep breath, choked, and coughed. The pain was excruciating. I felt consciousness slipping away, and I thought of Ana.

87

Darrien

I HAD TAKEN OFF ACROSS the lake to get my shit together. I needed to tell Cora. I promised Pearl. She was right, it had to be done, but that didn't make it any easier to do. I needed to pump myself up for it.

The look on her face…it was going to kill me. She's going to hate me. But it would be worth it if it meant that she would be safer.

That's when I heard the scream. It was short, like it was cut off. I turned my head so fast, I could have gotten whiplash. *Cora?* I shot through the water, to where I saw her last. She had just been standing near shore, in less than waist-deep water.

"Cora?" I called. Nothing. Panic was starting to rise.

Midira wouldn't have come out into the lake water. She wouldn't dare. That was a direct infringement of Mer territory. It would be considered an act of war. Whatever she planned for Cora wouldn't get off the ground before our forces stormed Stronghold and laid waste to her Siren clan.

So, where was Cora?

I dove under and started to search. I was going as fast as I could, and trying to tap into something that would let me know where she was, but I was getting nothing. It wasn't until I heard the song echoing through the water that I clued in. She was near the gate! SHIT!

I sped up. When she finally came into sight, she was only a few yards away from the gate, floating midwater, completely unconscious. I shot to her, lifted her into my arms, and streaked for the surface as fast as I could.

88

Cora

I WAS COUGHING. The air was life giving, and I choked it down. Exchanging water for air made my lungs burn like a gas-fueled fire, but breathing felt....it felt like being *alive* again.

I wasn't aware that Darrien was holding me until I got my breath back. He was shaking. His eyes did a quick scan of me, and then he smiled and released a tense breath, in a sigh of relief. I did too.

I was alive. I was okay...again, thanks to Darrien. I threw my hands around Darrien's neck and buried my head into his shoulder.

"I don't know what I did to deserve you, but you are literally my lifesaver." I was smiling and holding onto him tight. I let my breathing return to normal, feeling my heart slow and my lungs clear.

Finally, my head stopped buzzing. Darrien's strong arms held me up. I felt safe again. He was perfect. *I don't deserve him.*

I knew that, one day, the weird spell that made him fall for me would lift and he would find someone else, someone perfect like him.

I'll never be that perfect person for him.

I didn't want to believe it, but deep down, I knew it was true. I held on to Darrien tighter, wanting to savor this moment with him a little longer. Darrien closed his arms around me tighter, too.

My eyes took in Darrien's flawless features, from his stunning eyes to the curve of his chin, to the single freckle on his left cheek...*I love him.*

My heart exploded in my chest as I said it to myself again...*I love him.* I didn't know until that moment, and now that I felt it, how could I have missed it for so long? My heart didn't belong to me anymore. It *was* Darrien's.

I'm his.

I could feel tears well up in my eyes.

"Cora, are you okay? You're crying." His eyes were full of concern, but mine were full of joy. I beamed at him.

"I'm fine. Everything's fine...great...perfect, actually. This is perfect." The tears slowly dropped down my cheeks, stopped by Darrien's fingers as he wiped them away.

I pressed my forehead against his chest.

I want this moment to last forever. I want to stay in his arms forever, be with him forever.

The water felt amazing, and I could feel its warmth sink into my skin. I was completely relaxed, and completely happy.

"Whatever you are thinking right now, don't stop. Close your eyes." Darrien's voice was soothing and soft. I didn't know what he was getting at, but I trusted him.

I closed my eyes, relaxed, and thought about him. I thought about his arms around me, and the feel of the water on my skin. His arms relaxed, though he was still holding me. With a light and gentle touch, he stopped supporting me in the water. I tried not to think about it and do what he asked.

Relax.

"Keep going, Cora. You're doing great."

Don't think, just relax.

"Okay, now I want you to keep doing what you are doing. Stay relaxed and calm, and open your eyes." *Relaxed...calm...got it. Open eyes....*

I nearly screamed. I was freaking floating!

We were in the middle of the lake, and I was *floating.*

Everything above my waist was above the water.

This isn't possible. I should be in the water over my shoulders. How is this possible?

I wasn't moving my legs at all, or my hands. I was rapidly looking around myself to see what was keeping me above the water, and slowly, I was sinking lower and lower.

"You've got to stay relaxed, Cora. Close your eyes again and calm yourself."

Calm? I was magically floating in the water! How was I supposed...okay, okay...calm...calm.

I willed my panicked thoughts away. As the calm spread through my body, I could feel the water move down my body, as my chest rose above the surface.

"Excellent, Cora! You're doing really, really well! I'm impressed! You're a natural!"

"A natural what?" My relaxation gone, I fell into the water. Darrien reached across and picked me up into his arms.

"Seriously – enough!" I yelled, swiping at the water on my face. "I'm done with the questions and the mystery. I'm done. Either you tell me what the heck is going on with me, or I'm out of here…as soon as you take me to the shore."

I stuck my chin out, and narrowed my eyes. I meant it.

This is getting ridiculous, already.

Darrien sighed and lowered me into the water again.

"You're right," he uttered. My jaw fell open. I was ready to have to fight for some answers. I wasn't prepared for it to be that easy.

"Alright, then start." I maintained my serious expression and stared pointedly back at Darrien.

"I'll tell you everything when we get to shore, but first, take a deep breath." I eyed him, unsure of where this was going with that.

"Do you trust me?" he asked. His face was so close to mine, our noses touched. His eyes were swimming in greens and blues. My heart thumped deep in my chest.

"I trust you," I admitted. If this was what it took to get some answers…

I took a deep breath. Darrien pulled me into his arms and gently dove under the water. Panic started to rise in my throat and my eyes snapped open, wide with fear, but Darrien smiled reassuringly at me and held me tight.

Between the feel of Darrien's strong arms around me, and chanting *"I'm safe, I'm safe, I'm safe"* to myself, I was able to stay calm. After all, Darrien would never let anything happen to me.

His body was so graceful and strong, I wasn't holding him back a bit. We were moving fast, deeper and deeper, and the water got darker and greener the further down we swam. I knew Darrien was an incredible swimmer, but the speed we went at was well beyond an Olympic champion, and his body was barely moving.

I trusted him, but the further down we went, the more nervous I got. How were we going to make it back to the surface in time? My hero was down there with me. If we both ran out of air, there was no way we would make it back.

I looked at Darrien, my worries clearly written across my face. He smiled reassuringly back at me, but it didn't help.

Deeper and deeper we went. It got cool, then cold. The water went from light to almost complete darkness. Then, a small glow winked to life. We swam for it. When we were just on the edge, I could hear the melody again.

"Can you hear that?" Darrien's voice echoed in my head.

He was looking at me, but he wasn't moving his mouth. His words had entered my head and interrupted my thoughts. I started to open my mouth to respond, but he quickly reached across and put his hand across my lips. I stopped. I knew if I opened my mouth, I'd breathe, and that would be it.

"Don't try to talk. Think of your answer and visualize sending it to me. Try."

306

My eyes were as wide as they could be. I focused on what I wanted to say, and visualized sending it to him.

"What...what on earth is going on? How are you doing this?"

I was running out of air. *Does Darrien know? He doesn't seem worried at all.*

"Hey, Humbug, you sound just as beautiful in my head as you do in my ear."

His gave me a watery kiss on the cheek and held me close. The melody floated all around us. There was a part of me that wanted to open my mouth and sing along, but I knew better than that.

"I'm running out of air, Darrien." Panic sat at the edge of my nerves, ready to jump into play. It took a lot of concentration to keep calm.

"You won't run out of air, Cora. Trust me. Everything will be fine." He turned me around, staring me in the face. His hands on my arms were firm. There was sadness in his eyes when I looked at him. His face became resolute, determined, and it erased the sadness completely.

I realized then that he was holding me in place, not embracing me anymore. It hit me hard...*we aren't going back.* Panic pounced, slamming the calm right out of me.

"What are you doing?" I screamed.

He's going to drown me! I squirmed against his grip, but his arms were like stone.

"I'm sorry," he said, but held on tight.

"You're hurting *me! You're going to* drown *me! Why? Why are you doing this?"*

I struggled to keep my mouth shut, but my body needed air. It wouldn't be long before it betrayed me and opened. I kicked at Darrien as hard as I could, but he felt nothing. I clawed and punched as much as I could, but nothing. I was using up my air supply faster as I struggled.

With the last bit of strength I had before I lost consciousness, I sent one last message to Darrien.

"I trusted you! I thought...I thought you cared about me! I lo-"

I didn't get to finish my thought. My body demanded air and opened my mouth. For the fourth time in my life, I felt water enter my lungs and waited for the pain. It came with the same ferocity as each time before. Burning and searing on its way.

I glared at Darrien as I choked on the water. I tried to cough it out of my lungs, only to inhale more. My body screamed at me, but there was nothing I could do to stop the onslaught of pain.

89
Darrien

THE LOOK ON HER FACE was like having a firing squad take their sweet time with my heart.

She hated me.

As she fell unconscious, I hugged her tightly. I needed to be close to her one last time.

I love you, Cora.

I'm so sorry.

90
Cora

EVERYTHING WENT DARK, and then shook.

"Breathe, Cora! Take a breath! Now! Breathe!" His voice was resonating in my head, but I couldn't make sense of what he was telling me. My mind was fuzzy and my vision was blurred.

I have no air, I can't breathe.

Darrien betrayed me. Why?

I want to let go. I'm done fighting.

I felt Darrien shift, and a sharp pain erupted in my side. I opened my eyes and mouth wide, and gasped in pain.

A warm, electric current ran through me. I felt the pain in my lungs disappear. I gasped again, as another blast to my side ignited pain. Inhaling more water, warmth spread through me again. I could feel my lungs fill with water, but I could breathe again.

How is this possible?

I took more deep breaths, giving my body time to adjust to the new sensation. My vision cleared.

I'm alive? I'm alive!

Darrien was holding me, not to restrain me, but gently, tenderly. His expression was heavy, but relieved.

"Are you okay? How do you feel?" Darrien asked.

I pushed away from him. What did he think? I just drowned! I was *not* okay! What was wrong with me? Why was I alive? He drowned me! *He drowned me!*

My body resigned to the emotions I was feeling, and I was wracked with tears. I floated deep in the lake and sobbed. Darrien tried to reach out for me, but I shoved him away. He looked hurt, but he kept his distance.

"How could you do that to me? You know…you know what it took for me to trust you and get in the water! Why?" I screamed through my tears.

The betrayal of trust I felt at that moment was almost paralyzing. I took a deep breath. *Calm down.* I willed myself to bring my emotions under control.

What happened to me? Why am I still alive?

"Cora?" Darrien's voice was soft, unsure. He didn't make a move to comfort me. He raised his eyes to look at me, but couldn't keep eye contact long. Guilt flowed from him.

Good.

"I'm sorry, Cora.," he spoke, his tender voice entering my mind. *"I asked you to trust me because I knew you would be okay. I also knew if I told you about this, you would never have believed me. You needed to experience it for yourself. There's so much more to your story that you don't know. And it's time you learned it."*

He moved closer, but didn't reach out for me. I didn't want him to. The trust I felt for him had disappeared with the air in my lungs.

He doesn't deserve my trust.

"And who asked you to do all this?" I barked. *"Who asked you to do that? Why you? And why me? I'm no one special. I'm no one...no one!"* I yelled.

My fight was waning. I wanted to scream, but there was little energy left in me to do it. I could feel the tears burning in my eyes, but they never fell, just joined with the rest of the water around me.

"You're wrong, Cora. There's so much more to you than you know. You are special, very special. I wish there was some way I could have helped you without betraying your trust, but this was the only way I could keep you safe, if there was another way...I know you don't trust me, and...." His voice broke. He looked away from me, his shoulders drooped and his head dropped down.

"Cora, it wasn't supposed to be like this. I had a simple job to do. But then, the first day I met you...you...no one has ever spoken to me like you did, or stood up to me like that. You got under my skin. I couldn't stop thinking about you, not for a second. You changed everything. You changed me.

"This was supposed to be just another job, but instead, against everything I believe, I fell for you. You mean more to me than the job I was sent to do, a job that I love, that I have dedicated my life to. I will lose everything I've worked for when they find out what I've done.

"Somehow, that doesn't matter to me anymore. Since the day I met you, you have been the only thing that matters to me."

He lifted his eyes to mine. They were sincere and genuine, and – damn it - there was love in them too.

Against my wishes, my heart thumped excitedly in my chest. Darrien's green-blue eyes looked at me. He didn't expect anything. He didn't want forgiveness; he knew he didn't deserve it. As much as it pained me to admit it, that was endearing. It would be a while before I could completely forgive him, but my feelings for him warmed at the thought of having him next to me again. I cursed myself for being so weak, but it didn't matter...*I still love him.*

"I don't understand what's going on, Darrien. I'm hurt, I'm confused, and I'm floating. I'm having a very hard time digesting this. If you know so much about me, then help me." I wasn't mad, I was just desperate. It was all so overwhelming.

My anger was gone; I was too exhausted. I just wanted it all to be done and over. Even my curiosity was disappearing. I wanted to just give up. It was all too much.

"It will be okay, Cora." He smiled at me, and put out his hand. I looked at the hand. Did I trust him enough to take it? My heart wanted so badly to reach out for him, but my head told me not to.

"I'll follow you," I said and kept my hands to my sides, letting Darrien take the lead. Somehow, without moving my body much, I was able to carry myself swiftly through the water to the surface.

Breathing air again was like drowning all over again. This time, though, it was water I was running out of. Darrien transitioned flawlessly, but I choked and coughed. The air burned. Darrien carried me in his arms after I started losing consciousness again. I didn't want to, but I couldn't help it, I always felt safe in his arms.

After several breaths, the air felt life-giving again. He held onto me as we slowly swam for shore. I had to wrap my arms around him as we stepped out of the water and onto the sandy beach. I was exhausted. It was a long swim from where we were to the surface, and then from the middle of the lake to shore. I wasn't used to it, like he was.

"I need to sit down for a moment." And suddenly, my legs collapsed under me. I tumbled to the sand. The sky was pitch dark.

"So much time passed. How were we down there for so long? It seemed like only minutes!" I said.

"Time functions differently when you're...um, when you're in the water." He half-smiled and lifted me to my feet. "We don't have far to go. I can carry you if you want."

"I can walk...thank you." I picked myself up off the sand. *Time for some answers...finally.* I followed Darrien right to Pearl's door.

"What are we doing here? I thought I was getting some answers! Oh, don't make me face Pearl yet." Darrien smiled at me and knocked on the door. Pearl answered quickly.

"Darrien! Cora! So nice to see you...um, come in." She stepped aside and let us through the door. I exchanged a look with Darrien. *What are we doing here?*

The inside of Pearl's cabin was warm and friendly. The furniture was old, with lots of plaid browns and yellows spread across a fluffy couch and chair.

The room was small, with just enough space for a couch, chair, and small TV. I could see a small kitchen in the back, though I'm sure she did very little cooking. The floors were hard wood and matched the natural color of the logs. The room was inviting, just like she was. We sat on the couch and faced Pearl, who fell into the overstuffed chair across from us.

"And what brings you two here so late?" She smiled at us. Her eyes were sparkling, but concerned.

"We went for a swim, Pearl. She knows." Darrien looked intently at Pearl. Her smile faded slightly, and her eyes became clouded and concentrated.

"Well , then…we're going to need something to drink. It's going to be a long evening." She stood up and went to the kitchen, then returned shortly with a tray of drinks and a bowl of fruit.

"So, Cora, how was your first swim?" She gave me a small smile and sipped from her cup.

"Wait…you? You know too?" I looked at Darrien, "Pearl knows too?" I sighed.

This is crazy! Well, if Pearl's behind all this that would explain why I got this job. "Okay, I'm listening. What's going on? I think it's time I was told."

"There's a lot to tell you, Cora. How about we start with something simple, like how you survived today." She smiled. I grunted. If this was going to be the simple part of my answers, I'm not sure I wanted to know what I'd gotten myself into.

"Okay, so why did I survive the water today without drowning, like every other time?" I took a cup and started to sip. I gave Pearl my undivided attention.

"Today, you fully drowned. The other times, you *almost* drowned, but you were pulled out and your lungs were filled with air again. Today, your body filled completely with water."

I watched her carefully over the top of the cup. Darrien was at my side, he didn't drink or eat anything. Instead, he was watching me.

"When your body totally resigned itself to there being no air left, it started to breathe water instead. There was a change that happened in you. Your body started to process water as if it were air. It filtered the oxygen out and into your body, like a fish. You might have noticed that you were gasping for a bit; your body was getting used to less oxygen in each breath. The more you practice breathing water, the less the change between air and water will affect you. Darrien is able to do this smoothly, although most Guards are." Pearl took another sip from her cup. She looked at Darrien, and there was pity in her eyes, a sadness that wasn't there before. She broke her gaze and focused it on her cup.

"You're a guard? You didn't mention that," I said, and stared at Darrien. He was a guard, maybe *the* guard I was to be looking for? Then, I remembered he was sent to me to do a job; was he guarding *me*? Ana said...*holy crap*. Puzzle pieces were starting to come together. Granted, it seemed unreal, but at least they were forming a picture.

"There are a lot of things I never mentioned, but that's why we're here, so you can get some answers. I promise, I'll tell you everything you want to know about me. But that will have to wait. First, you need to hear what Pearl says." Darrien, my personal saviour...was a guard. *My* guard? His eyes flicked to Pearl, and my focus reluctantly shifted back to her.

"He's right, Cora. Darrien's story will come. Right now, you need to hear yours."

"But I- okay, I'm listening." I set my cup down and placed my hands in my lap. "I'm a fish." I focused my eyes again on Pearl.

"You aren't a fish, but you can adapt to living in water. Your body knows how to survive underwater. You're not the only one of your kind. However, you are a special case. Most of us grow up in the water and experience land in short bursts. There hasn't been someone born on land with no water experience at your age, ever. But I'm getting ahead of myself. The best way I can explain what you are is to give you the history of our people."

"Our people?" I asked, looking at Darrien again. "There's more like me, like you? Lots?" I gazed back at Pearl and searched her for an answer. Pearl and Darrien smiled and shared a knowing glance. Darrien rested a hand on my knee.

"Lots more, Cora, lots," Darrien slid further back into the couch.

Things were never going to be the same, but I already knew that.

Is Bree like me too? What about Dad and Mom? Ana? Are we all the same? If not, why am I different?

I still had so many questions. Just as I learned an answer to one, I had twenty more to ask.

"Our history goes back thousands of years, to around 9,600 B.C. At that time, there was a thriving island continent called Atlantis," Pearl started.

"What?" I shook my head. *You've got to be kidding me. The lost city of Atlantis? Right.*

"Oh, of course, you've heard of it. Well, then you'll have to suspend your belief just a little and let me get through this...no more questions." Pearl eyed me up, lifting her eyebrow.

"Okay, no more questions. Atlantis. Go on." I sat back in the couch and rolled my eyes.

Pearl leaned back in her chair. Her eyes unfocused, as if she were recalling the story from a distant memory. I watched her and listened.

313

"As I was saying, it all started thousands of years ago. The island of Atlantis was a thriving, growing place. It was a startlingly beautiful continent, possessing all parts of nature possible, to make up its round shape.

"Two deep rivers ran in concentric circles inside the island, and a third cut through it from the heart of the island to the ocean. Inside the smallest circular river was an island, and the government for Atlantis was located there.

"Surrounding the rivers were plains, where the people of Atlantis grew their crops. They had fields for their animals to graze, forests to hunt in, and plenty of water to fish. Everywhere you went, the land was taken care of, and used to supply the people with everything they needed. Everyone worked, everyone contributed, and everyone benefited. This was a utopian society, with no war or greed, and the people were happy.

"The gods, specifically the Greek gods, blessed the people of Atlantis with technology and knowledge far beyond those of their neighboring countries. They gave these gifts to see the true potential of humans and to witness how much they could accomplish, but mostly because they loved these people.

"Poseidon, especially, took much pride in Atlantis. He created soft and gentle seas for their fishing and boating. After all, living on an island, Atlanteans were a water people.

"Poseidon visited Atlantis in the form of a man, many times. During his time there and, as happened with many gods, he had relations."

"Relations?" I blurted, cutting her off. Pearl looked at me out of the side of her eye. "Oh! Relations," I enunciated, finally understanding.

The gods got busy with the humans.

"Gods are not permitted to have relationships with humans," Pearl clarified, "but a lot of them broke this rule. So, their time on land was monitored closely, and they were not allowed to stay on land long. Though his time was short, Poseidon's affection was strong and true. Because Atlantis was in the care of *all* the gods, Poseidon kept his visits secret. He knew it would upset the other gods to know he carried on with their people.

"In the years that Poseidon came to the island, his passion resulted in children being born. But Poseidon was not able to stay to see them grow. Gods weren't permitted to raise their human offspring. His times were short and spread out over many, many years. It isn't known how many children he fathered over the centuries he visited.

"Anyway, the people of Atlantis had everything a wealthy country needed to survive: a plentiful food supply, rich minerals to mine, and wealth; more wealth than they needed blessed its people. Most on Atlantis were very happy with this, but there were a few who were not content. They wanted *more*. They weren't satisfied with *only* the riches that came from Atlantis.

314

"Over the years, those greedy voices grew louder and multiplied. The utopia in Atlantis was in jeopardy of breaking. Though it took a few hundred years, eventually, the greedy voices outnumbered the happy ones. All but one member of the government was corrupt.

"Marcus Titus was the only leader left on Atlantis that still valued his country the way the gods had intended. The other leaders wanted to expand their borders by taking over neighboring countries. They wanted to claim others' treasures for their own and add to their wealth.

"Marcus argued that Atlantis had all the riches its people could ever hope for, and there was no need to resort to violence. But he was ignored and, eventually, cast out of government for his views.

"Battle ships were launched, and the army deployed to battle. Marcus stayed behind to try to convince the people that their greed would lead to their demise. Again, he was ignored.

"The battle for more wealth was lost, heavily. It seemed that even though they were technologically superior to their neighbors, they had never experienced war and had no idea how to fight in one. And so, the army retuned defeated, not just in battle, but in spirit. However, Marcus's message still fell on deaf ears.

"The gods, having watched the greedy grow to power, were enraged. They gave the people of Atlantis more than any other people, and they still wanted more. The greed and corruption of the government was absolute. The land had gone wild from neglect. People had grown lazy; instead of working for what they needed, they expected others to provide for them. When the armies left, they expected them to return with riches so great, that no one on Atlantis would have to work again. Of course, this didn't happen, and now there was nothing left of Atlantis for its people to use.

"Infuriated by the selfishness and greed of its favored people, the gods made the decision to smite Atlantis and bring it to its knees. They would sink it, and let it be a lesson to those seeking wealth they didn't need. 'Greed shall bring on the fury of the gods.'

"Poseidon watched all this in utter sadness. He cared for the people more than any other god, and was not in agreement with the other gods' decision. In an effort to find something in Atlantis that would change the gods' minds, he made another trip in human form. He sought out Marcus Titus. Surely, the gods would change their minds if they focused on the words of a man still honoring their gifts.

"Poseidon had watched the efforts Marcus made to change people's minds. His faith in the people of Atlantis was renewed through this. Surely, there were more that shared Marcus's views, those who remembered and cherished Atlantis for what it was meant to be.

"Poseidon found Marcus in a temple dedicated to the gods, at the center of Atlantis. Marcus was asking for forgiveness for the greed of his people. He asked that the gods not doom all to the fate that only some had earned. Poseidon interrupted Marcus's prayers. In his human form, Poseidon embodied an old man, so Marcus was unaware of who he really was speaking to.

"Marcus talked to Poseidon about all the good people that had found him. There were many in Atlantis that still believed in the gods' vision of their island. He spoke about his frustrations at not being listened to in the government, and how the men he once respected turned on him and cast him out. He was no longer permitted to speak in government, or in public. Marcus had even been arrested several times for trying to educate people about the corrupt government. He lost his family, his home, and the respect of his fellow Atlanteans. Poseidon was saddened; this story would not convince the other gods to spare Atlantis.

"In his ever-generous manner, Marcus brought Poseidon back to the home of his friend. Marcus was living there with this man's family. Even though food was hard to come by, they welcomed Poseidon to sit with them for supper. Poseidon sat around their table and listened to their stories.

"The people in this home were a happy family. They celebrated all the gifts the gods placed upon Atlantis, and they strove to teach their children how to care for them. This was a story Poseidon could use. He gave the family his undivided attention.

"They shared with him all the struggles they went through that year: losing loved ones, gaining loved ones like Titus, and keeping their ideals a secret from the public. They feared, should they reveal to more people that they were against the war and conquering outside of Atlantis, that they would lose their land and their homes. There were very powerful people in Atlantis that would not stand for those who spoke against them. They commended Titus on his bravery, for he had suffered the most.

"Poseidon left that night with a heavy heart. It was clear to him that there was just too much greed in Atlantis, and he would never be able to convince the other gods differently.

"He returned to his home in the sea that night to think. He decided that he would save those that still valued the gifts of the gods, for only those people were worthy of any gift a god could bestow on them.

"The gods had debated, and they would not change their minds. They would destroy Atlantis. Of course, the people of Atlantis were not aware of their fate. They went about their daily business, unaware that their world was about to be fatally shattered.

"Then, an old man showed up on the doorstep of the home of Titus. When the family and Titus answered the door, Poseidon revealed to them who he really was. He told them of the gods' decision, and not to be afraid, for he was going to save them.

"He ordered Titus to bring all the people he knew that honored the old Atlantis to a special boat Poseidon docked on the island. They were to board the boat that night, take it out to sea, and wait for Poseidon. Titus did as he was ordered. That evening, he arrived on the shore with one hundred people, which was a small number compared to the thousands that lived on Atlantis. They boarded the boat and took it out to sea.

"In the middle of the night, the old man appeared on deck. He asked all on board to join him. He told them of the gods' plan to destroy Atlantis, and that he would be unable to stop them. Instead, he chose this group of people to join him, to live out their Atlantean ways under the sea.

"They would be able to start over, and would be allowed to use all knowledge they gained living on Atlantis. The people were very honored that they had pleased the sea god, and that he was going to save them. They rejoiced at the mercy of Poseidon.

"He told them that they would have to return home and face the destruction of Atlantis without him, for if the other gods knew what he planned, they would destroy him *and* the people he chose to save. They must not reveal themselves to anyone, or all would be lost. The passengers all agreed to this.

"Poseidon thanked Marcus for opening his eyes to so many good people on Atlantis, and told them all that it was Marcus Titus who saved them. The people on the boat were all immensely grateful to Marcus for what he had done.

"Then, Poseidon made it rain. The rain landed gently and softly on the passengers of the boat. It was a blessed rain, Poseidon told them. All that were touched by it would survive the destruction to come, and would be able to join him for a new beginning.

"A few days passed, and the day of destruction was upon the people of Atlantis, but only one hundred people knew about it. They scurried from their homes to their jobs and back. A nervous energy filled the air that no one could explain or speak about." Pearl paused for effect, taking a slow, steady sip of her drink. She set her cup down and watched me.

"It all started with a rumble," she continued.

"The ground shook, just a little at first. Dishes were broken, furniture moved around homes, and animals were startled. The people of Atlantis were struck silent. An event such as this had never happened before, so they stopped what they were doing and waited. An eerie stillness spread across the island.

"What was to come was the single most destructive combination of natural events the world has ever seen.

"The shaking grew stronger and stronger until the earth gave way. The ground tore and broke along the shoreline, and it fell in great pieces into the sea. The land was shattered, and a great spider web of canyons was created. Buildings toppled and were thrown to the ground. People ran, screaming for shelter, but there was nowhere to hide from falling debris. The ground swallowed buildings whole, and anyone standing near. It was mass chaos. Atlantis was breaking.

"After the earthquakes stopped, people came out of their shelters to assess the damage. There was nothing left standing; not one building remained. People openly wept at the loss of their possessions, at the loss of their homes, and then, at the loss of their loved ones. If the destruction would have stopped after the earthquakes, the people of Atlantis would have survived, but it didn't.

"Next came the water. The sea swelled, causing the rivers to flow backwards, overflow, and flood the land. The land was completely immersed in water. The sinking of Atlantis had begun.

"It only took a few hours for the island to completely vanish underwater. The sea never dropped down again; instead, it beat against the remaining land and tore it apart more and more. The people that survived the falling buildings and earthquakes were lost to the sea.

"But not all perished. There was a small group that found themselves alive and unharmed by the events of that day. These were the passengers of Poseidon's boat. Somehow, Poseidon's rain had protected them from the devastation around them.

"Poseidon's people floated in the water, on collected debris from Atlantis, and waited. Now what? They were alive, but where were they to go? Hanging onto whatever they could, they waited all night and into the morning for their answer.

"As the sun rose, Poseidon came to them. He told them he had bestowed on them the ability to breathe underwater, but in order to come with him, they would have to shed their love for the land. To do this, Poseidon explained that they had to drown their land selves to give birth to their water selves.

"The people were horrified. How was it possible; breathing underwater? If they drowned, they were dead, there was no question.

"There was an outburst. The people shouted their mistrust and anger at this horrifying feat. It was Marcus that silenced them. He reminded them of

318

the sacrifice Poseidon made for them, and of the gifts that the gods gave them that their people wasted away. He scolded them for their selfishness. If this was the price Poseidon demanded so that they could live, they should be happy to give it.

"Silence fell upon the people as they watched Marcus sink himself below the waves. They waited and waited for him, but he did not return. Marcus's faith in Poseidon's word gave the people the strength and courage to do what Poseidon wished.

"Many tears were shed in having to do this. These people often mourned the loss of those that drowned in ship wrecks and other water deaths. It was a horrible duty they were asked to do.

"None were as hard as the parents of the young children, who, in order to save their children, first had to drown them. Soon, there were no survivors on the surface. They had all sacrificed themselves to be saved."

I stared in wide-eyed horror at her. Drowning children! What kind of monsters where these…things? No!

I wanted to leave. I didn't want any part of it. Darrien reached over and wrapped his fingers around mine. He looked intently into my eyes. It stilled my breath. This was his history, too. He had done this to me. He drowned me to help me see what I really was.

Was that saving me?

"Cora, they were all saved." Pearl's voice broke through my thoughts. I tore my eyes away from Darrien and looked to her. The woman that I came to know at camp hadn't really disappeared, but she was changed. The confidence I so admired in her was cracking.

"Poseidon greeted each one as they joined him under the waves," she continued. "He led them to their new home, deep under the surface, in a hole in the seafloor. Poseidon had created a new Atlantis for them. This new home would shelter them, and generations to come.

"He taught them what they could eat, what they could plant, and what sea creatures they could tame to help them. They were to earn their keep in this new city by maintaining the land around it and caring for the buildings. If they could do this and be happy with what they had, they would always have a home there.

"The Atlanteans named their new home Titus Prime, to honor their hero, Marcus Titus.

"Titus Prime adopted the ideals that made Atlantis so prosperous. The people thought that it was fit that Marcus be their first leader. After all, it was his passion and leadership that saved all of them.

"Marcus ruled Titus Prime until his death. He led with a firm but kind hand, and was loved by all the people of Titus Prime. Marcus also had the ability to command the water. All those touched by Poseidon's rain could breathe under water, and were able to propel themselves through water at speeds their land bodies would not have been able to. But commanding massive amounts of water was a gift only a few possessed.

"They found out that Marcus was, in fact, a descendant of Poseidon himself. Poseidon's children could control the seas, a great power that a city underwater could use if it ever needed to defend itself.

"A great dome was created over the city. It kept out the elements from the sea and any dangers it held. Poseidon tied the dome's strength to the ruler of the great city. After some debate, they decided that the ruler of their fine city would forever be a direct descendant of Poseidon.

"Titus Prime has been the center of our people for thousands of years; since the sinking of Atlantis. Our people have grown in numbers so great, two other cities have been created to house all of our kind. Wherever the ocean is at its deepest, you will find an underwater city. Not one has ever been discovered by land people, and it's essential that it stays that way."

I looked at Darrien and Pearl. Their eyes were on me, watching and waiting. Suddenly my world cracked open, revealing a hidden side I never knew existed.

Who am I? What am I?

91
Cora

"SO, CORA, THIS IS A SACRED secret you now hold. You can tell no one…not even Bree."

"What? Why not? If I'm one of these people, isn't she?"

She's my sister. Shouldn't we both be an underwater whatever?

"We don't know if Bree is one of us, yet. You are a special case, Cora. Let's just deal with you, for now," Pearl explained. As frustrating as that was, I could tell that was the end of the conversation.

No talking to Bree about this…that's going to be tough.

"Okay, so what happened to Titus Prime? Does it still exist? Where is it?" I watched Darrien and Pearl for the answer. Pearl sipped her drink and answered.

"It still exists," she said. "But there was a time when our numbers were getting low, and it was essential that new blood was introduced into our society. It was then that we started seeking out land people to join us."

Interesting. She had my full attention.

"At the beginning, the desperation of it drove some people to kidnapping. Eventually, we learned how to coax people, willingly, to join us. Our voices can lower inhibitions, making people calmer and relaxed, and more willing to come with us."

Pearl continued, "Even though we're not permitted to talk about what we are, that doesn't mean we haven't been seen in our water activities by people on land. In the beginning, the adjustment from land to water was difficult for some. They would spend time near the shore on the surface and watch people on land. I guess, they were missing the life they used to have. There were lots of sightings back then, but the idea of water people was so outrageous that they were waved off as folklore, legend, myth…you name it. Every part of the world has stories about us," she said, with a flick of her hand.

"Do you mean *mermaids*?" I blurted. "But they have fins, like a fish. Wait, am I going to sprout a huge fin and have to wear shells on my...you know?" I said covering my chest with my arms.

Darrien laughed out loud. I shoved him.

How am I supposed to know? I'm new to all this!

Pearl was laughing too.

"No, Cora, those half-naked ladies in cartoons and movies are *not* us. We don't need fins to swim fast, because we're able to control a small amount of water around us. This enables us to be propelled forward at great speeds. We use the water to push us along.

"The sightings that people on land had were of us moving very quickly through the water. The only explanation of that would be a fin of some sort. It was a wrong, but logical, conclusion," she explained.

"Wait! I've seen something moving around in the lake early in the mornings. It glides through the water fast, and makes no sound. I've never been able to get a good look at it. Was it-" Darrien raised his hand, sheepishly.

"That was *you*?"

That explains a lot, actually.

The way he moved in the water was similar, which was something I didn't connect until then.

"So, what do we call ourselves, then? Ex-Atlanteans or Titusians? What?" Darrien and Pearl exchanged a glance. Pearl cleared her throat.

"You're not going to like it, but it is what it is. You are a Mermaid, Darrien is a Merman, and we are Merpeople. Mer for short," Pearl explained. I burst out laughing.

"This is a joke! *Mermaids*! No way, no, *no*. It's not possible. Me? A mermaid...ha-ha!" I couldn't help it, I was laughing...a lot.

Darrien, a merman! No, no way! Poseidon's children...that's crazy! This has got to be a joke...albeit a very elaborate joke, but still a joke.

I looked at Darrien and Pearl, but they weren't laughing. My giggles stopped short in my throat.

Please, let it be a joke.

But then, I thought of the experience I had in the water. Pearl said Poseidon demanded that the people drown their land selves to give birth to their water selves. I had to drown to breathe water. Then, there was the way these people moved in the water...the water pushed or propelled them forward. When Darrien took me down into the water, we moved very fast, but he wasn't kicking his legs to move us and he was holding me in his arms, so what moved us?

I guess, that part fit in too, if it was the water that propelled us.

322

But, Atlantis? That couldn't be possible, no. Atlantis is a myth, a fairy tale…not real. But then, so are mermaids.

Is this really possible?

I sat there in stunned silence, as my brain frantically tried to figure all this out.

Me, Darrien, and Pearl were…merpeople?

"So…mermaids. I'm a mermaid," I mumbled shaking my head. "Forgive me, but I'm going to have a hard time processing that. How did I become one? I mean, how am I a mermaid? As far as I know, Mom and Dad are as normal as normal can be." I stared from Darrien to Pearl and back.

Something has to fit, so that this puzzle finally makes sense.

"Your father is Mer," Pearl said. She and Darrien exchanged a knowing glance. My initial shock was replaced by my old anger.

"Of course, all this would be his fault," I spouted. "That makes sense. Everything that goes terribly wrong in my life revolves around him. How do *you* know about Dad?" I asked, pointing at Darrien. "Pearl, you said you knew Dad way back when, but Darrien, how do you know him? *I* haven't seen him since I was *nine*, yet I get this feeling that you know him."

"We know your father, Cora," Darrien admitted. He turned his body toward me on the couch. His eyes were heavy with worry. "The best way to explain this to you is to tell you my role in all of this." Darrien eyed Pearl and she nodded.

"I work for your father," Darrien began. "He sent me here to find you. My job was to protect you, keep you safe, and get you in the water. That last part, I wasn't doing a good job of until today."

I crossed my arms and willed the beast of rage building in my gut to calm for a moment.

"Sorry. I know it wasn't great for you, but I couldn't figure out any other way to get you to this point."

"Really?" I cut in. "You couldn't have just *talked* to me about it? You went straight for drowning me?" My words were dripping with sarcasm, but I didn't care. The beast growled in my gut.

"Oh, yeah," he nodded sarcastically, "and you *totally* would have believed me. 'Cora, you're a mermaid, you can breathe underwater…oh wait, but first you have to drown yourself. So, let's get at it!' I'm sure that would have been much simpler. You're right," Darrien barked back at me.

I wanted to yell at him, but I was starting to understand things a little better from his perspective. This was hard for him, and frustrating.

How do you tell someone what they are when it's such an unbelievable story?

I didn't know if I could have done it any better. I heaved a great sigh. My anger and mistrust in Darrien left me with my breath. In the end, he was protecting me, and helping me discover who I was. But I was right about one thing...I *was* a job.

"You're right," I admitted, sagging into the couch. "Sorry. You did what you thought was best. It really wasn't a choice for you; you had to show me, not tell me. I wouldn't have believed you. I would have thought you were nuts." I smiled at him, and he smiled back. He reached out and held my hand. I let him.

"Cora, things are going to change now," Pearl commented. "There's a few things that you still don't know that are more important right now. Let's discuss those first. You two will have time to figure your issues out soon enough." My eyes drifted away from Darrien, to Pearl.

"What things? I'm a mermaid, I got that. It's hard to believe, but I got it. Don't tell anyone...got that. That's it...right?"

Oh, pretty please, let that be all.

Pearl sat up in her chair and looked deep in my eyes, "No, that's not it, Cora. Darrien was sent here to protect you because he's a guard, a *royal* guard." My heart leapt.

A royal guard? I smiled.

"He was sent here to help you discover who you are," she continued. "*I'm* here to give you the support you need to move on, and do what needs to be done next."

"Needs to be done? What does that mean?" I asked.

Just when I think I'm getting the tiniest hold of what's going on....

"Darrien was sent here...by your father." She was waiting for a reaction from me, but I just sat there, not sure how to process that information.

Dad sent Darrien to me, to protect me and help me discover what I am. Okay...why? Why, all of a sudden, did he care? Where's he been all this time? Why couldn't he have protected me? Taught me? That would have been easy if he would have just stuck around.

"Okay...Dad sent Darrien. I'm not surprised he didn't do this himself. I'm just wondering why, suddenly, he's taken an interest in my life. Where's he been all this time?" I looked at Darrien. The moment stretched out until, finally, Darrien broke the silence.

"Pearl said I was a *royal* guard, and your *Dad* sent me here...." He watched me for a reaction I was unable to give him. This was all flying high over my head.

"Cora, your Dad is the ruler of Titus Prime. You are the heir to the throne. I'm here to protect you and bring you *home*," he said slowly and gently as if speaking to a child.

"Home?" I asked, then everything crashed down on me as light bulbs started firing off. "Titus Prime? He's the ruler? That means that I'm..." I looked at Darrien and Pearl and they nodded.

324

A princess.

"So all the weird things that have been happening to me are because of Dad? Because he's a Mer? Did Mom know?" I asked, looking at Pearl and Darrien.

"Your Mom knew," Pearl said and looked at Darrien. There was more to this.

"I don't understand. Is this all because I'm a…a Mer?"

"No. You are more than that," Darrien pressed.

"What?" What weirder freaky thing could I possibly be?

"You are part Siren too," Pearl said gently.

"What is a Siren?" I asked loudly, searching them both again.

"A Siren is a different kind of Mer, a close relative of our species," Darrien said, as he eyed Pearl.

"But how am I both? That would mean…."

No! That can't be.

"Yes, your mother is a Siren," Pearl said gently. "You are a hybrid. And the first of your kind."

"A hybrid." I couldn't wrap my mind around what that even meant. But something had occurred to me, "Wait…the woman in the woods. The one at the pond. She's a…a…"

"A Siren," Darrien admitted in a hushed voice.

"Like me?" I asked.

"No! She is nothing like you, Cora," Darrien implored. His eyes searched mine. They were loving and tender. My heart ached. I didn't know who I even was anymore.

Dad was Mer. Mom was a Siren. Their world was so far removed from the one we lived in. All these years they had kept it hidden from us.

But why? What was so bad about their world that they couldn't live in it anymore? I searched the faces in the room for answers, but none came.

My tiny little world was crumbling around me. If I didn't find something to hold on to, I was going to be lost.

Darrien's hand wrapped around mine. My eyes flitted to his as a smile tipped the corner of his lip.

Darrien. He was still there.

A swell of determination broke through me in that moment, as if a knowledge I didn't know I possessed was released. I could feel the change in my body. Strength and courage pulsed through me.

As long as I had Darrien, I could face this. I smiled back at him, causing his dimples to deepen.

Even though I had no idea what I was getting into or what was going to happen after this, I knew with all my heart that as long as Darrien was by my side, I would be fine.

Okay, let's do this.

Keep reading for a peek at Mer: Book Two of the Water Series...

About the Author

Emory is an Arts Education teacher, a mother to two lovely little ones, and writer in the spare minutes she gets between those two things. She loves everything Harry Potter, Disney, and mythology based. She is a bibliophile with a towering to-be-read pile that she will never get through, but loves to look at. Emory lives in Regina, Saskatchewan with her husband and two kids. Find out more at www.emorygayle.com.

A Freebie from Me!

Because you are amazing and read my book, I want to thank you with this FREE copy of Celia's Journey, Vol 1.

In this novelette you will get to dive into the hidden world of the Sirens through the eyes of Cora's mother, Celia. Find out the history behind Cora and Darrien's world. You will also see familiar characters such as Midira, Pearl, and Zale.

This is the first in a series of stories that will be coming out as freebies in my newsletters.

Type this into your browser and get your copy today, don't be afraid to share it with a friend too!

https://www.instafreebie.com/free/sLRMO

Keep updated...

If you are interested in getting information on new books, promos, and giveaways, plus freebies for my subscribers only, head over to my website and sign up for my newsletter!

www.emorygayle.com

Help a girl out...

If you enjoyed Water, don't hesitate to let others know with a book review. Every review is SO appreciated!

https://www.amazon.com/Water-Book-One-Emory-Gayle-ebook/dp/B01L4T5R4O/

For the fun of it...

I am very active on social media too and would love to hear from you! Come find me and my crazy ramblings on Facebook, Twitter, and Instagram! If you love GIF's of Harry Potter and the frustrations of writing, pics of swoon worthy book covers, and some sarcastic banter...I'm your gal.

Just for you!

I've added a **sneak peek** at *Mer* for you, now available on Amazon!

Happy Reading!!
Emory Gayle

He would drown the
world for her...

Mer

BOOK TWO OF THE WATER SERIES

EMORY GAYLE

Prologue

IT WAS LIKE DROWNING. Drowning in fire.

Smoke choked my cry for help. My eyes searched endlessly for an exit, but there wasn't any and the ceiling was coming down. I watched the main beam give way with each lick the flames gave it. Around me the fire spread. It crawled up the walls like great spiders with flaming legs. The heat was like hell fire.

Coughing and stumbling in the smoky room I began to lose hope. Then, his arm was around me. *Darrien.*

I could hear the crunch of broken glass that was strewn around the floor, as we made our way to the window. Darrien grasped me by the hips, picked me up, as if I weighed nothing, and put me on the sill. Glass shards bit into my hands and through my clothes as I maneuvered to jump out.

"Go!" he shouted. That's when we heard it. The groan and great *crack*. Both our eyes flashed up as the main beam finally gave way.

Darrien's eyes met mine as the boathouse roof caved in…right on top of him.

"No!"

It was more than just a scream. It was a demand, a vow…a challenge. No. They wouldn't take him from me.

The world stopped.

In that moment, the flames stilled, the roof stayed and I felt the hum of a power, I didn't know I had, bloom in my core.

My fear. My anger. My love.

It was all there, riding the electric current coursing through me. In that one second, the world took a breath and shuddered, as if it knew what it had woken. Inside me, the cord of power snapped and unleashed.

Everything pulsed and then…*Boom.*

1
Cora

I'M A MERMAID. I am a mermaid.

It didn't matter how much I said it to myself, it was not sinking in. I wasn't entirely sure how to go about accepting this new person that I was supposed to be. Who was she? Where did she fit in?

Also, I just found out that my estranged father was, in fact, alive and well and ruling an underwater kingdom named Titus Prime. It's a city that Poseidon made for the survivors of the fall of Atlantis. Yes, the lost city of Atlantis; the one that sank into the sea. The one that is a myth, a legend…not supposed to be real. And, because my father rules it, that makes me a descendent of Poseidon himself. I had magical powers too, that were thus far mostly untapped. *Yay me.*

My mom is a Siren. A breed of deranged Mer that hate everything and everyone it seems. Which makes me this new hybrid underwater being that no one knows exists and everyone is afraid of.

Oh, yeah. I also found out that my boyfriend is a royal guard for my father and was sent to protect me. *He drowned me today.* My camp administrator is a mermaid, and my boyfriend is a merman, but my sister, Bree, is….a maybe.

Sitting on the shore of Crystal Lake I wondered what had happened to my life. It was quite a shock to the system, hearing that you were underwater royalty. How does a person even process that? I grabbed a handful of sand and threw it out over the still water. *A few hours ago I could barely stand in water over my knees, now, I was a child of Poseidon?*

How was I going to face my sister, Bree? She had no idea any of this was going on. How was I supposed to hide this from her? She's my sister and my best friend. And then there was my boyfriend, Darrien, what was his role in all this?

Mermaid. *Mermaid.* I am a *mermaid.*

Yeah, no matter how I said that it still sounded completely crazy.

I sat and stared blankly out at the lake, watching the reflection of the trees waver slightly in the water, knowing that my new home laid far below the surface. *Home. Where was home now?* Until then, home had been Yorkton with Mom and Bree, in our house that was falling apart, in the town where nothing ever happens. But, where was it now? Was I supposed to leave them and go to Dad? *Do I have to choose between Mom and Dad....Bree and Dad?* The thought of it hurt. I could feel a pain rise in the back of my throat. No, I would never abandon Bree. Too many people had left us; we were a packaged deal. Where I went, so did she. She was a mermaid too, I just knew it. And, that was a really weird thing to say. *Mermaid...*

"Hey."

His voice wrapped around me and sent an electrical shock through my body. Though I knew I should be horribly angry at him, I couldn't stop my heart from beating hard in reaction to him. Darrien sat down beside me on the cool sand. He wrapped his arms around his long legs, his black hair, a messy, sexy mop, moved slightly in the wind. He rested his head on top of a knee, turned, and looked at me. I knew there were a million things that he wanted to say, but to his credit he kept quiet. There was a shyness and sympathy in his face that shattered the wall I put up against him. He had earned my anger and my mistrust. After all, he did drown me.

"Hi," I said quietly, keeping my eyes on the water and not his beautiful face.

"You okay?" His voice was gentle, concerned. I could *feel* his gaze on me. I struggled between wanting to be mad at him, for keeping everything from me, and throwing my arms around him, just to feel his lips on mine. I took a deep breath, closed my eyes and exhaled slowly.

"I'll be okay..." I half grinned and nodded slightly, "eventually. But, right now? I'm not." I tried hard to keep my tears under control, biting the inside of my lip to distract myself with pain. The day's events came crashing down, overwhelming me and intensifying the grip my teeth had on my lip. I would taste blood before I would let myself cry in front of him.

Finding out about Dad had been a shock. I knew he was alive, at least I had always assumed so, but to hear that he was something out of a mythology text was completely different. And Mom...a Siren. The worst, most violent kind of creature you could imagine. Though Mom wasn't like that, she had left the Siren City when she was young, when she met Dad. She was still one of them, though, a magical water creature that I had no idea existed until I came to Camp Crystal.

I felt like I had been betrayed in the worst way. I didn't know my parents anymore, not really. All the stories that they told us as kids, were a lie. They showed us their childhood homes for goodness sake! Why would they do

3

that? What part of my family was true? What was real? I didn't know anymore, and I really didn't want to speak to the people that would solve those mysteries for me.

I had hated Dad for years because he left us right after Ana, my twin sister, drowned and I had hated Mom for retreating right out of Bree's and my life when it happened. Now, I hated the both of them for keeping everything from us. If they would have told us who we really were, maybe we would have understood our lives better and the choices that they made. I wouldn't have felt like it was my fault for years. I wouldn't feel so lost…

I could feel the rise of emotion in the back of my throat. It didn't matter how hard I clamped on my lip, the tears were coming. It all was just too much. Tears broke out and flowed freely. I stifled a sob, struggling to keep my emotions under control. I could feel Darrien's warm arms wrap around me.

As much as I wanted to yank his arm off and beat him with it, after everything that we had been through, after everything that had happened to me, he was the one that I depended on. I needed the safety he gave me. The comfort. But most of all I just needed him. So, for the moment, I allowed his comfort and I allowed myself to enjoy it and find solace in it.

Darrien was a surprise. I had sworn off loving someone because of what happened to Mom. The hollow shell of a woman that she was after Dad left, made me see the damage that love causes. I never wanted to be like that. I *swore* I would never be like that. Then, Darrien came along and everything changed.

He wasn't like anyone I had ever met, and maybe that should have clued me in about who he really was. But I fell for him…hard. His charm and kindness; his sweetness and humor. Although I didn't want it, I found love. But I hadn't told him that. I didn't want to scare him. I didn't know if he felt the same. At times I thought I felt it or saw it in the way he looked at me, but after him drowning me, I wasn't sure what was there anymore. That had changed everything. *Everything.*

Darrien's embrace tightened and warmed my heart. I don't know what it is about love, but it can forgive just about anything. I always thought that was weak and stupid, but now I understood. I was so in love with this boy, it was scary.

"Cora, there's something that I've been wanting to tell you. If I don't tell you now, I'm not sure I will have to courage to say it once…once you…." The words died on his lips as he stared out at the water. I watched the muscles in his jaw tighten. His breath caught in his throat as he cleared it. I pulled back from him. His blue-green eyes were focused somewhere else. I reached up and pulled his chin with my finger, willing him to speak. When our eyes

4

met he smiled and brought me further into him, each of us resting our head on the others' shoulder. A long sigh escaped his lips, the hot air rushing across the back of my neck. I could feel his cheeks rise in a smile I couldn't see, and in a whisper so sweet he said: "I love you."

My heart exploded, sending euphoric sensations shooting through my body. My head was light and my heart was beating wildly, frantically trying to leave me for him. A shocked and excited giggle erupted from my throat as I sat up. I looked deep into those gorgeous eyes and said the words that had been dying to get out: "I love you too! Oh my god, I do! I love you!"

Darrien's face lit up like a Christmas tree; he scooped me up in his arms and pressed me hard against him and kissed me. Not just any kiss, but a kiss to outshine all the other kisses that came before it. I thought our first was one I'd never beat, but this one had no competition.

Darrien and I pulled away from each other to catch our breath. He held my face with his hands, stroking my cheeks with his thumbs as he watched me. His smile was glorious, angelic…I never thought I could make someone that happy, or that I could ever be that happy. *This is crazy…insane…incredible! I could die a happy person right now.*

2
Darrien

I LOVED HER. I had been wanting to say it for a long time, but it just didn't seem right. I knew it with very fiber of my being, but nothing could have prepared me for hearing it back from her. I thought it was just me. I thought I was being the crazy one; but there it was, she said it. "I love you too!" The sweetest words to ever come from her perfect mouth.

Then a wave of fear and desperation washed over me. Love was not a small thing in my world. It came with a promise and I had every intension of fulfilling that. I would do *anything* for Cora. I couldn't lose her. I wouldn't. More than ever I realized how impossible of a situation I had put us in. I was in love with a princess that I would never be allowed to have.

But she loved me back, and right now, that's all that mattered.

3
Cora

MY HEART THUMPED WILDLY. *Love*. It was something I wasn't sure I was capable of giving to anyone before Darrien. He awakened it in me. The sensations, the passion, the frenzy. It was all glorious and terrifying at the same time. How could a person want something so much and yet be scared of it at the same time? I wanted him, more of him. I wanted every part of him. And, that was terrifying.

His kiss ignited something in me I didn't know existed. I turned my face toward him and he locked eyes with me. His love burned in them and behind it, a hunger stirred. I needed him. My world was so beyond my control, I felt like I would be swept up in it and be carried away from everyone. I had no control, I felt no control...except for this. Except for him. I needed something to make sense. Something that I was in control of. Something I *wanted. I want Darrien...now.*

I reached out for his face and drew myself up to him. His soft lips found mine, butterflies erupted from my chest and coursed through me. My body craved more and I pulled him in for a deeper, harder....more passionate kiss. I felt him respond, pressing against me, matching my thirst. Our breathing sped up as our hearts matched pace.

My hands curled around his back, I could feel his muscles flexing as I ran my fingers down his spine. His hands were strong on my back, pulling me in. I pushed today's events out of my head and just let my body do the talking. We fell to the sand as Darrien pressed up against me hard, he wanted this too. *He wants* me. His kisses became more daring, more passionate with each one. His hands were on my waist, my back, my shoulders...then he pushed away from me.

"What? What's wrong?" I demanded. My heart was racing and my skin was tingling. I needed more. I *wanted* more. When I reached for him again he grabbed my hands, gently in his, and pushed them slowly away from his chest.

"Don't, Cora. We shouldn't do this." His voice was weak.

"Why not? What's wrong?" I said, frustration leaking out.

"You aren't yourself right now. You just had some seriously shocking news. You're not thinking clearly at all. This isn't you," he said, turning slightly away from me. I moved in front of him again, forcing him to look at me. There was passion behind his eyes, stifled passion. Frustration boiled in me.

"You're wrong! I want this. I *need* this. I need *you*. Don't you want me?" My voice pleaded more than I wanted. I didn't want to be that desperate, but…I was. I was desperate.

"Of *course* I want you," he said, wrapping his hands around mine, "But you aren't doing this for the right reasons. I won't take advantage of you like that. You'll regret it, you'll regret *me*. I won't do that," he said sitting up and away from me. My breath caught in my throat. Disappointment weighed down on me. The passion I felt a moment ago died out slowly. I could feel it drain from me as I sat there on the cold sand.

"I just….nothing makes sense anymore!" I yelled, "You're the only thing that's real to me, and I don't even understand you," I cried in frustration. What was wrong with me? What was I doing? *I just threw myself at him…he's right, I'm not me.* I was going crazy. It was too much.

Darrien's arms wrapped around me. His tight embrace calming me.

"Ugh! I'm sorry," I dropped my head into my hands. I couldn't look at him, I was left with some serious embarrassment. *He must think…*ugh, my stomach dropped knowing what he must think of me. "I'm so embarrassed. You must think I'm…" I couldn't finish. I buried my face in my hands.

"I don't think any differently about you. You've had a very stressful day, I don't know what I would do if I were in your shoes. What do you need, Humbug? What can I do?" His voice was calm, kind, and exactly what I didn't know I needed. *But what* can *he do?*

I sat there, curled into Darrien's arms. I wanted to run. Get out of there and away from this mess. Maybe I could just pretend I didn't know all that stuff, and just go on being normal, boring me. I wouldn't have to hide anything from Bree, because even though we share the same parents, for some reason she wasn't allowed to know anything about what was going on. I wouldn't have to think about Dad and I wouldn't have to think about getting back into the water to drown myself again. And Darrien….I could pretend he was just a gorgeous swim instructor that miraculously fell for me. I could….*maybe.*

I looked at Darrien. *Maybe not.* This wasn't going anywhere and neither was I. I needed to put on my big girl panties and face my future.

8

"There is something that I would like to know. Mostly about you. So, please, no secrets." I looked intently at him. His eyes were genuine. He smiled at me, his beautiful, kind, understanding…gorgeous smile.

"No more secrets, I promise." He squeezed me tight. In his arms, I felt safe. Darrien bent his head down and rested a delicate kiss on my forehead. The heat from his lips radiated from the spot of contact.

"Thank you." I exhaled deep as I said it, relief running through me. I relaxed into him. I could feel his heart beating, steady and strong. "Okay, here we go. You said that you were sent here by Dad, to bring me back to him, but I'm sure that falling for me wasn't part of that plan. Or was it? Was it?" It was the hardest question to ask, but it was the one I needed to know the most. The rest could wait, everything about my Dad and mermaids and everything, it all was bearable if…if we were *real*.

Darrien grabbed my chin and tipped it up to him, he looked deep into my eyes. "You are more real to me than anything I have experienced in my life." He kissed me, the softest, gentlest and sweetest kiss. My heart grew, as a warm calm spread through me, like sinking into a hot bath.

"Was this relationship a plan from the start? No," Darrien affirmed. "You know I was sent here, and maybe this is the time to tell you my side of things. But, before I start into that, you have to know, that no part of my feelings for you were part of a plan. *Everything* I have felt for you has been surprising and completely genuine. I hope you never forget that. I never expected to fall for you, but I did," he chuckled, "and *hard*."

I felt his heart thunder in his chest and another hot kiss was planted on my forehead. I gazed up at him. He was beautiful, and he *really* was *mine*. I didn't think that would ever sink in, it seemed too good to be true.

"You have no idea how much that means to hear you say that. I feel like I can get through this, as long as I have you with me," I gushed and smiled big. *I can do this, I can do this.* "So, you're a guard. Tell me more about that. And your brother too. So much of what I thought I knew about my life has been a lie, tell me something true." I prepared myself for a completely different Darrien story. His past was what I identified with, it's what drew me to him. It scared me to think that all those things I felt a connection to, might not even exist. His feelings for me were genuine and real, but were mine?

"Everything I told you about my past was true. I have a younger brother, Tyde. We grew up in a military school as kids because our parents were killed in a Siren attack on Titus," he gave me a sad smile and shrugged. My heart broke for him; that was awful. To lose both of your parents like that. He didn't dwell but just kept going on.

9

"Now, as far as my job goes…..it's not a swim instructor." I chuckled lightly, I figured as much. "I am a soldier. Even though I'm only twenty, I'm high ranking. I'm actually the highest. I work very close to the king, your father. I control all aspects of his security and safety. I was sent here on a very secret, very special mission…to protect the future queen and bring her home." He was so serious and straight when he spoke, I almost started laughing. It was so hard to take seriously….*future queen?* Darrien's eyes turned to me.

"Sorry," I apologized. "It's just so ridiculous, when you say "future queen". That's not me," I said. I was still trying to keep from laughing when Darrien turned his body toward mine. He *was* serious. My giggles stopped short in my throat.

"I know it's going to be hard for you to truly understand who you are and how important you are. But, you *are* the future queen of Titus Prime. And I am here to serve you and to protect you." His eyes were piercing; I couldn't look at him. He was serious, so serious it completely deflated all the humor I saw in the situation. He said "serve"; he was here to *serve* me. My mind just couldn't wrap itself around that.

"Sorry. I don't mean to…..I just don't know how to deal with that right now," I said, shaking my head. I looked at Darrien, "Please, I want to hear more about you…not me…you." I gave him a half grin. I was discovering a new person. The swim instructor that saved me in the woods was melting away and a new Darrien was taking his place. Someone I don't know at all.

4

Cora

DARRIEN'S EYES WERE ON ME, gentle and gorgeous.

"Me? More about me." His voice was soft and sweet as he shifted on the sand, grasping me just a little tighter. When he started to speak I could hear the nervousness in his voice. *Maybe I'm not the only one who's not sure how this will turn out.*

"Okay, well when my parents died I was only nine, Tyde was five. We had no other family to look after us and were too young to stay on our own; so, we were put in military school. Titus Prime doesn't really have a place for orphans because, until us, it had never happened before. Typically children who lost their parents were placed with other family, but we had none." Darrien's eyes were stormy as he gazed out across the lake. "Tyde doesn't remember our parents very well, he was too young. We grew up having only each other we could depend on. We've been through a lot. He's my family, all of it." I couldn't help the smile that crept across my face. *This is the Darrien I fell for.*

"When I was eleven, I was chosen to be in the Junior Military Academy, it's something that was created by your grandfather as a way of jump starting the military at a younger age. The Junior Military Academy educates its students, it's a section of the live-in school we were at. I was a good student; a great student, actually. I was always at the top of my class. The soldier part of the program trained us to defend our city, our people and our king. Where I'm from, where *we're* from, being chosen for the J.M.A. is a high honor. I was lucky to have been chosen at such a young age." I could hear the pride swell in his voice, though he was not boasting. "By the time I was fifteen, I was teaching some classes and training with the adult army. No one had done what I had before." He stopped and shifted.

Darrien cleared his throat, "I know you wanted to know about my past, but I feel like I'm bragging, telling you all this." His voice was quiet, he

11

blushed. I thought it was incredibly sexy. Not only was he stunning to look at, he had brains too! Is there is nothing that this guy can't do?

"You're not bragging," I assured him. "I asked you to tell me all about *you* and that includes a lot of good stuff. I trust you're telling me the truth." I nudged him and squeezed his hand. Darrien grinned from the corner of his mouth and a dimple came out. He dropped his shoulders and nodded slightly. I could tell he didn't feel comfortable talking about himself; it wasn't something he was used to doing I guessed. He was either a private person, or everyone around him already knew everything about him.

"Okay, I'm glad you feel that way, 'cause this is really uncomfortable for me," he said, still not looking at me. I placed my hands under my chin and looked at him expectantly. He smiled, finally turning his eyes on me, and sighed. "Alright, I'll keep going. Uh…I advanced quickly up the army ranks. It wasn't until three years ago that I was assigned to guard duty at the palace. During one of my posts, there was an attempt on the king's life." My eyes shot wide. *Someone wanted to kill Dad?*

"I was able to find and capture the person that was responsible for it. King Zale, your father, was grateful. He asked that I be assigned as his own personal guard." I let go of the breath I was holding. "I stayed with him. Everywhere he went, I went. The only time I'm not with your father is when I sleep, even then I'm close by in case something happens. I became close with your father, we were…friends, we *are* friends. At least, I hope we still will be when he finds out what I have done." He paused, his eyes shifting away from me, fogging with thoughts I wasn't invited into. I ran my hand down his arm to shake those thoughts away and his eyes focused on me again.

"Anyway, in the last year there have been several attempts to kill your father, he has survived all of them. We were able to stop the assassins before they were able to do any damage, but still, your father was noticeably shaken. Our society is based on respect and responsibility and in the whole history of our people there had never been an attempt on a king's life. You have to understand that it's not coming from our people, though. The Sirens…never mind." My heart was racing.

"Sirens? You mean, *my* people?" I said, leaning away from him.

"No, Cora. You are *nothing* like them. They are monsters. You don't know what they are capable of. They hurt people. They kill people," he protested, grabbing my hand and holding on tight.

"And I'm one of them. So is my Mom."

"Look, I can't pretend that I like all Sirens but I have come to realize that Mer have painted Sirens with a broad brush. They aren't *all* bad. Pearl helped me realize that."

"Pearl?" I asked.

"Yes. Her sister was a Siren. She knows more about them than I ever thought I did. She changed the way I see them. You are a *good* person, Cora. I know that to the bottom of my soul. Siren or Mer, *you* decide who you truly are."

I was struggling to come to grips with the fact that I had mythological blood running through me. The idea that my parents were something out of a Greek myth or Disney cartoon was far from sinking in. I could look at Darrien and see the man that I had fallen in love with, but I could *not* see a king's guard or a merman. I definitely couldn't see myself as anything other than a sub-par teenager.

Darrien continued. "I don't want to dive too deep into King Zale's personal life, but in Titus Prime, your father has no heir. You are the only one left that can take the throne, and you're on land. Your dad has kept you and your sister a complete secret. None but a handful of us know who you really are."

"Does Pen know?" I asked.

"Well, she's a Claire," he said, like that answered my question.

"What's a Claire?"

"They can see the future and they can read people," he explained.

"Pen is Mer too?"

"Yes. Um, all the Leads are Mer," he admitted sheepishly.

"All of them! Even Aurelia?" *How did I miss that?*

"Yes, even her. We dated remember?"

"Right, of course." I nodded to myself. "But how - why are you all here? Is everyone here because of me?"

"No, well yes…actually they don't know about you. Zale sent them up to watch humans and bring back information that we might be able to use to better our culture. They all still think *that* is the reason they are here," he said with a shrug.

"Okay wow. I hope they aren't disappointed."

"They won't be. Once they find out that they have been working with the heir to the throne, trust me, they'll be thrilled."

"Heir to the throne. That is still a lot to take in. You keep saying that I am the only one that can do this stuff, but what about Bree? Can't she? She's got to be just like me right?"

"Yes. She should be just like you, but she is still too young. You are the oldest and therefore are the only one that can take on the responsibility of the dome."

"What's the dome?" I asked, starting to feel overwhelmed again.

"It is what protects us against the dangers of the ocean. It keeps the elements out and keeps us safe from the Sirens. In order for the dome to work, it has to be tied to the life force of a ruler. Right now, it is tied to your Dad."

"So, I'm going to have to tie my life to this dome thing once I go to Titus Prime?" I asked.

"Not right away, but if something happens to your father, it will pass to you," he said and took my hand. "This is all getting to be a lot for you. Are you sure you want to talk about this now? Some of it can wait." He brushed a hair behind my ear with a gentle hand. I didn't want to hear anymore, but I needed to. This was my new life, I needed to know what I was getting into. The more I knew the better I would be at handling it all; at least that is what I told myself.

"Keep going. I'm fine," I said, attempting a nonchalant grin.

"Okay," he said, drawing out the word, and unsure if I was really telling the truth or not. "Like I said before, King Zale and I have become friends, he trusts me. Even though we were able to stop the attempts on his life, we knew that there was someone in the castle that was a spy. The attempts were too close and the chance that they would succeed was getting too great, the heir had to come home. Zale didn't know who he could trust. To my great honor, he picked me, over guards and other palace officials he had worked with for a decade to bring his most prized and valuable possession home...you."

How was I Dad's most prized possession? *I don't like being called a possession, he doesn't own me. I don't owe him anything either.* I sighed, it's great that Darrien was able to get my dad to trust him, confide in him...but I just couldn't trust my dad, not yet. Not after the things that he put my family through.

I sat back and shook my head, "I don't know what to think of my dad right now. For years, all I've known is that he abandoned us. There was never an explanation; we never knew why...he just left. It's a little hard to believe that I'm the most important thing to him when I haven't heard anything from him in such a long time. I'm still so mad at him. I'm not sure if I even want to see him." I looked at Darrien knowing that I would see disapproval. A part of me felt ashamed of what I said. I could feel the question burning in his eyes...*How can you not want to see your family?*

But I meant it, he hurt us badly. A part of me wanted to hurt him back. If he needed me so bad, he was going to have to do more than sending a henchman to get me. *Why isn't he here himself if I'm so important? And Bree...she would give anything to see him again, and I can't even tell her that he's alive. I can't even begin to think what this would do to Mom.* I was finally getting some answers, but they just keep making things more complicated.

"What else do you need to know...*anything.*" He held me tight. My eyes lifted to look at him, I couldn't help it. I leaned in and kissed him. The heat

14

from his lips melted every cold feeling I had inside me, leaving warm butterflies fluttering around inside me. *As long as Darrien is with me, I will make it through this.*

"Right now, honestly, I just need to be held and told it will all be okay. I need to hear you say that. If *you* say it, I'll believe it. I don't believe it when I say it to myself." I could feel his arms stiffen.

He didn't say it.

5
Darrien

I COULDN'T LOOK AT HER. I didn't want to ruin this for her; for me either. I didn't want to lie to her, though. I sighed. I felt heavy with the weight of knowledge I couldn't bring myself to tell her yet.

"I don't know exactly what's going to happen from here. My job is to bring you home, to Titus Prime. After that, my job is done. You will be welcomed home a royal heir. A long lost princess is going to be a big deal. As for me, my future is a little harder to see, I've done something that I could get into a lot of trouble for." I smiled….*it was worth. She was worth it.*

"You've hinted at that a few times, what did you do that's so bad?" She asked as she bit her bottom lip.

"I'm just a soldier….who fell for a princess." I shrugged and closed my eyes. When her lips touched mine it sent a pulse straight to my core. A warmth spread through me with lightning speed and I groaned against her.

When she moaned she nearly undid what little I had left of my self-restraint.

6
Cora

A PRINCESS AND A SOLDIER, is that what we were to each other now? I figured that things were going to get confusing and that they were going to change, but I didn't think that would include Darrien and me. *Why do we have to change?* Being with him was the only thing that I trusted at the moment, the only thing I knew and the only thing keeping me together.

"Darrien, I can't handle things changing between us right now. You're not allowed to leave me, understand? You can't leave me..." Then it struck me. "You don't *want* to leave do you?" Maybe this is his way of backing out of everything.

"Of course I don't *want* to leave you! *Never.* But there may come a time when *you* don't want *me* anymore, and I want you to know that I understand and don't blame you. If that time ever comes, I will support whatever decision you make. As long as you want me, I'm here." His smile made all of my fears evaporate immediately...*he wants me.* I felt lit up from the inside out.

I grabbed him around his neck and hugged him hard. *I will never let him go.* Nothing would make me let him go.

Darrien brought his soft lips down on mine. His kiss was sweet, hot and more passionate than before. *Why can't we just stay here? I don't want things to change, I want to stay like this.* My smile faded as I realized that was not going to happen. The future was hanging above us and it wouldn't go away.

"I don't ever want to lose those kisses...ever," I whispered and rested my head on his shoulder. Listening to his breathing relaxed me and lulled me into a calm I desperately needed.

We sat on the beach for a long time, not moving, not talking; just being together. I needed to feel this one more time before my life started in a direction I had no control of. I leaned against Darrien's strong chest and closed my eyes. Would this be the last time we'd able to be together like this? With everything I had inside me, I hoped it wouldn't be.

As the sun was setting over the lake, a storm brewed. The sky turned from a beautiful pink and purple to greys, dark and foreboding. I could feel the change in the air beginning and knew I was stepping into a storm I was not prepared for.

7
Darrien

THE FEEL OF HER AGAINST my chest and the sweet flowery smell to her hair were driving guilt spikes through me. I wanted to tell her that she was going to be fine. That I would never leave her and that I would always be with her, but I couldn't. Her life course was on a different path now, one that I couldn't control. She was going to be the future queen and there was no stopping that. I was just a soldier, a guard. There was no changing *that*.

Her trust and her love were everything to me. I ached, knowing that I would end up causing her pain. In the end, she would have to choose between me and her duty to the throne. *What have I done?*

I looked down at her.

She was killing me in the slowest, sweetest death. I was happy to die.

8
Cora

THE MORNING WAS AS GLOOMY as I felt. A storm had come during the night, leaving behind thick clouds that hid the sun but the birds were up and happy with the fresh clean air. Their glad chirping woke me, and annoyed me. It was dark in the cabin when I opened my eyes. The others were still sleeping, but I was restless. I tiptoed to the bathroom, brushed my teeth and washed my face. Quickly, I ran a brush through my hair, changed into jeans and a sweater, and snuck out the door. The girls' side of the camp was quiet but for the chirping of the birds and the swaying of the trees. The fresh rain smell woke me up further and did its best to soothe my anxious mind.

The weather was turning darker and colder by the minute by the time I made it to the beach. A chill ran up my arms and settled into my chest. But, it wasn't just the weather that was getting to me, it was everything that had happened in the last few weeks. I was supposed to go back to teaching the girls in my cabin. Swimming lessons resumed and craft time. Going back to reality was something I wanted so deeply yesterday, but today it just seemed…weird. *How do you go back to being "normal" after being told you're a mermaid princess? How?*

The wind picked up slightly, goose bumps prickled my skin and I was officially cold. It started to rain just slightly, but the rain was oddly warm for the prairies. *Well, since no one is around, I'm on the beach getting wet anyway, and I really need to get into the water...*

I walked over to the lake's edge, removed my shoes, rolled up the cuffs of my jeans and dipped my feet in. The air may have been cool, but the water was like a bath, warm and welcoming. I took a careful look around the beach; no one was there and not a light on in Pearl's cabin. I quickly slipped off my jeans and bunny hug, standing there for just a brief moment in my undies before I stepped further into the water.

20

It took my breath away. The feeling of the water rising up my body and closing in around me. It was suffocating in a way and made me gasp. I was warmer in the water than I was out of it, which was a blessing. I impressed myself by going on further than I had in years, past my waist. I wasn't ready to glide far out into the lake yet, so, when I finally slid fully in the water, I stayed relatively close to the shore. Memories of my swimming days came flooding back. The weightlessness, the freedom, and the agility I could never feel on shore. A surge of courage bloomed in me. I planted my feet in the sand, under the water, and pushed off toward the center of the lake.

The water rushed beneath me, running around my arms and legs like silk, warm silk. It felt incredible.

I didn't need to remind myself to breathe anymore, air flowed in and out of my lungs freely. The water was still and the rain was warm on my head. *What an amazing morning.* I could feel the water speeding around me. I just let my body do its thing, keeping as relaxed as I could. If I thought about it, I'd panic and sink for sure.

Darrien said that being Mer you could move water. The way water had been acting around me now made sense. I was able to call water out of fabric when I wanted something to dry, but I didn't understand what I was doing or how it worked. Though I still didn't know how I did it, at least I knew where I got the power from.

As for my swimming skills, Darrien said that Mer were able to move the water around them to swim at great speeds. I looked down at my hands, but I was treading water, there was nothing supernatural going on there. Concentrating more than before, I willed myself to go out further into deeper water. Usually the deeper the water was, the cooler it felt, but not Crystal Lake, no. It's warmth wrapped around me and I smiled in spite of myself. I did a few turns in the water, feeling graceful for the first time in forever. Being Mer was starting to make sense in a strange way; I always felt free in the water. Maybe that was because I was meant to be in it.

As I made my way slowly out into the middle of the lake I couldn't help but think of Dad. How was I supposed to start a relationship with him after all those years? He didn't know me anymore; I didn't know him anymore either. I wasn't sure if I even *wanted* to know him. A hot anger filled me the more that I thought about it. Why couldn't he have just told us he loved us and had to leave? Why did he even come on land if he knew he would have to return to Titus? Why do all that knowing you would hurt everyone that cared for you? How selfish is that? I could feel the heat of my rage bubbling beneath me....*wait.* It wasn't my anger bubbling...it was the water!

I looked down at my feet in the water. Bubbles were erupting all around me; popping, throwing fizzy spray in my face.

What's going on? Am I doing this? Was it some of those "powers" Darrien was talking about? My thoughts were cut short as water filled in over my head. My concentration lost, I sunk under the waves. The bubbles were so thick I couldn't make out the surface anymore and they blocked all lines of sight around me. I looked down at my feet.

How do I stop making these damn bubbles? Stop feet! Stop bubbles!

Didn't work.

Then I saw it. A giant bubble-shaped object was rising from down below me, and it was coming fast. I couldn't help it, I opened my mouth and screamed. Water surged into my mouth and into my lungs. Now familiar with the burning, I waited for the searing pain. It came on fast. Lightning flashed behind my eyes as the sharp pain spread across my body. The giant bubble was almost on me now, its light shining and blinding me. The curtain was lifted as darkness overtook me. With my last shred of consciousness, I felt strong arms grab me, shoving me toward the surface.

Mer is now available on Amazon

22

Also by Emory Gayle

The Water Series:
Mer: Book Two of the Water Series
Siren: Book Three of the Water Series
Tempest: Book Four of the Water Series

Celia's Journey: A Water Story
Volume One
Volume Two
Volume Three (Spring 2018)

The Triton Series
Triton's Daughter

Made in the USA
Columbia, SC
07 January 2019